What The Glass Eye Sees

What will you find in the woods today .. ?

Simon Kippax

Copyright

All rights reserved.

The characters and events portrayed in this book are fictitious. Any similarity to real persons, living or dead, is coincidental and not intended by the author.

No part of this book may be reproduced, or stored in a retrieval system, or transmitted in any form or by any means, electronic, mechanical, photocopying, recording, or otherwise, without express written permission of the publisher.

First published 2023

© Simon Kippax

This is dedicated to my family for all their encouragement and support, with a special thank you to my dad for his invaluable time and effort.

This is my second novel. I hope you enjoy reading it as much as I've enjoyed writing it. If you do, I would be very grateful if you would take five minutes to rate it by going to the Amazon website where my book is listed. Thank you.

I also invite you to meet me and say hello at my website, simonkippax.my.canva.site and to leave your comments about the book, good or bad. I really would like to know what you think (including letting me know if you've found a mistake). All feedback is very useful, especially for me as a new author.

My first novel, "Arlene and the Music Box" is also available on the Amazon website. It follows Arlene and her mysterious relationship with a music box, given to her by a gypsy woman at an early age. If the music box speaks, does it live?

1

Intro

The floor was icy cold. The dark flooded the hall with unquestionable solitude. The silence was deafening as he took one step, then another down the corridor. He came upon a door. It creaked open to reveal more darkness, only this time a lot heavier. A tall figure stood facing away from him with his head stooped over – a silhouette in an already blackened room. The revenant figure was breathing, echoing through the deathly silence. In a slow, baleful manner, the figure turned its head. One bright, burning eye stared directly into Jack-Jack's soul making his heart ache –

"I see you".

Three children, an orphanage, a glass eye and endless tales of superstition. A town steeped in forgotten history resided with forgotten people. Only one man was not so forgotten, just cursed and banished to a cabin deep in the woods. They say long after he was gone, his glass eye could still see into your soul.

This is the story of Old man Joe.

Prologue

I'm frightened.

He is here, again.

He always comes without warning and takes things - things that aren't his to take.

All I can think to do is lie here under the bed and shake. There's no-one to be scared with me.

He walks around my room very slowly. I can't even see him but this is only because my eyes are shut tight. I never open my eyes on one of his visits.

I can't bring myself to say anything. My stutter will get the better of me and I know it won't do any good - not with him.

This is just something he does. He visits other boys too and takes their things. It's not just me, but he visits me the most. I am his favourite. He's been doing it to me for some time now. I have got used to it but I'm always afraid it will be more than just taking things.

Under my bed is dusty and the old wooden floorboards feel damp beneath me as I huddle myself into as small a ball as I possibly can. I don't know if he knows I am under here - clinging onto my pale blue blanket that has holes all over it. It doesn't matter to me though. It could be the oldest, dirtiest blanket but it's still mine, unless he takes that too.

I knew he was coming tonight. Maybe it's because of how long he has been visiting me. I carefully crept under my bed and decided to stay there no matter what happened. My bed can be a scary thing when I lay on top of it but my safe place when I'm underneath it.

4

It feels like ages and ages and even though I can't hear any footsteps on the wooden floorboards, I know he is still here. It's like he is just gliding around my room; his feet not touching the ground at all.

I want so badly to sneeze with all the dust that is hiding there with me, but everything I have inside of me stops that from happening. I just know I can't.

I often wonder what he thinks about or even if he does think. Maybe he doesn't think at all. Maybe his mind is empty.

I wait a while after I can't hear anything anymore before I can bring myself to move. When I do, it's small, jerky movements which make the floorboards creak. I don't have as much room as I used to under here as I am bigger than I was when I first started hiding.

It is dark but I force myself to open my eyes, first one then the other. I don't know why I don't open them together. I can't see anything at first but then the darkness turns into shapes and shadows.

Nothing.

I crawl out from my shelter as quietly as I can and get to my feet. My blanket is still in my right hand, by my side, half under the bed.

Is that it? Is it over? Is he gone, at least for now?

I have to check if it is still there. Up to now he hasn't taken it. Each time he visits me it's the first thing I check when he's gone.

This time though, it isn't there.

My pendant.

We meet Robinson

My name is Robinson Harvey.

I want to tell you a story if you're willing to lend me your time; a story about a particular year in my life.

The year was 1919. I was thirteen.

That was the year a storm revealed a hidden treasure.

It was also the year of the boy - and the body.

This is a story about Old man Joe.

What can be said about Old man Joe? The only factual thing I can tell you is that no-one truly knew anything about Old man Joe. His name was legend and still is to this day.

The story I would like to tell you I have never told anyone before. It goes back to when I was a young boy living in middle-England just after the conclusion of the First World War. The town I was living in was still reeling from the war but at the same time seemed to be segregated from reality. I was living in an orphanage called Saint Vincent's as both of my parents had died during the war; my father having been killed in the trenches and my mother being victim to our house being bombed when I was at school one fateful day. But more on that later.

There were about a dozen or so children at Saint Vincent's at that time, too few for the size of the building in my opinion. Saint Vincent's had been around for many years, which was clear to see in the lack of structural integrity of the building. I was the eldest but there were children of different ages and both sexes.

As you read about an orphanage that takes in children of suffering, you might be falsely led to believe that this was an upstanding place of good deeds. Let me assure you, having lived there, this was not the case. The orphanage was a place of disrepute, at least in the eyes of its unfortunate residents.

A nun by definition is a woman who vows to serve her Lord under chastity and obedience - a person of understanding, compassion, patience. I saw very little of these values in the nuns who looked after me. When I say very little, that is because my dismal view of what a nun embodied was saved slightly by Sister Athena, the only pleasant nun I have come across to this day.

The orphanage where I lived was situated in the very remote small town of Fellowood Marsh. A lightly populated, superstitious town, surrounded by marshland and forest. I lived there for a relatively short spell with the other children, two of whom I was very fond of; Mollie and Jack-Jack. I was thirteen and Mollie was a year younger than me - I called her my voice of reason. Jack-Jack was just a boy of nine whom I felt a great deal of affection for. He was sort of the runt of the litter, so to speak.

Now, as I mentioned, this town was steeped in superstition. Back then there was a lot of superstition, but it took on a whole new meaning in Fellowood Marsh. Tales of old had manifested themselves into folklore by the time I arrived. People do strange things because of superstition. If it is not properly dealt with, it can consume a town and everyone in it. That is exactly what happened in Fellowood Marsh, because of superstition, because of fear and because of a glass eye.

Chapter I

"Let the punishment be proportionate to the offense."
Marcus Tullius Cicero

'I d..d..didn't lose, Robbie!' exclaimed Jack-Jack.

'Yes you did, but like I've told you before, it doesn't matter. You're supposed to lose in running races, you're younger than us. That's just the way it goes.'

Jack-Jack struggled, as he always did, to get it into his head that ability usually came with age as a child. He insisted on competing with the older boys but couldn't accept that most of the time, he was going to lose. It wasn't always the case. There had been times when the other boys had let him win but he didn't like it that way. He had protested afterwards. The older boys couldn't win either way.

The race in question was the foot race that Robbie and some of the other boys Robbie's age in the town had participated in earlier that day. It was a race like so many others before it; nothing at stake but pride and bragging rights. A small form of entertainment in a town where very few things of interest happened. Jack-Jack had insisted to Robbie that he wanted to be a part of it, even though Robbie had tried to persuade him against it due to the aftermath that Robbie knew was inevitable.

Robbie had felt compelled to look out for Jack-Jack ever since he had arrived at Saint Vincent's. He didn't really know why. After all, it gave him more grief than reward. Or at least, that's the way it felt. It might have had something to do with Jack-Jack being younger than him or it might have been on account of Jack-Jack having a stutter which, subconsciously, Robbie always felt pity for.

The boys were now laid on their respective beds in the communal sleep hall. The beds were uncomfortable at best and not exactly the cleanest. Prison-style beds may have been pushing it. However, they weren't far from it. This wasn't the worst thing about night time at Saint Vincent's; the worst thing was that there was no privacy. There were around a dozen or so children living in the orphanage at any one time and these were separated into two fairly large halls. The halls were clearly not meant for sleeping arrangements, but this is what they were used for nonetheless. Not only that, but they were gender neutral. Not that this was too much of a bad thing amongst most of the children as it meant that Mollie was able to be with Robbie and Jack-Jack during the night. The good thing about the halls being the size they were was that the other children were far enough away so the three of them could talk quietly and still be unheard..... if they were quiet enough.

The three children, even though staggered in age, were best of friends and were usually together most of the time. Mollie and Jack-Jack had been at the orphanage most of their lives but Robbie had only been there a short time. The other two were used to what life was like at Saint Vincent's, but Robbie had yet to adjust and couldn't understand how they had been there so long without losing their minds.

'One day I'll w..w..win on my own b..b..back, you'll s..s..see. I'll be faster and q..q..quicker than everyone here. One d..d..day!'

'You will Jack-Jack, you will. But you have to accept that that might not be for a long time yet,' Mollie explained. She was on her bed just next to Jack-Jack's. There were more beds than children but that only meant, at any given time, another child could arrive and have that bed.

'One day,' Jack-Jack responded, but only by muttering it to himself quietly. He was a sore loser, but maybe that came from being on the wrong end so often.

It was getting late. The problem with sleeping in a communal hall was that the slightest thing could keep you awake. Or if one child wasn't tired and wanted to talk, he or she kept the others from sleeping. This was a common occurrence and usually left one or two of them tired the following day. Breakfast came at an early time at the orphanage so lie-ins were uncommon, even on weekends.

The night was a warm one. The spring was coming to a close as summer was beckoning. This was a good thing because the old building became excruciatingly cold during the winter months. There were not enough blankets to go around and even the ones that were available did not provide as much comfort and warmth as was desired. During winter, a lot of the children suffered with maladies as a result of the temperature dropping well below freezing; the candles did not exactly give off much heat.

Robbie whispered while lying on his side with his hand under his head, 'Tomorrow we'll have another race. I'll show that Richie who's really the quickest. He clearly saw that I stumbled on the rocks that were on my side of the path, but he kept going on and on that it was even terrain and it was a fair race. I'll make sure I go on his side of the path and see how he likes it.'

'Shhhh.' Mollie could hear the familiar sound of footsteps.

They were the ominous footsteps of Sister Meredith - the Mother Superior at Saint Vincent's and by far the strictest of all the nuns. Just her presence sent fear shooting through just about every child in the orphanage aside from Robbie. He didn't like the way she carried herself and abused her position of power. Still, he knew it wasn't worth getting into trouble just because he objected to the way she ran the orphanage.

Her footsteps were melodic and consistent with a steady rhythm, like she was taking her time on purpose in case there were any children still awake who could hear her approaching. She didn't like children being awake when they were supposed to be asleep. To her it was a simple form of rebellion.

As she entered the hall from the corridor, the large heels of her shoes echoed on the cold concrete. It was unclear how many children were awake, but not a peep was to be heard as she meticulously made her way down the side of the beds along the side wall, then her footsteps faded as she went around the corner to the other hall.

This was the nightly routine. It wasn't always the same Sister, but there were always checks done throughout the early stages of the night to make sure the children were sleeping and behaving. Usually, it would go without incident. Several times, one of the Sisters would do the checks by walking up and down the two halls and back to the nuns' quarters before bedding down themselves.

Not tonight however. Robbie lay there with his eyes open in the dim candlelight and thought to himself that he could very faintly hear another voice coming from the other hall. This was confirmed once Sister Meredith entered as she heard it too. The boy's whispers were evidently too loud for him to hear her footsteps as Mollie had done. And now Sister Meredith had heard him too and caught him whispering when he should be sleeping.

What followed was a combination of slaps and whimpers, which in an open room like the hall, amplified the sounds and resonated around the walls to their hall. Robbie, Mollie, Jack-Jack and the rest of the children lay as still as could be, having no choice but to listen to the act of discipline taking place in the next room. Each slap was immediately followed by a whimper and Robbie wanted nothing more than to get up and go to the aid of the boy. However, he knew this would help in no way whatsoever. In fact, through experience he knew that, not only would he get himself into trouble, he would more likely make it worse for the other boy.

What was apparent in the whole process was that the discipline didn't come with any words; no form of teaching, no attempt to explain what the discipline was for. It was all just physical. Robbie thought Sister Meredith enjoyed dishing it out, for no reason other than to exert her power over the children.

And just like that, it was over.

The other hall went as silent as its neighbour. Robbie couldn't even hear the other boy's whimpers. The next sound was Sister Meredith's shoes once again on the concrete floor coming back towards them in the exact rhythm as when she walked through before. No-one dared move. You couldn't even hear anyone breathing, although Robbie suspected every breath was heavy. Robbie kept his eyes open and turned his head to see the silhouetted figure of Sister Meredith float on past back down the corridor.

Then it really was silent.

~

The sun was rising earlier and earlier in the lead up to summer. There were no curtains or blinds covering the windows so the children were usually awake before a bell-wielding nun would come down the corridor disturbing the quiet with the metallic instrument. This was one morning that Robbie was awake long before the need to be. He had spent most of the night wide awake thinking about the boy in the other room. He had an idea who it was but couldn't be sure. The discipline at Saint Vincent's made him angry and fuelled his rebellious streak.

Robbie was named after Robinson Crusoe due to his father being an avid reader of the *"Classics"*. Only the adults called him Robinson. The other children didn't refer to him as this. It was too formal and not fitting to his character. The common trait he had with his namesake was the appetite for adventure. Robbie was always looking for the next adventure and discovery. When he was younger, he was always out and about making his mother worry. But the arrival of the war put a stop to all that. He became more reserved and agitated.

He had been at the orphanage for almost a year. A series of unfortunate events had left him without both his parents. His father was killed in the trenches somewhere near the western front. He was at home with his mother when a knock at the door revealed a young boy with a letter in hand. The sight of his mother as she fell to her knees was a vision he doubted he would ever forget.

It was only a matter of months before the conclusion of the war when he was at school the day his house was bombed with his mother inside. The fact that this had happened so close to the end of the war made it even more difficult for Robbie to comprehend. The past year had been a complicated one and Robbie's dealing with losing both of his parents at times was clear to see.

His only living relative had been a grandmother further north who was more of a stranger than anything. After a brief spell, it was clear that she did not have the capability to look after him, therefore he had been assigned to the orphanage at Saint Vincent's, which predominantly took in children who had suffered the casualties of the war. It wasn't his choice but at the time there had not been other more favourable choices for a boy his age.

Saint Vincent's orphanage had been around for many years but, because of the war, was struggling to cope with the pressure of taking in new residents. The beds were available and it was certainly a sizeable building, but it couldn't house many children due to insufficient funding.

Standing on the concrete steps at the large front doors, the first nun he saw was Sister Meredith and instinct told him this person was not to be taken lightly. He was clutching his few belongings that had been salvaged from the house, including a splendid-looking compass that had been given to him by his father, which he kept with him at all times. He had also been given a selection of donations since the bombing; a few items of clothing, some personal possessions and a few books – most of which had not been read.

The bell rang out - time to get up. Breakfast was a somewhat miserable experience in the orphanage. The food was questionable at best and there was not a lot of it to go around. Robbie didn't know much about the general funding of Saint Vincent's; he never cared to find out. But wherever the money came from, it certainly wasn't by the bucket-load. Meal times took on a certain prison-feel, the children lining up with their metal trays to be dealt spoonsful of God-knows what. Maybe God did know, although if He did, Robbie was sure He wouldn't have allowed it.

Meals were set up in a different room to where they slept - next to the kitchen. It was a lot smaller than the two halls so there was not as much of an echo. Robbie, Mollie and Jack-Jack always lined up for breakfast together. There were so few children at the orphanage, all ages and genders were grouped together for night time, meal times and lessons.

Ordinarily, orphanages were predominantly gender specific; nuns would look after the girls and monks would look after the boys. Saint Vincent's was different in that aspect.

Even though the building itself was large, it had always had minimal staff and from its early years had taken in children of all ages and genders. However, the lack of standards had meant the upbringing of the younger children had been quite poor. They just weren't given as much attention as was required.

The boy who Sister Meredith had disciplined last night was a few places in front of them in the queue. His name was Linton. Visible bruising could be seen on the side of his face. He wasn't making any attempt to hide the markings and was remaining quiet with his head down in line, as all the children were. One by one, they were dealt the near-inedible swill before taking their seats on one of the two long tables that were set out. Today's selection looked like some sort of porridge with one slice of stale toast. As Robbie took it, he thought to himself that the colour of the porridge resembled the same colour as the walls in their sleep hall.

Not one of them had said a word since the three children had entered the room and this continued after they were seated. Robbie looked over at Linton and couldn't help but compare his portion to the others around him, including his own. Not that it was a bad thing considering the dish, but he noticed Linton's portion was considerably less than everyone else's. The only sounds echoing through the room were of chewing, swallowing and cutlery clanging together. Two nuns were walking around slowly as if supervising an exam.

When no nun was close by, Robbie leaned over in the direction of Mollie, Jack-Jack and a few others in earshot and whispered, 'Something has to be done about those nuns.'

16

Mollie was the first to react, 'Quiet Robbie. They'll hear you. This is not the time. Wait until the waterhole.'

'Pipe down. They can't hear me.' He looked quickly over his shoulder. 'Besides, those two bats are almost dead. Probably couldn't hear me if I screamed down their lugholes. Look, Linton did nothing wrong. How many times do we whisper and talk in a night-time? Like that's a crime? We only think it is because they make us think it is. Kids should be allowed to talk whenever they want, not just when they say so. We haven't done anything wrong to be here and yet that's what the rules suggest. It's all just bull.'

'I know that. We all know that, Robbie,' Mollie responded as the other children listened on, in fear that this little debate would indeed be overheard and get everyone in the close vicinity in trouble. 'It's not like we all follow the rules and think it's right. This place is an orphanage run by nuns..... nuns, Robbie. It's the only way they know.'

'Don't give me that. They enjoy it. They use this place to exert their power over us and they know that no-one is going to stop them. It sounds like you're defending them.'

'I'm not defending them at all! I hate this place and everything in it, but it's where we are. We have a roof over our heads and food in our stomachs, if you can call it that. Other children are not so lucky.'

'That may be so, but does it have to come at that price? Just for keeping us here does not give them the right to treat us that way and they know it. God's work my arse. If that's what it's like up there with this bunch of cretins doing His work then I don't want to know. Look, all I'm saying is.....'

The whispering stopped as Robbie sensed one of the nuns coming closer. He thought he might have noticed too late, but the nun just walked on by and then once again was out of earshot. 'All I'm saying is maybe it's time to stand up against them, somehow.'

'And just how are we supposed to do that, Robbie? You know we can't. We're trapped here. If we did, it would only end up worse for any one of us or the whole group.'

'So Linton just has to take a beating and rationed food for no good reason. Is that it?'

'I don't like it any more than you do, but there's nothing we can do about it right now.' She looked over at Linton who was visibly upset, looking like he could burst into tears at any moment.

Just then, a girl on the other table to them started to be sick on the floor. It drew the attention of every child in the room as well as the two nuns who made haste over to the girl.

One nun in particular was distraught about her being sick. She stood over the girl with her hands on her hips. 'Sister Beatrice, go and get one of the kitchen staff to come and clean this up. Wasting food is unacceptable. Unacceptable indeed. Now come along. We need to get you cleaned up. Good gracious girl, you're a mess. Just look at you. You should be ashamed of yourself.' She grabbed the girl by the arm and pulled her away from the table and marched her down the corridor, all the while chuntering something under her breath which the children were unable to make out.

Once out of sight and with Sister Beatrice off to fetch someone to do the dirty work, Robbie continued, 'Do you see? Do you see what I mean? Punished for something that isn't a crime. No compassion at all. I'm surprised more of us aren't sick to our stomachs eating this crap.'

'We know, Robbie. Do you think we all don't see? Just because you're the eldest here doesn't mean you're the only one with a set of eyes and ears. Look, just keep your wits about you until we get out of here, otherwise you're going to regret it.'

Mollie always was the voice of reason. It seemed to Robbie that, even though she was a year younger than him, she played the role of his conscience very well. He kept quiet from then on and finished his breakfast, as did all the other children. Debate finally over.

The girl didn't return to the dining room.

~

After breakfast it was time to get washed up and dressed for the day. No-one could understand why it didn't make more sense to get washed and dressed before breakfast. It certainly seemed more hygienic, but as Robbie had pointed out before, it was probably in case of any spills or mishaps.

This too was not a pleasant task. The water in the orphanage was usually cold, tepid at best, and was only slightly more endurable at the moment due to the warmer months. Many a child during the winter got sick because of the cold but, as usual, nothing ever got done about it.

The washrooms were all communal. There were a number of showers and basins all lined up next to each other in a sort of changing room set up. There was no gender separation in the orphanage and this was no exception. The girls were forced to wash in the same room as the boys, which embarrassed some of the girls terribly – especially the older ones. Boys being boys, didn't seem to mind or pay any attention to it most of the time. But some of the girls would wait until the boys were finished before washing themselves, which at times made them late for any lessons they had to attend. Being late to a lesson was never a good idea so it meant that some of the girls didn't spend as much time washing themselves as they should have.

The pyjamas given to the children were a dirty grey colour and all went in a large washing basket before going into the washroom. This too was usually supervised by a nun, even though at times there wasn't one available, mostly due to attending what needed to be done after breakfast. This was one of those times. Maybe it was on account of the girl being sick but there was no nun in the washroom this morning.

Robbie thought this might be a good opportunity to get one over on the nuns, at least in his mind.

'I'm not going to wash,' he said. He had already put his pyjamas in the wash basket and entered the washroom.

'Robbie no, what if a nun walks in and sees you haven't? Why take the risk?' Mollie pleaded.

'They're not going to be able to tell. Besides, look, I'm not dirty.' He lifted his arms up totally naked and did a twirl.

A little embarrassed, Mollie turned her back and couldn't deny herself a rare smile. She said, 'Yeah well. Remember when I did the same thing and got caught? I didn't think any of them would see me or even care, but they did.'

On that particular occasion, Mollie had tried her hand at her own attempt at rebellion. With Robbie's encouragement, she had gone to leave the washroom just as a Sister had entered the room, so it was obvious Mollie wasn't going to wash and was going to go straight to the hall to get dressed. The Sister had been incensed at this and taken Mollie to the washbasin and washed her herself. Mollie recalled this being dreadfully embarrassing and the Sister was anything but gentle during the process. She used the scrubbing brush that the children never used, which was incredibly scratchy, and was particularly rough with her throughout. Mollie was left with red marks all over her body and a few scratch marks that had broken the skin. These had agitated her throughout the whole day. She told herself it wasn't worth risking it after that.

'Nah, I don't care anyways,' Robbie announced a little louder now with an air of cockiness about him. He picked up a towel, wrapped it around himself and left the washroom, dry hair and all, and went to the hall to get dressed. He passed two nuns who were having a quiet chat while some of the other children who had washed were getting dried and dressed, neither of them noticing a thing. Once dressed, he sat on his bed with a smug smirk on his face as he looked around the room. It was a small victory but a victory nonetheless. Robbie loved getting one over on the nuns, even if it was one as insignificant as not washing oneself in the morning.

Chapter II

**"What the mind doesn't understand,
it worships or fears."**
Alice Walker

It was a sunny day and sunny was good. It meant the children could go outside as they loved to do and escape the confines of the orphanage, providing there were no lessons to attend. There was nothing to do inside the orphanage. The nuns were there constantly and the children did all they could to avoid being in their presence.

Fellowood Marsh was a small, forgotten town which had remained stagnant in its own past. For whatever reason, it couldn't get over its relationship with superstition and legend. It swamped it like a dense fog. The tribulations of the recent war had done little to shunt the town into the present. It was almost as if the last several years had passed it by like a silent ship on a still night.

The town was picturesque. Because of being completely surrounded by trees for miles in all directions, it was unique and stood alone, as if in another world. There was only one main road in or out of the town, which led to the much larger town of Savannah's Bridge. To say this was a road may have been pushing it a little.

The town consisted of one main, dusty unkept street that was quite wide in structure. The orphanage stood at the top of this street with the street declining away from it towards the mines at the foot of the town. Either side of the street was lined with a select number of shops and businesses. There was a small path that led to a quaint little church hidden amongst the trees and some small rundown houses situated at the back of the town on the opposite side. About half way down the street was a small island made of stone on which once stood a tall wooden cross. Some of the town-folk who had lost family during the war wanted a memorial built on the island but were not confident that the town council would ever get round to it.

When Robbie arrived almost a year ago with his one rustic green bag slung over his shoulder and a heavy step, he thought to himself that the town and its surroundings were actually quite beautiful and steeped in mystery; the kind of place you would see in old history books under the heading "folklore".

Once breakfast and other menial tasks had been completed, the three friends left the orphanage to enjoy the hot morning sun, stepping out onto the concrete steps down into the dust. Robbie was still feeling smug about his tiny success after breakfast and with that, Mollie was also feeling slightly aggrieved at having her advice ignored.

It was evident the day was going to be sweltering. The sweat was already starting to bead on Robbie's forehead. Good, he thought. That meant they could be out for a large part of the day; a bit of respite from that dreadful place.

There were not many people out and about just yet. Fellowood Marsh was awake but in its early stages. As they walked downwards towards the end of the town they passed a sleepy looking two-storey wooden house. A man was sitting on his porch as he always did early in the morning, rocking back and forth with a pipe hanging from his mouth, whittling away at whatever project was in progress. The house looked ashen with its white paint chipped away in all areas and dirt-stained glass making the windows almost impossible to see through.

The whittler was called Virgil. He was a content, retired gentleman who had lived in this particular house in Fellowood Marsh all his life. He was a creature of habit and never deviated away from his routine. Some people called him the Godfather of the town, always watching over everybody from his porch throne.

His house sat towards the bottom end of the town and was far too big for just one elderly man, but Virgil didn't mind. He had lived there from a small boy with his family and taken on the family house by himself, having never been married or had children. He was a simple man and he liked it that way. He liked his porch, his tobacco and his wooden art. As he used to say: *"A complicated life makes for a confused mind"*.

It was a house with the front door and porch positioned on the corner of the house rather than in the centre. Inside was littered with "whittlings", looking like a wooden museum; mostly of animals like small rodents or birds, mixed with some trees and other little artefacts. They were not of a great standard considering how long Virgil had been trying to perfect this craft, but Virgil was not interested in being a craftsman or artist. He liked what he did and it was his habit.

This morning as the children approached him, the piece of wood forming in his hands looked like it was taking the shape of some sort of fish.

'Morning children,' he said with a glance up over the top of his glasses. 'Lovely morning, isn't it?'

'Hello, Virgil. What are you working on?' replied Mollie.

Virgil held it up, as if inspecting it closely, 'What do you think?'

'Looks like a fish to me!' exclaimed Mollie.

'Uh uh, I think it looks more like a squirrel,' said Robbie playfully looking down at his feet, hitting a few small rocks with a stick.

'Mollie, that is why you are the brains of the outfit and Robbie,' Virgil looked at him as he took off his glasses, 'I think maybe you need these, my boy,' before laughing mockingly.

Robbie pushed the hand holding the glasses away. 'I know, I know it ain't no squirrel. I was only having fun. I like it though. Looks like the kind me and Jack-Jack catch sometimes down at the river – only those are less wooden. Is this one to go inside too, Virgil? You're soon enough going to have nowhere to stash those things.'

'Oh, I'll find a place. Think maybe this one might look quite good next to my bed.'

'You could try selling 'em.'

Virgil looked at Robbie. 'These aren't for no selling boy. They've got more value to me in there than any coin in my hand. I do this to keep my mind at rest and seeing them all around makes me feel at ease. Don't you have anything like that?' It was a poor question and slipped out before Virgil could catch the words. He was well aware how few possessions the children had to their name.

'Uh uh. Nothing like that anyways. Wouldn't have anywhere to put them even if we did. I really would like to live in a big house like this one day though,' Robbie stated as he looked up.

'Yeah, me too. I'd have that room right up there,' agreed Mollie playfully, pointing to the window right above her head.

'I..I..I would too, Robbie. One d..d..day I'd like to live in a big house like th..th..this one,' Jack-Jack also agreed. He didn't say much around other people due to his lack of confidence, but Virgil had always made the children feel very comfortable around him and had never made any remark about Jack-Jack's speech impediment.

'Well, maybe one day you will,' Virgil looked over at the orphanage further up the street. 'You won't be there forever you know.'

'One more day is too damn long,' Robbie said with a hint of anger.

Nothing else was said among the four of them for a few moments until Mollie asked, 'Are you going to live here for the rest of your life, Virgil?'

''Til my dying day, child. No-one's ever taking me away from this place. I'll not be dying in no hospital or resthouse. They're no place for the likes of me. They'll have to take me kicking and screaming first. I was born right up those stairs when my parents had me. I've seen my family go one by one and remained here ever since. This place is filled with memories, not all pleasant mind you, but they all make up what I am. That's the most important thing.

'So what are you lot going to do today? Swan it off no doubt like you always do?'

'I..I..want to go fishing, Robbie. C..c..can we go today?' Jack-Jack pleaded.

'We went only yesterday. Darn if there aren't more things to do around here than catch stupid fish all the time. It's so boring around here. A boy can't have adventures like in the olden days,' as he continued to rearrange the stones underfoot.

'So it's adventures you want is it?' said Virgil. 'I've seen many an adventure round these parts. This place isn't as boring as you might think my lad.' The knife grated on the piece of wood in his hand as he spoke. 'I wear these glasses, but they only help me see so much. Now Old man Joe, there's a different matter altogether.' Robbie looked up, suddenly attentive. 'Yes sir, as it's told, he never needed glasses to see more than I'll ever be able to see.'

Just at that moment, the story was interrupted by the tall lonely figure of a man walking slowly past where the children were sitting. It was a walk that demanded attention. They watched him walk past without acknowledgement. To him, they weren't even there. This was a rare sighting of this man. The children had seen him before but, like waiting for hours on the side of the river for your line to jolt, it was sporadic.

With the man out of earshot, Virgil continued, but not on his story. Instead he said, *'There he goes - the rogue that bears the name..... Fletcher Mane.'* This was a saying that had become popular among some of the children in Fellowood Marsh. One boy had said it one day and because it rhymed and sounded good, it had stuck.

Fletcher Mane was a man pitied by some, feared by others and misunderstood by most. People are always afraid of what's different, and Fletcher Mane was different. He had a walk about him that stood out from the rest; it was slow, steady and deliberate. It was almost as if he walked without his head bobbing up and down.

He was a thin man with long arms and light brown hair. He lived alone in a house tucked around the back of town at the bottom of the street and had done for as long as anyone could remember. The house was rundown, but boasted a sizeable back garden decorated with lines of rose bushes with a fence surrounding it. There was only a small garden in the front with a cobbled path leading to the front door.

He was a long-time resident of Fellowood Marsh but was treated as if he were a common rat which came out of its house once in a while, making everyone feel uncomfortable with its presence. He would mind his own business and in return, the town would let him.

Today he was carrying some garden utensils under his arm. Having a garden meant he could spend his time outside but still in the confines of his home, out of sight from the rest of the town; a luxury that not many others had. Some of the town-folk were somewhat envious of this.

'I've not seen him for a while,' said Mollie.

'He's reclusive to say the least. Yes sir, that man's got problems I'd say. But he ain't willing to tell nobody, so nobody knows nothing about him. I can't remember him saying more than a nod to anybody. Why, I don't even know if the man *can* speak,' replied Virgil.

'He lives in that big house at the bottom of the street, doesn't he?' asked Mollie.

'Yes. It was empty for a while. Nobody seemed to want it and then, one day, Fletcher Mane appeared in town and moved in. Nobody knows where he came from and he must have money from somewhere because he was only a young man at the time and, as far as I know, has never had a job while he's lived here. People don't like him because he's different and because he never speaks to anybody, even when he goes to the store.'

'He ain't so bad if you ask me,' said Robbie. 'He's just trying to get along. Best thing to do is leave him be. He ain't hurting nobody.'

Virgil held up his masterpiece. 'He just tends to those rose bushes and keeps himself to himself. All that work and I doubt if he'll ever find any use for them,' he said as he inspected his craftsmanship. All the while, the children had been talking to him, not noticing him finishing off his fish. 'So, what do we think?'

'Splendid Virgil. Just splendid,' was Mollie's answer, sounding a little over-zealous.

'Your best yet,' Robbie said, slightly sarcastically.

'I'm not so sure,' replied Virgil giving it a closer inspection. 'Right, my little rapscallions, time for you to be moving along. I'm going to find a place for my new friend here and the days moving along fast, so I think you should be too. Go get into trouble, but not too much mind you. Don't want to be getting on the wrong side of those nuns, now do we?'

The children acknowledged Virgil's request and stood up, dusting themselves off. They walked off towards a familiar but hidden, overgrown path that led into the trees. Before too long they arrived at the waterhole.

29

~

The waterhole was a sizeable hole that sank into the ground with natural spring water at the bottom of it. On really hot days, the children would climb down to drink the water which so far hadn't done any of them any harm. The water tasted so pure and fresh and was a welcome saviour from the hot days in the forest. They would only do this on rare occasions as it was quite slippery and treacherous.

The waterhole stood in a clearing in the trees and acted as their sanctuary away from everything and everyone. It was only a short walk but, as far as they were aware, no-one else knew of the waterhole, which made it even more special. It was a place where they could escape and hang out without being bothered by anyone. The surrounding area, as far as they knew, was densely populated by nothing but trees and wildlife. The only thing they could hear aside from the birds and the rustling of the occasional visiting animal in the undergrowth was the gentle sound of the spring water. This was a steady, calming trickle that never stopped; they didn't even understand where it came from or if it ever would stop.

Robbie sat on the edge and swung his legs down into the waterhole, dangling them there as he liked to do. Mollie and Jack-Jack were always a little more cautious and sat or lay down on the side but not too close to the edge. There were also several large rocks that acted as seats if so needed, but some of them could be quite uncomfortable, and there was a nearby small tree that had a few low branches that the children could climb up and sit on. It was their own little, natural camp site.

'That Fletcher is a strange man.' They hadn't spoken since leaving Virgil's house to traipse through the undergrowth and Mollie was the first to speak. 'Why does he act that way all the time?'

'What way?' Robbie answered.

'You know, creepy-like. He never speaks to anyone or looks at anyone. He's always up to something too.'

'He ain't up to nothing. He's just a lost soul is all. That's what happens when you don't live with folk all your life or have anyone to speak to. Fellow goes a bit stir crazy.'

'Wh..wh..what's stir crazy m..mean Robbie?' Jack-Jack asked after thinking for a second.

'Stir crazy means after a while, a chap can go insane. Starts talking to the walls and howling at the moon. Many a man has had it happen to them. Lose their mind and run around the streets with no clothes on or nothing.'

'H..howling at the moon? Like a..a..animals do?'

'Yeah, just like animals do,' Robbie swung his legs while throwing tiny twigs inside the waterhole.

'Leave it off Robbie, it's enough to give Jack-Jack nightmares that is. And I'll be the one staying up with him trying to keep him quiet so the nuns don't hear,' Mollie pleaded.

'I w..w..won't have nightmares. I'm much more g..g..grown up than to worry about silly things like th..that. I know it ain't real.'

'Insanity's real alright, all too real for them that it happens to and for those they murder.'

Robbie had a curious affliction for teasing Jack-Jack. Most of the time it would just be older boy winding younger boy up as kids do, but sometimes the line would get blurry and Robbie would go too far, which usually resulted in him feeling bad afterwards and having to cheer Jack-Jack up somehow.

There was a four year gap between the two boys and Jack-Jack meant the world to Robbie. Robbie acted like a young father figure and felt compelled to watch out for Jack-Jack whenever he could.

Jack-Jack had never known his father. For that matter he had never known his mother either, but he had at least had a connection with her, if only for a brief spell.

He wasn't an orphan. His mother's family had brought him to the orphanage when he was just a baby due to their strict religious beliefs. She was very young, unmarried and had fallen pregnant. She had given birth at a shelter for young mothers, but once Jack-Jack was born there was no room for them to stay there permanently. For the mother there was no other option. She couldn't go against her family's beliefs and she couldn't look after the baby by herself with no money or place to stay. The family thought leaving him in the hands of an orphanage would give him the best start in life where he would be safe, taken care of and taught in the ways of the Lord.

It was the hardest thing she had ever had to do in her young life. The family had gone late at night to the sleepy town and left Jack-Jack on the concrete step in a baby basket – he didn't even cry. It had broken his mother's heart.

After a short while, when Jack-Jack's family had long gone, he had begun to cry and alerted the attention of the nuns. They had found him on the step unharmed and taken him inside without knowing anything about him, not even his name. The nuns had named him Jack but had declined to give him a last name, so when the subject had arisen, he was simply named Jack Jackson.

'Before Fletcher walked past, Virgil was going to tell us something about Old man Joe. Something right interesting too, I reckon. Which reminds me. I heard something the other day.' Robbie was always telling of rumours he had heard while sneaking around various nooks and crannies in town.

'Oh, yeah?' enquired Mollie. 'Where were you when you heard this then?'

'I was hiding behind Marley's Store with Drayton. I heard a few women having a talk about him so I earwigged.'

'Okay, so what did they say?'

'It was just this one woman. She was all in a panic you know, like she'd just seen a ghost or something. I couldn't see her face but I bet it was as pale as breakfast. She was telling the others that she had had a visit from Old man Joe a few nights back. He had come into her room and taken her hairbrush. She was in a mighty fix I tell you.'

'A hairbrush, is that all?'

'It's not the hairbrush, Mollie. The hairbrush ain't the thing. It's that this woman swears that it was Old man Joe. And now she's telling everyone that he's visiting again, like he done before. She's getting them all riled up. I tell you, this town will never leave that story behind. It's like..... I don't know, like they're suffocated or something. This Old man Joe, for example, has anyone ever seen him on one of these visits?' Robbie had been sceptical ever since he had first heard of the tales. He had no doubt that this man was no myth. He had yet to see any evidence of any supernatural behaviour, but that wasn't to say that it wasn't all true. The town was so steeped in superstition and he was just an inexperienced young boy. What did he know? He would put on this sceptical exterior, especially in front of Mollie and Jack-Jack, but deep down, if he was being totally honest with himself, the legend of Old man Joe frightened him more than he would like to admit.

'It must be true, Robbie. It's happened to so many people, how can it not be? I believe it.'

'Of course you would, you're as impressionable as the rest of them.' Mollie tried not to take offence. 'Alright, look. Let's say it is true. Why does he do it? What's the point?'

'It's that eye, isn't it, that witch cursed it all those years ago.'

'That's the most interesting part of the whole story, that glass eye.'

'Wh..wh..what about the glass eye, Robbie?' Jack-Jack had heard many stories about Old man Joe's glass eye but, just like other children tell scary stories around a campfire, he enjoyed hearing about the tales even though they usually stopped him sleeping. The waterhole was the children's campfire.

Robbie pulled his legs from out of the waterhole and turned towards the other two. 'Many years ago, in the dark times, there was this witch - a witch so evil she was scared by her own reflection. Everyone in the town was afraid of her and her spells. One day, she apparently put a curse on the Constable for something he had said to her in the street. He had called her a meddling witch, or something like that, so later that night she had put a curse on him. The next day, he was dead.'

'How did he die, Robbie?' Mollie interjected.

'It don't matter what he died of.' In truth Robbie didn't know. 'The fact is he died, all because of her and the curse she put on him. Well, the town were in uproar so they were. They put two and two together and that was that. A big witch-hunt took place. They all went looking for her with pitchforks and spades and lanterns and all that, like you hear in all them tales, every single one of them.' Robbie's voice lowered, 'Well, they found her and dragged her kicking and screaming to the cross which stood in the town centre and stood her dead set in the middle of this pile of wood against the cross. They tied her arms behind her back as she was mumbling something that weren't English, then they all stood back.'

The other two children were riveted. Every time they heard the story it was as if it was the first time. The story had been passed down through the years. There hadn't been a legal burning at the stake in England that century. Fellowood Marsh was a forgotten town and rooted in the past. Nothing was ever told of the burning for some reason, so therefore the story only lived on within the town.

'Now, guess who spoke next,' Robbie continued. 'That's right - Old man Joe. He was the brother of the Constable and was the one who did the sentencing you see. It was him who gave the go ahead for the wood to be set alight. And he did it, just like that. He said in a booming voice: *"Witch! You have brought this upon yourself! For the atrocity you have committed against my family and this town, you shall perish by fire and so your soul will be purified!"* And then he said: "Do you have anything to say?"'

'What happened then, Robbie?' asked Mollie intrigued.

'Well, you see Old man Joe had lost his right eye some years earlier due to a bad infection, or so I'm told, so the witch she turned to him and looked him dead in his good eye and said: *"I curse you for sending me to the grave. After I am gone, even long after you are gone, you will be feared by this town. You will no longer be able to walk the streets."* Then she tilted her head back and closed her eyes, *"I curse that false eye you keep in your head. I give it the ability to see into people's souls. You will visit them in their sleep. You will watch over them even long after you are dead. You will no longer be able to rest in peace as I shall do. I curse you!"'*

He took a long pause. 'Then came the lighting. The pile of wood beneath her got lit and then the flames grew bigger and bigger. It weren't fast neither. It was slow, starting at her feet and moving up her body. Everyone expected her to scream but she didn't make a sound. Even when it got up near her face and covered her whole body she was dead quiet. Just let it happen. Burned to death right there as everyone watched. So I'm told, you could smell the burning flesh and people had to put cloth or whatever they had up to their mouths. Some even took to throwing up it was that bad.'

Both children listened with their mouths open as Robbie continued, 'You see, the whole town was there so they all heard her curse, and once more they all believed it too because of what had happened to the dead man she had cursed. From that day on, Old man Joe wasn't welcome in the town; too many people feared his glass eye.'

'So what happened to him, Robbie?' Mollie asked.

'He had to leave is what. Leave and never come back. He vanished and no-one knew where to. Since then, some say he went to live in a cabin deep in the woods where he lived until he died right there in that same cabin. That's where he remains still with his glass eye, still visiting folk. They say if you get visited, when he looks into your soul, it burns – burns just like the fire underneath the witch's feet.'

'S..s..stop it now, Robbie, I'm g..getting scared,' Jack-Jack said suddenly.

'Aw c'mon Jack-Jack, you've heard all this before. And besides, it ain't real.'

'Y..yes it is so real.'

'How can you say it isn't real Robbie?' asked Mollie. 'You've seen and heard what people say.'

'Yeah, but you know what this town is like. They're all crazy, the lot of 'em.'

'I hope he doesn't v..v..visit me in the night. He w..w..won't, will he, Mollie?' Jack-Jack pleaded.

'See, now look what you've done. These stories are all well and good until it goes too far. Jack-Jack's only nine you know. It's too much for him sometimes.'

'I ain't trying to scare him, you know.' Robbie hated scaring Jack-Jack and it was usually too late before he realised he had. He stood up and brushed the foliage from his trousers. 'Come on, let's head back.'

The story was over, for now.

Chapter III

**"When people talk, listen completely.
Most people never listen."**
Ernest Hemingway

Lessons in the orphanage were nominal. The nuns were more bothered about discipline than education. Children from Saint Vincent's were not allowed to attend the schoolhouse in town under the schoolhouse's strict policy. This was the way it had always been. It meant the children at the orphanage were vastly uneducated compared to the other children in the town which, in itself, created a divide between the children in Fellowood Marsh.

The schoolhouse was a collection of small classrooms. The rooms contained small, one seater wooden desks and chairs that all faced towards the teacher's desk at the front. Windows covered the walls and there was a low wooden fence that encircled the building around the outside. There was also a small garden at the back which the children tended to as part of their extra-curricular activities.

One reason for the divide was that children attending the schoolhouse had to go to school every day, whereas children at the orphanage could go outside when they didn't have lessons. Many of the parents had argued persistently about this because it was distracting to their own children, but the Town Council had done nothing to quell the divide; just another example of Fellowood Marsh being behind the times.

All the children at the orphanage attended the lessons therefore the classes were made up of children of both genders and all ages, just like at meal times and bed times. It just wasn't big enough. This made it particularly difficult to accurately teach age-related material to the children; either the subject wasn't challenging enough or it was too difficult.

Robbie hadn't been at the orphanage long, and had attended a city school before the war and before the tragedy that had killed his mother and sent him to Saint Vincent's. He had been doing rather well at school, showing enthusiasm and high potential. However, the past year had greatly affected Robbie's confidence and focus. His concentration in class was deteriorating, resulting in his education declining rapidly. Again, the orphanage seemed to do little or nothing to spot this and do anything about it, so it just continued. Robbie just became more and more distracted and would only focus on things like adventures or what he could get up to in the sleepy town after getting out of lessons. Lessons, after all, were horrible for the children. The fact that they didn't have to attend lessons as much as their fellow peers in the schoolhouse was little consolation for how bad it was during lessons. Not only was it dreadfully boring, but it was unpredictable as to how harsh the nuns were going to be on any given day. At times, children would get caned for the slightest thing, it seemed. The cane was used in city schools also, but it seemed to be more prolific in the orphanage.

The morning's lesson was about as tedious as the rest. The lessons were always in this one room so everyone had their own individual desk: Robbie being on the back row next to a window, Mollie just in front of him and Jack-

Jack a few rows to his left. Robbie was thankful for his position in the room as it meant he could spend most of his time staring out of the window at the sun-soaked leaves on the trees, lightly blowing in the breeze. He loved the trees and the greenery. He always wanted to be outside exploring and to be in the fresh air. If he could, he would live outside, lying under the stars listening to the sound of nothing but the creatures around him and the rustling of the trees.

Sister Beatrice had given the lesson this morning. To Robbie, she was boring and had a monotone voice that went right through him. The lesson itself had been uneventful. The subject had been about something to do with history, mainly focusing on the eighteenth century but, if he was honest, he couldn't tell you exactly what about.

The best thing about it was the overly high-pitched ringing of the bell that left every child there with temporary tinnitus, signifying the end of the lesson. After trying to get in the final bit of the lesson having run out of time, Sister Beatrice gave the signal it was the end of class.

~

After class, all the children would take their books back to the sleep hall before going off to do whatever it was they chose to do before lunch and another lesson in the afternoon.

'I'm going over to The General. Are you coming?' Robbie said to both Mollie and Jack-Jack, setting his books on the bed.

Jack-Jack looked up, 'I am R..R..Robbie. I want to go with you to The General. I l..l..love The General.' At times,

Jack-Jack's stutter subsided when he was excited. The words would flow out without obstacle, but it was a rarity.

Mollie nodded her head imperturbably; what else was she going to do with her time? And besides, it was a nice day outside.

"The General" was a tall, thick oak tree that stood in the middle of a thicket of trees just beyond the town. They had called it The General when Robbie was introduced to the tree because he said that it stood majestically in the middle of the thicket and was taller and bigger than all the other trees around it. He thought it looked as if it was the "general" of a small army, with the other trees acting as the soldiers.

Jack-Jack had learnt to climb here when he was younger. When Robbie had arrived, he had taught him how to go higher than he'd ever been before, much to the worry of Mollie, who had always been used to seeing Jack-Jack get to a certain point before stopping as he had climbed too high. Under Robbie's tuition, Jack-Jack had become braver and felt the need to push himself more and more. There was one time when Jack-Jack had had a stumble and grazed his arm quite badly after falling. They had done their best to conceal the wound from the nuns who would undoubtedly question what had happened; they were never happy with the burden of an injured child.

The General looked inviting today, the branches swaying in the gentle breeze. Robbie was first to ascend the big tree from his favourite starting point. There was no moisture on the branches as it hadn't rained for a while, so he found it easy to get a good footing. It was the perfect day for tree climbing. Robbie was fairly high up before Jack-Jack started to climb. He was of course slower than Robbie. Mollie watched from the ground. She waited for Jack-Jack to get to a point before she started. She felt it was her duty to watch him go up first even though he was quite capable; sort of like a mother figure.

Up and up they went, with only the squirrels to share The General with. Jack-Jack stopped, looking down to the ground with Mollie just below him.

'I'm h..h..high up, huh Mollie?'

She stopped and looked up – then down to assess her own position – then back up to Jack-Jack. 'You're pretty high already. Are you stopping there? Hang on. I'll be there in a second.'

Jack-Jack just looked around, making sure he had his footing correct. It was a scary feeling being high up in a tree, one false move away from tumbling down between all the branches. He looked up to see the underside of Robbie, who was still going up higher but slowing his pace.

'Robbie, wait would you!' Mollie shouted. She always hated the way Robbie would leave Jack-Jack in his wake, just because he was older and more experienced at climbing than he was. She felt he was just showing off.

Robbie looked down to see them both looking up at him; Mollie almost up to Jack-Jack's level. 'Come on you slow-coaches,' he teased. 'It's great up here, the air is so fresh. I feel like I'm on top of the world.'

This tempted Jack-Jack to go higher, so he continued up the tree, one branch after another. 'I'm c..coming up to where you are R..R..Robbie. I want to b..b..be as high as you are.'

Robbie didn't stop. He just carried on up the tree without a care in the world. He heard what Jack-Jack had said to him but, in all honesty, didn't think Jack-Jack would get up to where he was. He knew he could go further up, but even this height was higher than Jack-Jack had ever gone before.

Jack-Jack was going slowly. This was difficult for him. Inside he was scared, but he didn't want to show it and desperately wanted to be bigger and older than his body would allow. This was just another foot race with the older boys.

Before he could take his next step, he heard Robbie's voice from above: 'Hey! Hey, you two. You got to see this. I can see Old man Joe's cabin! It's right over there! Clear as the morning sun!'

'No you don't. Don't be silly, Robbie!' Mollie shouted up.

'I tell you it's right there. It's all surrounded by trees and I can see the roof poking out. It's got a chimney coming out the top too, and it's smoking. Someone must be inside! Hell's bells. He's still alive, I tell you. Old man Joe is still alive! I bet if I shouted loud enough he could hear me!'

Mollie and Jack-Jack were motionless, hanging in the tree like a pair of owls perched up for the night. Jack-Jack in particular was very excited now. He had more incentive to make it up to where Robbie was. Truth be told, he wasn't going to go any higher. He was getting too scared and wanted to go back down. But this changed everything. Before he could think, he had started taking more steps up the branches. Up and up he went, fear a forgotten memory. Mollie watched from below, getting increasingly worried.

Just then, one of Jack-Jack's feet slipped because he was trying to go too fast. Fortunately, there were a lot of branches all around him. The General was a dense tree so he didn't have far to fall before he hit the branch below him. He struggled to hold on and get his balance. It happened so fast. As he hit the branch, he let out a little cry which alerted Mollie. She looked up to see Jack-Jack holding onto the branch in a sideways position, looking like he could fall at any moment.

'Jack!' she yelled, the panic denying her the subsequent "Jack" in his name. 'Hold on! Robbie!' Her yell alerted Robbie who hadn't heard Jack-Jack as he had slipped; he was still looking out over the treetops.

As he looked down, he could see Jack-Jack was trying to hold on, desperately trying to swing his flailing leg up onto the branch, with no success. Robbie could see he was slipping so he moved as fast as he could down the tree. It wasn't easy. The situation he was now in had caused him to be careless and he too almost lost his footing a few times. This was no time to panic. Easier said than done.

He was just a few branches above where Jack-Jack was now, almost in touching distance. Jack-Jack looked up to see Robbie, a look of fear on his face. 'Robbie! Help me!'

No stutter.

Robbie steadied himself at the base of a branch protruding from the tree. He reached out to Jack-Jack's hand and placed it firmly on the piece of branch in front of him and held his shoulders tightly. 'I've got you now. Pull your leg up on to the branch. You'll be fine,' he instructed.

Jack-Jack did as Robbie said and was able to lift his legs up. With a bit of shifting around and a struggle, he was secure on the thick branch as Mollie looked on from below, helpless.

With the situation a little more relaxed, Robbie and Jack-Jack continued to get slightly more comfortable as Mollie made her way up to the two boys and steadied herself next to them. Breaths were heavy and hearts were pounding. They knew that was a close call and even Robbie couldn't deny he felt a pang of guilt run through him for goading Jack-Jack to climb higher with his hoax.

'Are you okay Jack-Jack? I'm sorry, I should have known you were going to try and climb higher if I told you I could see Old man Joe's cabin.'

'Yes, and how is the cabin?' Mollie said irately, obviously annoyed with Robbie's antics.

'Okay, okay. So I couldn't see the cabin. I thought it would be fun to mess with you. I didn't think.'

'You're damn right you didn't think. Look what could have happened to Jack-Jack.'

'Look, I've said I'm sorry.'

Jack-Jack was still steadying himself, not wanting to seem frightened.

Just then, there was a sound of rustling approaching them. The children went silent all of a sudden as though they'd been caught doing something they shouldn't. They looked down through the copious branches and leaves to see two men approaching the tree. The men sauntered over to the tree and sat down with their backs against the thick trunk. Even though they weren't doing anything wrong being up in the tree, the children all felt a need to be discreet; the childlike secrecy of being undetected.

The two men were difficult to identify from above as they were both wearing hats. Robbie thought they must work down the mines.

The mines were where most of the men living in Fellowood Marsh worked. The town was mainly a small mining community. Unless you were a skilled professional or man of stature, you were a miner. They had been there for a great many years and had a long history within the town. The families of the men who worked there all lived in small terraced houses that were situated close to the entrance of the mines. The houses were cramped with poor facilities. They were nothing like Virgil's big old house - these were built for purpose. Most of the time, the houses were damp, draughty and poorly maintained. The town council was meant to look after the houses, but rarely made any substantial improvements. It was not a high standard of living, but working down the mines was a fortuitous position to be in and only a fool would overlook such an opportunity. It provided a roof for a family and food on the table.

The mines themselves were very hazardous and detrimental to the men working there. The toxic fumes and dust often shortened a man's life but were necessary risks to take. Working down the mines was hard. The hours were long and it was unhealthy. Most of the men got aches and pains that would last a lifetime – a lifetime that wasn't expected to be all that long.

The two men sat poised with an intensity about them; elbows on knees and leant forward. The fact that they had sat down signified they may be there for a while. This was not good news for the children who at this point didn't want to be seen as eavesdropping.

'So, how are we going to do it?' one said to the other. Robbie listened to the short sentence with his head tilted to the side. The man had spoken quietly but, with enough concentration, you could still just make out what was being said.

'I ain't sure yet. I told you that. Darn if you aren't always pushing me to make decisions all the time. We got to be clever about this. If anyone sees us we're done for. I say we do it in the daytime. At night, everything is locked up and quiet which will make it harder. People are always more suspicious at night too. What we'll need is a distraction. That's your job, you hear? Then I'll slip in and take the money.'

'And what will I do as a distraction?'

'I don't know yet. Blast it all, am I going to have to come up with every little detail of this plan? I'll think of something. Now, the store in town usually holds quite a lot of money on a weekend, so I think that's when we do it. Hell, there'll be enough for me to set myself up real proper like, away from this festering pit of a town.'

'And me, it'll set me up too, right?' said the other man.

'Yeah, yeah sure. It'll set you up too, that's what I meant,' without conviction is his voice.

Up the tree, the children realised they were now eavesdropping on what was clearly some sort of plan to rob the general store in town. The need for stealth was much more important now. If they were to be caught, the consequences could be disastrous. Even Jack-Jack knew this and had never been as still and quiet in all his life. Not a leaf rustled.

The first man continued, 'Now you ain't going to mess this up like last time, are you? Christ knows I can't go through that again. I'm counting on you and you ain't going to let me down.'

'No, you can count on me this time. I swear I ain't going to mess it up like last time.'

'Good. You just see that you don't.'

A few moments passed in silence, which was bad news for the children. In the quiet, any little noise from them could alert the two men. Robbie was finding it difficult to hold on to his position and wanted desperately to move. It's funny how when you know you mustn't move, you suddenly want to.

Thankfully, the meeting was over. Both men got to their feet and without another word wandered off, their footsteps in the undergrowth getting quieter as they got further and further away from the tree.

No-one knew what to do. *Who should speak first? Should they move? Was it safe?*

Without saying a word, Robbie moved and started to carefully climb down the tree, the other two following his lead.

With all six feet on the ground, it was Mollie who spoke first but with a cautious tongue, 'What are we going to do? Robbie, are you going to tell the Constable?'

He looked at her patronisingly. 'And say what? If I go to him and tell him that cock and bull, he'll laugh at me and say I was just making it up. He'd say I was being troublesome and, hell, I'd probably get lashed for it.'

'We've got to do something. I mean, if those two are serious, they're going to rob the store.'

'Maybe they won't. I mean, they didn't exactly sound like professional bank robbers, now did they? Did you hear them? Sounded like a right couple of scoundrels and not all too bright at that. I ain't saying nothing. It'll be worse for me if I do and you know it, Mol. No-one takes no notice of a poor troubled orphan boy, do they? They'll just think I'm daft.'

There was nothing else Mollie could say. She knew what Robbie was saying was, unfortunately, quite true. You could be telling the whole truth and nothing but the truth and most, if not all, people in town would just think you were making it up for attention or to cause mischief. She also knew that the same would go for her. Yes, Robbie was making a name for himself as a bit of a troublemaker, but she would get the same response if she went to the Constable herself.

There was nothing they could do and with all the excitement - if you could call it that - they had completely lost track of time. They were surely going to be late for the afternoon's lesson.

All three children knew that was a bad idea so they forgot about the two men and promptly made their way back to the orphanage where Sister Meredith, who had noticed their absence, was waiting on the front steps.

Her demeanour was sombre, with a stern look in her eyes; a look that would stare down even the deadliest of snakes. *How long had she been standing there?*

Her title of "Mother Superior" came with great responsibility and great power. She thrived on that power.

She had been at Saint Vincent's for quite some time now, seeing children come and go. She was old but still had her wits about her. The look on her face usually presented the same portrait; cold, grey, and unforgiving.

She stood on the steps looking down on the children with their heads bowed, the height of the steps giving her a greater advantage than usual. Her arms were crossed, her long, crooked fingers lightly tapping in rhythm on her outer elbows.

'You're late,' she said gravely.

Robbie was the spokesman. 'Sorry Sister, we lost track of time. We were.....'

'I don't care where you were. Where you weren't, was here. That's all that matters. Now, you know what's to come. Hold out your hands, one at a time. Who's first?' Robbie looked up slightly to notice her arms unfold to reach for a cane which was resting against her tunic.

Knowing there was no escaping the inevitable, he stepped forward and held out his hand, palm facing up. With his eyes closed, he felt a swift burst of wind before a sharp pain on his hand. He had felt it before. It wasn't that bad until the swelling would appear.

Mollie was next, then Jack-Jack. Sister Meredith didn't relax the blow for either of the other two, even though they were younger. The lesson paused and the other children watched as they entered the classroom - one hand a lot redder than the other.

Chapter IV

"Compassion is the basis of morality."
Arthur Schopenhauer

The throbbing was, at times, unbearable. Tiny needles pricking his palm. Robbie's hand felt twice the size of its neighbour and would possibly explode at any moment. He sat there on the back row next to the window with one arm resting on the desk at an angle and the other hovering just under the table in the dusty air.

Small welts had begun to appear. They smarted to say the least. He looked over at Jack-Jack, obviously still upset from the caning, but trying to appear not to be. Robbie wasn't upset though, he was angry. Oh, he had had canings before but he felt that Sister Meredith had put more emphasis into the blows today. Maybe she was already having a bad day and had taken it out on them. If *his* hand was on fire, he wondered what Jack-Jack's must be feeling like.

Robbie wasn't good at dealing with anger, especially when it was aimed at the nuns. It was as though they could get away with anything and he couldn't do a thing about it. That didn't sit well with him. He would vent his anger in other ways. He never liked to lose.

Today's lesson was, ironically, about religion and discipline. *Brilliant*, he thought. *Just what we need, more rubbish teachings on how religion is the light and discipline is the tunnel. Or whatever they keep going on about.*

What irritated him the most was looking ahead at the other children, all taking it in. A sea of brainwashed minds. They hadn't chosen to be there yet they were having to be subjected to this tripe and with the Sister's patronising voice reverberating through his bloodstream, it was more than Robbie could take.

The Sister was coming towards the end of a sentence: '….. for the end of all eternity. And for that reason, it is essential that you follow these rules.'

'Yeah, right,' came a mutter from the back of the classroom.

Everyone heard it and, subsequently, the sea of heads turned in unison. The Sister's head didn't have to turn, it just moved up slightly with no change of expression.

'Did someone say something?' the Sister queried, extending her neck.

'I said, "Yeah, right",' was the short response, not giving too much away.

'Who said that?' she asked rhetorically. 'Robinson Harvey, was that you? Have you got something to say to the class?'

'I just don't buy it, is all.'

'You don't buy what exactly?'

'This religion thing, I mean….. it's a bit far-fetched, isn't it? First you tell us about all these things that apparently happened, what is it you call them….. *Miracles*? And now you're feeding us all this pish about discipline and self-righteousness when really it's just abuse, isn't it Sister?'

The tone and level of the disrespect and disobedience was staggering and by the time Robbie's sentence had finished, every child in the room was left with their jaws dangling. Robbie knew how to push buttons and this was a deliberate attempt; a successful attempt.

'What are you talking about, young man?'

'Let's face it. There's no proof any of this happened is there? You might as well tuck us up every night with other fairy-tale stories rather than the ones you teach us from the Bible. At least those would be more entertaining.'

The level increased. The Sister had never come across such insubordination before and she wasn't quite sure how to handle it. 'Robinson Harvey, you stop talking like that at once!'

'I mean, come on. People walking on water? Angels flying in the sky? And about that Jesus fellow,' he was just warming up, 'why, he's just about as made up as the rest of them.' Robbie's hand was starting to feel a little better. 'Like he could do that with bread and wine. Are you lot all really that gullible?'

The rant begun to stir up the whole class and some of the children started snickering and snorting in the most unflattering ways. Like the way you're not supposed to laugh at a funeral, children couldn't help themselves sometimes. Some began to laugh at what Robbie was saying and, for a brief moment, he enjoyed being centre stage. A feeling of vindication swept over him.

Jack-Jack was one of the children who began to laugh, but his laugh seemed to amplify over the rest.

'Jack Jackson, come up to the front of the class this second!'

This was an unexpected turn. The laughter stopped. Robbie stopped. Jack-Jack had been summoned up to the front, and for what? He wasn't the only one laughing and he wasn't the one having this outburst. *Why hadn't she called Robbie up to the front?*

Jack-Jack did as he was told and got out of his seat like a guilty puppy and made the six or seven treacherous steps up to Sister.

'Do you find the mocking of our Lord Jesus Christ amusing?'

Jack-Jack said nothing. He stood stagnant, arms by his sides looking down at the floor.

'I'll ask you again. Do you find humour in the ridicule of our Lord?'

Robbie wanted badly to jump to the boy's aid but he didn't know how. The Sister's request had thrown him for a loop.

Jack-Jack attempted a mumbled response, embarrassed in front of the whole class. 'I..I..don't, Sister. I..I.. don't find it amusing at all.'

'Speak properly boy. If you don't find it amusing, why pray tell were you laughing?' The uncompassionate teasing of Jack-Jack's speech hit Robbie hard.

'I was just l..l..laughing as e..everyone else was.'

'Not good enough. Detention for you. Stay behind after class.'

This made Robbie feel awful and he watched Jack-Jack return to his seat with a forlorn look on his face. He didn't look up – to Robbie or anyone else. Deep regret flowed through Robbie for mocking the lesson and for the remainder he sat quietly, guilt eating him up inside.

He didn't like to lose, but Sister had won.

~

The room echoed more when no-one else was there. He could swear even his breathing echoed. The room seemed bigger and more daunting. As the bell had rung, the children had flooded past him like salmon in a stream, including Robbie and Mollie. He had felt a light tap on his shoulder which he knew was Robbie's, and he knew why.

Jack-Jack rarely got detention and never on his own. If he was party to a mass detention, it was only because he was present; wrong place at the wrong time. But he never did anything to warrant a solo detention. This was new territory. New territory he didn't like.

The walls were meant to be white but they presented more of a creamy, stained finish. There were large windows down one side of the room with a solid wall on both the other side and the back wall, both of which sported gallant efforts of children's art work, with mixed results.

The dust was still attempting to settle after the joyous stampede, each speck floating around trying to find a good place to rest. It clouded the room with a light fog that tickled the back of Jack-Jack's throat. Even though there was no-one around to supervise him, which he found a little strange, he knew there was nothing he could do but allow the time to pass. Time that would be exactly the same speed as any other time he had experienced, but somehow he knew this would seem to pass a lot slower.

To say there wasn't anyone supervising him was premature as the heavy door opened and in walked Sister Athena.

Sister Athena had been at the orphanage ever since she had decided to become a nun. It was the only place she had ever known and served. In the children's eyes, she was the only decent nun at Saint Vincent's, the reversal black sheep.

For whatever reason, she was a different breed to the others. She had kindness in her eyes and voice. She cared, and not because it was her duty; it came naturally to her. She had always wanted to serve the Lord and she loved children. All those years ago when she had been placed at Saint Vincent's - this strange obscure place in this strange forgotten town - she hadn't quibbled once. She didn't care where she was as long as she could care for children and be the best that she could be.

It pained Sister Athena to see how the orphanage was run. It hadn't always been like this. There was a brighter time, but that time seemed to be as forgotten as the town itself.

Jack-Jack was pleased to see her. It meant he had someone here who cared about him and now he didn't feel as lonely. Sister Athena could see how upset he was. She sat in the chair next to him without saying a word.

After a prolonged silence, the dust finally at rest, Jack-Jack spoke, 'W..w..why did I get d..detention? All the other ones w..w..were laughing too. I..I..I was just laughing with them. The other n..n..nuns always pick on me.'

'I don't have an answer for you Jack,' she said softly. To Sister Athena, his name was Jack. It was only the other children who referred to him as Jack-Jack. 'Sometimes things just happen and there is no accounting for it. We all know what this place can be like. Don't you worry yourself, you did nothing wrong, nothing at all. Now, is there anything I can do to make you feel better?'

Jack-Jack doubted there was anything. Make time go faster maybe? No..... she's not that powerful a nun. Instead, he just shook his head glumly. It was okay, the time would soon pass. But he was thankful for the company.

Sister Athena could see he was upset and knew she needn't say more. She stayed with him for the remainder of detention until the Sister who gave the lesson came through the door to release him. She didn't seem to mind that Sister Athena was there with him. She seemed to be more concerned with not having the burden of Jack-Jack in detention anymore. And so that was it, his first solo detention over. At least he hadn't been alone - for some of it anyway.

~

Everyone had gone. Off on their own meagre adventures; to cause mischief, to be bored, who knew? All the children would go their own way after lessons, unsupervised. In reality, the nuns couldn't care less as long as they weren't under their feet.

Jack-Jack knew that Robbie and Mollie would likely be at the waterhole today. There had been no organised plan as they had usually had, because of the sudden unexpected turn of events in the classroom.

He was never on his own after a lesson. If they went to the waterhole, or anywhere else for that matter, it was usually as a threesome. Being the youngest, he was hardly ever on his own anyway. Part of him hoped the other two would have waited for him in the sleep hall but he knew why they hadn't - it was because of the nuns. He understood that.

He could make it to the waterhole by himself. He was braver than he used to be. It wasn't as if it was night time; the sun was shining and the day was bright outside the dark, stricken, porridge-coloured walls of the orphanage.

Jack-Jack started for the waterhole. It took him longer with his short legs than the other two, but it wasn't too far. Through the overgrown bushes and brambles he trekked, snagging his clothes on some wayward thorns along the way.

He couldn't hear any voices as he came into the clearing. His heart stopped when he saw that they weren't there. He was so sure they would be. *Where are they if not here?*

He looked around, his head turning frantically, like a child that suddenly realises they are not by their mother's side. After a few quick turns, he saw something. *Was that them?* Yes, he could just about make them out through the trees. They were almost completely out of sight behind the thick trunks and low hanging branches.

He eagerly made his way over to them. As he got closer, something struck him as slightly odd. They had their backs to him and just stood there, looking down like statues. He could swear, if he reached out to touch them right now, they would be made of stone. There was no breeze for their clothes to be blowing in. They must have been able to hear him coming through the brush, but didn't turn around to acknowledge him.

Jack-Jack slowly joined them by Robbie's side and yet still there was no acknowledgement. The reason they were so enamoured with the ground became clear. The silence was broken by the sporadic sound of flapping wings. There was a chicken that had got caught in a rat-trap but was still alive; its body contorting to try and desperately free itself from the death-grip of the jagged, rusty metal teeth. The grass and soil surrounding the victim was painted in crimson red. No noise was coming from it. The only sound was the slapping of feathered wings hitting the ground on its next attempt to escape.

All three children stared, the compulsion too great to turn away from the misery.

'It must be getting tired,' Robbie said finally. 'I think it's been like this for a while. Look, it has to take a break after trying to get loose. Then it goes again.'

'Poor thing,' Mollie sympathised, 'those traps are brutal. Why do they have to be around?'

'People set them up to stop the rats. There's loads of them round here. I reckon Arnie Took set this one up. His farm ain't too far away from here. It's just on the edge of the woods.'

Robbie took his eyes away from the helpless chicken for the first time since Jack-Jack had joined them. 'Somewhere over there I think,' he nodded, before reverting his attention to the helpless creature.

Meanwhile, Jack-Jack hadn't said anything. He hadn't taken his eyes off the chicken. He had never seen such horror before, the morbid fascination captivating him.

'It's half dead it is,' Robbie continued. 'It won't get out of that.'

'What should we do?' Mollie asked.

'Only thing we can do. Put it out of its misery. It's too far gone and now it's just suffering.'

No-one said anything. Robbie knew it would be down to him to kill it. He was the eldest. No-one would have expected one of the other two to do it.

He looked around. There weren't many stones large enough to do the trick.

Flap, flap, flap.

The chicken's next attempt made Mollie and Jack-Jack jump. Without saying anything, Robbie walked off, leaving the other two still staring, then returned moments later with a sizeable rock he had found near the waterhole.

With one swift up and down movement, the rock came crashing down on the chicken's head.

Dead.

There was no question about it. Its misery was finally over.

Compassion undertaken.

Robbie threw the blood-stained rock away. Blood was now a rug under the chicken and a light smattering had burst onto Robbie's sleeves.

'Now what do we do?' Mollie asked.

'Well, like I said, I reckon this chicken got loose from Arnie Took's farm and wandered over here. Maybe we should take it back to him. I don't know what he'd do with it, but he might be able to use it somehow and I'm sure he'd want it back. Probably doesn't even know it's gone.'

The statement seemed logical enough.

Robbie crouched down and released the chicken from the trap. He had to be extremely careful. These traps were dangerous and he could injure himself profusely. It wasn't easy.

After it was free, Robbie picked it up by the legs, blood dripping from it. Then they made their way in the direction of the farm.

Sure enough, the farm was where Robbie had nodded to, not too far away but enough for the waterhole to still be secluded. By this time, the chicken was almost bereft of blood, hanging from Robbie's hand, swaying in motion with his walk.

Arnie Took's farm was small. It boasted a generous area of land but the farmhouse and barn were modest in size. He didn't have anybody working for him and he liked it that way. Arnie Took was what you might call a loner. He had a short fuse and many people in the town were intimidated by him. A farm on the edge of the forest was probably the ideal location for someone like him.

The farm had been passed down to him many years ago and it was all he knew. The chicken would feel like a substantial loss as he didn't keep many and it was all he could do to keep the rats and foxes from destroying what few he had.

As the children knelt down peering through the fence, it didn't seem like there was any life anywhere. Arnie certainly wasn't anywhere to be seen but that didn't mean he wasn't home. He could be inside the house or in the barn. A farmer very rarely left his work; up at the crack of dawn until the night came. The hours of a farmer were long and strenuous.

'What are you going to do?' Mollie asked. Now that they were here, carcass in hand, she felt a twinge of nerves creep up from her stomach to her throat.

Robbie thought for a moment, 'I could just throw it over the fence. Then it would seem like a fox had got it or something.'

'This chicken is going to be a big loss for him. Times are hard enough as it is. He won't be happy when he finds out one has gone missing, if he doesn't already know. I think we should leave it somewhere he will find it so he at least knows what happened to it and he can use it if he wants to.'

'I don't know. If he's not around maybe I could sneak up and leave it on his porch.'

'B..b..be careful, Robbie,' Jack-Jack said, worryingly peering through the fence.

Robbie climbed over the fence and stealthily crept up to the porch, keeping his head low. Still no sign of Arnie. He set the chicken on the wooden porch. Before he could think, he was running back to the others.

They disappeared into the woods with the chicken safely delivered.

The next problem was that Robbie knew he needed to get inside the orphanage without being seen. He had rolled his sleeves up so the blood splatters were hidden. Still, he didn't want to take any chances.

The front door was open as it usually was in the middle of the day. They entered cautiously. The coast seemed clear. Just before entering the sleep hall, Robbie felt a hand on his shoulder. It was Sister Beatrice.

She looked down on him, tight-lipped. 'And what have you been up to?'

'Nothing, Sister. Nothing at all.'

'Then what's that all up your trouser leg?'

They all looked down in unison. Sure enough, blood had splattered on his trouser leg too. He simply hadn't noticed. He was too focused on hiding the blood on his sleeves.

He had no answer at hand.

'Come with me.' Sister Beatrice moved her hand from his shoulder to roughly grab his arm and marched him off to the Mother Superior, leaving the others standing in the corridor.

Like a naughty child, Robbie was dragged down the corridor. 'You're hurting my arm!' he pleaded, but it was no good. She didn't relax her grip before getting to Sister Meredith's office.

She knocked once on the door before letting herself in. Sister Meredith looked up startled, not having time to say *"Come in"*.

She set her pencil down, interrupted from her task, and entwined her fingers together on the desk in front of her. 'Sister Beatrice! What's going on here?' she inquired.

'Excuse me, Reverend Mother. Robinson here has some blood on his trouser leg and refuses to tell me where it has come from.'

'Is that so? Well, Mr Harvey, shall we try again?'

Robbie still had nothing to say. Usually, he was quite adept at coming up with answers. For some reason, today he was drawing a blank, so he just stood there looking down at the base of Sister Meredith's desk.

A prolonged sigh left her mouth. 'You are proving to be a very troublesome young man. And if you continue down this path, we may have to act with harsher discipline. Don't you think so, Sister Beatrice?'

She didn't wait for a response. 'Now, I sincerely hope that blood isn't from one of your fellow students or any other child in the town, because if I find out it is, you'll wish you were never born my boy.'

The message was clear. A momentary look was shared between the two of them, Sister Beatrice still holding on tightly to his arm.

'For now, a simple cane to both hands should suffice.' She stood up from behind her desk and picked up her cane, which was in a stand next to the window behind her.

'Hold both hands out in front of you, face up.'

He did as he was told. *Thwack, thwack*. The pain was instant. First one then the other. The swelling hadn't even subsided from the previous one.

'You may be excused. Go and wash your clothes immediately and don't let me see you in this room again anytime soon.'

Sister Beatrice released her grip and he went off to the washroom.

The water was cold which stung his hands as he washed his clothes in the basin, a trickle of red liquid cascading around the bowl down the plug hole. Mollie and Jack-Jack came to see him, knowing full well he had probably received the cane for his troubles.

'This is what you get for trying to do a good deed. We could have left that chicken in that trap to suffer or left it in the woods and I wouldn't have got any blood on me at all. Typical.'

'You did the right thing by it though, Robbie,' Mollie tried to reassure him, 'you know that.'

The annoyance was clearly written across Robbie's face. 'Might think twice next time though.'

The next morning as they all woke, Robbie sat up in bed. Mollie pointed out his upper arm. A large bruise in the shape of a hand enveloped it.

My Fate

Less than a year before I arrived at Saint Vincent's, my life changed forever. Being so young, it was hard for me to comprehend. A lot of what I felt about the war resonated from my peers. At times I didn't feel like I had my own mind with my own thoughts; just a twig floating downstream with the current.

You don't ask for a war to begin. You don't ask for a war to continue and you don't ask for a war to take away the people who are dearest to you. A war just happens. There is no warning. There is no manual for how to deal with it. Most of the time you don't know what is happening. You wake up and wonder what the day will bring.

For the majority of the war, life was as normal as it could be for me. After a while, you fall into a regime, a way of life. The longer it goes on for, the more normal this reality becomes and you forget about the one prior.

My mother and I had come to accept what had happened to my father during the war. Not that it was expected, but it certainly came as no surprise, even though this does nothing to quell the nightmare that ensues when it happens.

He was killed in the trenches as so many were. I can remember my mother always expecting the worst every day. The waiting can make you very pessimistic. He was there and we were here. So many soldiers had died that, the longer the war carried on, the more my mother's (and I suppose my) hope faded.

I was in the garden when the knock on the door came. Knocks on doors were infrequent; a neighbour maybe or a postman. I heard it and came inside just as the "angel of death" was leaving. He was a boy around my age. I saw the back of him. It was as if he was running away from me, but I knew what he was really running from. He didn't want to remain after handing over the telegram to my mother. Tears were already forming in her eyes before he could turn his back. The delivery was complete and came with no compassion; the shoulder to cry on was already half way down the street.

She fell to her knees with the door still open. The whole street was able to see if they so chose. She didn't care. Privacy was not the priority. I knew what it was - the dreaded telegram that all families feared to receive. Boys around my age would be used to deliver these messages of horror, earning them the nickname.

I slowly approached her from behind and could think of nothing else to do but lay my hand on her shoulder as a faint act of comfort which resulted in her hand being placed atop mine. I wasn't thinking about myself at that moment. My grieving could come later, which it did.

The weeks and months after that were hard. I guess hard was an understatement. But life continued, as it had to.

As for my mother's death, the thing that made it harder was that it was only a few months before the end of the war, although obviously at that time I wasn't aware of this.

I was at school when a bomb landed too close to our house. I was informed that she felt nothing. Still to this day, I don't know how anyone could have possibly known that.

And so my fate was decided. I had no parents, a grandmother who didn't want me, no home and no real place in this world. That was how the powers that be came to decide Saint Vincent's was the place for me. I'd sure like to know who made that decision. If it was God, I'll deal with Him later.

The aftermath of the bombing was just a blur to me. It still is all these years later. Everything became so frantic. The "normal" life I referred to earlier was no longer normal. Normal took on a whole new meaning. Either that or it ceased to exist.

Somebody told me I was to be sent to an orphanage, at least until something else could be done. I was now an orphan so I guess it made sense. I had no other family around, you see. It was just the three of us before the war. A lot of my friends had large families, but not us. Both of my parents were only children as I was, and all but one of my grandparents were dead. I had no uncles, no aunties, no siblings and no cousins. I had no-one.

When I got told, I didn't care. I was numb from the neck up. What was to happen to me was immaterial. I had not long lost my father and now I had to deal with losing my mother too.

That's all I can really tell you about that. I was twelve and forced to grow up at an alarming rate. The events took their toll on me, mostly bad. I became a different boy to the one I was before. Understandable I feel. What life would have been like if the war hadn't have happened in the first place, I'll never know.

But then again, isn't that the same for many families?

Chapter V

"In the name of God, stop a moment, cease your work, look around you."
Leo Tolstoy

Names written in stone.
Birth dates.
End dates.
The occasional message of love and loss.

All finely carved with acute delicacy, decorated in moss and wilted flowers - some still erectly poised - some leaning as if looking to lie down and rest.

Legacies come and gone. To always be remembered, or just temporarily?

Cold, stone memorials in hope of lasting as long as physically possible.

As Robbie looked around, he was fascinated by how many people long gone were somewhere underneath his feet right now; a multitude of skeletons doing nothing but lying on their backs (most probably with their arms across their chests), never to be seen by a human eye ever again.

Mollie and he had gone for a walk the next morning and ended up at the cemetery. There was no reason for this. They had been talking and one step after another had led them there.

It was very secluded. The old church stood poised on a small mound overlooking its cemetery. Little maintenance had been carried out recently and it was clear to see. The iron fence that encircled it was in disarray, entwined with vines and weeds. The grass was overgrown and the headstones looked abandoned more than remembered.

Truth be told, Robbie had always been drawn to the appeal of a cemetery, of being laid to rest and generally of the afterlife itself. If anyone asked him outright, he wouldn't be able to tell you what he truly believed in. He had a few ideas but nothing he could raise a decent argument over. Here he was, having religious beliefs rammed down his throat on an almost daily basis and yet he was being more and more lured away from it all. This may be down to his need for rebellion against the nuns or the fact that both of his parents had been taken from him. Either way, he couldn't come to a firm conclusion.

Mollie was a little way off doing her own inspection. She didn't have as much interest as Robbie, but was still interested in looking at the dates of the deceased. It was strange to think back to when they were laid to rest and what this place would have looked like at the time.

They had inadvertently created their own game of trying to find the oldest headstone, a game that was almost impossible to play as a lot of the older ones were unreadable.

'1823. I've got 1823 over here!' bellowed Robbie from closer than he seemed from the outburst. So far, the winning ticket was a chipped and worn headstone that had 1830 still visible. They both knew that there were much older ones but they wouldn't be able to tell as the carvings were too worn or gone completely. Robbie was hoping to find one that dated back to at least the eighteenth century but so far the search hadn't proven fruitful.

'No you don't. Don't believe you,' was Mollie's response. He was always pulling her leg, so the need to believe what he said was always with an air of doubt.

'I'll beat you Mr Harvey, you just see if I don't,' she mumbled to herself under her breath.

'I wonder if Old man Joe's grave is here somewhere,' Robbie said.

He had discussed Old man Joe being in the cemetery before, but the conclusion was always that he couldn't have been because he disappeared after his eye was cursed by the witch, never to be seen again. No-one knew where he went, even though most people rumoured that he had gone to live in a cabin deep in the woods. The reason this had become the unofficial truth was because of the visits that people had claimed had happened. No-one believed he could do this if he wasn't at least fairly close by, keeping his eye on everyone.

'You can keep looking but you won't find it here, Robbie. You know that.'

The voice of reason.

'Imagine if we found it though. That would change everything around here.'

'1802! Ha, beat that if you can.' Robbie knew he was defeated. *Where had she found that one?* He had to see for himself.

Sure enough, on a headstone that was half sunken in the floor and leaning to its left was the date *1802. "Alma Marie (something)"*. It was too distorted to tell. Robbie thought the *something* began with a C but he wasn't sure. There was something else written but too unclear to make out. In all fairness, the headstone was relatively clean for its age. *Who was this lady? What did she mean to those who knew her and did anybody know or care that she was still here?*

It all seemed very hollow.

'Well, I suppose you win. This must be the oldest one here that we can tell. At least we know how long this has been here - over a hundred years and counting.'

They both sat on the floor staring at the stone in front of them, Robbie with his usual stick of some kind in his hand scraping the mossy floor, poking around in sandy holes that looked like the beginning of an ants nest.

'I ain't going to be buried here. That's for sure. If this lady has been here for over a hundred years and probably a hundred more to come, I don't want to spend that long in this place, doomed to not be able to escape. No thank you. I'd be buried in a better place, somewhere far from here.'

'Don't think you have to think about that right now, Robbie,' Mollie said in a mocking tone.

'You always have to plan ahead, don't you know that? The best laid plans, so to speak,' he said, looking around and up at the sun shining through the trees, warming the headstones. 'Come on, let's go. If you're in a cemetery too long the spirits lock on to you and then stay with you until you join them.'

Just like Robbie to pull Mollie's leg. This time though, joke or not, she didn't like the idea of finding out. So they got up and left.

~

Robbie enjoyed walking around the outskirts of the town. That was one thing that Fellowood Marsh had going for it; it was picturesque to say the least and free from the hustle and bustle of the larger town of Savannah's Bridge. Yes, it could be boring, but in a way it suited his nature of wandering, exploring and not having to barge past people or have anyone see where he was going or what he was up to.

The walk to and from the church was particularly pleasant. The path was surrounded by greenery and they had only the sound of birds chirping in the trees to accompany them. It was very similar to the path to the waterhole. Robbie loved walking along, hitting the branches and leaves with his chosen stick of the hour.

Mollie, on the other hand, had always been more reserved. She was a thinker. Not that she found herself having a great deal to think about but, regardless, thinking was what she was best at. She was always trying to analyse things, put pieces in their respective places. She never did anything without carefully contemplating it first.

Mollie was a particularly pretty girl with shiny, long dark hair that was her pride and joy. It was what made her stand out from the crowd. Most of the other girls were jealous of her hair; the way it would glisten in the sunlight and had so much bounce to it. They struggled to keep their hair in any kind of respectable health, but Mollie's just seemed to take care of itself. It made her face very prominent. She boasted chiselled cheek bones that allowed her hair to accent her face. Everyone could see that she was going to be a great beauty.

Her life had been one big confusion. Mollie, like Jack-Jack, was also not an orphan, although this was not for certain. Probably the biggest thing she had to think about was where she came from. She had never known. She had been found wandering around the streets as a small child in Savannah's Bridge. No parents or guardians of any kind were to be found and of, course, she could do nothing to shed light on the situation. The only conclusion was that she had been abandoned. This had brought her to the orphanage where they had named her and "taken care" of her ever since.

Now at the age of twelve, this had left her confused and without a place in the world. She had no idea who her parents were, why they hadn't wanted her or if they were even still alive. And if they were still alive, where were they? To be abandoned was one thing, but to not know the reason for it was even worse.

Mollie seldom spoke about her past. The orphanage was all she knew as she was too young to remember anything about her parents or anyone else. Her earliest memories were of the orphanage, the nuns, the food, the discipline. It was her life.

Coming out of the thicket, they were faced with Fletcher Mane's house. And there he was, through the window, walking around in what was presumably his living room. This was another opportunity for Robbie to be secretive and discreet. Mollie would just have to follow suit.

It was daylight so, if they could see him, he could see them. They didn't like the idea of him seeing them just staring at him, so they both quickly took cover behind the fence. It wasn't the greatest. The fence was slatted and could be seen through quite easily but this was the only cover they had. They chose a point of the fence that had a shrub on the other side for extra invisibility. Every child at some point or another wants to be invisible, don't they?

They looked on. *What were they hoping to see?* Neither of them were sure. The excitement of watching someone who doesn't know you're watching was enough for Robbie.

'Do you think he's mad?' Mollie whispered in Robbie's left ear.

'Nah, what makes you say that?'

'What Virgil was saying. He sounds like an oddball. And Virgil must know. He's been around for ages and knows everybody.'

'Just 'cause someone lives alone doesn't make them mad, Mols.'

'I know that, but he's weird, isn't he? He looks weird. He walks weird. And no-one's ever heard him speak, have they?'

'Virgil was saying that maybe he can't speak. If he's been around these parts for this long and no-one has heard him speak, maybe that's 'cause he can't. It doesn't make him mad.'

'Yeah, but Virgil said he's got "problems". What do you think he meant by that?'

Robbie thought a while, still focusing on the strange character in their manufactured theatre.

'Problems could mean anything. I feel sorry for him. Must get lonely in there. All those years without anyone to talk to.'

'That's what I'm saying. Years on your own without talking to anyone can send someone mad, can't it? What if he's dangerous?'

'Don't let your imagination run away with you. Heck, he ain't done nothing to no-one, has he? And I bet my last toenail he won't ever do nothing to no-one neither. Look at him, harmless I'd say. Like a stray dog in a pound.'

'Yeah, but I heard people say he's done stuff.'

'What stuff?'

'Just stuff, I don't know what exactly.'

'See, there you go, listening to rumours again. I swear, this whole town's been built on a whisper floating on a breeze. I bet I could go say anything to anyone and a few days later I'd be hearing it back to myself, only a lot more exaggerated.'

The two children watched as Fletcher went out of sight.

'This is stupid, Robbie. What if he sees us or comes out and catches us spying on him?'

'Dare you to go up to the window and peek inside. You might see him doing something awful.'

'Don't be daft. I'm not going up there,' Mollie whispered in a lower tone. 'If I did that he might.....'

At that moment, Robbie felt a strong hand grab him right on his bruise. It sent a thumping pain straight to the area. Before either of them knew what was going on, he had been spun around by his arm and thrust up to a standing position by a tall, ugly looking man with anger in his face.

It was Arnie Took. He pinned Robbie against Fletcher's fence, which hurt Robbie's lower back as the pointed tips of the fence dug into it. Mollie stood up, but instinctively took a few fearful steps backwards.

Arnie looked mad as hell, leering over Robbie, still maintaining a firm grip on his bruised arm. Right now, the pain in his arm was the last thing on Robbie's mind.

Saliva hung from Arnie's lip like a rabid dog, snarling through gritted teeth.

'It was you, wasn't it?!' he sneered. 'It was you who killed my chicken! Confess boy!'

Robbie had yet to notice the dead chicken hanging from Arnie's non-bruise-grasping hand; the dead chicken that only yesterday he was holding himself.

He said nothing in response. At this moment, he didn't know which answer would get him out of Arnie's clutches. Instead, he froze. He was outmatched in size, weight, strength and Arnie was angry. Robbie had no chance against this man who was pinning a young boy half his size up against a fence.

With no answer from Robbie, Arnie shook him as if trying to shake the confession out of him.

'Answer me boy! I know you did this. Do you know how valuable these chickens are? And you just go and kill it for sport. I should do to you as you did to my chicken. That's the way it should be!'

He dropped the chicken and smacked the side of Robbie's head with the palm of his hand, which sent a ringing straight to his ear.

Mollie, who was standing to the side, jumped on Arnie's back to get him off. It was impulse. *Brave or stupid?*

It was like riding a bull. With one violent jolt from Arnie she was cast aside, landing on the floor and rolling in the dust. Arnie didn't even look at her. She had been like a fly that he had swatted away without a thought.

The second smack came before a commanding voice came out of nowhere; a voice that demanded attention. It was Sister Athena. She was behind Arnie. 'Let him go!'

He turned and released his grip on Robbie, letting him fall to the floor with his back against the fence. He marched up to Sister Athena and stared at her in the eye.

'And what are you going to do about it?' he growled. 'I thought you people were all about justice anyway.'

Sister Athena stood firm, looking him dead in the eye. She could show no fear. *The mouse to the snake.* That's the way it had to be in her head. Not another word passed her lips.

Arnie looked her up and down and backed off, still sneering. He went back to pick up his chicken from by Robbie's feet.

'This isn't over boy,' he whispered before walking off, the chicken swinging by his side, this time with no dripping blood.

There had been no sign of Fletcher.

~

After the children had dusted themselves off, Sister Athena escorted them back to the orphanage.

'Wow, Sister, you were really brave. He could have hurt you really badly,' Mollie said as they walked back up the street.

'Confidence usually wins against cowardice children. I don't know much about that man but I want you to stay away from him at all costs. What was that all about?'

'He thinks I killed his chicken. Which I didn't, well..... I did. You see, we came across it in the woods. It was caught in a rat-trap and was in agony. I killed it for its own good. I didn't kill it for fun like he thinks I did. I went and left it on his porch 'cause I thought he could use it for the meat or something if he still wanted to.'

Sister Athena gave him a concerned look through the side of her eye. 'You know it's dangerous to be wandering the woods. I've told you this before. Anything could happen to you and no-one would know about it.'

'We really didn't mean any harm, Sister,' Mollie interjected. 'We didn't expect to come across the chicken. And we thought we were doing the best thing by it.'

'I didn't know how to tell Sister Meredith and Sister Beatrice yesterday,' Robbie said. 'They had me in her office and quizzed me about some blood that was on my trouser leg. I wanted to tell them where it had come from, but I thought it might make things worse.'

'I understand,' Sister Athena said softly. 'I will talk to Sister Meredith and explain what really happened. I'm sure she will understand.'

Once they got back and were in the sleep hall sitting on their beds, Sister Athena left them with one last piece of cautionary advice: 'Now remember children, you mustn't go wandering off into the woods. These woods are strange. They are dense and filled with danger.'

The words "strange" and "danger" intrigued Robbie. 'Is Old man Joe's cabin deep in the woods?' he asked.

The concerned look returned to Sister Athena's face. 'What have you heard about that man?'

'We've heard lots of things,' said Mollie, 'but it's all just people talking and superstition.'

'That man was feared by the whole town.'

'So he did exist,' Robbie said excitedly.

'Of course he existed, but I don't pretend to know much about him.'

'But the glass eye, it's cursed isn't it, by the witch?'

'Now you know there's no such thing as curses, Robbie. And there's certainly no such thing as witches. Haven't I taught you better than that?'

A sudden guilt pulsed in his chest. He knew he didn't wholeheartedly believe in the actual curse but wanted to know what Sister Athena thought about it. 'It's just what people say. It's like Old man Joe is a myth and a legend but is still real in people's minds to this day.'

'He left the town because of what that woman said to him. She instilled fear into the hearts of everyone in the town, which is why he had to leave. I do believe he relocated to a cabin far into the woods, but no-one knows where. The only thing I know is it is meant to be to the east.'

To the east. Robbie had never heard that before.

~

Grating chalk down a blackboard; Robbie had always hated the sound. The white, dusty stick screeching across the slate stone sent shivers through him. It felt as though the chalk was being scratched along his brain. It was torture to be endured during every lesson.

Today was no different. *Screeeeeeech, schreeeeeeech.* It was unbearable. The Sister with her back to the class was quietly writing something meaningless on the black canvas – something for him to be taking note of, to be copying maybe. But he wasn't. Not today. He just couldn't be bothered.

The one person whom he thought he'd never be glad to see saving him from this hell appeared in the doorway. Sister Meredith interrupted the lesson to pull him from class and take him to her office, again. This was too frequent even for him.

She left him standing in front of her mahogany desk as she took her position behind it, fingers once again entwined as she leant on her elbows.

'Sister Athena informed me about the mysterious blood on your leg. So, a dead chicken.' She looked over her glasses at him, 'Is that the best you could come up with – chicken blood? I thought your imagination was better than that.'

She didn't believe him. He knew she wouldn't.

'You find new ways to insult my intelligence.'

Silence. He knew she was just goading him into saying something he would regret.

'Still nothing? No admittance? No responsibility? You disappoint me, young man. Off back to class with you. I shall ponder upon you some more and may see you again before the day is out.

Robbie turned and left the room, uttering not a single word.

"Work Detail."

The term was not sweet sounding to any child above the age of ten. Many years ago, Saint Vincent's had a handyman by the name of Billy who took care of all the work that needed doing around the orphanage and was a friendly figure to have around, especially for the children. This was the way it had always been until, one day, Billy stopped showing up for work. No-one knew the reason why, he just disappeared. Instead of recruiting another handyman, the nuns decided to distribute the work between the children. Ten was deemed to be the desired level for some of the tasks, so any boys above the age of ten would tend to the more masculine chores and any girls would tend to the more feminine chores.

This of course meant that Robbie had been on Work Detail since arriving and Mollie for the past two or so years. This also meant that Jack-Jack was exempt, at least for now.

The nuns had been very pleased with their decision. It was a simple solution at the time and they couldn't believe they hadn't thought of it sooner. There were times when certain children needed to be taught to toe the line and, in any case, some of the work was deemed too undesirable to undertake themselves. This was usually followed with some form of punishment but, all in all, this had become the new routine.

Work Detail was three times a week and not always for a specific length of time. If work needed to be done, it needed to be done. Time was not of the essence.

Not all Work Detail was that bad. For example, chopping wood for the fires and the kitchen was Robbie's favourite of all his tasks. It felt manly. It felt primal, wielding the axe above his head and crashing it down onto the log, separating it into two parts with one almighty blow. He was particularly bad at it at first but soon got the hang of it, with a few sharp *thwacks* with the cane when he got it wrong. It bode well for him to improve quickly.

The chopping of the wood was his task for today. The sun was beating down today too. He didn't mind the sun when he was fishing, climbing trees or lying in the grass as time ticked by. But today it was scorching his back and making it exceedingly difficult with every piece of wood to continue to lift the heavy tool high up in the air.

The wood storage was at the back of the orphanage just beside the garden. Tending to the garden was also one of Robbie's chores, which he shared with one of the other boys. The sweat was dripping off his brow and hands making it difficult to grip the axe.

He was almost finished before Sister Meredith came around the corner behind him. He immediately stopped what he was doing and looked around. She approached him and perched on the end of a bench.

'Robinson Harvey, hard at work,' she said patronisingly. 'I wanted to have another quiet word with you away from the other Sisters. I told you I would ponder upon you a little more and well..... I have. It is quite clear to me that you are fast becoming the "black sheep" of the orphanage. You insist on breaking the rules and being, quite frankly, a nuisance to the Sisters here, including myself, and it is becoming tiresome.

'Now, we took you in, or have you forgotten? You came to us with nothing and all we have tried to do is guide you in the ways of the Lord and help you in becoming a man. For this, you repay us by causing mischief and if you don't change your ways, Mr Harvey, I'm afraid I can see your time here being a little less enjoyable than it should be.'

A few silent moments passed between them.

'Furthermore, I urge you not to test me on this. You know I have the power to make your life miserable here and, Lord help me, I don't want it to come to that. Believe me I don't. Now, I think you need a little time to absorb what I have said.'

Sister Meredith stood up and walked over to a large pile of un-chopped blocks of wood. 'Here, you can chop these up while you think. Yes,' she nodded to herself, 'that should give you enough time.'

And with that being said, she walked off, leaving Robbie to his extra work.

Chapter VI

"We all come from different paths in life but we can find common ground."
Nanette Mathews

Rebellion is a funny thing. Why does one rebel? Is it for attention? Is it manifested from anger? Does anger in fact use rebellion as a way of communicating through oneself? Largely, we are led to believe that we rebel because of a sense of powerlessness and insecurity stemming from early childhood.

In my case, it is arguable that this was more from later childhood rather than early. I could argue I had good reason to rebel. Some would say it was a childish way of trying to outdo my authority figures. To me, rebellion was not a prized venture. I didn't feel good about being everything my parents had taught me not to be. It was just those nuns. That was it. You can spew out all the psychological jargon and hypotheses you want, but the simple fact was the nuns annoyed and angered me. I hated how they would use their position of power to bully and intimidate the other children. If it meant getting into a bit of bother, fine. But I would have the last laugh.

A few days passed without incident. There had been no more sign of Arnie Took. No-one had gone to confront him since he threatened Robbie. After all, no-one had even seen it. Sister Athena had simply warned the two children to not cross paths with that man again. If Fletcher Mane *had* witnessed it from inside his house, it was unlikely *he* was going to take any action.

One thing was true: Sister Meredith was correct, Robbie had been getting himself into more trouble than usual in recent days.

Today was a nothing day.

Some days are like that with no meaning to them, no substance. But the day doesn't stop.

Time doesn't stop. It has to carry on. It doesn't get tired. It doesn't have to rest or sit down for a while. It doesn't sleep and it won't die when its "time" is up. The sun will rise and set whether we want it to or not.

As usual, there was very little to do. Children struggle when there is nothing to do. They need stimulation, excitement, something to help pass the mundane time away.

They were sitting on a wall looking out into the street. The familiar goings-on were in full flow. People trying to make their own use of the time that they all shared. One of those people could quite easily have been Arnie Took but, thankfully, he was nowhere to be seen. That wasn't unusual. He would often keep tucked away on his farm out of everyone's reach. Robbie was keeping a particularly keen eye out in case he was around somewhere so they could quickly skulk out of sight.

A number of subjects had been talked about as they sat on the wall but nothing of major interest; just little snippets of inane chit-chat to pass away the time.

Robbie held his signature stick, banging it lightly against the wall between his legs. (It wasn't always the same stick of course.) He always felt better with a stick in his hand.

A lady walked past. A familiar lady. The same lady that Robbie had heard talking about Old man Joe when he was lurking behind Marley's Store. The town had always been superstitious after the witch's curse but this lady seemed to be the kindling that fuelled the fire.

'Out on your own today? Old man Joe not with you?' he couldn't help himself. The words were out before he could cage them.

The lady stopped but didn't turn towards him. Instead, she stared straight ahead as if paralysed by a magnetic force. Robbie instantly felt regret.

As calm as you could imagine she simply said, 'You should not joke about such things. He'll hear you. It is not only his eye that lives on. It is him as a whole. I hope you never have to find out.'

The words were chilling and Jack-Jack became visibly distressed, but the lady didn't care.

'He sees you even now. Oh, he will not visit you here. He only does that at night. But rest assured children, he sees all: your souls, your fears. He plays on them. He feeds on them. There is nothing to stop him. If he wants to visit someone he sees..... he will. Then when he sees you, it'll burn like the blazing fires of hell.'

Robbie could see Jack-Jack's discomfort at what the strange lady was saying and, feeling guilty for starting her off, he tried to stop her. 'Quiet! Can't you see you're upsetting him? Shut up you crazy old fool!'

The lady stood rigid, still not having looked at the children and not deterred by Robbie's demands.

'No amount of insults towards me will keep him at bay. You have no choice. He will come at some point, that you will see.'

'You're just a crazy old bat. What do you mean going around scaring young kids with your tall tales? Anyone who listens to you is crazier than you are!'

The lady sharply turned her head now with a scowl on her face. Robbie looked her right in the eyes. He could see she meant business. Her skin was loose and withered, covered with brown dots and worn from years of tiresome worry. Like an old oak tree's recognised age is told by its rings, her forehead showed signs of years of storytelling.

Scorn quickly turned to sadness. She looked weak now. Pathetic. She said in a low voice, 'He does not like to be mocked. He does not like to be scoffed at. He sees you doing this and will take vengeance. Maybe not now, maybe not soon, but he will come. He comes to us all, eventually.'

Before Robbie or the other children could say anything else, she strode off.

The encounter had left all three of them humbled, Jack-Jack especially although he hadn't said a word. Having been put in his place, Robbie looked after her, the back of her disappearing down the street. He still didn't believe it, regardless of what the lady had said. He hadn't been surrounded by the superstitions long enough for it to be embedded in his mind, unlike Mollie and Jack-Jack who had grown up here.

For them it was all too real - not surprisingly.

~

They went to the waterhole, the place where everything seemed better; their place. The lady and her words could not touch them here. It was as if it had a protective bubble around it that no-one could penetrate. Not angry farmers, strange ladies or overbearing nuns.

Robbie sat on a rock, still holding his stick. Mollie and Jack-Jack hadn't said a word since they left the wall.

Finally Mollie asked, 'Jack-Jack, are you okay?'

'Of course he's okay, Mollie. He's not going to take any notice of that daft old hag.'

She ignored him and remained focused on Jack-Jack. He was quite visibly upset by either the lady's words or Old man Joe's legend. Either way, he was only young and clearly perturbed by it all.

'I..I..don't want Old man Joe to visit me. I..I just c..c..couldn't bear it.'

'Don't let her and her superstitions get to you, Jack-Jack. She's just trying to scare you.'

Jack-Jack started to form tears in his eyes.

'Stop it, Jack-Jack. Stop crying at once,' Robbie insisted.

Jack-Jack ran off, leaving the other two alone. Mollie got up to go after him.

'Leave him be. I don't know what's up with him. I really don't.'

'Can't you see he's upset, Robbie? Why do you have to be like that? He's younger than you, younger than both of us. And he's lived here with all this all his life. It's real to him, if not to you.'

Robbie sat there and thought. Mollie was right. This was all that Jack-Jack had known. He instantly felt regret and bad about himself. He cared greatly for Jack-Jack. To him, he was like a younger brother and he should be looking out for him. Jack-Jack after all, looked up to him.

'I'm sorry. I don't know what got into me.'

'I do. It's that woman. The things she said got under your skin and you took it out on Jack-Jack.'

'Yeah, I guess you're right. I don't know why it gets to me. I think it's because I want them to shut up about it and leave it alone. I don't want it affecting Jack-Jack. Can't they all just leave it be?'

'Why don't you believe it, Robbie?'

The question threw Robbie off track. He wasn't used to such a direct question, even if it did come from Mollie.

He answered, 'It just sounds crazy to me – witches and curses. If I've learnt anything from being at this orphanage, it's that you can't always believe what you're told. Look at what they teach us in that place. It's not the same stuff as what they teach in the schoolhouse. So why do they have to teach it to us?

'Yes, but you don't know it's not true, do you? There are a lot of things that go on in this world that no-one can explain, Robbie. And things have happened in this town for people to believe it. They won't be easily budged. You're fighting a losing battle trying to convince anyone around here otherwise.'

Robbie knew she was right, as always. He was the elder of the two but Mollie seemed to have a much more grounded head on her shoulders.

He'd catch up one day.

Robbie didn't see Jack-Jack for the rest of the day, which was unusual as there were not many places to go. The altercation between the two of them had been playing on his mind all day. Jack-Jack *was* like a brother to him and let's face it – brothers argue.

Jack-Jack was in bed as Robbie entered the sleep hall to get ready for bed. He was in bed awfully early and Robbie had a sneaking suspicion that he wasn't asleep. It was more than a suspicion - he knew.

He approached him. He was facing towards the wall. Robbie knelt down.

'Hey, Jack-Jack. You okay? I'm sorry. I didn't mean all that earlier. I didn't mean to vex you. That old lady just got me wound up is all. And you know what I'm like when I get wound up. What d'you say, you forgive me? Pax?'

Jack-Jack turned around slowly. He still wasn't himself but he also couldn't be mad at the big-brother figure that he admired so much.

'O..O..Old man Joe w..w..won't visit me w..w..will he, Robbie? P..p..please say he won't.'

His stutter seemed to get worse when he was stressed. Robbie knew that so he tried to reassure him. 'No, Jack-Jack. Old man Joe won't be visiting you. He won't be visiting any of us. Those stories that lady tells are just rumours. Take no notice of them.'

Did he truly believe that? Even as he said the words, he wasn't sure.

'Look, we won't talk about him anymore, okay? He doesn't even exist. He never did. Just forget about it. And besides, even if it was true, he wouldn't get in here, would he? This is a place of worship and no evil spirit can come in, can they? That's why he's never been here before and why he never will.'

Jack-Jack had never thought about it like that before. Robbie was right, how could Old man Joe visit them in an orphanage with nuns around. It was a place of God and God wouldn't allow it. This sat very well with Jack-Jack and he appeared to perk up, if only a little. His stutter however was still strained.

'I g..g..guess you're r..r..right, Robbie. H..h..he couldn't get in here if he t..t..tried.'

Sister Athena overheard the last thing Jack-Jack tried to say and came over.

'Are you talking about that man again?' She came over and sat on the end of the bed. Looking at Robbie, she said, 'You really should stop about that man, that curse. It can't be good for Jack.'

Jack-Jack tried to sound like he wasn't bothered, 'I..I..I'm okay Sister A..A..Athena. He d..d..doesn't scare me.'

It sounded anything but convincing. Sister Athena didn't like seeing Jack-Jack upset. She too felt protective towards him, as Robbie did. She was always trying to find the right things to say to make him feel better about himself. Any little story or anecdote she could muster. One in particular had occurred to her recently about a boy that stayed at Saint Vincent's a long time ago. She had forgotten all about him until now.

'You know Jack, there used to be a boy who lived here who also had a stutter just like you. I can't recall his name, but he was a quiet boy and spoke just like you and did just fine. He was always very pleasant when spoken to and was a very clever boy too.'

Sister Athena was struggling to recall things about this boy but she could see it was having a positive effect on Jack-Jack so she continued, 'The point I'm trying to make is that you're not the only one. There have been other boys and children with the same problem as you and there will be a lot more to come after you, but you can't let it hold you back. You are the same as everyone else. You can be the same as anyone, just like that little boy was.'

Just then, Mollie came into the hall. She had been on Work Detail in the laundry room. The laundry room was one of her "girl chores", but she had hated it ever since turning ten, having to help out with the washing, ironing and folding of clothes.

'I hate it in there,' she interrupted.

'Mollie, shhh. Sister Athena is telling us a story,' Robbie said firmly.

A look of embarrassment covered Mollie's face. 'Oh, sorry Sister. I didn't mean to.....'

'It's fine, Mollie. Don't trouble yourself. Sit down, won't you? Now, I was telling the boys here about a fine young man that used to live here years ago. He had a stutter just like Jack.'

'What was his name?'

'I can't remember, dear. There have been so many children pass through these doors. I was a lot younger of course and Saint Vincent's was different then. I don't mean to sound glum but it was a lot happier than it is now.'

'Why have you stayed here this whole time?' asked Robbie. 'I don't understand. You can go anytime you want to. Surely there is somewhere better than here.'

'I love the children. As a nun, where you are and what sort of place you are in isn't important. I love my work here with you children and nothing will make me leave.'

Robbie lowered his voice somewhat, 'But how can you stand being around..... them?'

Sister Athena knew to whom Robbie was referring. She gave him a wry smile. 'Well, they're not all that bad really, just a little rough around the edges when it comes to the softer side of life.'

'That's putting is loosely.'

'My point is. Even though it was different back then, this boy was just like you, Jack. He reminds me a lot of you. He was a good boy, and smart too.'

'Y..y..you really think I'm s..s..smart?'

Another wry smile, slightly larger this time. 'Of course you are. You can do anything you put your mind to. Don't let the way you speak hold you back. It didn't for that boy all those years ago and it won't do for you.'

It was time for bed. Sister Athena, having done her duty as an empathetic lady of the cloth and, more importantly, of someone who cared, left the children to sleep.

Jack-Jack was indeed feeling a whole lot better about himself. He thought about the boy. He thought about what he must have been like. Even though the times were different and many years separated them, maybe he *could* be just like him. Stutter or no stutter.

Chapter VII

**"Stupidity is the same as evil
If you judge by the results."**
Margaret Atwood

There are times in life where a good decision can be a bad choice. This would often happen to Robbie – a good decision at the time, a bad choice in the end.

It had rained non-stop for a number of days. This was unusual for the time of year, but England had always had unpredictable weather. You could never be certain that the weather was going to coincide with the seasons, so it made it very difficult to plan anything.

Rain was not a good sign. This meant they would have to stay inside. Inside the orphanage.

Porridge walls.

There was nothing to do, but even worse was that the nuns were there. Summer was their escape, their freedom; it meant they could be outside and free, whereas rain didn't put a stop to lessons or Work Detail - those could still be done inside. Robbie was even sent outside in the rain to chop wood, which always made it twice as difficult.

The days felt twice as long if they couldn't go outside and no-one felt it more than Robbie. He was the most adventurous out of the three and Mollie and Jack-Jack were used to it, having lived at the orphanage all of their lives. The winters were cold, dreary and long.

Very long.

The rain had cleared up but the sky was still cloudy. A grey blanket hung over the entire world. It stretched as far as the eye could see. No creases. Like when you stretch a blanket over your body as tight as it will go, pulling at the threads. The sky was smooth today; a closed lid sheltering them from the blue sky above.

It was good enough for Robbie. He had been out in the cold for a while before he came back and ushered the other two outside, much to the reluctance of Jack-Jack who didn't appreciate being dragged out of the warmth into the chill of the day breeze. But he had acquiesced. Robbie could be very persuasive.

He led them to the cemetery. He needed them to not be interrupted, unlikely due to the temperature and the fact that the cemetery was a solemn place.

'What are we doing here again, Robbie?' Mollie said, as she lowered herself down as respectfully as she could on to a horizontal gravestone, as the ground was still damp.

Alma Marie looked on.

'You'll see. Jack-Jack, sit down..... there will do.' He pointed to a large stone that in all fairness was impossible to distinguish as an old half-buried tombstone or not. He reached into his back pocket and took out a handkerchief that was folded in half. The other two had never been so intrigued by a simple handkerchief before. He placed it down on the matted blades of grass and unfolded it like it was the crown jewels. As the other two laid their eyes upon it, they could see it wasn't the crown jewels but some odd-looking brown material that looked like dried up mud.

'What is that stuff?' Mollie enquired.

'Why, don't you know? You never seen it before?'

'No. Should I have?'

'It's tobacco. You know, what the old folks smoke in their pipes.'

'What are you doing with tobacco, Robbie? Where did you get it?'

'I got it from Drayton.'

'Sneaking around the back of Marley's Store trying to hear more gossip I suppose?'

'No, he asked me to go there and gave it to me. He said I should try it because it's what the soldiers smoked in the trenches just like my father would have done.'

Mollie gave him a bothersome look. 'And where did he get it from?'

'I dunno. He didn't say. Look here, you're not supposed to be lecturing me about it.'

'What would happen if you got caught with that?'

'Well, we're..... I'm not going to, am I? That's why I brought you here.'

'So what are we going to do with it?'

'What d'you think, dummy? Smoke it of course.'

'With what?'

'Drayton gave me some matches and I ripped out some pieces of paper from some old books. We can roll them up just like a cigarette.'

'And you what, want us all to smoke it? We've never done anything like that before. Not even you.'

'That's what makes it so dandy. I reckon my father would have smoked a few cigarettes lying in the cold and the mud with his buddies. Drayton said they would do it as a form of relaxation when the fighting got too stressful.'

'There are other ways of honouring your father, Robbie, if that's what you're looking to do.'

'Yeah, but this one is right here and right now. Come on, don't be a spoilsport.'

'Well, I don't know what I'm doing, so whatever it is you have in mind, you'll have to do it.'

Taking that as an invitation, Robbie took out his crumpled up pieces of paper littered with black words and smoothed them out on a flat stone. Next, he poured the tobacco carefully into the middle and did his best to roll it up to resemble a cigarette. It was shabby work but it was the best he could do. The makeshift cigarette was quite long and not exactly tube-like, but it was going to have to do.

Robbie put the end to his lips and took out the matches, of which there were four. He already felt like a "big man" holding it in his mouth, one eye almost closed as if pondering a fascinating statement.

Lighting the matches was not going to be easy as all there was to strike them on were the rocks and they were still somewhat damp from all the rain. Still, there must be some with some dry patches somewhere. Robbie looked around with the cigarette in his mouth and saw a rock embedded in the ground that was quite dry and rough. It would have to suffice.

Kneeling in the mud he struck one match hard over the serrated coating. To his surprise it lit straight away. He put it up to the end of the cigarette and held it there until it lit. It worked. He puffed like he'd seen the old men do and sure enough, it began to glow as the smoke rose.

He didn't even cough, not at first. He puffed and puffed like it was a campfire he was stoking and the tiny end of the worded paper fell away. Then came the cough. He took it out of his mouth and held it in front of him.

'Here.' *Cough, cough.* 'Your turn,' he said, holding it out to Mollie.

She took it. The voice of reason held the home-made cigarette. What harm could it do, really? She emulated Robbie's actions and puffed on it gently. Her cough was instant. Robbie laughed, then took it back and had another turn. He felt great. He felt like his father all of a sudden and there was a fire in him that burned like the tip of the paper he was holding.

After a few goes, he turned to Jack-Jack. 'Come on. This is your big chance to be just like one of the big guys, like you wanted.'

'Robbie, I don't know about that. Look how much it made you cough, not to mention me.'

'Oh, give over would you? He's got to be a man sometime, ain't he? This is just growing up, so it is.' He offered it to Jack-Jack like a stick of chewing gum. Sure enough, Jack-Jack, being so easily led, took it and did what Robbie and Mollie had done. He took his first drag on a cigarette and tried his best to hold in the tickle in his throat. It felt like someone had just lit his neck on fire.

Because he was trying to hold it in, when it came, it was indeed monstrous. He coughed so hard he felt like his innards were going to come out, making Robbie laugh.

'That's it my boy!' he praised. 'That's how you know it's gone right down.'

'I..I..I don't like it, Robbie. It tastes..... f..f..furry.'

'Ha ha, furry. That's as good a word for it I guess.'

The cigarette was running low, but Robbie was having a great time with it. It was passed to the other two a few more times before it reached the nub and had to be put out. He felt quite chuffed with himself and if the other two were being honest, so did they. It was also another one over on the nuns. Here they were, smoking a cigarette in the cemetery and no-one knew. He almost wanted to rush to tell them. How they would scowl. Oh well, this particular victory was going to have to remain a secret.

~

The walk back from the cemetery had not been as joyous as Robbie had anticipated after their sneaky smoke in the woods. The feeling of triumph had been replaced by a feeling of nausea, with Jack-Jack cradling his stomach and looking rather pale.

Robbie had decided not to go back to the orphanage right away with the other two. He had forked off when they had come out of the clearing to go and see if he could find Drayton. He had a good idea where he would be.

For a pittance-a-week, Drayton helped his father by carving names into headstones. Cliff, Drayton's father, was a stonemason and, occasionally, a headstone was required. It would not normally be a job for a boy of such young age but Drayton had a very steady hand and Cliff had been impressed with his level of concentration and skill. He was a natural and his father had noticed this. Drayton had practised on a few slabs and the results had pleasantly surprised his father, so whenever a request for a headstone had come in, Drayton had been called upon.

Robbie was right. He was round the back, chipping away at a blank slab.

'Drayton.' He wanted to announce himself, rather than creeping up on him and forcing him into making a mistake.

'Now then,' he replied, looking up from his work.

'Who's this for?' Robbie indicated towards the slab laying on the worktable. Drayton had only just started. The only letters carved so far were a capital *J* and a small *e*.

'This here's for the late widow, Jean Hawkins. She died in her sleep a few nights back.'

The boys stood looking at the headstone like it was the first time seeing one.

'That's too bad,' said Robbie.

'Aye, well, she was old. And a widow. Didn't have much to live for. Maybe just gave up.'

Robbie shot him a questioning glance. 'Doesn't mean she had to die though.'

'Better yet. I reckon she didn't give up anyway.' He lowered his voice slightly, 'Some are saying Old man Joe had something to do with it.'

'Not that old hag spreading her disease again?'

'I don't know, maybe. But she ain't the only one. Heard folks saying he visited her and gave her a heart attack.'

'If she died, how does anyone know it had anything to do with Old man Joe?'

'Heard one of the old girls say she wasn't dead when she found her the next day. Said she had suspected something was wrong when there were no lights or nothing on in the house and Jean here was supposed to meet her friend that morning. She'd gone over and let herself in as the door weren't locked. Found her upstairs she did, lying on the ground, not dead yet. She said she died in her arms, but before she did she mouthed the word "Joe". Creepy, huh?'

'That don't mean nothing. Maybe her dead husband was called Joe or she thought someone called Joe was holding her. She was probably delusional after having a heart attack and lying there all that time.'

'I dunno. Maybe. But there's still a bit of a "to-do" in town over it.'

'There's always a bit of a "to-do" in this place. Nothing can just happen without someone thinking it's witchcraft or something.'

Drayton didn't answer. He was just glad of the break in his work. The carving was delicate work and it took an immense amount of focus. Bending down over the slab also took its toll on his back. The etching on the stone couldn't be done upright.

'Hey, how was the smoke?'

Robbie's grown-up feeling came back to him. 'It was great. Just like my father would have done, right?'

'Right. Like I told you. Could you take it?'

Robbie didn't like the question. It showed lack of faith in his grown-upness. 'Sure I could. It tickled a little but nothing I couldn't handle. Heck, it's nothing. I never asked you anyhow. Where did you get that stuff from?' Robbie asked finally.

'I swiped it.'

'Who from?'

'That fellow down the street there.'

'Which fellow?'

'You know, the one who just sits on his porch all day, smoking his pipe and making his wooden creatures.'

'Virgil?'

'Is that his name? I don't know. I've seen him sat there most days. His pouch of tobacco sitting next to him on the table. I snuck up down the side of his fence and swiped it from under his nose. Poor fool never sniffed out a thing,' he laughed.

Robbie all of a sudden felt angry towards Drayton. He thought a lot of Virgil and he didn't like the idea of him being taken advantage of. Especially as smoking Virgil's tobacco himself made him feel more like an accomplice than anything.

He stepped over a blank headstone that was propped up against the wall, knocking it over and breaking it in half before grabbing Drayton by the scruff of his neck. He stood him up and pushed him against the wall.

'Don't ever steal from that man again, you hear?'

Drayton pushed him back sternly. Having heard the headstone crack before being pushed against the wall, he looked down at it, laying in two separate pieces. 'What's the big idea? You broke a headstone. They ain't cheap, you know?'

Robbie didn't even look back at the headstone. 'Why did you steal his tobacco?'

'It ain't nothing. He won't miss it. It's not like he's your dad or anything.'

The words went through Robbie like a steam train. Before he knew it, he had balled his fist and struck Drayton around the face, sending him back into the wall, then to his knees. Drayton held his face.

'What the hell, Robbie?' he cried out, slightly bewildered.

Robbie, although hurt from what Drayton had said, felt immediate remorse. 'Look, I'm sorry. I shouldn't have hit you. But you shouldn't be stealing from Virgil. Don't do it again.' They looked at each other before Robbie finally said, 'I'll see you around.'

He turned and walked off, stepping over the broken headstone and leaving Drayton to complete the rest of the late widow's name with a somewhat swollen jaw.

~

Guilt had probably made him hit Drayton. Robbie hadn't hit anyone since coming to Fellowood Marsh. He had got into arguments and squabbles before but it had never materialised into anything physical. He wasn't sure what his relationship with Drayton would be like now. This was their first real argument as friends and it had resulted in one of them being punched.

The saving grace (if you can call it that), was that he knew he hadn't connected well with the punch. It had put Drayton off his feet but Robbie hoped that may have just been the shock more than anything. He knew he was kidding himself.

He also knew he was going to have to tell Mollie and Jack-Jack where Drayton got the tobacco. Jack-Jack might not be bothered that much but he could almost guarantee that Mollie would be. He could keep it to himself but that wouldn't sit well with him.

The afternoon brought with it another lesson; another boring lecture about something trivial. Another session of facing whichever mundane, pompous nun sent to try and attempt to teach "the rabble". Another chalk-dust filled classroom with nothing to do but dream about the outdoors, about adventures.

Sister Klara was the chosen one and arithmetic was the afternoon's selection. Probably the only thing worse than learning about religion. Was there a god of arithmetic? Did arithmetic hold all the answers?

They sat in their usual chairs. As Mollie was just in front of him, maybe he could use this time to tell her about the tobacco, so there would be witnesses around when she found out what Drayton had done. Jack-Jack was too far away but he wasn't as important to disclose to.

Nun-mumbling was going on at the front. He took up his ruler and poked Mollie in the shoulder. She turned with a start and gave him a look of confusion and annoyance. Not a good start.

She mouthed the word, 'What?'

In as faint a whisper as he could, Robbie started, 'I spoke to Drayton, you know, about the..... stuff.'

'And?' Again mouthed.

'He says he stole it from Virgil.'

'What?!' This time in a faint whisper. 'Robbie. How could you?'

'I didn't know, did I?'

Mollie had to turn back around so as not to get caught by the teacher, but when he felt it was safe to do so, Robbie continued with her back turned to him. 'Hey, it wasn't like it was me. I feel like you do about it. I told him not to do it again. Somehow, I think he got the picture.'

There was no response this time from the chair in front. Maybe telling her wasn't the best idea after all. Maybe he should have just kept it to himself.

The confirmation that his stupid stunt of the day became even more apparent as, unbeknown to him, during their conversation, a few rows to his left Jack-Jack had been trying to keep his composure and not succeeding. He was holding his stomach and looked awfully pale.

A high-pitched screech filled the room as Jack-Jack pushed his chair back and hastily left the room without any notion of asking for permission. He fled through the door as if Sister Klara wasn't even there. The lack of respect and disruption of her class irritated her so she went after him.

Quiet gossip swept the room and a few moments later, she returned.

'Right, class. Listen up now. Stop that. Here. Jack is currently being sick in the corridor. He has just tried to apologise to me for doing "it". What is "it"? Who knows what he is talking about? Come, come. Somebody must know something.'

Gossip turned to silence throughout the room as her wandering eyes hovered over all heads. She was annoyed and meant business.

The momentary silence was broken by a boy who spoke up, 'Maybe he's been smoking, Sister.'

She turned in his direction. 'Smoking? What do you mean? The boy's only nine.'

'Dunno, Sister. Maybe someone gave it to him then. Or made him do it.'

The Sister wasn't expecting this response and was shocked. The boy had obviously found out about their little rendezvous in the cemetery. Maybe Robbie had whispered too loud or they had been seen. He was pretty sure they had been alone. He had double checked.

'Right, class. This is terribly upsetting. Does anyone know anything about this? Come now. It'll be all the worse for you if caught with no confession.'

No movement, no ownership. Just heads turning left, then right, looking for a guilty party.

'In that case, I shall have to conduct an inspection. Everybody stand up at once.' The class did so. 'Now, I want all pockets emptied on the desks in front of you. Do not leave anything unearthed. I warn you, I shall find out.'

Everybody did as she asked. Nobody had anything to hide aside from a few things that weren't ideal to bring into class, but nothing that would overshadow what she was looking for: a few marbles, rocks, toy soldiers and a tiny unfortunate newt, half dead.

Robbie was in a quandary. He had the rest of the tobacco that they didn't roll up in his pocket. He knew he should have got rid of it but there was too much to fit in the piece of paper and at the time there was something stopping him from discarding the rest of it. How he wished he had now. There was no way to dispose of it here. And Sister Klara was keeping her beady eyes on the whole group. It felt as though she had a set of eyes for every child in that room.

He did as he was told and emptied his pockets. The tobacco was still inside the ragged handkerchief. He hoped that by just laying a simple handkerchief on the table, she would think nothing of it and pass him by. As he got it out, he was careful to make it look like there was nothing of interest. It lay there, still, lifeless on the desk. He wished he had more in his pockets so it didn't look so conspicuous on its own.

Sister Klara made her way from desk to desk – searching, inspecting, finding nothing of interest. The newt had stopped moving when she got to its table, earning the owner a clip round the ear.

The one and only disadvantage to sitting at the back was that Robbie was the last person she came to and, having found nothing and being close to defeat, she approached him with a look of determination on her face.

She stood in front of his table with her arms behind her back. He looked down at the table, signifying guilt. Without hesitation, she unmasked the tobacco lurking under the handkerchief and Robbie's heart felt as though it would stop. He was in trouble, again.

Before he knew what was going on he was frogmarched out of the room and down to Sister Meredith's office.

With a brief description of why he was there from Sister Klara, Sister Meredith listened with a most intense look on her face.

Once alone, she looked at him some more before getting up and coming around to stand in front of him.

'I'm glad to see you took note of our little chat the other day. Seldom do my words have such little effect. It's quite impressive really. In one ear and out the other. I warned you to toe the line and I also urged you not to test me.'

There were no following words, only actions. The rest of Robbie's time in Sister Meredith's office was spent with his hands outstretched. The end result culminated in welts and raw red markings, the likes of which he had not experienced at Saint Vincent's before.

She had said not to test her, and she had meant it.

My Shortcomings

The last chapter was not my finest hour. I hope your perception of me did not dwindle too greatly so early on in the story. Remember now, I was young and stupid. Only through times like those can we learn from our mistakes.

The forthcoming chapter also does not put me in a shining light as you will soon see. Reflecting back is not easy. Even now, I see the look on Jack-Jack's face as he tried so wholeheartedly to inhale the smoke and the vision of him getting up mid-class to go and throw up. He looked up to me and I had an unfortunate habit of letting him down. It was never intentional. I suppose the only explanation (not an excuse) is that I was the eldest and quite often felt a lot of pressure in being the so-called leader of the group. I wasn't just the leader of our small group but I was the oldest of the current residents of Saint Vincent's at that time. I had a need to act a certain way, to not let it seem like I was being controlled by the nuns.

I felt immediate remorse for giving Jack-Jack his first taste of tobacco at such a young age. Even as I was at the mercy of that evil witch, Sister Meredith, (yes, I called her an evil witch. I hope I won't go to hell for that) I kept thinking about his watering eyes as he held in the smoke or how he said he felt like his neck had just been set on fire. Looking back now, he looked like he was going to explode, a bit like Monstro the whale when Geppetto lit the fire inside his stomach so he would sneeze the raft out.

It was also the first time I had hit a friend. Drayton and I had argued before but it had never come to blows. For this too I felt regret, even though you might not believe it. Drayton had never said anything about my father before that. I know it shouldn't have pushed me into jumping over the headstone and hitting him but, like inside Monstro's stomach, a fire was lit inside me too.

I hadn't really had time to grieve for my father and I certainly hadn't had time to grieve for my mother. Everything had happened so fast. Bang, bang: *like a double-barrelled shotgun. One bang for each parent.*

I think the only thing that had helped me come to terms with my father's death was that he was a soldier and it was a war. Death goes hand in hand with war, doesn't it?

It might have made it easier if I had known someone else whose father or family member had been a casualty of the war, but amazingly there was no-one. Certainly no-one I considered close to me.

I was all alone. And do you know what makes it even worse to this day is that I was so wrapped up in my own little world, I was ignorant as to what my poor mother must have been going through. I obviously knew she had lost her husband but I wasn't there for her like she was there for me. And then she was taken too and I had no chance to rectify the situation.

Back then, it was as if my life mirrored a theatre production, with an intermission somewhere in the middle. I was two versions of myself: Robinson 1 came before the deaths of my parents and Robinson 2 came after – Act 1 and Act 2 so to speak.

In Act 1, I was a bright boy with potential and was a proud sparkle in my parents' eyes. I think I'm forgiven in saying losing both parents so close together changed me; I'm sure it would anyone. Changed for the good however, that was not the case. I was acting out and I knew it. Maybe I still am to this day.

I would never return to Act 1. Act 2 had a very long encore.

Chapter VIII

"Look at how a single candle can both defy and define the darkness."
Anne Frank

There are times in life when we just aren't ourselves. Not so much as an out-of-body experience but more when we lose all track of our personalities. Our identities.

A lot of the time we all put on an act in some way or another. Life is a play. Just as Robbie said, *his life mirrored a theatre production.* This term rings true for us all. Ask yourself when the last time you were your complete self, without having to put on a face or persona for the benefit of someone else. In all honesty, you'll probably find it's not very often.

The little episode in Sister Meredith's office had had an effect on Robbie. As he lay on his bed with his neck bent up against the wall, blanket pulled up tight to shield him from the world, he felt as though he had lost a piece of himself. He had, of course, been in her office before, but this time felt different. There was a seriousness about her he had not seen before and her demeanour had angered him greatly.

How dare she? How dare she act the way she did, just because he had a bit of tobacco in his pocket? His hands were so hot under the blanket, he was sure it would go up in flames at any moment. He hadn't even gone to soothe them under some water after leaving the office as he knew it would just sting and hurt. The sight of them afterwards bore the marks of her vengeance. He took it personally. This was not just a routine caning to an unruly student. This was a statement to him for not listening to her word. Her word was always adhered to and his defiance had echoed straight through the cane and onto his palms.

Instead of sending him back to the classroom, she had dismissed him back to the sleep hall with strict instructions not to leave until the end of class.

Porridge walls.

Whether he wanted to or not, he knew someone would be watching him, to make sure he was toeing that ever-so-distinctive line. She couldn't trust him and he knew it.

He didn't want to see anybody. Talk to anybody. The whole world could take a flying leap as far as he was concerned. At some point, the class would be over and that would mean the stampede would break the silence. Up to now, since leaving the office, he had been alone with his thoughts; his anger; his resentment. He didn't want the silence disturbing. Something that was near impossible when you share a room with a dozen or so other children.

The inevitable happened. First there were distant voices from down the hall. Next came the faint padding of little footsteps. Then one after another, child after child, they came bounding in. Jubilant from no longer having their brains numbed and their thinking stunted. That's what made it even worse. Smiles and frivolity everywhere and here he was, scorn-faced with a tattered grey blanket pulled tight up to his chin.

No-one even acknowledged him. All except Jack-Jack. He came in without Mollie. She had gone off to do some Work Detail of some kind. He came over and sat on the bed, too young to grasp the aura Robbie was giving off.

He looked at Robbie like an innocent puppy. 'Robbie, w..w..where did you g..g..go to? You didn't c..c..come back to class.'

Robbie didn't answer. He just squeezed the blanket tighter and let out a sigh.

Jack-Jack waited for an answer but not for long. With no answer forthcoming, he continued, 'It's a n..n..nice day outside. Maybe we c..c..could g..g..go to the..... caves.'

The caves were about half a mile away behind the mines. They were infrequently visited as most people regarded them as too dangerous, but the children didn't see the danger. To them it was another place to be adventurous and another place that was adult-free and, more importantly, nun-free. They weren't the biggest caves you would ever see but they were home to many a winding tunnel with small alcoves around every corner. In parts, it was like someone had designed them that way. Jack-Jack loved them because, apart from being home to many tunnels, they were also home to a family of bats. They had found this out once when a wayward pebble had been thrown too close and disturbed them all. Fairly deep inside there was a small pool of water that had a consistent drip from above. The children had found this with just enough candlelight to see it before falling in. They had decided to throw small pebbles into the centre of it, but Jack-Jack had lost control of one of his pebbles and then all hell had broken loose.

Jack-Jack again received no response. He didn't know why, but Robbie seemed to be in a world of his own. He shuffled around a bit in a subconscious attempt to get Robbie to answer him. He really wanted to go to the caves.

Robbie didn't give Jack-Jack the answer he was looking for. Instead he just said, 'I'm going to get out of this place one day.'

~

The grease! So much grease. It was caked in the stuff. Rusted metallic items surrounded her, all of them dirty. One of Mollie's duties (and probably her most hated) was to help clean the pots and pans that were used to prepare another unsatisfying lunch before class. Today, she had been sent there as soon as class had finished to get to work on them.

Scrubbing and scraping made her hands feel funny. This was all she needed after class. There surely had to be some sort of lasting affect to doing this. She was just glad it was usually only once a week that she would find herself standing in front of a bath sized sink, the grime facing her.

After Work Detail, Mollie entered the sleep hall to a subdued and reclusive Robbie, just as Jack-Jack had. He was, however, up off his bed and sorting something in a drawer. She still felt dirty even after a wash – the scrubbing of herself more vigorous than that of the pots and pans.

'What are you doing?'
'Looking for something.'
'What?'
'Doesn't matter.'
'Okay.'

Conversation done, she noticed Jack-Jack wasn't with him. Jack-Jack was always with him - his shorter shadow.

'Where's Jack-Jack?'

Robbie's shoulders shrugged as he stood up. 'I can't find it anywhere.'

'What exactly?'

'Doesn't matter. What did you say?'

'I said, where's Jack-Jack? Isn't he with you?'

Robbie looked around as if it wasn't obvious that he wasn't there. 'He was here, a bit ago.'

'What do you mean by a bit?'

'I don't know. A bit ago. He's probably in the toilet or something.'

Mollie looked around again as if by doing so would magically make him appear. But it didn't.

The smell of grass and the trees sailed up his nose. It was something that Jack-Jack loved about being outside. That and the magnificent colours of nature: the blue of the river; the greens and reds of the leaves; even the brown bark that clothed the trunks of the trees.

He had always been interested in the outside but too timid to go out on his own. Lately, he had started wanting to be more and more like Robbie. He wanted to go on adventures, be brave, be daring. Robbie always looked like he was having so much fun when he wasn't confined to the indoors. That's what made him look up to him.

Jack-Jack had never had a father-figure growing up at Saint Vincent's. He was surrounded by nuns who were all women. Fair enough, Robbie was by no means old enough to be a father, or indeed *his* father, but the sentiment was still there.

Okay. So Robbie hadn't wanted to go to the caves. Actually, he didn't even know that. He hadn't said he didn't want to go. He hadn't said much at all, just that he wanted to leave the orphanage. Jack-Jack knew that already. In truth, he didn't know what was wrong with Robbie. He was acting all strange.

He had left Robbie's bed and wandered outside. That's when the smell and the gentle to and fro of the trees had given him a thought: just because Robbie didn't want to go to the caves, he hadn't said *he* couldn't go. The idea filled him with excitement. He had always been the follower, the proverbial sheep. It might be nice to go there on his own, to experience it for himself.

Something inside his young brain had told him this wasn't the best idea. And something inside his young brain had told him to ignore that last statement. Now he was walking down towards the caves. No-one had stopped him or asked him where he was going. He had just carried on and before long, everyone was out of sight.

Now it was just him. He liked it – no-one in front of him to follow or lead the way. The path was his to take. So take it he did.

'Well?'

'He's not in the boys' toilets.'

'So, now what, Robbie? You tell me you can hardly remember him talking to you apart from he said something about wanting to go to the caves, and now he's not here.

With what happened with Arnie Took, it's still not safe out there.'

'Look, we don't know where he is. Don't be such a flapper, you're getting me all worked up. He talked to me while sitting on the bed, but never said he was going to go down there. You know what he's like. He doesn't like going places on his own, so why would he?'

Robbie had a point, but Mollie couldn't shake the uneasy feeling she now had in the pit of her stomach. This place was weird enough but not compared to the town and the people in it. She and Jack-Jack had grown up here and she knew what kind of place it could be.

'What were you so engrossed in sat on the bed that you can hardly remember him talking to you anyway?'

Porridge walls.

That wasn't what he had been engrossed in, but it had been what he had been staring at while picturing wrapping his hands around Sister Meredith's scrawny little neck. If he had two pairs of hands, he might just extend the gesture to Sister Klara as well.

He didn't want to admit to the feelings that had been cooking up inside him. 'I don't know, I was just thinking about stuff. You know what it's like when Jack-Jack talks, it's hard to focus on what he's saying anyway. I was just not interested in going to the caves.'

'Well, you never returned to class after Sister Klara took you out. I thought you might have been stewing over what Sister Meredith said to you in her office.'

'Maybe I was, maybe I wasn't. Anyway, what does it matter? I'm sure Jack-Jack is somewhere close by.'

'The only thing that worries me is that he came to the waterhole to find us after his detention. That might have given him the confidence to go alone.'

Robbie didn't want to agree with Mollie but he knew she was right; *the voice of reason*.

The entrance to the caves was half covered under a hill and was easy to miss if you approached it from town. They were dark but not too dark to not be able to see. The light entwined its way through the passages like a bright tube. Jack-Jack knew the light didn't go very far but he wasn't planning on going far in anyway. He just wanted to have an adventure, as long as those annoying bats would stay out of his way.

Now that he was here on his own, he felt a spark of excitement wash through him.

'We need to go and look for him,' Mollie proclaimed.

'Alone though. I'm not telling the nuns that we're going to search for Jack-Jack in the caves. There'll be hell to pay.'

'We should tell someone. What about Sister Athena?'

Robbie pondered a moment before agreeing that telling Sister Athena would be okay. He was pretty sure she wouldn't get him into yet more trouble.

They found her outside, tending to a few menial duties.

Mollie approached her. 'Sister Athena, can we talk to you?'

'Of course, children.'

When she was out of earshot of the other children, Mollie described their predicament.

Sister Athena said urgently, 'We need to go looking for him right away. If you say you think he's gone by himself to the caves, I'll need to get a candle first. A large one at that.'

The orphanage didn't have gas lanterns that would have done a better job than a poxy candle. As mentioned before, the orphanage was lost in time. Candles had always been the chosen form of light at night time. It gave the place an eerie look to it.

Sister Athena returned, candle in hand with some matches. She had declined to tell the other nuns what was going on as she also saw that this may bring more trouble than was needed. She collected the other two and they were off.

It was not as adventurous as he had first thought. Jack-Jack was starting to get cold the further he went, and the light was dimming quicker than he had wanted. He had wanted to be brave, just like Robbie. He might even go as far to say he would welcome seeing some bats just so he could go back and tell the other two they didn't scare him. They would hang on his every word and be mightily impressed. *Who was he really trying to convince?* He had wanted to make it as far as the pool of water and throw a few pebbles in, but now he was thinking of giving up and heading back.

His eyes must have been adjusting to the dark because now he could see the sides of the walls instead of just feeling his way down the damp, jagged stone. He hadn't realised how many steps he had taken and his eyes were now playing tricks on him. He couldn't tell where the tiny bit of light was coming from. It seemed like it was coming from the right but then would shift and come from the left. He now didn't know which tunnel to take to get back to the daylight.

In fact, the daylight had gone.

A long flowing tunic wasn't the most ideal attire for traipsing through the tall grass and undergrowth. But Sister Athena didn't have what you might call "hiking gear".

'What have I told you children about these caves? Goodness me, there are so many unsafe places around these parts, it's a wonder the whole area isn't condemned.'

Robbie and Mollie didn't answer. They knew Sister Athena was the only kind nun at Saint Vincent's but they didn't want to disappoint her or put her in any kind of predicament with the other nuns.

They were going slowly towards the entrance to the caves. Sister Athena was getting on in years and even though they were in a hurry, they could only go at a mere walking pace, if that.

Jack-Jack had lost all sense of direction now. When a child is scared or confused, the most logical thing doesn't spring to mind. The only thing he thought to do to get out was to keep walking and eventually the light would come back, then it would get brighter, then he would be back at the entrance.

That was not the case.

Instead, unbeknown to him, he had kept walking in the wrong direction. He hadn't even gone in the direction of the small pool. They hadn't been this way before. It was unknown territory. The tunnels intertwined like intestines and Jack-Jack had been turned this way and that. Someone might as well have put a blindfold on him and spun him round ten times with a pin in his hand. But there was no donkey missing a tail - this was not as fun.

Because of the structure of the caves, it wasn't as simple as just turning back on yourself. There were too many tunnels. He was starting to get really scared now. He was old enough to realise what sort of predicament he may have got himself into.

For the first time since entering the caves, he stopped. If it was possible, everything became even more silent and even colder than before. Now his clothes were wet from scraping up against the wet walls and the cold air was prickling his skin. He started to shiver. Then he started to sob. Then he leant with his back to the wall and slid down to the floor, wrapping his arms around his legs and burying his head.

He was lost.

Finally: the entrance to the caves. Robbie knew what they were like inside. He was scared now they were here. In the back of his mind, he was hoping all this was going to be futile; getting all panicked, informing Sister Athena and dragging her out here. Now they were undoubtedly going to go in. He secretly hoped that Jack-Jack was back at the orphanage wondering where they were.

Sister Athena lit the bulky candle on the first attempt. The flame was big. Good.

In they went. The candle lit the whole place up well. None of them wanted to admit it, but all three of them were on edge.

'Should we just call him?' Mollie asked.

'I suppose we could,' replied Robbie. He was hesitant but then filled his lungs – 'JACK-JACK!'

It reverberated around the walls as if it was the only sound in the whole world.

Jack-Jack lifted his head up. It had reached him, breaking the silence he was sitting in. He coughed. His lungs were suddenly quite tight. His shivering had got worse. He hadn't been in there very long at all but he had gone quite far in and down to the colder, damper tunnels. He wanted to shout back but his stuttering came on fully fledged. All that came out was a pathetic stuttered whisper. He tried again but his chest hurt.

Again he heard his name called. He could swear it was Robbie but he couldn't be sure. Could he get up and follow the sound? It was too distorted and echoed too much to tell where it was coming from.

He stayed where he was so as not to get further away. He was too cold to move now anyway. He just hoped his name would get closer.

They were getting further in, one after the other with Sister Athena leading the way. The candlelight was doing the trick as long as it didn't go out. *Oh, how a lantern would have been so much better*, thought Robbie. This would have to do.

Robbie shouted Jack-Jack's name a few more times. If he was indeed in here, they would have expected to hear a reply as it echoed so loudly, but as yet they had heard nothing. None of them knew if that was a good or bad sign. Seeing as they had light, they had to go further and hope for the best, as long as they could get back. Robbie knew the tunnels as far as the small pool but there was obviously a vast amount of tunnels they had yet to explore and probably never would. There was a reason everybody considered the caves to be a dangerous place.

The sound was getting closer. The closer it got, the more he shivered. He coughed again. His throat felt as though it was going to close up.

Then, he saw a flickering of light. Or were his eyes playing tricks on him again?

The light got steadily nearer and then he could hear footsteps.

It was them. He tried to shout again which came out as another pathetic whisper but it was loud enough for them to hear. They rushed over to him sitting balled up on the floor.

'Oh, my dear. Look at you. What are you doing all the way down here? You must be catching a fright of a cold I shouldn't wonder,' said Sister Athena.

She handed the candle to Robbie and gave Jack-Jack an instinctive hug, feeling how cold and wet he was as the other two stood by, Robbie trying to stem the guilty feeling that had crept up on him.

'Come on. Let's get you out of here. We need to get you back as soon as we can and out of those clothes.'

Sister Athena had been taking a mental note of exactly what tunnels and directions they had gone, admittedly made easier by the aid of candlelight. They managed to get to the entrance without any problem and helped Jack-Jack limp back to the orphanage.

There, Jack-Jack was de-robed and washed (in tepid water at best) before being helped into bed.

The commotion had alerted a few of the other Sisters who in turn had alerted Sister Meredith.

The doctor was called.

Sister Meredith was displeased.

~

The onset of a fever was the diagnosis. Nothing to worry about, just to keep warm and drink lots of fluids. And bed-rest. Jack-Jack was not to leave his bed except for toilet needs and such like.

Robbie meanwhile had escaped the iniquitous clutches of Sister Meredith's claws and was wandering around with a serving of guilt – table for one. How could he have been ignorant of Jack-Jack when he was talking to him on his bed? Anything could have happened to him in those caves. Contrary to Jack-Jack's estimation, he hadn't actually gone that far in. But that didn't mean Robbie hadn't been careless and irresponsible.

Jack-Jack had a lot of growing up to do – he knew that. Being brought up (if you can call it that) by these nuns as your guardians or, dare he say it, parental figures, he was surprised Jack-Jack had as much fortitude and common sense as he did.

He needed to do something for him, but what? Some sort of gesture to say he was sorry. He knew Jack-Jack didn't blame him for getting lost in the caves, but that did nothing to curb the feeling he was having.

Hands in pockets and scuffed ends of shoes from kicking up dust, Robbie ambled through the street with his head lowered. No-one questioning what he was doing – the town-folk were used to the children being around under their feet, especially the ones from the orphanage.

'Now, there's a boy with the weight of the world on his shoulders.'

It was Virgil, sitting in his favourite spot, meticulously carving another one of his creations. Robbie stopped and looked up. He was in such a trance, he hadn't realised he was casually walking past Virgil rocking back and forth on his chair.

'Oh, hey, Virgil. Yeah, I guess you could say that.' He padded over.

'So sit. Talk.'

Robbie sat on the rim on the porch. 'Jack-Jack went to the caves on his own and now he's sick as a dog, laid up in bed.'

'I see. And that's got you looking like tomorrow might not come, has it?'

'Well, not just that. He wanted me to go with him, but I was so caught up in my own stuff, I ignored him and he went on his own. Got lost didn't he and we had to go looking for him. By the time we reached him, his clothes were all wet and he was shivering, crumpled up in a ball in the corner. It was a sorry sight to see. I felt ever so sorry for him. And also felt pretty rotten too, I tell you.'

Virgil digested this for a moment. 'Hmm, I see. Yes, you will feel pretty bad about that I shouldn't wonder.'

Was that it? That was Virgil's evaluation? He was good at storytelling but not so good on the advice front.

After giving Virgil a puzzled look, Robbie continued, 'I'd like to do something for him to say I'm sorry and also cheer him up, but I'm not sure what.'

Neither of them said anything. The only sound was the chipping and scratching of Virgil's knife on an as-of-yet unformed chunk of wood.

That gave Robbie an idea.

'Hey, Virgil. Do you think I could maybe whittle him something? Something he'd like. Like a fish or something. Nothing too difficult.' A chirpiness arrived in Robbie's voice.

Virgil stopped what he was doing and shot Robbie a patronising look. 'You think this comes naturally? You think it's easy just to do it, just like that?' He snapped his thumb and middle finger together in conjunction with the word "that".

Robbie all of a sudden felt as small as a grain of sand.

Virgil laughed – a dirty cackle sort of laugh as he threw his head back. 'I'm just playing with you, boy. Here.' He threw the piece of wood he was holding into Robbie's lap before extending his arm, holding his knife towards Robbie. 'You can use this. But be careful now, it's my best one. And it's the sharpest.'

Robbie felt a wave of pride wash over him. Virgil had given him his best knife. He wasn't used to anyone having such trust in him, especially with something like a knife. 'Thanks,' he said with an uncontrollable smile on his face. 'I'll make sure to be really careful with it.'

He went to the stream that fed the river further down the bank where he and Jack-Jack sometimes fished. Maybe he thought the ambience and location would inspire him to do a better job than he was anticipating.

In an instant he went from: *"how hard can whittling be?"* to *"this is difficult"*. The knife didn't want to serrate the wood. He wasn't doing it as smoothly as Virgil. Instead, he was just hacking away at it like a lumberjack trying to overthrow a large tree. His time at the chopping block had done nothing to aid in the delicacy of this matter.

By the time he had finished, his feet were embedded in the sandbank and his legs had gone numb. He surveyed his creation with an air of pride as well as one of embarrassment.

A fish – it could be. It would have to do.

He hadn't realised just how long he had been sitting there, but by the time he got up and returned the knife back to Virgil, the sun was sinking, making long shadows.

Jack-Jack was asleep. They had put his bed in a secluded room away from the other children so as not to make them sick. He looked content so Robbie was reluctant to wake him. He needed his rest. He placed the wooden fish by his bed and left, pleased at least a little with his accomplishment and hoped Jack-Jack would be too, when he woke.

~

The floor was icy cold. His bare feet were numb. The dark flooded the hall with unquestionable solitude. The silence was deafening as he took one step, then another down the corridor. Ahead of him, the walls began to close in with no light at the end of the tunnel. *Was he back in the caves?* No, he knew where he was. But he wasn't here. Not alone anyway. *Another step – Where do you think you're going?* Icy fire danced around his ankles stretching to reach up his legs. His heart sounded hollow in his chest. *Another step – I'm coming.* He turned around to see the inevitable "nothing" following him, pushing him ever closer. *Closer to what?* He was unsure but took yet another step.

He came upon a door. It was old, wooden, with a bedevilled past. His hand reached out to push it open before he could stop it. *Where are you going?* It was coated in something sticky. It creaked open to reveal more darkness, only this time a lot heavier. With the door fully open, a tall figure stood facing away from him with his head stooped over – a silhouette in an already blackened room. The revenant figure was breathing, echoing through the deathly silence. In a slow, baleful manner, the figure turned its head. One bright, burning eye stared directly into Jack-Jack's soul making his heart ache – "*I see you*".

He sat up with a bone-chilling scream that made Sister Athena drop her Bible. With heavy breath, he stared straight ahead.

'My goodness!' Sister Athena gasped with her hand on her chest. 'Jack, are you alright?'

The stare remained. Locked to a focal point straight ahead of him. He couldn't catch his breath. His palms were clammy, his mouth was dry. Sister Athena could see he was in distress and enclosed him to her bosom. She could now feel how fast his heart was beating. She held his head into her as he breathed in and out, in and out.

'It was just a dream. Just a dream.'

It *was* a dream. But it wasn't like any dream he had had before. There was something chillingly real about it.

As he tried to compose himself, the only thing that went through his mind was that if Old man Joe could visit him in his dreams, he could visit him when he was awake.

Orphanage or not.

Chapter IX

"If history were taught in the form of stories, it would never be forgotten."
Rudyard Kipling

The fever brought on the nightmares. At first it didn't look like it was going to be too bad but after a few days it had taken hold and Jack-Jack had gone from burning up to having cold sweats. He had a high temperature and at times would hallucinate. The nightmares were the worst part. Sister Athena had been assigned to watch over him day and night; a job she accepted cordially.

He had been pleasantly surprised by the makeshift fish left to him on the bedside table by a remorseful Robbie, which is where it remained.

As the days progressed, Jack-Jack was able to return to his own bed in the sleep hall but was still fending off the back end of the fever so was still not allowed to go outside.

The orphanage was pretty quiet during this time, but the town was not. Word had got around from the start about what had happened and by now, people had formed their own exaggerated versions. Most people had pointed the finger at Robbie, he being the older of the two boys and being viewed to be some sort of role model to Jack-Jack - *"How could he just let him go off like that by himself?"* - *"It's his fault alright. Anything could have happened to the young boy."* - *"I hear he was close to death by the time they got him back."* - *"He almost killed him. By leaving him on his own, he damn near killed him dead."*

Whispers - like a ball of snow running down a hill - can collect dirt along the way and manifest it bigger and bigger as it goes.

Because of his speech impediment, some people felt sorry for Jack-Jack. Others were not so kind and treated him as though there was something wrong with him. Even in his younger years, people would treat him badly making him withdrawn. Other boys would imitate him and mock him. Adults would ignore him or stay away from him as if it was contagious and at any moment, their speech might alter.

The ignorance of man can be staggering.

Hasn't she read that book enough? Jack-Jack watched as Sister Athena thumbed her Bible with great delicacy as if it were a relic. Looking at it, *relic* might not be too bad a word for it. It was a dark brown shade with patches where it looked like something had been spilled numerous times. The corners were frayed and had lost their leathery points. The pages were a dull yellow. Jack-Jack wasn't sure they were supposed to be that colour.

She was poised with a straight back and bent neck on the end of his bed, her relic on the bed, open at some evidently key passage. He often thought to himself that if the Bible doesn't change, why do the nuns need to read it over and over?

Surely they knew the ending by now.

Each nun was assigned their own personal Bible and Sister Athena always had the same look on her face when she read hers; concentrated and lost. He wondered why she found it so fascinating.

Jack-Jack liked her just as the other children did. The contrast between her and the other nuns was vast; night and day; summer and winter; cat and dog. He wished more of them were like her. She was old now but had a youthful smile, her hair hidden away under her habit. He wondered what she was like when she was younger. She had been a nun most of her life which had been a tradition in her family.

'Have you al..al..always been nice, S..S..Sister?' he decided to ask innocently.

She looked up slightly dazed, drawn out from her Biblical world. 'I'm sorry dear, what was that?'

'Y..y..you're always so k..k..kind. Were you always like th..th..that?'

She smiled youthfully. 'Well, thank you, Jack. I have always tried to help others and be there if anyone needed me. It's what I live for.'

He contemplated her a while. 'You t..t..talked before about when..... you were h..h..here long ago. About that other b..b..boy.'

'I did. Do you want to hear more about him?' She sensed Jack-Jack was interested and would benefit from hearing more.

Jack-Jack nodded.

She closed her Bible. 'Well, like I said before, I struggle to remember details. My mind isn't what it used to be. I have been living inside these walls for many years and I have seen many children come and go. It pains me when I have to see them go, but I know that it has to happen sometime or another.

'I recall this boy being very charming, just like you, and a smile that would bring me to smile also.' She took a moment. 'From what I remember, he didn't always have a stutter. Unlike you my love, who has had it all your life, his came on when he was a certain age. To me it was unique – something that set him aside from all the other children. Difference doesn't have to mean bad. And after a while, I don't think I noticed it anyway, just as I don't hear yours most of the time.'

By this time, Jack-Jack had his head rested on his hand with his elbow angled on the bed very casually. One thing about him, he was very attentive. Whether it was listening to Sister Athena, the teacher in the classroom or Robbie at the waterhole. Jack-Jack loved listening to stories. They were tales of a world outside of this one. And anything outside of the current world was usually better.

Noticing Jack-Jack's attentiveness, Sister Athena carried on, 'Now you have to bear in mind, Jack, that the orphanage was very different back then. I'm fully aware of what it is like now, but it wasn't always like this. It has always been a place of worship, but it was a place of happiness too. The children were very happy back then and there were more of them too. There were smiling faces everywhere I looked. We had a bigger garden than what we have now and it was so vibrant and full of colour. One of my jobs was to help out in the garden, but I can't do that now due to my back.'

'D..d..did the boy help you in the g..g..garden?'

'I don't think so. Oh, my memory. Sometimes I do despair. He was very shy and didn't like getting involved in activities. Not before Billy. He was our handyman here.

Unlike us, he didn't reside here. The orphanage had always had a handyman ever since I can remember. Oh, he was brilliant for the boy.' The edges of her mouth turned up a little. 'Billy would get him involved in some of the work that needed doing around the place. It worked. The boy would follow him around and do as he was doing. He really came out of his shell. We thought it was good for him so we left him under Billy's wing. He was really good with him. I don't know if he felt sorry for him or just liked the company. I guess being the sole handyman in a place like this could get quite lonely. Don't you think so?'

Jack-Jack was hanging on every word. Sister Athena was a good storyteller. She had a voice that flowed like water down a sacred stream.

He liked stories if they were real rather than made up. Maybe that's why he enjoyed hearing about Old man Joe all the time. He wasn't sure if he would enjoy the stories quite as much now after having nightmares.

'Anyway, that's how it transpired for a while. The boy's confidence grew. He was more active and seemed to find a friend in Billy. It's a shame we don't have a handyman around nowadays. Lord knows there are enough things that are in need of some attention.' Her eyes lifted towards the ceiling as if to find some fault with the roof. 'And who knows, if we did, maybe the past would recreate itself and you would follow the handyman around, help him with the work and it just might have a profound effect on your confidence too.'

Jack-Jack thought about this. It did sound like things were better back then. Let's face it, it couldn't be much worse than the present time.

Sister Athena looked at him staring into space - a small hint of a smile etched across his face. She cared about him, she wanted to help him. And if telling history through the means of story was going to help with his confidence and his stutter, then so be it.

She stood up, feeling like she had done some good comparing the two boys. She would check in on him in a while as she had been doing since he took ill. But for now, she was satisfied there would be no more nightmares, at least for a while.

~

History both teaches us nothing and everything. We can either learn from it or allow it to dictate to us. Like Sister Athena telling Jack-Jack the history of the orphanage with Billy and the boy with the stutter, the history of Fellowood Marsh had less of a positive effect on the town and had been doing since the burning at the stake.

That one event had set the tone for the town ever since. The results had stunted the progression of Fellowood Marsh into modern day society. Instead, it had kept it hidden away in the depths of the woods with its dark secret as its only companion.

Burning at the stake had become illegal in the early eighteenth century in England. It was prevalent a few centuries before with many a witch-hunt taking place. It was a public form of capital punishment for both men and women for the crime of heresy.

The last person thought to be burned at the stake for witchcraft was a woman in 1727. She had been accused of witching her daughter to make her hands and feet grow into horse's hooves so she could ride her. Both her and her daughter had been sentenced to being burned at the stake. Her daughter had managed to escape but the woman had been stripped, smeared with tar then paraded through the town on a barrel where she was burned alive.

The burning of witches was less used in England than in other parts of Europe as a legal form of punishment. However, private burnings still took place for a number of years in small colonies or villages.

This was what happened in Fellowood Marsh. The so-called witch that cursed Old man Joe's eye was an illegal burning in the mid-nineteenth century, many years after the punishment had been abolished. It was one of those things that sort of just "happened". Everyone was swept up in it at the time but was too afraid to acknowledge it in the aftermath. It stayed within the confines of the town and the town-folk. But it did more than just stay with them; it haunted them.

It haunts them to this day.

Regret swept through the town in the years to come but no-one would dare admit it for fear of the repercussions. Instead, they dealt with it in the form of rumours and whispers.

Ironically, fuelling the fire.

Chapter X

"Real learning comes about when the competitive spirit has ceased."
Jiddu Krishnamurti

Jack-Jack was improving day by day. He remained in bed as a precaution but his temperature had subsided and the nightmares had stopped.

The guilt inside Robbie had also subsided. It had been a surreal time for him with talk of him being the cause of Jack-Jack's illness. He had endured stares and inane tittering as he had walked past people. It had made him feel extremely excluded (not that he had felt a part of this strange town in the first place, or would want to be).

Some of the other children had given him the cold shoulder in class as well. At least that showed what people thought of Jack-Jack, he thought.

Some comfort.

Robbie and Mollie were walking through town when they noticed something going on near Fletcher's house. There were some children crouched down behind some crates and barrels. It looked ominous.

They thought they should take a look and strolled over.

'What's going on?' Robbie said, looking around at a few faces to see who they were; a few he knew, a few he didn't. None were from the orphanage.

They pulled him and Mollie down by their clothes to join them in their stealthy position.

'Shhh. You want to get us seen?' one of them said.

'Seen by who?' What are you doing?' Mollie interjected.

'We're spying on that weirdo, of course.'

'Fletcher Mane?'

'Duh, who do you think we mean?'

This was some sort of boredom-meets-curiosity child prank. There wasn't a great deal to do in Fellowood Marsh and children being children would sometimes resort to trivial entertainment at the expense of others.

Today, it seemed the target was Fletcher.

'What are you going to do?' asked Robbie.

'We're going to try and get him to react and do something, that's what.'

'What like? What do you think he's going to do?'

A shrug replaced an educated answer. Just then, Robbie looked down to see a brown bag containing the likes of what can only be described as the remnants of someone's rubbish; tomatoes, lettuce, even a few eggs.

'Look, shut up will you. You're going to get us caught.'

All faces and eyes were aimed towards Fletcher's house. No-one could be sure if he was inside or not. As of yet, Robbie had seen no sign of life. But then again, he was a rare sighting.

His house was ideally secluded for a man such as Fletcher Mane. If anyone wanted to be detached from society, this would be the place to choose. The day was bright enough to not need any lights on inside and the vantage point they had from behind the crates wasn't quite good enough to see all of the windows.

Richie, who hadn't spoken yet, picked up the bag. 'I'm going closer.'

'Where?' another boy said.

Richie looked. 'There, behind that big tree. If he is in, he won't see me.'

They all looked on as Richie scuttled low with the bag towards the tree. Once there, he placed his hand inside the bag and took out a large tomato. He turned and threw it at Fletcher's house. It hit the wall with a splat. The sound acted like a starting pistol at the start of a race. It invigorated the other boys. One after another, they all ran from behind the crates to join in the fun. Robbie and Mollie were the only two to remain behind the crates; the only two non-conspirators. In a second, a barrage of more tomatoes, eggs and something soft and green was raining down upon the outer walls of Fletcher's house.

Each boy got away only one or two shots before they ran away as fast as their mischievous legs could carry them. Not wanting to be blamed for this act of vandalism, Robbie and Mollie ran too, in the same direction as the boys. They ran into the thicket of bushes, out of sight.

Richie was particularly pleased. He was out of breath, stooped down with his hands on his knees. 'Ha. That got him. Did you see? Did you? He'll be cleaning that up for a long while I should think.'

'What did you do that for?' Mollie asked in a slightly breathless voice.

'Because he deserves it, don't he.'

'But you said you wanted to see what he'd do. You just ran away before there was even a chance to see him. He might not even have been at home.'

The point had Richie stumped slightly. 'Yeah, well. Whether he was home or not, he's bound to do something once he sees it. You watch, he's mad is that one. I'll bet he goes on a right mad streak. There's no telling what he might do.'

'Pipe down, would you?' Robbie said finally. 'He ain't crazy. Just because he lives on his own?'

'That ain't all. He's done stuff, I reckon. Bad stuff. People have said it.'

'What stuff? What people?'

'My dad for one. And his dad, and his.' Richie pointed to a few of the other boys.

'And they tell the truth of course. I swear, this town has got nothing better to do than spread talk about stuff they don't know anything about. It's a hive, I tell you. That's all it is.'

'Hey, don't you say nothing about my dad. He's a good, honest man so he is.'

'I'm not saying nothing bad about him. But he's caught up in the way this town operates. That's all I'm trying to say.'

'You're just jealous because I have a dad to tell me stuff.'

The comment was a low blow and came out of nowhere. It rocked Robbie back slightly that a boy could be so readily cruel with his words. Richie was a son of one of the miners who considered himself above anyone in the orphanage. For some reason, being in the orphanage had the same connotations as being disabled or inferior in some way.

Robbie - not wanting to lower himself to what he could see as being an inevitable argument with no beneficial conclusion - considered Richie. 'Whether you have a dad or not, you're still stuck here in this God-forsaken cesspit like the rest of us. But I won't be here forever like you will. I'm going to do something one day that will get me out of this place and be remembered for a very long time.'

'Oh, yeah? Like what exactly? You daren't do anything of the sort. What, you going to go and find Old man Joe's glass eye or something?'

'If I did, there's nothing to that. All that about the witch and the curse is just all nonsense.'

Richie reared up a moment. He wasn't happy to hear that the tales passed down from his father were being questioned by Robbie. 'They are so true. My dad told me so!'

By now, the other boys (none of whom had said a word during the dispute) were all enthralled by the tit-for-tat going on.

'Your dad's just been duped like everyone else around here. There ain't no truth in the superstitions I tell you.'

Mollie could see this was going to escalate and decided to run back and maybe tell Sister Athena before Robbie could get himself into any more trouble.

She turned without a word and ran fast, not caring much for anything except getting back and fetching Sister Athena for yet another possible rescue mission.

She arrived out of breath, bursting into the orphanage, trying to locate Sister Athena, hopefully without alerting any of the other nuns. Mollie couldn't find her anywhere. She must be here. The nuns never went anywhere. This was the only place she could be. She searched the classroom, the garden, even the washroom.

Still no sign.

Eventually, once returning back to the sleep hall, she sat on her bed to catch her breath. Robbie came in. He had a busted lip and a trickle of blood leaking down one corner of his mouth. The conversation turned argument had resulted in what looked like a brawl, just as Mollie had suspected.

'What happened?' she asked.

'I gave that Richie what for, didn't I. He had it coming. I didn't want to, but he got mad at me and faced up to me. He was the one who swung first, honest! But I got the better of him and he ran away with the other little cowards.'

Sister Athena walked around the corner into the sleep hall as Robbie was finishing up his sentence.

Where had she been hiding? Mollie wondered.

'Robbie?' She came over and inspected his face. 'What have you been doing? Goodness me. You really do get yourself into some bother, don't you?' She took a piece of cloth and patted his face with it, mopping up the line of blood. There wasn't much - only a small cut on the edge of his mouth. But any blood to Sister Athena was enough, even though she had seen many a squabble in her days and was used to cuts and bruises.

He felt a tang of embarrassment, being cleaned up like a toddler. 'It weren't nothing. Just some boys hanging around getting up to no good.'

'You need to be more careful. We can't have you going around getting into fights.'

'I know. I'm sorry. It's just some of the boys here are so stupid sometimes. They're just like everyone else around here. They're all caught up in rumour and superstition. It drives me mad.'

'Superstition about what? That man and his glass eye again?'

Robbie went quiet. He didn't want Sister Athena thinking that was all he ever talked about.

'Like I told you before, I don't know much about those kinds of things. But it goes against everything we stand for here,' she said.

'You don't stand like the others though, Sister.'

'I may not conduct myself in the same way, but I share the same beliefs. It worries me that you are getting too interested in all these superstitions. I know they have been around for a long time, but you just have to let people get on with their own lives and concentrate on yours. It can hold you back if you let it.'

'Like it's held this town back?'

'It has done damage before, yes. A few men in the past have tried to prove their bravery by going to look for the man's cabin in the woods. Not one of them returned.'

Robbie thought about what Richie had dared him to do.

'That is how I believe we lost Billy.'

He looked at her quizzically. 'Who's Billy?'

She collected herself. 'Oh, Billy was the handyman here. I was telling Jack about him.'

'Why?'

'In the hopes of boosting his confidence. You see, Billy was friends with the young boy I told you about who lived here many years ago and who also had a stutter. I thought by telling Jack about them together and the relationship they had would allow him to see that his stutter doesn't have to burden him.'

'So, what about Billy? How did you lose him exactly?'

'Well, nothing's for certain, but we think he went looking for that glass eye one day, just like the others. He never returned. You see, Billy had very childlike mannerisms. He was what people around here called a "simple man". He sometimes struggled with interaction. I suppose that's why he connected so well with the boy I was telling Jack about. Billy was very innocent and naive. When talk of the man with the glass eye arose, he became very attentive. We think that's what drove him to go looking for the cabin and the eye.

'After that, we didn't get another handyman. Instead, the nuns collectively decided to share most of the work between all the children over the age of ten. That is why you have Work Detail.' She looked apologetic at this statement. 'Of course, the big jobs couldn't be done by the children. And that's why this place is slowly going to ruin.' She looked around as if the walls would crumble in on them at any moment.

'I don't know what to think about it all,' Robbie said dejectedly.

'The only thing I know is no good can come from that eye. Whatever it is, it has ruined people's lives and I don't want you getting swept up in the conspiracies.'

After that, Sister Athena got up and left, having quelled the trickle of blood.

Robbie sat there a while and thought about what she had said. He thought more about what Richie had said. He also thought it would be a mighty big adventure, going to look for Old man Joe's glass eye.

He liked adventures.

~

Sister Meredith's office was a depressing place to say the least. Decoration wasn't an important thing to the nuns. There was no warmth in there – only artefacts of a religious nature perched on her desk. A large cross hung above the desk on the wall. The size of this alone was enough to bring down the disintegrating walls around her.

There was a meeting going on today. Meetings often took place to discuss the running of the orphanage and any matters that were in need of attention. In reality, they were just a ruse to allow the nuns an excuse to get together and have a good gossip; something which they all knew they shouldn't be doing. But if it was part of a meeting, somehow that made it okay.

They were all in there, all apart from Sister Athena. She was regularly left out of the meetings due to her objecting to many of the ideas that circulated the table. As far as they were concerned, she was a nuisance and was better left out of the proceedings.

Today though, she would do her best to muscle in on them. She knocked on the door and waited for the invitation to come in. It was hesitant but it came. She opened the door to several sets of beady eyes burrowing deep into her over several sets of beady glasses. The most distinctive being those of Sister Meredith at the head of the relatively small table, crammed into a corner of the office. The table appeared to be shrouded in darkness in the tiny corner.

'Yes, Sister? Can I help you with something?'

'Excuse me. I was just wondering if I could bring your attention to a matter.' She entered and closed the door, ignoring the cold welcome.

'Matters to be brought up are solely on this list I have here in front of me, Sister. No other business can be brought up until the end of the meeting.'

'I appreciate that. But as you can see, I am not officially in the meeting, therefore the matter wouldn't be able to be brought up.'

Sister Meredith could see her point, although she was reluctant to admit it in front of the others.

'Well, what is it? Speak up.' The eyes burrowed deeper.

She stood facing them like a naughty schoolgirl sent to the Principal's office. 'I am concerned about the superstitions going around lately. It is distracting the children.'

A few glances at each other, then back towards her.

'Superstitions you say? Come, come now, Sister. They have been around for many, many years. Why do you feel the need to burden us with this problem now? There are so many other pressing issues to attend to.'

Sister Athena could already see she was going to get nowhere, but still she tried. 'I am concerned for the children. They have over-active imaginations and it is weighing heavily on their minds. Some of them are even having horrendous nightmares over it.'

'You know as well as I do that these myths have been around for as long as any lady in here can remember. And we've never spoken about such matters as we know there is nothing to discuss.'

'But there *is* something to discuss if it is detrimental to a child's learning or beliefs.'

'And what do you propose we do about it?'

'I thought maybe we could include something about it in our lessons. We concentrate so heavily on the teachings of the Lord, maybe we could use it in a more beneficial way and then maybe they will see there's nothing to be afraid of.'

'Afraid of indeed. Sister, you know better than to get yourself involved in the over-imaginative mind of a child. They will always let their heads run away with them, fantasising and concocting up the most ridiculous stories. The best thing we can do is to leave the ideas of this town to themselves and focus on what we do here.' With a wave of her hand she returned to whatever was in front of her on the table.

As one, the other nuns turned from her, signifying her moment was over. She was back to being ignored - unofficially dismissed. She opened the door and left without acknowledgment.

Matter dealt with..... or not.

~

The church at the bottom end of town would have been picture perfect had it not been so rundown. *Rundown* seemed to be the operative word for most places in Fellowood Marsh.

It had white paint chipped off it and planks of wood were coming away exposing tiny holes. The mound that it sat upon was riddled with tree roots that were eating away at the earth beneath the church making it look like it might topple over one day.

The surrounding area was overgrown with trees and bushes which didn't allow much sunlight to shine down upon it, rendering it helpless, lurking in the dark and the shadows. It didn't have the beaming ambience a place of worship should have.

Every Sunday, there was a service run by an Anglican vicar, whereas the orphanage service was run by Catholic nuns, which Robbie had to attend. The world of God and religion in general should all be one team shouldn't it? Not in this case. In fact, the children of Saint Vincent's were not allowed to attend the services of the town church. They were to stay separate in the teachings of the Lord, which was one thing that seemed very peculiar to Robbie. He also didn't like that there was somewhere in town that he wasn't allowed to go.

Forbidden territory.

The term "forbidden" in Robbie's mind was something to be challenged. So of course, Robbie had always wanted to attend the church services just because he wasn't allowed. If he was allowed and there was no forbidding him, he wouldn't want to go.

After a while, he had left the idea behind. It just wasn't much of a bother anymore – he wasn't allowed to go and that was that. What was he missing out on anyway? He had stopped caring.

It was Sunday. There was even less chance of the sun shining down upon the roof and front steps of the church. It was dreary outside with a chill in the air; most unusual for the time of year. The attendees this morning were going to have to wrap up warm if they weren't to catch their death of cold in that draughty church.

Even though he wasn't allowed to go, at times Robbie would linger while everyone gathered around and then went wandering down the path that led to the church, leaving him behind.

He tried not to get in the way though. To the churchgoers, he was just a pest.

He spotted Drayton, whom he hadn't seen since their fight; something which had been weighing heavily on Robbie's mind ever since. He looked at Drayton dressed in his Sunday best. He did look like a prize turnip. The two boys looked decisively different now with Drayton dressed like that. He looked more like a small adult than a child. That was one good thing about being banned from the church - he didn't have to look like that.

Drayton looked mighty uncomfortable. Should he go over and try to make amends?

Before he could decide, Drayton spotted him looking and came over before Robbie knew what to do. It caught him off guard. *Was he going to hit him? Was he angry?* There was no time to react. Within seconds he was standing in front of him, the two boys looking like they were auditioning for roles in *The Prince and the Pauper*.

'So..... how do I look?'

It wasn't the opener Robbie was expecting. 'Like a bit of a pillock.'

It was all the two friends needed to break the ice. They both fell to laughing. There was no need to bring up the fight. The code between the two boys spoke for itself.

Drayton's Sunday mornings consisted of having to dress up for church but it was the only time he would be seen in such clothes. He hated it. Church was boring. It was a chore and he looked stupid. His family would drag him along every week just like most of the other families in town. It was a ritual but he didn't get it. He often got confused and most of the time couldn't understand the ramblings of the vicar.

'Sort of glad I can't go. Then I would have to wear that stuff too,' Robbie said, looking at Drayton in his Sunday suit with his knee length socks and his knee pants.

'Yeah, I will be changing out of all this as soon as it's over. That's for sure. What are you doing hanging around here anyway?'

'Nothing much. Just thought I'd come see the fashion parade in all its splendour,' he teased. 'What goes on in there anyway?'

'The usual: preaching, praising. The vicar will no doubt ramble on about some topic or another like he does and everyone will listen silently and then say "Amen, Amen" over and over whether they know what he's going on about or not.'

'Sure does look different to what goes on over there.' He nodded to the orphanage.

Drayton contemplated a moment then looked around as if someone was earwigging on his plan. 'Hey, why don't you come in?'

'I can't, can I? I'm not allowed.'

'You're not allowed as you. But what if no-one knew it was you?'

'What you getting at?'

'If we're quick, there's another outfit like this one at my house. We could fit you out in it and sneak you in.'

'That's crazy. I'll be caught.'

'No you won't. All you have to do is blend in. You won't be able to go in with us, but no-one will notice if you don't make a fool of yourself like usual.'

The jab went over Robbie's head as he reflected on the opportunity to get one over on the church instead of the orphanage for once.

'Okay. But we have to be quick.'

'Let's go.'

The two boys went off like a shot. The congregation was in no hurry to meander down the path towards the church just yet. It was a chance for people to catch up and show off their Sunday best.

Within minutes, the boys were back amongst the gathering, looking more like twins than polar opposites. Robbie stood there in clothes he had never worn before, even in his days before the war, aware that at any moment somebody could recognise him and land him in yet more trouble. Trouble he could do without. But being in disguise was exciting. It was like he was invisible. Drayton had told him to stand a certain way and if God-forbid anyone would speak to him, to speak properly and clearly. This he hoped wouldn't have to be put into practice.

The time came for everyone to follow one another to the church. Just like Noah's ark – they all came in two by two, with the occasional child in toe. Robbie tried to blend in and look like he belonged.

So far so good. He made it to the front doors of the church. The vicar was welcoming everyone inside. This was it. This was where he would be spotted. He should turn back. But that would definitely get him caught.

He followed a steady looking chap who was easy enough to hide behind and when the vicar greeted him, Robbie slid past without being seen. He had done it. He was in. The first time inside the church. He soon realised he wasn't missing much. The inside was just as deplorable. It wasn't warm outside but was colder in here. Whether it was the chill in the air or the setting, Robbie felt an icy spike climb up his spine.

Single file, everyone quietly took their place in the pews. Robbie did the same, still with no-one batting an eyelid at the impostor hidden amongst them.

He was in – a churchgoer.

The vicar was a Reverend Morse: a stern, rather overweight, pale-looking man with minimal amount of hair. His demeanour fitted in just right with the coldness of the church, Robbie thought.

He took his place in the pulpit. The congregation was so quiet, all you could hear were Reverend Morse's footsteps on the concrete slabs. He took a moment before looking up at all the faces staring back at him.

'A good morning to you on this somewhat wearisome day. I thank you for making it out. It's a good gathering.'

Robbie looked around cautiously. He still couldn't believe he was sitting there now, listening to the Vicar.

'My friends, I would like to talk to you today, as I have done so many times, about the curse that was brought down upon us all those years ago. A curse so evil, it has eaten away at our very lives – our souls. Now you all know that our beloved Mrs Hawkins passed away last week. I don't want to upset you, but I think we need to address the nature in which Jean passed on.'

Robbie's mind suddenly jumped back to what Drayton had told him about Mrs Hawkins mouthing the word "Joe" to her friend before she died.

'I had spoken with Jean not more than a few days before she died and there was nothing to suggest she was of ill health. Her death came quite abruptly.' The congregation remained silent. 'I'm afraid, my friends, that this looks likely to be another devilish errand by the cursed man. I will not utter his name in the house of the Lord, but it seems to me that Jean had been visited again and this time it had cost her her life. I went to Jean's house after she had passed and I can tell you I felt there was something very wrong there - something not of this world. I do not know what took place on that night, only Jean would know that.' His voice raised now. 'But I do know that he continues to haunt us! I will not let this man's spirit condemn us to purgatory. He will not defeat us!'

In disbelief, Robbie sat there listening, taking it all in. He realised then that Reverend Morse had been the one keeping the rumours and superstitions alive. *"I would like to talk to you today as I have done so many times"*. Was he using the church and his sermons to preach to everyone about Old man Joe and infect their minds with his words? No wonder the town could never let it go. Up to now, he had thought it had been the poisonous gossip from a few of the older ladies who had nothing better to do than scare everyone with their tales.

The vicar continued, 'I look around this church and I see faces; faces that have also been visited. Once someone has been visited by that monster, it never leaves their face. You can always tell.' He searched the room. 'You madam, yes you. I see it in you. He has visited you, has he not?'

In unison, everyone turned to the target of Reverend Morse's finger. It was a woman with a perplexed look on her face. She screamed out, 'Yes! By God, yes, he has!'

'I knew he had. Come up to the front, my dear. I shall relieve the burden he still has over you.' Within an instant she was up and kneeling in front of Reverend Morse. He placed his hand upon her forehead. 'He still sees you. But no more. I shall cast him aside. You shall be released from his sight.' With his other hand he splashed her with water from something shiny he was holding and the woman fell back onto the floor. Everyone gasped, as if a miracle had just happened right in front of their eyes.

A few of the men helped her back to her seat. And again, the vicar chose someone who had answered with an over-exaggerated "yes" and performed the same so-called miracle on them. One after another, Robbie watched. Is this what happened every week? Again and again, the hand on the head, the splash of water and the fall to the floor before being escorted back to their seat.

Robbie was so beguiled by what he was seeing, he didn't notice when it all went quiet. He looked up. The vicar's finger was pointing at him. He had failed to answer as all the other's had done when Reverend Morse had asked him if he had been visited.

He froze. He didn't know what to do. He had been careful to be inconspicuous and now he had a finger pointing at him and everyone looking.

'I..I..err.' Now he was the one with a stutter.

A queer look appeared on the vicar's face. He came closer.

'You, boy. I don't recognise you. I know *everyone* who comes here.'

Robbie sat still.

'He's one of those orphans from that place,' a woman said from a few seats across from him.

'Is that right?' bellowed Reverend Morse. 'What are you doing here? And dressed like one of our own children too. Why, that's sacrilege. You are not allowed in here!'

Before anything else could be said and before anyone pinned down exactly who he was, Robbie got up and bolted for the door like a pursued rabbit. His legs carried him through the door, along the path and into town. He ran to Drayton's house and to where his clothes were hidden. He quickly got changed out of the Sunday suit and left it for Drayton in the same place he had got it from.

His first church service hadn't exactly gone to plan but he now knew what went on in there. The superstitions were being kept alive through the church. Had this been going on ever since it had happened? One thing Robbie knew: it had seemed more like a religious cult than a church service.

With the orphanage and now this, he was starting to think if this was all that religion was.

Some sort of cult.

My Beliefs

Religion. Belief. Are they the same thing? Many of you reading this now will believe in something. Ask yourself, what exactly that is? Is it what happens to you after death? Is it what comforts you in life? Whatever it is, the subject is ambiguous.

I am sitting here now, still not knowing what I believe. I probably never will. Some may frown upon that. To some, making their way through the journey of life is treacherous without some sort of faith to guide the way, to rely on - a metaphorical shoulder.

To some, belief can be scary and to others it can shelter you from the things that are scary. Throughout my years, I have seen things that could only be construed as Acts of God. Does that mean He exists? Have I seen and experienced enough to make me a believer without any shred of doubt? Someone who doesn't have any doubt: what does that mean? Does that mean they are forever content? No room for manoeuvre?

Sorry if that is a lot of questions, but religion is littered with questions. I was thrown into a cauldron of questions when I arrived in Fellowood Marsh. Before my life changed, I was not part of a religious family. We didn't go to church like a lot of people did. I wasn't taught in the ways of the Lord. My mother and father were good people, they were honest people and yet there was no Bible in our home. I think if they were alive today, they would be the same.

I realise I have not depicted religion in a positive sense here. Maybe this is just my take on it. Saint Vincent's was supposed to be a place of God, of positivity. We were living in a spiritual habitat surrounded by an ungodly presence. If I had been a boy of God at the time, I might have been more afraid of the tales I heard from the moment I arrived. My younger friends, of course, had spent their whole lives in the orphanage - something I am in awe of to this day. That is where we were very different, and at times it showed. They had a different mindset. I realise that now, more so than I did back then. But bear in mind, at that time I was struggling with many conflicts and I do not believe my mind was functioning on the right levels.

The people of Fellowood Marsh were desperate to deflect the curse of Old man Joe away from their small, simple lives. It wasn't working. They were drowning in legacy. The town wasn't able to shake it and leave it in the past. It was stuck. I could see it was stuck. And to me, it was all because of religion.

Chapter XI

"An eye for an eye will only make the whole world blind."
Mahatma Gandhi

No-one had reprimanded Robbie since he fled the church. Ironically, it was as if he was running away from evil, but evil hadn't caught up with him. He had kept his head down for a while afterwards. He hadn't heard of any talk of an impostor but that didn't mean he could relax - anything to stay clear of more trouble with Sister Meredith.

Speaking of the good Sister, she was a wily one. She was always trying to catch the children off guard. She acted more like a Regimental Colonel than a Mother Superior. One of her favourite tricks was to spring an inspection on the children's dorms. Supposedly, she wanted to make sure the children's sleeping areas were up to her standard but, in essence, she just liked the power. They were never planned and there was no schedule. They could come at any time so the children had to keep on top of their sleeping areas.

Today was one of those days. The announcement came at the end of breakfast in order for all the children to be present and to not allow any last second adjustments. When it came, it sent shivers down each child's spine.

They would be escorted by the other nuns and supervised before lining up in front of their beds.

Sister Meredith appeared - slow steps on the concrete tiles in her heavy shoes, echoing around the hall. Her beads hung next to her tunic, clattering together. Her stare bore deep into each child as she made her way down the row, making them acknowledge that she was the boss.

Each sleeping area was thoroughly inspected, ensuring each child was keeping a tidy and clean space. The one thing Sister Meredith couldn't tolerate was a messy living area. It happened in silence, awkward tension resonating around the hall as the other nuns stood by like bodyguards. It really was the most unsavoury, cold act of militant behaviour for children so young and vulnerable.

She must have been in a rational mood as every area seemed to be satisfactory, but there was one girl at the end of the row in Robbie, Mollie and Jack-Jack's hall who wasn't looking as confident as the others. Like a lion to red meat, Sister Meredith could smell this. She took her time making her way to the girl. It was as if she wasn't concentrating on the other areas as she knew she would get to the girl eventually, biding her time.

She stood in front of her, looking down her nose at her. The girl started to sob quietly.

'And what is the reason for the sniffling?'

The girl wiped her nose with the sleeve of her slightly stained grey night shirt that she had worn to breakfast. 'I don't know, Sister.'

'You don't know? On the contrary, I think you know very well. Look at this mess.' She looked over the girl's shoulder, making her inspection; clothes falling out of drawers, the bed quite clearly not made and books from the bookshelf open and strewn over the floor. The girl said nothing.

'I feel I am reasonable in what I expect from you children.' She turned to address the rest of the hall and raised her voice slightly so the other hall could also hear. 'I do not ask the earth. What kind of Mother Superior would I be if I just allowed this place to become ruinous?'

Ironic considering the state of the whole orphanage, Robbie thought.

'Now, you know what happens when things are not kept up to my standard. I do hate that you insist on making me do this but I have to make an example of you if you persist in ignoring my rules.' She turned back to the girl and took out her cane from underneath her tunic, as if expecting it would need to be used. She turned the girl around to face the wall before striking her across the back of her bare legs. The girl shrieked but tried to stay as quiet as possible. Another one came. The other children jumped in unison like a bolt of electricity had gone through them with each blow. Robbie felt sick to his stomach. How could he just stand there and watch as this girl got a beating for something that was so trivial? The third blow came, then a fourth. Tears fell from her eyes as her legs developed coarse, red lines.

Enough was enough. 'Hey! Stop that! She's had enough, Goddamn it!'

Robbie's outburst was both shocking and relieving to the other children – the red-legged girl in particular. Sister Meredith stopped abruptly and turned to face Robbie with a look of sheer indignation on her face. She padded over briskly to him, cane in hand. 'What did you say to me?'

He stared up at her. He had said what he needed to say. He had stood up for the girl - regardless of the consequences.

'How dare you speak to me in that manner when I am carrying out my duty and use the Lord's name in vain. I should give you a dozen lashings at the very least.'

All the other children dared not look up. The girl hadn't moved, still facing the wall with the back of her legs on fire. Sister Meredith stared at Robbie with a look of contempt.

'But no, that will just not do. Instead, I shall give you demerits for your unruly outburst. I know how much you adore the outside world. A little extra work will do an unruly boy like you no harm at all. That is the way you will learn some respect.'

Sister Meredith turned and walked away without even going into the other hall to inspect the rest of the children. The inspection had taken an ugly turn and the fact that the other hall wasn't that important to her, showed it was more an excuse to discipline a child than anything else.

~

Demerits this time. His act of defence towards the girl had landed him in hot water yet again. But this time felt different. Robbie could acknowledge that sometimes he was in the wrong and that was fine. But he had felt justified in sticking up for the girl. As he sat on the wall at the back of the orphanage, he wondered how the girl's legs were. He could still hear the cracking of the cane on her skin as it had cut through the air like a knife. He hadn't seen her since Sister Meredith had left the hall. Once she had, the girl had gone running off somewhere, crying. He felt bad - bad for her; bad for himself; bad for every child in that stinking place. Sister Athena aside, the nuns were evil. Their tunics just a garment of falseness of what truth lay beneath.

He needed to get away, even for just a little while. To be on his own. To gather his thoughts. He didn't want to be around anyone, not even Mollie or Jack-Jack, which was strange to say.

There were some ruins a short walk away – the remains of some castle long forgotten. He didn't know anything about the history of it. The only thing they had been taught was to stay away from it as it was considered too dangerous. There seemed a lot of places to be warned off around here.

He had seen it once when he and the other two had gone for a walk when he first arrived. Mollie had told him about the ruins and how they were positively not to go anywhere near them. Robbie had wanted to at least go and see what all the fuss was about. Much to the protests of both Mollie and Jack-Jack, they had gone to see them without climbing on the perilous rocks. Back then, Robbie wasn't quite as rebellious as he was now, so just going to look at them was enough. At that time, he was new and respected the orphanage's concerns.

He stood up, checked no-one was around to see in which direction he was going, and headed off up the road that led out of the town. The walk took around twenty minutes. The second part of the journey was slower as it meant leaving the road and continuing on the beaten path. It was a struggle to remember exactly which way to go, having only been there once and almost a year ago.

He came to a clearing. He recalled this part now, fresh in his memory. Though the path had disappeared, he knew he was on the right track. Through another bundle of bushes and into another clearing and he should be there.

The ruins looked more magnanimous than he remembered as he parted the thick shrubbery with his hands and peered through. They also seemed bigger. It was true: the rickety rocks underfoot were loose and hazardous. But he didn't care. He wanted to climb up them. He wanted to see the view from the top. He wanted to do what the nuns didn't want him to do. No-one was going to stop him. It didn't seem like there was a single soul around for miles.

Climbing trees was one thing but this was even more dangerous than he had given it credit for. The problem with no-one being around for miles was that one slip and he would be in a very sticky situation.

Nevertheless, he had made it pretty much to the top. He balanced cautiously on the wall that was the side of the castle. One side of the castle was more intact than the other, for what reason, he didn't know. As he sat, he thought what the castle must have been used for. Great battles? Not so great battles? It wasn't big enough for a king or queen, but he bet some form of nobility had sat not far away from where he was now. He liked that. Right now, he would be the king of the castle.

The view was beautiful. It was like he was looking into a painting. The sky was clear and he could see for miles looking out across the copious treetops.

Time seemed to stand still. Not a care in the world. He wished every day could be like this. But he knew no matter how long he stayed there for, the cares would be waiting for him when he got back.

Just as he was about to get up and leave, his eye spotted something in the grass near the clearing. It was an animal of some sort. Squinting to make it out, it became clear it was a deer.

He started a steady, meticulous climb down from where he was, keeping a close eye on the deer, which as yet hadn't run off. He wondered how close he could get to it. It didn't even look like it had noticed he was there.

His feet now on solid ground, he gently made his way over the grass and foliage to a rock that was half buried in the ground. The deer turned its head in his direction and he stopped, a few feet away from the rock. Now it was a standoff, a stare-down and he was pretty sure he wouldn't win. Yet the deer remained, as still as a statue. He dared move slightly closer to the rock. Still the deer remained. When he reached it, he sat down, still being stared at.

He waited. A game of chess: who would make the first move? He certainly wasn't about to. To his amazement, the deer moved in his direction. Crumpling leaves and twigs cracked under its hooves as it walked up to him. Before he knew it, the deer was standing directly in front of him. Being in its presence alone signified to him the amount of danger he could possibly be in. Would it attack him? Would it be protecting its territory? It could have young nearby and wild animals will do anything to protect their young.

He had no idea, but he didn't care. He wasn't frightened.

The deer looked directly into his eyes and he looked right back. The animal was majestic. Robbie smiled. He saw more compassion and truth in its eyes than any person he had ever met in his life. It felt like the deer was trying to speak to him through sight. He lifted his hand up and touched the side of its face. Its hair was sharp and thin but with a warmth to it. It never moved. This wild animal was trusting him more than he had felt from anyone in a very long time.

As soon as he removed his hand, the deer calmly and steadily turned its head and trampled off slowly into the thicket and disappeared.

Robbie sat there a good while longer, secretly hoping the deer might return, maybe bringing its whole family with it. But that was not to be. The exchange had been magnificent and filled him with such power. It had felt like electricity surging through him.

The connection between man and beast astonished him.

~

The interaction with the deer had altered Robbie's mood. All the cares he'd had beforehand seemed to be superfluous now. Sister Meredith and the other nuns had been getting the better of him, but now he felt calmer and more at ease. A great load had been shifted from his shoulders.

He had declined to tell the other two about his small adventure. He didn't know why. Usually, it would be the kind of thing he would be desperate to tell them about. Maybe he wanted to keep the experience private; a personal moment between two beings.

They were on one of their walks. When there was nothing to do, sometimes walking was the most preferred option. Jack-Jack had recovered from his illness; Sister Athena had remained by his bedside the entire time to tend to his needs.

The day was bright. Beams of sunlight shone through the trees onto the top of their heads. The birds broke the silence with their chirpy calls. Walks through the thick woods made them feel like they were the only ones in the whole world, at least for a short while.

'Keep up slowcoaches.' Robbie was teasing again, just like he had done when he was climbing the furthest up The General. He was ahead of Mollie and Jack-Jack. For reasons they couldn't understand, he was full of life today. Spring was coming to an end, but it was still in his step.

'What's your rush?' Mollie shouted to him. 'We don't have anywhere to go.'

'That's not the point. We're exploring. We've got all these woods at our fingertips. Don't you want to see what we can find?'

'Find what? There's nothing in them for miles. I'm getting tired.'

'I'll have to go it alone then. I'll find something around here that no-one else ever has.'

'Simmer down, we're coming. Just slow down, would you?'

The feeling of being the only ones in the world evaporated when they came into the clearing. A familiar building stood before them. It was Arnie Took's chicken farm. They simply hadn't been paying enough attention to where in the woods they were.

The last time they were here was to deliver the unfortunate dead chicken.

Arnie Took had proven to be a dangerous man. He had grabbed Robbie hard by the arm, accusing him of killing his chicken and threatened him, not caring that he was a juvenile.

There was no sign of Arnie as they stood in clear daylight at the edge of the woods. They were in full view which was a bad thing. Quickly, they ran down to take cover behind a small shed. As they cowered, Robbie took a quick glance to see if he could see any life – still there was none.

'Robbie, we have to leave. He could be here somewhere and you know what he's like,' Mollie whispered.

'Hold on. I can't see him. This place is small. It's the middle of the day and the weather's fair. If he's not out here somewhere, chances are, I reckon, he ain't here at all.'

'And you want to take that chance? We need to go back into the woods, right now.'

Robbie, still looking, could see what looked like a container that must hold the chicken feed and a lever next to it with a funnel at the bottom. An overwhelming urge came over him to vent some revenge on Arnie Took for threatening him.

'Robbie. What are you looking at?'

'Nothing. You and Jack-Jack go and run back to the woods and back to the orphanage. I'll be there in a moment.'

'What are you thinking of doing? Don't do anything stupid.'

'He threatened me. He hit me. He said it wasn't over. So I'm just supposed to let him get away with that?'

'Yes, you're supposed to ignore it. Nothing good will come from playing tit for tat with a man like Arnie Took. Now, let's go.'

'I have to do something first.' With that he shot out of hiding and over to the chicken coop. The sound of chickens squawking became louder as they sensed the intruder. They sure could conjure up a right racket.

Still with no sign of Arnie, Robbie crouched with his back to the wall next to the container. Without thinking, he reached up and pulled the lever down hard. It was rusty and tough to pull down. As soon as he did, a waterfall of seeds cascaded onto the ground in front of him. It sounded like thunder, barrelling down, colouring the ground.

Finally it stopped. He hadn't taken into account just how much feed there was. He had made a colossal mess – an outdoor carpet of beige.

Now was time to leave. He got up and sprinted as fast as he could back to the shed where the other two were still hiding. They all ran as fast as they could back to the trees and out of sight. Once a good way into the trees, they stopped, hearts pounding.

Mollie tried to catch her breath. 'Well, that was a really dumb thing to do, you idiot!'

'I know. I didn't think that much would come out. I didn't know if any would come out at all.'

'Well it did, didn't it? And we can't go back and clean it up. Arnie's going to come back and find it and then blame you for it.'

Robbie regretted his decision immediately, but knew there was nothing he could do about it now. Again, he had let his impulsiveness get the better of him.

When would he learn?

Chapter XII

"No-one is useless in this world who lightens the burdens of another."
Charles Dickens

Town meetings occurred every so often, in the town hall - a chance for folk to raise their queries or concerns and debate matters of usually no importance, typically resulting in some form of argument.

Children were prohibited to attend.

Frequently, there would be some form of fallout following the meetings. The town could never agree to disagree and tempers would flare easily.

The meetings were hosted by Councillor Grayson – a somewhat odd-looking man who had been a Councillor for many years. He was tall, slim, with red hair slowly turning grey. He had big bulging eyes protruding from his head more and more with every year and a crooked smile. Freckles covered his face like a rash.

His voice was low as he addressed the crowd:

'Meeting commenced.

'Thursday – 7:30pm.

'All accounted for?

'Minutes to be taken by June to my right.

'We will start with the maintenance to the school. As you know, the wall has been in need of some attention for some time. I'm fully aware a number of you have raised your concerns for your children's safety. Let me assure you.....'

'Forget the damn wall!' The Councillor was abruptly interrupted by Arnie Took who had stood up sharply in the fog of the crowd. 'What about the nuisance those children are at that orphanage up the street there? What are you going to do about them, I'd like to know?'

Councillor Grayson turned to Arnie Took, trying to contain his anger at being interrupted. 'Mr Took, please. We can discuss other business at the conclusion of the meeting. We have topics here that are scheduled to be addressed.'

'I don't give a damn about your list. I want something done about them, now! They don't belong. They cause nothing but mischief and they're making my life a living hell. If you don't do something about them, then I will.'

'Peace, Mr Took. There is no need to raise your voice.'

'The hell there isn't. How else do you get your voice heard in this God-forsaken town?'

The rest of the crowd lay silent. Arnie Took was an intimidating figure. He stood firm in the middle of the room with annoyance on his face. Whether he was or not, the only person not to look intimidated by him was the Councillor.

'And what would you have me do about them exactly?'

'That's not my decision. All I know is my farm got vandalised the other day and I know exactly who it is.'

'Did you see who did it, Mr Took?'

'See? No, I did not see. But I swear, it's that no good boy who killed my chicken and left it on my front porch.'

'He killed your chicken, you say? Did you see him do that?'

'I did not. But I know it was him. He's been nothing but trouble ever since he got here. He's no good, don't you see? He killed my chicken for no good reason and now he emptied all my chicken feed I had stored up, all over the ground. Do you know how much that is going to cost me? I can't even get a delivery for another week. What am I going to feed my chickens until then?'

'Mr Took, I appreciate you're angry. And it sounds like someone did vandalise your farm. But if you or no-one else saw anyone, you can't just go around accusing people of such things, especially the children.'

'Don't give me "especially the children". Those children are the bane of this town and everyone here knows it.' Arnie looked around at all the faces staring at him, looking for some sort of validation. None came his way. Everyone in town was hesitant to say anything against the orphanage. The spiritual side of it just frightened them too much.

Suspicion can be ugly.

With no response, Arnie Took pushed passed the numerous legs in his row. 'In that case, I shall have to take matters into my own hands, Councillor. I shall not be responsible if anything else happens, you mark my words. Those children over there and that whole place has the mark of the devil. I swear to God it does!'

He marched off up the aisle and out of the door, pushing it open with venom. And just like that he was gone. Any other business accounted for.

It took a moment for anyone to say anything. When they did, it was a mid-to-elderly woman from near the back.

She had a shawl around her head and a pleasantness about her. She stood up just as Arnie had done to voice her point.

'Councillor, I would like to say something about the treatment that Fletcher Mane has had to endure at the hands of some of the children in town. Now, I'm not talking about children from that orphanage, at least I don't think I am. But I have witnessed some disturbing actions from some of the boys in particular. I do not think he deserves this and I would like to bring it to your attention.'

A man stood up a few rows in front of the woman. 'I disagree! That man deserves everything he gets. I do not want someone like him living in this town. He's an outcast and just plain weird.'

Fletcher Mane had never attended these meeting. He was an outsider and he liked it that way.

Councillor Grayson tried to regain some sort of order in the room. The meeting certainly wasn't going to plan and he wasn't prepared for all the outbursts. 'Silence at once. Now see here, I am conducting this meeting. We are supposed to be addressing the matters at hand. Other business comes at the end of the meeting as you well know.

'Now, seeing as this subject has come up, I would like to say that I am fully aware of the treatment of Fletcher Mane by some of the boys. In fact, I had to scold my own son, Richie, recently for behaving in such a manner, although I am sure his part in it was influenced by some of the other boys in question. Fletcher Mane is a resident in this town and he deserves to be treated as one, does he not?'

'Not!' Were the shouts of several other men seated. It was like they had practised it before the meeting had commenced. It was evident. The feelings of many in the town were clear. They did not like having Fletcher Mane as one of them. As far as they were concerned, he was a strange man who made them feel uneasy.

'Well, I'm sorry you feel that way gentlemen,' Councillor Grayson said. 'I ask you to try and be more open minded in this matter.'

'Why doesn't he attend these meetings?' one man shouted.

'And why doesn't he show himself?' another followed.

'And why doesn't he ever speak?' a third man cried.

All questions no-one, even the Councillor, could answer. People were always afraid of what's different. Fletcher Mane was a law unto himself and had been like that since anyone could remember. Every town had a Fletcher Mane: a man pitied by some, feared by others and misunderstood by most.

~

Arnie Took stormed down the wooden steps from the town hall onto the dusty street. No-one had listened or taken his side. He was angry now. He hated attending these meetings. They were useless and just an excuse for everyone to meet up in one big room and argue about the stupid things that only these maggots cared about.

Topics? Concerning what exactly?
A school wall that will fall over eventually?
The price of bread at the local store?
The welfare of some old codger on his or her last legs?

It was all stupid and they knew it. No-one ever concentrated on what really mattered – on what really mattered to *him*. All he knew was his chicken feed had been emptied onto the ground and it wasn't because of any fault with the machinery. And, one of his chickens had been killed. His chickens were too dear to him. Money was tight in this day and age as it was. Someone had committed these crimes and he wanted justice. And by the look of it, no-one was going to give it to him.

He walked swiftly away from the town hall feeling let down. He was good at feeling angry. Arnie Took could be intimidating when he wanted to be, but he also didn't want to get himself in to trouble. He knew that he would lose in relation to the town if he took on the boy from the orphanage. *What was his name? Robinson - something.* It wouldn't look good; a grown man picking on a boy his age.

He thought he had got him that day when he saw him outside that Fletcher's house and pinned him up against the fence. He wasn't planning on hurting the boy. He just wanted to scare him into not doing it again. But then that girl had got involved and, as if by magic, one of the nuns had shown up as well; a guardian angel so-to-speak that watches over them all the time in case of any danger. He wasn't "danger"; he just wanted to put the frighteners on the boy to scare him stiff. Teach him a lesson. But now, he had been caught by that nun and God knows what she's now said to the rest. (In fact, God probably did know.)

His name would be tarnished if he wasn't careful. He certainly wasn't about to let that Robinson boy get away with it.

Just then, in mid-thought, by coincidence, who should come into view but the Robinson boy. He was up near Marley's Store kicking along some random stones, making a dust-cloud.

Arnie stealthily made his way around the back of the store so as not to be seen. In a moment he was face to face with Robbie, taking him by surprise.

'We meet again, boy,' he said as he grabbed Robbie by both shoulders this time. He held him steadily, looking down into his eyes with a stern look. 'Now, listen here. I know it was you who vandalised my farm. Oh, I know you'll say, *"It wasn't me, Sir. I'd never do a thing like that"*, blah-di-blah. But I know better than these cretins around here and I don't take lightly to someone thinking they can wreck my things and get away with it.

'Now, seeing as no-one around here is willing to do anything about it, I will be keeping a close eye on you, my boy. Mark my words, if I see you anywhere near my farm again or if you think in that tiny little head of yours that you're going to mess with my chickens, I have a shotgun cartridge with your name on it. You understand what I'm saying?'

Robbie took a big gulp as he tried to absorb everything Arnie Took was saying. The only thing he could think to do was nod, which is exactly what he did. Arnie Took was a big fellow and no matter how cocky Robbie felt, he knew he was in big trouble. The regret he had felt after emptying the chicken feed had been validated behind Marley's Store.

With a squeeze of the shoulders for good measure, Arnie released his grip and went on his way as if nothing had happened, leaving Robbie disorientated and unsettled.

~

Just go for a walk, he'd told himself. *Get some fresh air*. Well, fat lot of good that had done him. Minding his own business and then, bam! - threatened again by that no-good Arnie Took. So much for staying out of his way. Mollie had told him it was stupid to mess with the chicken feed, and she had been right. He knew it as soon as he had pulled the lever, but by that time it was too late. Now, he just had to do as Arnie said and steer clear of his farm and, hopefully, him too.

Why did he have to get himself into these messes? He was never like this back home.

Home – he was not even sure where that was anymore. Was it here? Or was it still back with his parents where things made sense; where strange people didn't live; where magical, God-like legacies didn't rule every aspect of people's lives; where nuns were good people and the way of God was a good thing. Only one problem with that - his parents weren't there anymore.

Regardless, he had never been this troublesome. He needed to rethink a few things.

He was treading on thin ice and he knew it.

Don't cry. Big boys don't cry. But he could cry right now. The cocky persona had been sucked out of him. When Arnie had held his shoulders and peered down on him, he had felt like a small boy. Right now, as he walked solemnly down the street, he felt like he could cry; cry for his mother; cry for his father. Neither of them were there, that was the reality. His hard exterior had been his protective shield all this time but he knew deep down he needed them here with him to fight his battles and to comfort him when things were tough.

Things *were* tough. He knew it but had tried to bury it in a pit where no-one could find it. The thing was, no-one sat down with you and gave you a rundown on what it was like to be an orphan. No-one prepared you for it or let you know when it was going to happen.

He wondered how Mollie and Jack-Jack felt. He wondered how the other children felt who he was not as close to. Many of them were orphans and a few had just been abandoned. Which was worse - to not have your parents there because of death or to know that they were alive but didn't want you?

He struggled to answer his own riddle.

As he rounded the corner of the schoolhouse, (with the wall in need of some attention) he could hear a rustling. It sounded like feet frantically scrabbling around for grip in the dust, like a tussle was going on. Something in his gut told him it wasn't a good sound. He quickly made his way to the back of the schoolhouse to find three boys cowering over someone in the middle of them but he couldn't see who. The boys were slightly younger than him and he had an idea who they were.

One of the boys then said, 'Wh..wh..what's the matter, dummy? C..c..cat got your tongue or something?'

Oh God! He was mockingly stuttering. That could only mean it was Jack-Jack in the middle. Without any hesitation, Robbie ran straight into them like a bull to a red rag, knocking them over and nearly tripping over Jack-Jack who was indeed the target of the boys bullying, kneeling with his head in his hands.

The boys fell like skittles. They had been preying on the weak and now Robbie was the one towering above them as they gathered themselves on the floor.

'Hey, what gives?' one shouted.

Robbie knelt down next to Jack-Jack and parted his hands to see if he had any wounds to his face. He had yet to determine whether this was a physical or mental form of bullying - or both. The good news was he couldn't see any abrasions on Jack-Jack's face. His clothes were a bit dirty, probably from being pushed over in the dirt. Maybe that was what the frantic feet-scrabbling was he'd heard. But there was no telling how long this had been going on for.

He got up to face the bullies as they were getting back to their feet.

'What the hell do you think you're doing, picking on someone younger than you? Takes three of you too, does it?'

'We was only playing. And besides, what's it got to do with you?'

'With me? He's my friend and what does that matter? Think it's alright to pick on some little kid just because he talks different?'

'He's just a dummy. We wasn't going to do nothing to him. Just having a bit of fun is all.' The other two boys stood by idly, letting the "head bully" do all the mouthing off.

'This ain't fun. And I'd say I'm looking at three of the biggest dummies I've ever laid my eyes on.'

The words seemed to hit home with the boys. They didn't look so big now as they stood in front of Robbie, still outnumbering him, which made little difference.

'So get lost! And if I catch you teasing the kid again, I'll batter all three of you and give you all graves somewhere in those woods where no-one ain't going to find you. You'll just be nothing but worm-food.'

The boys sheepishly turned and walked away around the corner of the schoolhouse and out of sight. Robbie stood firm, anger boiling in the pit of his stomach and with his fists clenched so tight his nails were digging into his palms.

He stooped down to Jack-Jack, still slumped on the ground, quiet, but with tears rolling down his face.

'They're gone now, Jack-Jack.' He knew that made little difference. To him, bullying was one of the worst things a child could go through.

'How long has this been going on for? I mean, do these same boys do this a lot, or any others?' He wanted to know. He dreaded to think of where it might have gone if he hadn't have been walking around the corner.

'N..n..no, Robbie. Not happened a lot. I d..d..don't go places on my own too m..m..much. I've only seen them a f..f..few times before.'

That was something at least.

'You have to tell me if anything like this happens. Don't just keep it to yourself, okay?'

'I'm s..s..sorry for being a d..d..d..dummy, Robbie.'

Robbie felt a small crack split down the centre of his heart. 'Hey, you're not a dummy. And I don't want you thinking like that. Don't you be listening to boys like that. You're very bright and how you talk don't matter neither. Remember what Sister Athena told you about that other boy with the stutter? He did alright didn't he, helping the handyman do work and stuff? He was happy and didn't let his stutter get in the way.'

In truth, he didn't know what he was talking about. It just felt right to use the comparison as Sister Athena had done. She said it had raised Jack-Jack's confidence and he wanted to do the same.

Jack-Jack gave a little nod, still looking at the ground.

Robbie felt good about coming to his aid. The altercation with Arnie Took had left him feeling lower than a pregnant snail, but now he felt tall and important. He felt like a friend to a younger brother. Thankfully, Jack-Jack was okay, but he needed to keep an eye on any bullying from now on.

'Do you feel better?'

Another faint nod.

Just as he had needed his parents not more than ten minutes prior, he realised just how lonely Jack-Jack must feel and had felt all of his life.

The conundrum stood - to not have your parents there because of death or to know that they were alive but didn't want you?

Chapter XIII

"A woman of God is never afraid of any storm. She understands that the God she serves will calm the storm."
Gift Guru Mona

English weather can be unpredictable. The saying: "All four seasons in one day" can seem legitimate at times. The months leading into summer had been quite amiable so far. That was all about to change.

Speaking of which, Robbie had kept a weather eye over Jack-Jack in the days following the incident behind the schoolhouse. The young boy must have been more resilient than Robbie had given him credit for because he hadn't appeared to let it get him down. Although, Robbie knew what it was like to hide behind a tough exterior. It didn't mean it was the same on the inside. In fact, it rarely was.

Today, the rain was in full flow. Robbie was trying to ease the boredom with a book. Reading was something he hadn't done too much of since coming to Fellowood Marsh. The education he received here was different to before. The teaching methods were different. The nuns concentrated more on speaking rather than reading and writing. Mollie and Jack-Jack's reading and writing skills were far inferior to his but he tried not to make that apparent in front of them.

The bookshelf in the sleep hall was more for show than anything else. Seldom would one of the children use it. It was more of a housing area for dust mites and spiders who loved to cover the old books in their webs.

Robbie had picked up Frankenstein – a "classic". But he was struggling to feign interest. If he was being honest, it was a fascinating story (not that he would admit that to anyone). But he wanted to be outside. Being in this place was mind-numbing.

He wanted to be climbing The General or fishing down by their favourite spot. There was nothing like hauling out a flapping fish as it battled against the current of the river. Instead he was here, on his bed, listening to the rain hammering on the window sill above his head as he balanced Mary Shelley's finest on his lap.

The morning had consisted of another mundane breakfast followed by another mundane lesson. The rain had put a damper on doing anything fun or exciting like meeting stray deer or getting threatened by lone, middle-aged chicken farmers.

His concentration was waning. The rain was getting heavier and louder. It was angry now, appearing to rain vengeance down on their little habitat. He closed the book and lay there listening. The sky got darker and he could hear the build-up of the wind. A quick crash of thunder sent a shiver through him that was followed by flashes of lightning. It quickly went from relaxing to worrying.

A violent storm was upon them.

Everyone came in to the empty hall to take shelter from the storm. Some of the children were scared and the nuns were trying to calm themselves down, ignoring the needs of the children and focusing palpably on their own well-being.

Mollie had come back from Work Detail. They had all been sent back to the main dorms. 'Robbie, the storm's really picking up out there.'

'I know. I can hear it.' He stood up on the frame of his bed so he could see out of the window to the street. It was grey and blurry, looking through the rain flooding down the window.

Jack-Jack came in next. To say Robbie was keeping that weather eye on him, he had no idea where he had been. He jumped on Robbie's bed. He didn't look too bothered about the storm. If anything, he looked excited about it.

The outer doors were closed but making an awful racket in the wind and the window frames were clattering, looking like they would burst at any moment.

The nuns gathered in the corner, clearly discussing how to handle the situation. As yet, they didn't know how bad the storm was going to be, but it was getting worse by the minute and the orphanage wasn't the fortress it needed to be to deal with a violent storm.

A similar storm had hit the town some years back and had flooded all the rooms – fortunately not bad enough that the foundations had been undermined, but it had taken a lot of repairs. As a result, the damp and mould had made some of the children sick.

Sister Meredith addressed the children, all of whom were gathered in the one hall. 'Now, children,' she said as she clapped her hands together twice. 'We seem to have a storm outside. We hope it will pass but there is no way of telling. Right now, we just need to stay calm and not panic. I know it sounds scary out there but I don't want a mass of children causing a ruckus, you hear? Just stay on your beds, keep covered up to keep warm and stay quiet. The other nuns and I need to think and we don't need any distractions.'

Compassion levels at the maximum as usual, Robbie thought. In a time of crisis, (not that they were there just yet) Sister Meredith was the last person you wanted in charge.

~

The rain didn't let up. It pounded on the windows and doors like a madman trying to get in. It was turning dark. The day had ended but the storm had not. It didn't seem like it would until it had got what it came for. With the light fading, the persistent flashes of lightning were brighter, illuminating the halls with every crack. As time had drawn on, everyone had become subdued and quiet. Everyone - child and nun listened to the rain and wind with nothing else to do but wait.

Some of the children had been watching the rain from their windows which required them to stand on the backs of their bed-frames in order to do so. This had to be done out of eyesight of any of the nuns so was not able to be done now as the nuns were all sitting in the hall. That was until a trickle of water started to come in from under the big wooden door just outside the entrance to the hall. It was Sister Beatrice who came in to alert the others.

She broke the silence in the room with her hysterics. It was clear something was wrong but she only ushered the other nuns away down the hall to tell them and to show them the leak. With the opportunity presenting itself, Robbie quickly climbed his bed-frame to look out at the storm. It was just light enough to see the enormous puddles and the small river that had formed, running down the street, carving out a whittled path that looked like it had been carefully designed from the clouds above. It looked as though some of the other buildings were starting to be swamped by the muddy water but it was hard to tell in such bad lighting. One thing was clear: the storm was more aggressive than any storm he had ever seen. The thunder was immense and sounded like it was hovering over them with its arms outstretched like a monster, refusing to relinquish its hold on them.

The nuns hastily came back in, being chased by the steady trickle of water. Sister Meredith double-clapped her hands again.

'Children, we need to evacuate this hall and make our way upstairs. No amount of sheets or blankets is stopping the water from coming in from under our door.

'Quickly, now. There's no time to waste. I need everyone in single file and no pushing, no cutting-in and try to stay calm. Come, come. Up the stairs with you.'

Even the harsh coldness had escaped the Sister's tone temporarily. Everyone made their way up the stairs to the vacant rooms, mostly where the nuns slept.

This move was short lived, however. Before too long, the winds had reached immense velocity. Suddenly, one colossal gust of wind blew out two of the upstairs windows, shattering glass all over the floor, making some of the girls scream. There were most probably some downstairs windows blown out as well. The wind angered its way inside as did the rain.

Sister Meredith had no choice but to take further action. 'We have to go into the attic. It's not safe down here with the glass and the cold. Ladies, pull the ladder down from the hatch. Children, when the ladder is safely down, I want you to carefully climb up one at a time into the attic. Be careful now, I don't want any accidents. The very last thing we need is someone getting an injury. Is that clear?' She almost sounded caring.

Everybody did as they were told and before long every resident of Saint Vincent's was out of the wind, huddled up together in the attic.

~

The damp smelled musty. The ceilings were too low for a grown person to stand up straight. Candles had been lit and were placed on the wooden floorboards. The children sat in groups as the nuns sat together. There were boxes and chests, clothes stands and bits-and-bobs scattered all over the place. It was an unkept space - no-one had expected it have to house everyone during a crisis.

The size of the attic was big enough for everyone to be somewhat spaced out, even though it felt claustrophobic when they first got up there and closed the latch. Robbie, Mollie and Jack-Jack formed their own small group of three, fortunately in a corner some distance away from anyone else.

'How long do you think we're going to be up here?' Mollie whispered while holding Jack-Jack close to her like a mother would comfort her child.

'I'm not sure. That storm could last all night and then some,' Robbie replied. 'It's a good job they gave us some food before the water started to come through but folks are going to have to use the privy too. I guess they'll just let them down the ladder when they do, but the windows are blown out and it will be like being in a hurricane down there.'

'It's not much warmer up here. Glad we've got candles though. That warms it up a little. Smells though.'

'That's the damp. I'm not surprised though with the state of the rest of this place,' Robbie said as he focused on the floorboard in front of him. 'This is probably the biggest room in the building.' This last sentence petered out as if he couldn't be bothered to finish.

'What, Robbie? What are you looking at?'

He kept his attention on the floor. 'That floorboard. Look at it.'

'What about it?' Mollie looked confused.

'Doesn't it look different to you? It doesn't have any nails in it like the other ones do.'

He had a point. All the other boards were nailed down to the thick beams underneath. All the floorboards up there were very thick and covered the whole attic. This particular board didn't have any nails at either end. Once you saw it, it stood out like a sore thumb. Robbie leant forward inquisitively and tucked his fingers down the sides. It was tight and his fingers were too big.

'What are you doing?' Mollie whispered quietly as she looked behind her.

'I'm trying to prise it up, dummy, what does it look like?' But his fingers couldn't get the anchorage they needed to get down the cracks. 'Hang it all. I can't get it. Jack-Jack, your fingers should be small enough. See if you can pull this board up.'

Jack-Jack was quite excited. He was suddenly important. He did as Robbie asked and, sure enough, his fingers, albeit still slightly too thick, just fit down the side of the board and with a few attempts, he managed to pull it up, hurting one of his nails in the process. He didn't say anything. Again, Mollie looked over her shoulder, but no-one was paying them any attention.

Robbie pulled the board up, trying not to make too much noise. He placed it to the side on top of the one next to it. There was just enough candlelight to see. All three children peered into the hole.

Toys - just old dusty toys covered in cobwebs. They looked as though they'd spent an eternity down there. There were some wooden soldiers, a train with most of its wheels missing and an odd-looking horse with half of its face chipped off.

'What are these?' Mollie chirped in.

'What does it look like? Just a bunch of toys. But why are they up here though, hiding under the floorboards?' Robbie answered.

'Maybe some kid hid them up here.'

'Like treasure!' Robbie found the discovery very exciting. It wasn't exactly treasure, but it was as close to it as he was going to get.

'Could be. But look at them. It would have had to have been a long time ago. I don't think it was anyone who's here now.'

'It must have been a kid who used to be here. And looking at the toys, it must have been a boy too, otherwise there would be dolls instead of soldiers and trains. I guess the horse could have been either. Do you think he put them up here for someone to find years later?'

'I don't know, but it's creepy. I don't like them. They look alive or something. Like they're watching us.'

Meanwhile, Jack-Jack hadn't said anything. He was just looking at the toys like they had some sort of spell over him.

None of them were keen to pick any of the toys up with them being covered in cobwebs; certain creepy-crawlies might be lurking underneath in their homes just waiting to be disturbed.

'We should keep them hidden before someone sees.' Robbie carefully replaced the floorboard. No-one took any notice of what they were doing. 'This needs to be our little secret. No-one else can know about it.' The excitement in his lowered voice was evident.

'Isn't it strange to think that all that time ago, whenever it was, some kid stored these up here? Maybe it wasn't even one boy – it could have been two or three.'

'I don't know, Mollie. But the fact that we have found them is something, don't you think?'

'I guess.' Mollie was unsure what to think. It was still creepy to her but she had no desire to go telling everyone. 'But how would they have got them up here, in the attic? Not to mention, why?'

'Well..... maybe that answers it. There must have been more than one kid because then they could climb on each other's shoulders to pull the latch down.'

It made sense, Mollie couldn't deny it. They had stumbled on what they were deciding to call "treasure". Robbie was more into it than she was but that made sense – he was a boy and boys went looking for treasure, not girls.

~

The storm ended up lasting all night. A few children and nuns had gone down to use the toilet in this period and returned to impart the information that water was covering the whole downstairs. The storm really had come knocking and invited itself right in.

It was early morning by the time the rain had stopped and the wind had died down. The sun was attempting to shine a light on a dismal situation through the broken windows and the air outside was still; the calm after the storm.

The children were let out of the attic to descend into the water. The bottom floor was covered by a full inch apart from, ironically, the washroom as that inclined slightly from the sleep halls.

There was a murky smell from the dirty water. Some things had been ruined and were unsalvageable. Seeing as there was no cleaner or handyman, the children were put to work on the seemingly endless task of mopping up the water. There was only one mop and bucket so anything and everything was used: brushes, sheets and pots-and-pans from the kitchen. It took all day and the result was not a pleasant one. The walls were damp where the water had risen and a pile of ruined things had been stacked up around the back. The beds and cabinets had to remain as they couldn't be replaced.

The whole place was a mess, but after a lot of work, it was at least liveable again. The nuns hadn't lifted a finger; it was left exclusively to the children. The local blacksmith had noticed the damage to the windows and offered to board them up, so at least that was one thing the children didn't have to do.

Later on in the day, the three children decided to go and see what the rest of the town looked like. The picture wasn't pretty. The flood had eaten away at the ground and many of the buildings had suffered the same fate as the orphanage. People were trying to relieve their businesses from the destructive water and were throwing out damaged pieces of furniture and other possessions.

As they walked down the street taking in the tragedy, they noticed Virgil sweeping some water from his porch. His house had escaped being invaded as it was raised up from the ground.

'Hello, Virgil.'

'Oh, hello children. Just getting rid of some of this water. Fortunately, it didn't make its way inside. Good job really, some of my carvings are on the floor. They would have been destroyed for sure. Hell of a storm. Did you get through it alright up there in the orphanage?'

'It was terrible. The floor got flooded and the windows were blown out so we had to take shelter in the attic,' Mollie said.

'Well, I've never seen such a storm, certainly for this time of year.' He sat down on his rocking chair to take a breather, propping the brush up against the wall.

'We've been working since the early hours to get that place cleaned up.' There was a hint of anger in Robbie's voice. 'The blacksmith offered to board up the windows that blew out.'

'That's because there's been no handyman over there for far too long.'

'Yeah, Sister Athena told us about the last one.'

'Who, Billy?'

'You remember him?'

'Sure do. He was a hard worker over there, but it's a very long time ago. Must be decades. Everyone seemed to like him. But he was a simple man, so he was. He was there as a handyman and that was it. I'm not even sure where he lived. He never got involved in anything to do with the town. I seem to recall he used to get followed around all day by one of the boys that lived there.'

'Sister Athena told us about him too. She told Jack-Jack here about him because he also had a stutter and she was saying it never let it hold him back.' Jack-Jack lowered his head and Robbie felt a stabbing of guilt shoot through him for mentioning it like he wasn't there.

'That's true. He was always helping out with the work that needed doing. I think it helped him because he didn't have many friends there. I guess that must be why the two of them got on so well together. They were like two peas in a pod. We called them "Billy and the boy". Not very inventive. But it was a long time ago.'

Robbie thought for a second. 'Sister Athena said Billy disappeared one day because he went looking for Old man Joe's glass eye and never returned. Is that true? Do people who go in search of the eye just vanish?'

Virgil eyeballed him suspiciously. 'That was what the town concluded. He was the kind of person who would do such a thing. He didn't understand the seriousness of the superstitions surrounding that eye. I suspect he probably did go looking for it after hearing about it. Maybe he thought it was valuable.'

The story sounded very intriguing to Robbie. It was the kind of thing he had only read about in books. Yet this was so close to home. He had never been sold on the superstitions of Old man Joe's glass eye, but it was very suspect that whomever would go in search of it would not return. That was something even he could not ignore.

~

The rain hadn't returned which allowed the town to at least get back to some sort of order. The storm had left its mark on the orphanage. The windows were still boarded up and would prove difficult to replace on the orphanage's budget, which sufficed to say was miniscule at best. The damp smell permeated the inside due to the rainwater covering most of the downstairs. The bottom few inches around most of the walls now displayed a darker, uglier colour, if that was possible.

Robbie never liked staying inside and now it was even worse. It would be a long time until things got back to normal. Maybe a nice trek down to the river would clear his head.

The river was a good downhill walk through the woods. Robbie and Jack-Jack would go fishing when they could. He wasn't much of a fisherman but he enjoyed the soothing sound of the trickling water and teaching Jack-Jack the ropes. It made him feel like he was better at it than he really was. He liked the look on Jack-Jack's face when he caught something. They always threw it back; there was no way they could take their catch back with them.

The riverbank wasn't vacant. Drayton was fishing in his favourite spot. Robbie slid down the slope to join him.

'Hey. Caught anything good yet?'

'Shhh, you'll scare the fish away, you idiot,' Drayton replied.

'Nonsense. That wouldn't make a difference the way you fish.'

Drayton would have come back with a similar sarcastic remark but the truth was he had yet to catch anything.

'My father taught me how to fish. He usually comes down here with me but he's busy cleaning up after the storm. It's too nice a day to be inside, especially seeing as I was just getting in the way.'

'I never learned how to fish before coming here. My father never taught me and now he never will.'

Silence floated between them like the twigs in the river.

Drayton decided to break it. 'You know I help my father with carving the headstones?'

'What about it?'

'He wants me to be a stonemason because he says the mines are too dangerous. People have been killed by cave-ins because they use dynamite down there. He thinks being a stonemason will be better for me.'

'Maybe we should go look for it.'

'Look for what?'

'The dynamite. If we find it we could blow up the schoolhouse and then you wouldn't ever have to go there again.'

Drayton knew Robbie was joking but the idea seemed quite appealing, nonetheless.

'Well, it doesn't appear as though the fish are biting today and my arm is getting tired. It's Saturday afternoon, so there'll be nobody there, but it'll be very dark.'

'We need some matches then,' said Robbie.

'I've got a penny I found on the street a while back. We could go by the store on the way and get some,' he said, holding the penny in his hand.

The boys headed off but it was imperative not to be seen going into the mines. Skulking around the entrance, trying not to be caught was enthralling to Robbie. He was always looking for ways to be adventurous.

As they'd expected, inside was dark. The further they went, the more the light dwindled away. The room opened up where the work was currently being done. Drayton lit one of the matches. There was just enough light for the boys to see. They saw carts perched on the rails and pickaxes haphazardly left lying around.

It was so still. Dust hung in the air. Robbie wondered if it ever settled or if it just danced around all day and all night down there until the workers disturbed it again.

'Look at this place. It's amazing.' Drayton was in awe. He'd always wondered what it was like but never dared come down to see. The warning his father had given him many times had been enough to plant the fear of getting caught in him.

The match fizzled out so Drayton lit another. One of the shafts was high enough for them to explore a little further and they'd only gone a few yards when Robbie said, 'Hey, look at this.'

There was an alcove, almost hidden from the main walkway with a makeshift door which was wide open. They went through the open door and found a crate with its lid askew. Under the lid were some sticks of dynamite and some fuses in another box. Drayton automatically shielded the match with his other hand.

'This must be ready for Monday,' said Drayton, keeping his voice low as if to protect their secret, even though there was no-one else there to hear them. 'My dad told me that the rest of the dynamite is locked safely in a storage hut away from the diggings and the manager of the mine has the key.'

Robbie went over to the open crate of dynamite. He picked up a stick to inspect it. Holding the danger in his hand filled him with excitement.

All of a sudden in the tunnel behind them, there were footsteps. They both heard it and looked at each other. *That shouldn't be, it was Saturday. No-one was supposed to be down here.* But then again, neither were they. They stood still, listening to see if they were imagining it or not.

They weren't. Drayton quickly blew out the match.

Sure enough, the footsteps got steadily louder.

As the owner of the footsteps came into view, the boys did their best to stay hidden. If they didn't make any noise, they shouldn't be seen.

It was a man. He was creeping around as if looking for something, holding a small lantern. He was only a matter of a few feet away from the boys now as he knelt down and hid something underneath some rocks in the corner before covering it back up. They could see him from the alcove but he didn't look in their direction and therefore didn't see them. Once he was satisfied, he left.

The boys waited long after the footsteps had disappeared back up the tunnel before emerging from their hiding place. Drayton lit another match and Robbie realised he was still holding the stick of dynamite. He carefully replaced it in the crate and they immediately went over to the rocks to unearth what the man had hidden. It was a big wad of money wrapped up in a crumpled-up paper bag. They held it like discovering treasure – real treasure this time.

'Robbie, what do we do?'

Robbie thought for a moment. This must have been one of the men that were talking about robbing the store in town when they were above them in The General. Even though it was dark, the man had been so near to them. Robbie could swear it had been Arnie Took.

'We have to put this back. I reckon the store in town has been robbed and this is the money from it.'

'How could you possibly know that?'

He had made a blunder. 'I'll tell you later. Regardless, we need to leave the money here. Imagine if someone catches us coming out of here with it. They'll think it was us and that'd be a bind even I couldn't get out of.'

Robbie had a point. Getting caught being down the mine in the first place was one thing, but to be in possession of all this money warranted a whole lot more trouble. They put it back and covered it up as well as they could and left the mines quietly. Thankfully, there was no-one waiting for them at the entrance.

They walked up towards town. There was a whole lot of commotion. Everyone was in the street outside Fletcher's house with their fists pounding the air.

The boys joined the gathering. People were shouting things like: *arrest him* and *get him out of there*.

'What's going on?' Robbie asked a man he was now standing next to.

'That man's just robbed the general store.'

Chapter XIV

"Much remains to recover, repent now."
Lailah Gifty Akita

The general store *had* been robbed, just like Robbie had suspected. But why did the town think it was Fletcher? Robbie knew it wasn't, he could see that from his vantage point behind the crates in the mines. The figure appeared to be Arnie Took. He couldn't be sure. It had been dark, but at the time he had been so convinced.

As he stood there confused, the town-folk continued their mob-mentality towards Fletcher's house. They were yelling from behind his fence, but as of yet there was no sign of him. Robbie thought it would only be a matter of time before someone stormed the house and dragged him outside.

Constable Pennileason turned up at that moment. Although an inexperienced constable, he was a commanding figure who had fought in the trenches during the war and was well respected for it. He made his way through the crowd to stand in front of Fletcher's front gate. Robbie and Drayton both looked on. The crowd seemed more subdued now the Constable had turned up.

'People, please. Calm yourselves down. There is no proof this man robbed the store today,' the Constable started.

'But he was the last one seen in there,' one woman shouted.

'That's right. It had to have been him,' a man followed.

'I have just been speaking with the storekeeper. No-one actually saw the robber,' Constable Pennileason explained. 'The robbery was committed whilst the storekeeper was cleaning up after the storm. He was around the back and didn't see anybody. The mere fact that Fletcher Mane was the last one to be seen going into the store is irrelevant and I cannot arrest someone on that suspicion alone.'

'So you're just going to do nothing?' The crowd was now in uproar again.

'I will conduct a full investigation over this, I assure you. But what you're doing is wrong. Go back to your homes. This is no time for a man-hunt.'

The crowd evidently disagreed with the Constable. Deflated, they started to disperse.

There had once again been no sign of Fletcher Mane. It wasn't even clear if he had been inside at all, but Robbie figured he must have been; cowering in the corner most likely waiting for someone to storm his house and drag him outside to the waiting mob.

The two boys, having not moved, were left standing in the street as the rest of the crowd went home. Robbie thought about saying something to the Constable about his thinking it was Arnie Took. But yet again, doing the right thing would most likely land him in trouble. So he kept his mouth shut..... for now.

~

So many things were happening one after the other. For a town that was usually rather boring, it had been an eventful time. Now, as the two boys had vacated the deserted street to a more secluded area behind Marley's Store, Robbie thought about sharing his suspicions with Drayton. Surely telling Drayton wouldn't get him in trouble.

'I think I know who the man was.'

'The man down the mines?'

'Yeah.'

'So why didn't you tell the Constable about it?'

'Do you think he would take any notice of me? I'm the troublesome one around here, remember?'

As Drayton thought about it, he agreed. 'So who do you think it was?'

'That good-for-nothing Arnie Took, the chicken farmer. It was dark but I could tell it was him. You could say I've seen him up close recently.'

'Arnie Took? Why do you think it could be him? He's never done anything around here like robbing a store.'

'Maybe not. But a while ago, we were up The General and two men came and perched themselves right underneath us. They didn't know we were there. They talked about robbing the store and even said they would do it at the weekend – and today's Saturday. We didn't think anything of it. They had hats on and I couldn't tell who it was but now, after seeing him in the mines, I'm sure it was him. And what's worse, the whole town have their minds set on it being that poor fool, Fletcher Mane.'

'They were saying he was the last to be seen in there. And he's such a strange man, it makes sense, don't it?'

'I don't see no sense in it at all. It's just folks wanting to pin the blame on someone and he's the easy target. But they all weren't down those mines seeing Arnie Took bury that money.'

'But he doesn't work down the mines so why would he hide it there?'

'Well, don't you see? That's the perfect alibi. If anyone found it, they'd most likely think it was someone who worked down there who had hidden it.'

Drayton sat on a crate that was on its side and thought. 'Hey, we should go get the money and take it to the Constable.'

'Oh right, so he can think we did it? We'd be hung and quartered for sure.'

A puzzled look appeared on Drayton's face. 'Hung and quartered?' Drayton had clearly not heard of this term before.

'You know, like they used to do to traitors in olden times,' Robbie attempted to explain.

'Well, I don't know much about that.' Drayton was more focused on the matter at hand. 'Alright then, we go take the money to the storekeeper and he'll be so happy, he'll give us a reward no doubt. Might let us keep some of the money. We'll just ask him not to tell where he got it back from.'

'That might work. But whatever reward we get, we split it fifty-fifty.'

'Yeah, yeah. Fifty-fifty. He's a nice man, I reckon he'll give us quite a bundle for it too.'

So the two boys went back to the mines to retrieve the money. But when they uncovered the rocks, the money was gone.

The boys stared at the gaping hole between the rocks.

'Is this definitely where it was?' Drayton asked.

'Of course it is. He must have panicked and come back to remove it after seeing the crowd gathering on the street.'

'So, now what do we do?'

'We could go to his farm and see if we can find it there.'

'Woh, hold on. That's a whole big mess of trouble. Just coming back down here was risky enough. I don't want no reward that badly.'

'Don't be a scaredy-cat. He might not even be there. And you said we might get a whole big bundle for returning it. We can't pass that up.'

'I ain't no scaredy-cat. I just don't think that's a good idea, that's all. That Arnie Took can be a mean character.'

Robbie could relate to that. He had already risked going to Arnie Took's farm more than he cared to, but this was yet another notch on the adventure-post. Was he going to risk another trip to the farm? Arnie had told him not to go near his farm again, but this time it could be a lot more lucrative.

'Look, let's be quiet and not be seen and if we don't find anything, we'll leave. No-one will know we were there.'

After a few more attempts, Robbie finally convinced Drayton to go along.

The farm was just as eerie as the last time he was there. The only difference was the chicken feed had of course been cleaned up, which was no mean feat.

They took up station behind the small shed where Robbie had hidden with Mollie and Jack-Jack. Again, there seemed to be no sign of Arnie Took. Like last time, there could be a good chance he wasn't there.

'So, now what?'

'Well, we have to see if we can get close enough to see into the house. If he is inside, we should see him before he sees us. He's not looking for us so he won't suspect nothing.'

'This is not a good idea, Robbie.'

Robbie, taking no notice, was assessing a path to the house and on to the front porch where the unfortunate chicken had been delivered.

'We have to get up to the window. There is no curtain up. Maybe we can see something inside.'

Drayton followed Robbie as they crouched down and quickly moved around the edge of the shed and along the wall, up on to the porch. They sat with their backs to the wall under the window. Robbie turned around and peered over the ledge and took a look.

As if seeing exactly what he had imagined, Arnie Took was inside, sitting in his chair, counting a large amount of money on the table. Robbie had been right. It had been Arnie and here he was, plain as day, counting the stolen money in front of his eyes.

At Robbie's faint gasp, Drayton couldn't help but join him. He too peered into the window to see for himself. Arnie was scrupulously fingering his way through the notes as the boys looked on. The inevitable happened. At a break in his counting, Arnie looked up just in time to see the boys duck their heads from sight.

There was no denying it, they knew he'd seen them. There was no time to waste. Once again, Robbie found himself running as fast as he could away from Arnie Took's farm. They were quicker than Arnie and he had had to come outside after them. By the time he had, they were gone. The only thing Robbie didn't know was whether Arnie had recognised him.

How he hoped not.

~

The boys had parted ways with Drayton being less than amused that he had slavishly followed Robbie to the point of being seen by Arnie. Now he would be on edge and there was nothing that Robbie could do about that.

Robbie on the other hand was wondering what to do next. He knew where the stolen money was and he had also been seen skulking around Arnie's farm. He could forget about it and let matters take their course. He didn't like thinking that Arnie would get away with it and that Fletcher Mane would continue to be blamed by the town if the truth didn't come out. The other question on his mind was: *who was the other man?* Under them in the tree were two men talking about robbing the store, but so far he had only witnessed Arnie both hiding and counting the money. The other man hadn't sounded too bright and had made a blunder in the past, so Robbie thought maybe he had been dropped through incompetence.

He was at a crossroads. He needed some advice and the only person he could think to talk to in confidence was Sister Athena.

He found her in her quarters.

It was unusual for her to have a child come to her quarters so when Robbie knocked on her door, she suspected it must be important. Once seated, he told her in animated detail about what had been happening.

To say the least, she was taken aback. The first thing she said was not what Robbie had anticipated: 'I have to say, I'm disappointed.'

Robbie looked sheepish.

'You already know you have got yourself into far more bother than what is good for you recently and you insist on not keeping your head down. Robbie, you know I only want what is best for you and you getting yourself into trouble every second of your time here is not what I consider to be the best for you.

'Now, you find yourself in somewhat of a dilemma here. On one hand you say you know where the money is but you decline to tell me where. We may have to revisit that later. And on the other hand you say that if you tell someone where it is, you fear you will be in hot water. I think the best thing to do here is to be honest and face whatever consequences come your way. I do however, think that going to the Mother Superior is probably not the best thing to do, all things considered. You should go and tell the Constable what you know and, if it turns out to be true, you should have nothing to worry about.'

Sister Athena and her honest streak. Robbie didn't like the sound of going to the Constable. That was the exact reason he had come to Sister Athena in the first place. He did agree with one thing she had said - there was no way he was going to go to Sister Meredith. She would have him walking over hot coals before he could finish his story.

He left Sister Athena's room still no clearer than he was before. She was an honest soul and a dear one at that, but they were on two separate pages.

He decided to tell the other two about it at the waterhole.

The waterhole: the one place where everything made sense. It was the children's thinking chamber.

They all took up their respective places. Mollie could tell something was on Robbie's mind. 'Robbie what's going on? You know something about the robbery don't you.'

'I do. Dear Mollie, you know me so well.'

Robbie proceeded to tell them both about what he and Drayton knew, focusing mostly on Mollie rather than Jack-Jack; the latter staying silent throughout.

Mollie looked apprehensive. She had already seen what Arnie Took was capable of and had even had the unpleasantness of riding him like a wild bull. 'So, what are you planning on doing about it?'

'I want to go back and retrieve the money. The more I think about it, the more I don't want him to get away with it. It just wouldn't feel right.'

'Are you crazy? He saw you last time.'

'I'm not scared of him. And I don't even know if he knows it was me.'

'He's most probably hidden it somewhere now he's seen you.'

'Maybe. But he won't want to put it anywhere outside of his home with the town like it is. That's why he moved it soon after he put it down the mines. He's rattled, and that means he's not thinking clearly.'

'Since when did you become Sherlock Holmes?'

'Since I found out Fletcher Mane is being blamed for something I know Arnie Took did.'

'I agree, I don't want Arnie Took to get away with it, but I don't know why you feel so sorry for Fletcher Mane. We don't know him and most people around here seem to think he's bad news.'

'Look, are you with me or not? I can't do this alone. It needs two people to do this. We've got more brains than him.'

'W..w..why not me, Robbie?' Jack-Jack piped up.

'I don't want you coming along, Jack-Jack. Mollie's right, it's dangerous. You stay back at the orphanage and wait for us to come back, okay?'

Jack-Jack looked dejected but understood and deep down was a little relieved. This was one of Robbie's adventures that he was happy not to take part in.

~

It was King Henry V that once said: *"Once more unto the breach, dear friends"* when he rallied his troops to once again attack the walls of Harfleur. Arnie Took's farm was no Harfleur and this was no Shakespearian play, but Robbie found himself once again faced with the uneasy feeling at Arnie's front porch, looking through the gap in the fence.

He knew where he had seen Arnie counting the money before, but they had spooked him, so God only knew where it was now. If God were here, he would ask Him, seeing as He seemed to always be the only one who knew. But then, knowing God, He probably wouldn't tell anyway.

The only thing he could think to do was to go back to the window to see if the money was in the same place.

Why was he putting so much effort into this considering the danger? He knew. He didn't want a man like Arnie Took to get away with such a thing at the same time as an innocent man being accused of the crime. The Constable hadn't arrested Fletcher Mane, but that didn't stop the town from holding it against him, which would follow him around for a long, long time.

'So, what do we do now?' Mollie asked finally.

They had been staring through the gap in the fence for a while in silence, looking for signs of life. The one thing Robbie had taken from the times he'd been here before was that there was no way of knowing if Arnie was home or not. Their vantage point was just not good enough to see inside the house.

'I have to go and look through the window again. If he is here and we can see the money, we need to get it before he can see us and take it back to town.'

'I don't know how I let you get me into these things, Robbie, honest I don't.'

'We're doing a good thing here. People are always telling me I'm doing bad. Well, maybe they'll see I ain't so bad after all.'

Robbie crept around the same edges of the walls as he had done before. Before he knew it, he was in his not-so-favourite place under the window. Mollie, having moved from behind the fence to against the shed wall, stayed where she was. Once more, he turned and peered over the ledge. To his amazement, the money was still on the table, but Arnie was no longer counting it. He couldn't see him at all. Maybe he wasn't home after all. He was also not too bright; leaving it on the table after knowing the two boys had seen him counting it.

Robbie whispered as loud as he could to Mollie, 'It's on the table. I can't see him anywhere though.'

'So go and get it. Hurry up,' she whispered back.

There was a side door that led straight into the living room which he hoped would be open if Arnie wasn't here; farmers were renowned for leaving their doors unlocked if they popped out. He just might be lucky.

Before he could make an attempt for the door, a large hand gripped his arm, pulling him to a standing position.

Arnie *was* home.

He had seen him and now he was holding him firmly in his grasp, looking down on him with a sinister scowl.

'So we meet again, my boy. I knew it was you. You just couldn't keep your prying eyes away could you? And where's your friend?'

Mollie, seeing this, ran through the door Robbie had been talking about. She quickly snatched up the money and ran without thinking. At the same time, Robbie gave a swift kick as hard as he could to Arnie's shin. It did the trick. He let go of Robbie's arm, freeing him. He also ran as fast as he could away from the farm. The two of them ran as if in a dream where it feels like your legs are made of lead. It felt further than it really was and by the time they got to the orphanage, they were completely out of breath. They came at it from out of the woods so as not to be seen. Sister Athena and Jack-Jack were outside with some of the other children as they came rushing out of the trees.

Their sudden arrival caught everyone by surprise.

'Children, what is going on?' Sister Athena enquired, matching their panic.

'This is the stolen money!' Mollie held it out to her completely out of breath. Sister Athena took it before knowing what to do. 'We got it from Arnie Took's farm. He caught us! He's after us!'

As if on cue, Arnie marched towards them from the street with a spade in one hand. He had gone straight to the orphanage while Robbie and Mollie had gone through the woods and got there a lot quicker than either of them had anticipated.

'Now, Sister. What you're holding there is my money. Don't listen to these petulant children. They have just gone into my house and stolen that money from me. You're not going to believe some hare-brained concoction from some over-imaginative children are you?'

'Mr Took. From what I have seen of your behaviour recently, I am less inclined to believe any story that you tell me over these "over-imaginative" children you refer to.'

'I'd be careful whose side you take here, Sister. It might just disagree with you.'

Arnie approached further. He looked menacing holding his spade. Sister Athena was not about to be intimidated by him, but he was bigger, stronger and when it came to money, it seemed like he could be desperate.

They were face to face. Arnie towered over her.

'If you know what is good for you, Sister, you'll give me what's rightfully mine and we can forget this whole business.'

'Mr Took, you know as well as I do, this money is not rightfully yours and never has been.'

This displeased Arnie. He was getting nowhere. As the children looked on in horror, he raised his spade above his head. The look in his eyes was one of desperation and frustration. Sister Athena stood her ground. Robbie froze. He fully expected the spade to come crashing down on Sister Athena's head. However, Constable Pennileason appeared out of nowhere and tackled Arnie to the ground, sending the spade flying. He had seen what was going on from the street and come rushing over. Now he was subduing Arnie on the ground.

'Ahhh, get off me, damn you! That money is mine. They stole it from me!'

'We'll see about that later, Mr Took. For now, I'm arresting you for possible theft and attempted assault.'

The two wrestled on the floor for a moment before the Constable thankfully took charge of the situation.

With that, Arnie Took was arrested and marched off to the town jail, leaving the children jaw-dropped and Sister Athena still holding the stolen money.

My Voice of Reason

At that time, I had not been in Fellowood Marsh long, but Mollie and Jack-Jack had quickly become very dear to me. When I arrived, I knew no-one. I had just lost both of my parents and the whole town and situation was alien to me. I was frightened and I was lonely.

Mollie was the first one to reach out to me. One day, not long after I had arrived, I was sitting alone, hitting the dirt with my familiar stick of choice when she came over to me and struck up a conversation. That took courage because I was the new kid and could have been full of anger and bad attitude. I didn't want to look past that. We hit it off right away. She quickly became my metaphorical conscience and I found out that she was my voice of reason.

She always seemed to know what to say in certain situations. The phenomenon about Mollie was that she didn't know who she was or where she came from. Being found wandering the streets had always been an unsolved mystery. I would have thought the confusion of not knowing who you were and why you had been abandoned would be something that Mollie would let destroy her, but despite all this, she had a very strong head on her shoulders. She was mature beyond her years, younger than me, but I looked up to her. I valued what she said and tried my best to listen to her guidance. I didn't always follow it, however, as you have already witnessed. Sometimes I would ignore her advice, thinking I knew best.

Usually, I didn't.

The incident with Arnie Took and the money always bothered me. I let the whole thing control me. I was fixated on it so much I ended up putting Mollie in danger. I just didn't see it at the time. I would never want to put her in danger. Although, she did have a rebellious streak in her as you will see a bit later on in the story.

Mollie was an enigma to me. She was intriguing. One day she would be timid, quiet and sensible, the next she would be rebellious, brave and full of courage. Maybe she was just trying to find herself in a very confusing world that was just recovering from a war. After all, the orphanage was no place to grow up in. I still have no idea how both she and Jack-Jack had grown up and lived there all their lives. At the time, if I had had two medals just lying around, they would be the deserving recipients.

The one thing I remember most about Mollie from the first time I saw her was her hair. She was very proud of it. It fell down her back like a shiny black waterfall. No girl at the orphanage had hair even remotely close to as perfect as Mollie's was. It was her defining feature and made her stand out from the rest of the crowd. I could tell some of the nuns were jealous of it.

I respected Mollie greatly. Her ability to deal with her problems and brush off anything that bothered her was so fascinating to me. I envied her for that. She was a young girl with a much more mature head on her shoulders.

I am grateful she was there with me.

Chapter XV

"Never apologise, mister, it's a sign of weakness."
John Wayne

Fellowood Marsh was well in need of a break. The town had been rocked by the storm and then quickly thereafter by the robbery. Word spread about Arnie Took's arrest and as always, rumours circulated. Folk speculated about why he had been arrested, most of which was unfounded and exaggerated. All they really knew was that it involved the orphanage, one of the Sisters and some of the children. The blanks they filled in themselves.

Work on resurrecting the town after the damage caused by the storm was coming to an end. Anything that could have been done and salvaged had been. It had shaken the town and, after some time and hard work, it was beginning to resemble normality again.

Sister Athena hadn't appeared to be phased by her second altercation with Arnie Took in such a short space of time. It was like the woman had ice in her veins. As far as she saw it, it was just another duty she had to undertake for the children.

The children, on the other hand, had kept a low profile after the robbery and the arrest. The recent events were not something they were used to and neither was the town. This was a sleepy place with sleepy people whose slumber was rarely disturbed.

~

And so the days came and went. And once again, they found themselves up in The General on a hot summer's day. School for the other children in town had ceased but lessons went on as normal at Saint Vincent's. Rightly or wrongly, the nuns believed there was no reason to stop lessons just for a summer break. As far as they were concerned, the children had enough time away from study as it was.

The General now had more birds to disturb. They had returned some months ago and many had congregated, as they always did, in the plush shelter of The General. As the children ascended, every so often, they would come across a nest that needed to be carefully passed. They hadn't knocked one out of the tree as of yet.

Robbie was perched on his favourite branch, lying back on it as if it were a bench.

'Do you think you'll be here forever?'

As he asked the question, he was staring down at a piece of bark he had recently torn from the stump of the tree. It had a caterpillar slowly making its way from one end to the other, unaware of the young human eyes centred on it.

The question was clearly directed at Mollie, even though Jack-Jack was also there.

'I don't know how long we'll be here for. We're children and can't possibly look after ourselves. We don't have anywhere else to go.'

'That's not what I asked.'

'Well, no, I don't think we'll be here *forever*.' She couldn't help but emphasise the last word. 'Why do you ask?'

'I want my time here to mean something. This place; it's weird. It's got a hold on everyone I tell you, only they don't want to see it. I don't want to just be another local who gets smothered by all the superstitions.'

'You're older than us. You probably won't be here as long anyway. You came here because of circumstance unlike me and Jack-Jack. Chances are you'll go to a place far away from here once the fallout from the war has ended.'

'Look around, Mol. The rest of the world has forgotten this place. It's not bothered about it or what's inside it. In order to get out of here, a person's got to do something extraordinary; something that other folk ain't never done before. Then folk would take notice.'

'You're talking about going and looking for that glass eye again, aren't you?'

Silence.

Mollie shot him a look. 'I know you want to be recognised for something and you crave adventures. But that isn't the way to go about it. Grown men have gone looking for that eye and for some reason or another, haven't returned.'

'But we don't know why. There could be a perfectly reasonable explanation for it. And besides, how many men do you know have gone looking for it?'

'Well, alright. I don't know how many.'

'So it might not be that many. The only one we know of is that handyman, Billy, and that was a long time ago. And we don't even know if he went looking for it or not. His is the only name we've heard so far and we only have Sister Athena's word for it.'

'It's a pretty good word to go with.'

'I'm not saying she's lying. I'm just saying it's speculation. Like everything else around here.'

Mollie kept quiet. Jack-Jack just took it all in. He was never part of these debates. And the topic of Old man Joe always made him anxious.

'H..h..has Old man Joe e..e..ever come and taken anybody a..a..away?'

They both looked at Jack-Jack, surprised at the impromptu question.

'Taken away?' Mollie asked.

Jack-Jack just offered a steady nod as he looked at her.

'There hasn't been any talk of him taking anyone away, Jack-Jack.'

'B..b..but maybe that's what h..h..happened to the people.'

Mollie glanced at Robbie. Her concern was clear. 'No, I don't think so. As far as anyone has ever said he just visits people and takes things.

'Robbie. We really must stop talking about this in front of Jack-Jack. It's affecting him. And he's clearly not over those nightmares he was having.'

'I'm n..n..not scared. Those n..n..nightmares weren't nothing.'

Robbie relented, 'Okay, okay, enough about Old man Joe. But I'm getting pretty bored up this tree.

'I got an idea. Speaking of old things - let's go over to the old rectory.'

'Are you just trying to scare Jack-Jack today or are you fed up of him getting any sleep at all? You know that place is run-down and abandoned. There's nothing there but an empty old building that's just about falling down. It's creepy.'

'Everything's creepy around here: the old rectory; the mines; the ruins; Old man Joe's cabin. We're hardly living in a fairy tale. Come on. It'll be fun. We've been up here for ages and my bum's going numb.'

'But we've been there before, ages ago.'

'I know but it was cold then. We didn't want to hang around because it felt colder inside than it did outside. Today is warm. We can stay there longer. Who knows what we might find.'

'You and your adventurous mind.'

Mollie had to admit, the choices of destinations surrounding them were less than ideal. Robbie had a point: they were hardly living in a fairy tale. She did worry about Jack-Jack, but at the same time knew that Robbie could be very persuasive.

She conceded and they climbed down and headed in that direction.

~

The old rectory was not as pleasant a looking place as it once was. It was situated deep in the woods and most of the time was forgotten about. Standing on the outside looking up, Robbie had to admit, Mollie was right about it looking creepy. It looked like it should feature in a sinister novel where some unsuspecting vicar gets his head chopped off or something.

The place was covered in overgrown shrubbery and had empty holes that were once filled with glass. The big wooden door looked like someone had repeatedly tried to knock it down. It was littered with rotten holes and covered in silver cobwebs. Moss lay on top of the roof like nature's blanket and thick roots intertwined themselves up the walls like bony fingers trying to pull it under the earth.

'This place really does give me the creeps,' Mollie said.

Her heart was pounding fast as they stood in awe of the old building. There was an eerie quiet that seemed to envelope it. It was the kind of building in which the walls would tell stories if they could. But by the looks of it, not many of the stories would have been happy ones.

'I love it. It's got charm, don't you see? Look at the walls; the door; the gardens. Imagine what it used to be like when someone lived in it. Come on, let's get a closer look.'

Mollie had her reservations and, as for Jack-Jack, well, he just followed as per usual.

They crept over the weeds and twigs lining the ground, crunching their way to the front door. As to be expected, it didn't budge.

'Darn it. There must be another way in.'

Robbie went looking around the side of the wall and sure enough, along the west facing wall was a large, open window, big enough to fit them all in.

They clambered through, Jack-Jack needing a hefty boost up to reach the ledge properly, then Mollie, then Robbie.

Once safely inside, they all gawked at the rancid interior facing them. It felt damp and cold. The walls were peeling and chipped. They had to tread carefully as the floor boards were rotten and covered in holes. It seemed larger on the outside. In here, the walls appeared to close in on them. There was a large staircase that was evidentially too dangerous to attempt, even for Robbie, and three sizeable rooms that they could see into.

One particularly large room straight ahead of them was letting in a little more light than the others. This room looked different. It almost looked..... tidy. The reason became clear once they fixed their eyes on what was in the corner - a small, man-made campfire.

'Robbie, someone's been here, and recently. Look, you can still see small embers burning at the base.'

Right at the moment Mollie was making her observation, a rock hit Robbie in the small of his back. He turned, trying to ignore the sharp pain that had just shot up to his neck.

'That's right. Someone's been here recently. Well, well, well. Some call this breaking and entering. What do you think, lads? We go out for only a short while looking for some more firewood and when we return, we have guests.'

Richie and a few of his friends stood at the entrance to the other room. Richie clung onto a slingshot in his right hand; obviously the weapon used to fire the rock at Robbie's now throbbing back.

'What's the matter, couldn't face the whipping I gave you last time, now you have to carry that thing around with you as protection?'

The remark was more accurate a blow than the rock. Richie's pride had been bruised the last time the two boys had come across one another. He was not about to let it happen again. The problem was, he knew deep down he wasn't as witty as Robbie. Regardless, he was going to have to say something to save face in front of his troops.

'What are you doing here? This is our spot. And we don't want no unwelcome guests, you hear?'

'We're not planning on staying now anyway.'

'I thought you might be out looking for Old man Joe's cabin. Or have you not got the guts like I suspected?'

'We were doing nothing of the sort.'

'You know, I would have thought an outsider like you would know better than to lead these two innocent children out in to the woods. Strange things happen in the woods.'

The statement sounded threatening and Robbie knew that meant it was time to go, if not for his sake, then for that of Mollie and Jack-Jack's. The only way out however, was past the three boys.

He started for the exit and pushed past Richie.

'I should have expected nothing more from a simple orphan.'

This statement hit a nerve. It was different to the other things Richie had said. Without thinking, Robbie turned around and struck Richie hard, sending him tumbling to the ground. He hit it with a thud and lay on the floor holding the side of his face as Robbie leered over him with his bloodied fist still clenched. This was the second time he had hit Richie, only this time there had been venom in the strike. It wouldn't have surprised him if he had inadvertently broken his jaw.

Without even looking at the other two boys - both of whom knew better than to rush to the defence of their comrade - Robbie turned and left via the large window, Mollie and Jack-Jack on his tail. No leg up or help getting out, they just wanted to leave.

~

At home, before tragically losing his parents, Robbie never got into fights at school or outside of school. Arguments – yes, but nothing that ever warranted hitting another boy. It was either this place or what had happened to him that had changed him in that way. It didn't take much to push his buttons. The resentment he was feeling deep down didn't need much to be surfaced. A dormant volcano just waiting to erupt.

Maybe it was the feeling of injustice of having his parents taken away from him in such unfair circumstances. Whatever it was, in truth Robbie had never really dealt with the loss of his parents; he hadn't yet had chance to.

The next day, Robbie and Mollie both had Work Detail. Mollie's chores involved washing and folding the laundry whereas Robbie's presence was needed in the gardens. Fortunately, he loved being outside and even though he protested wholeheartedly about being given Work Detail, he had to admit that being outside was a great deal better than being inside the orphanage. He was also still working off the extra demerits Sister Meredith had given him.

Little did he know, his time outside would be short-lived. He had not been set to work long before being ushered into Sister Meredith's office; a somewhat common occurrence as of late.

The room seemed darker than normal despite the beaming sun – now taunting him to come back outside. He stood with his hands behind his back staring out of the window as Sister Meredith sat in her chair – *probably writing some inane drivel*, Robbie thought. She loved the power, making him wait; at her beck and call, sucking every second she could out of his patience.

Putting her pen down next to the inkpot, she lifted her head up to look at Robbie over her glasses; her beady eyes staring into his.

'It appears as though we've been here before, doesn't it?'

Condescending as always.

Robbie just stood still, refusing to answer her rhetorical question.

'Only this time, apparently we're here due to you attacking another boy. Are you just trying to find ways to get yourself into bother?'

Again, no response.

Sister Meredith gave a shake of her head. 'So, is this true? The boy's father contacted me this morning as it seems his son has a rather nasty black eye and a swollen cheek. The blame is being solely pointed at you and I have to say, I'm not at all surprised. Now, I'll ask you again, is this true?'

Robbie stood firm, staring out of the window behind Sister Meredith.

'Your silence will do you no good. I warn you not to antagonise me.' Sister Meredith got up from her chair and came around to the other side of the desk, picking up her cane on the way.

Guilty until proven innocent, Robbie thought as he was instructed to put his hands on the table in front of him and bend over.

The first *thwack* came without warning. The second came followed by a statement: 'The boy's father has a good standing in this town. I don't want you tarnishing this establishment with your evil, boyish acts. You need to go and apologise to the man for your behaviour.'

'He called me an orphan,' Robbie protested finally.

'But you are an orphan. You can't alter reality.'

'He deserved what he got.'

The next one came with a bit more venom behind it. Robbie wasn't listening. The clash of personalities was evident. Robbie's posterior was stinging and he could feel his palms leaving sweat marks on Sister Meredith's oak desk.

She wasn't done. Enjoyment may have been a stretch but there was certainly no remorse for what she was doing.

'You will go and apologise. It is not up for discussion. You are living under this roof and any child – and yes, you are a child – will live under the rules of this orphanage. My word is law. Do you understand?' There was no time for an answer before the next blow came.

'Do you understand?'

'I will not.' The words came out through gritted teeth. Fortunately, Sister Meredith relinquished her assault and returned behind her desk, leaving him in the compromising position.

Robbie did his best to stand up straight. He was not about to give her the satisfaction of getting the better of him. He stood looking straight ahead and put his hands behind his back again, with his chin raised as if standing to attention.

The look on Sister Meredith's face was one of torment and frustration. She hated not having full control over a situation. But did she hate this boy that stood defiant in front of her more? She scowled.

'So,' she said calmly now, 'you're refusing to apologise to that young boy, are you? I see. In that case, you leave me no choice. If you do not want to go and say how terribly sorry you are for almost breaking his jaw, then I suggest you don't go anywhere for a while. It seems to me, the only reason you end up getting yourself into all this bother is simply because you are much like a wild animal trying to claim its territory. You go gallivanting around this town like you have no care in the world; like you own the place. Well, I think the town could use a well-earned break from Robinson Harvey for a while.'

Robbie listened but couldn't believe what he was hearing. Here he was, in an orphanage, not his home with his parents, but in an orphanage, about to get grounded like a petulant little schoolboy who had just stolen the teacher's daily apple.

'Until further notice, you are not allowed to leave the orphanage. You have everything you need right here and some time inside to reflect will do you good. I do not want you thinking you can cause more trouble within these walls, however. Like I warned you before, I urge you not to push me. Life at Saint Vincent's can either be a pleasant one or a tough one. The choice is yours alone. Now, leave my sight and I advise you to adhere to my instructions.'

Dismissed.

He had officially been grounded for the first time since arriving at Saint Vincent's. He felt small and insignificant. He'd never even been grounded by his parents, never mind some wrinkled up, sour-faced old nun.

Robbie went to his bed and laid there for a while, contemplating. Brilliant – *porridge walls*. How dare she? She wasn't going to get one over on him, not after everything. He would make sure of that. He would have the last laugh, if not now then some other time.

Chapter XVI

"Solitude is the house of peace."
T.F. Hodge

Grounded; isolated; imprisoned.

Call it what you will. It didn't change the fact that he was trapped in this stupid place. Grounded was exactly what it meant. For the past year, the only silver lining – if you could call it that – was the fact that there was an escape from this God-awful place. The outside was Robbie's haven; his very own Garden of Eden. Okay that might be overdoing it a little but, regardless, anywhere out there was better than in here.

It had already been two days – two days of nothing. Time really could stand still it seemed.

Life carried on as normal for everyone but him. By now, word had got round as to why Robbie was spending every waking hour inside. He was quickly making a name for himself in the orphanage as well as the town.

He didn't care. In a way, that was what he wanted - to somehow be remembered. This place wasn't going to defeat him. He knew what Fellowood Marsh was and he knew what its people were about. They were metaphorical sheep, herded by tales and folklore. When he had arrived, he never would have guessed he would be steeped this deep in it. They were drowning, if they hadn't drowned already. He regarded the whole town much like a withered leaf that falls from a naked tree – once so vibrant and full of life, now to fall to the ground and rot away in the earth.

Apart from lessons (which did nothing to relieve the boredom), for two days he had done nothing but think, fidget and frown.

He fidgeted because there was nothing to do and he longed to be outside. Forbidden fruit can be a burden to one's mind. The mere fact that he wasn't allowed out made him want to be out even more.

He frowned because of the injustice he felt towards the orphanage and every one of those useless nuns that inhabited it, Sister Meredith most of all.

And he thought. He thought about everything that had happened in such a short space of time: Arnie Took; the chicken; those mysterious toys in the floorboards; Richie and his stupid little followers. But most of all, he thought about Old man Joe. He couldn't deny that the tales intrigued him greatly. It was like living inside a real life fairy tale – only fairy tales didn't usually come with nightmares..... or did they?

He had never believed in magic, ghosts or being haunted in dreams. But like most things, if enough people believed it, did that make it real? After all, he was just a novice in the extensive life of the world. *What did he know, really?* Were all the people claiming to have been visited by Old man Joe lying? Or were they simply confused?

It is true, in olden times there had been witches. There had been things unexplained; strange goings on, if you will. There were things happening now that were unexplained. Just because we think we know what's real because of what we see with our own eyes, doesn't mean we can allow ourselves to be deceived. Our eyes can be our worst enemy.

Look at Old man Joe: he would argue that at least one of his eyes had become his worst enemy. Was the witch that cursed him that day real? Did she really put a curse on him to be able to see into people's souls with his glass eye even after he was gone?

At first hearing, it had been nothing but a child's campfire story gone wrong. Robbie felt indifferent about it all. He just let the town get on with their daily obsessions with this other world and kept himself to himself. But he couldn't deny, after living around it for a while, he was feeling rather eerie about the whole thing.

Just like the Old Rectory to Mollie, this place gave him the creeps. Being alone in a place like this would give anyone the creeps.

With nothing to do, he had taken to checking out a few of the dust-laden books on the bookcase in the sleep hall. He had been taught to read at a young age. His parents had thought it important for a young boy to be literate in the modern world. He didn't often use this skill, however. He was more interested in exploring and having adventures. The only thing he had to admit to himself was that, truth be told, he hadn't really had any. The closest he had come to having any kind of adventure at home was going down to the fields and climbing trees. Occasionally, he and a few friends would catch tadpoles in an empty jam jar, but nothing that would make it into a Mark Twain novel.

He watched the nuns getting on with their daily business. He struggled to figure out what they did all day. They just seemed to wander around a lot. But then again, if he was in their shoes, he would probably do the same.

He hated the nuns, sauntering around with their hands held together, tucked inside the sleeves of their oversized tunics. All but one. Sister Athena wasn't like the others. She was everything the others weren't. She was the closest thing to a mother figure at the moment. He liked talking to her, whether it be about what he had been getting up to outside or the many stories she would tell them just before going to bed. She had been around for a long time and had many fascinating stories; some not so, but he wasn't about to tell her any of her stories were boring.

The latest one, of course, was that of the handyman that used to be here and his so-called apprentice that followed him around everywhere. She had found that telling Jack-Jack about another boy around his age who also had a stutter, but been quite happy and hard-working, had helped with Jack-Jack's confidence. That was what she did; she found ways of relating one thing to another for a purpose and it usually worked. She was far too clever to be here. He still didn't know why she remained.

But remain she did, and so did he – within these walls, within the confines of Saint Vincent's, left to waste away and become part of the furniture. Maybe one day he would be just as forgotten as a bunch of toys under a floorboard.

What made it even worse was that Sister Meredith hadn't told him when he would be free. It could be a few more days, or a week, two weeks! He didn't know if he could stand that. Maybe that was the plan, to drive him to insanity. Great, then he could be like the rest of the town. A small, inner chuckle resonated inside of him as he clutched onto a book, plucked from the bookshelf not ten minutes ago.

Moby Dick. He had heard of this. A true classic as far as he was aware. Silly title though. He knew, as he stared at the grey and red cover with the gold wording down the spine, that he wasn't going to delve into it right now. He was thinking too much and didn't really fancy sitting here on his bed, reading a book like a scholar. Or worse, a wrinkly old man who had to hover a magnifying glass over each word.

He was still to attend lessons when they came around, which fortunately wasn't that often. But he was to go straight back to the sleep hall afterwards where there would always be at least one nun at hand to keep an eye on him. To say Sister Meredith didn't trust him not to try and escape was an understatement.

There was only one good thing about this whole "grounding" thing – and he still couldn't believe he was using the term – and that was that he had been taken off Work Detail. The reason why hadn't been explained to him, but it was probably because it involved a lot of being outdoors and Sister Meredith knew in the circumstances, just like a prisoner, that would be a treat for Robbie.

Mollie was still assigned to Work Detail and hers would be over shortly. He didn't know where she was or what she was doing, but she should be coming up from the corridor fairly shortly and there was one thing he needed to sort out.

Food.

The food at Saint Vincent's was below standard anyway, but he had been put on rations as well as being grounded. That was not discussed in Sister Meredith's office but seemed to have been an afterthought on her part, just to turn the screw a little tighter. He was living on wall-coloured porridge and water, with the occasional bit of stew thrown in. The stew normally would sound appetising to any normal ear but it had hardly any taste at all and the taste it did have wasn't exactly anything to write home about.

He needed something more substantial and he wasn't about to let Sister Meredith and her band of witches keep him from it. Among his thoughts had been exactly how to get the better food from the kitchen. There were too many nuns around to see him sneak off and, even if he did make it by them, there were the kitchen staff. It didn't deter him from at least the idea of trying but his better sense warned him off.

So, he didn't want to, but the next best thing he could think of was recruiting an accomplice. That's where Mollie came into the equation.

He felt bad at the prospect but he felt his hunger more so.

Just then, as Moby Dick hit the floor with a thud which created a mushroom-shaped dust cloud, Mollie did indeed walk up the corridor with her apron on smattered in grease stains. Evidentially, she had been in the kitchen. She plonked herself down on her bed, which was parallel to Robbie's, ripped her apron off and lay down.

'Rough day?'

'Not funny.'

'Kind of funny.'

'Kind of not funny.'

'You look ten years older every time you come out of that kitchen.' Maybe this wasn't the best approach to buttering her up.

'Thanks. My feet are screaming at me and I don't even know what they're trying to tell me.'

'How is the kitchen?'

'Dark, smelly and greasy. I feel like it's stuck to me.'

'You don't feel like going back down there, do you?'

She sat up resting her weight on her elbows and turned to look at him with an innocent confusion. 'What do you mean?'

'Mollie, I'm going crazy up here. I've got to get something better to eat. Prisoners of war eat better than I do.'

'Oh no, you're not going to make me steal food for you. Are you trying to get some company during your grounding?'

'I just can't live on what they're giving me and I don't know how long I'm going to be in here for. It could be more days yet. I'll waste away or get sick. Neither of which I want to do. You wouldn't want that either, would you?'

'Look, I know it's unfair that you're grounded. What Richie said to you was unforgivable and he got what he deserved, I admit that. I think even his little followers thought the same thing. But that could get me into a lot of trouble – stealing from the kitchen.'

The guilt of asking washed over Robbie like a tidal wave. He realised what he was asking was a bit much and very selfish. That was what hunger did to you. The temptation was too high.

As they both sat on their beds contemplating, Robbie opened his mouth to begin to retract his request but Mollie beat him to it:

'Okay. I'll do it. I'm not saying I'll be able to, but I'll give it a go.'

He quickly changed his mind. 'You mean it?'

'I hate the idea of you up here starving. And like you said, who knows how long it's going to go on for. I don't like the way this place treats us anymore than you but the difference is, I've been used to it all my life. I don't know any better. But I do know it's not right what they do.'

What a star she was. She was like his sister and even though he really didn't want to get her in to any trouble, he knew it was a strong possibility.

~

Mollie was always in the kitchen so she knew where everything was and she also knew the usual whereabouts of the kitchen staff. Saint Vincent's did not operate under a huge budget, especially in the aftermath of the war. The kitchen staff were sparse, which resulted in the delay of food being prepared and its poor quality. Work Detail for the girls helped the staff a lot as they were usually assigned the more undesirable jobs.

Being an undercover thief was not in Mollie's arsenal. Before Robbie had arrived, she would mostly keep herself out of trouble. She was a good pupil in class and wouldn't complain about much. However, she had to admit, her life hadn't been near as exciting. Since then, they had explored the area - some of which she didn't even know existed – and flirted with danger on many occasions. Robbie was like an older brother: always risking getting her in to trouble or pulling her leg about something or another, but she loved him like a brother also. She had no real siblings that she knew of and had only grown up with the children in the orphanage. Robbie and Jack-Jack were the only two she had ever felt a close relationship with. She didn't like seeing Robbie get himself in to trouble and hated knowing he was driving himself crazy being grounded. If she could help him out, she would.

So, being crouched down behind the large table in the corner of the fairly extravagant sized kitchen must be what she considered helping him out. As she had approached the kitchen, she didn't really know what she was aiming to steal. She had a pang of nervousness but at the same time didn't feel any guilt. Why should she when the food they were usually given was of such insufficient quality?

She knew no-one would be suspicious of her being there but she didn't want to take any chances. If she could do this without being seen, that would be the best thing.

On the table top was a rather large loaf of freshly made bread. That was too big for her to carry back and it would be too risky to break some off. What she needed was something she could grab quickly and wouldn't be too hard to carry.

Just then, someone came in. She quickly ducked her head behind the table. She was only small and keeping hidden was not as difficult as first thought. The staff member came straight over to the table and put a tray of muffins down. Perfect. That would do nicely. But she would have to be careful not to take too many; just enough so no-one would miss them.

Once the room was empty again, she quickly emerged, gathered up several muffins and, without thinking, a jar of apricots and hastily headed straight back up the long corridor back to the sleep hall.

Success.

Crime committed.

No-one saw and she couldn't deny herself the rush of blood that was pulsating through her as she made her escape. If she was honest with herself, she was so nervous of the prospect of bumping into someone in the corridor she could have easily peed herself.

Robbie had better be grateful, she thought as she made her way back to him.

He was grateful. When she showed him her haul, he was mightily impressed and beside himself with joy. It was more than just the food - it was the never-ending need to get one over on the nuns. This was just another bead on the abacus to his side.

He offered to share the goods with Mollie but she declined. Maybe consuming the stolen items was a step too far. Regardless, he would have been happy to share, but he was so hungry, he was glad she declined.

Jack-Jack was off helping Sister Athena with something Robbie had been meaning to pay attention to but hadn't – something in the garden, that was all he knew. This was good as Jack-Jack wouldn't be able to inadvertently give the game away.

Because there was always a nun lurking around making sure Robbie didn't leave, it proved very difficult to eat the items without being noticed. The advantage was that they didn't come over to Robbie's bed. Just knowing he was inside was sufficient and he could see they weren't putting their heart and soul into the task.

So he cowered behind his bed, kept a sharp eye on them and delighted in scoffing the whole lot discreetly. It wasn't hard. He knew half way through the second muffin that, depending on how long Sister Meredith was going to keep him locked up for, this may not be the last time he would ask Mollie for her help.

~

A few more isolated days down the line, as Robbie was yet again lying on his bed, ankles crossed and staring straight up at the damp-stained ceiling, he heard a male voice. This was very unusual in the orphanage. No male voices were to be heard in here, at least not as deep as this one.

He sat up, intrigued. At this moment in time, a beetle scurrying across the cold concrete floor would probably intrigue him, but he wanted to hear who this intruder was and what was being said.

The answer was nowhere near as interesting as he would have wanted. It was the Reverend Holland, coming by to check on the general running of the orphanage. This happened every now and then, but the last time Robbie recalled seeing him was some time ago.

The Reverend was representing the Bishop, who was head of the diocese. He remembered him to be an odd-shaped, balding, overweight man with a lasting frown on his face. He was the kind of man that had a deep-rooted ugliness to him; the kind of ugly that even when you smile it looks like you're constipated or just stubbed your toe.

Last time, he had disappeared outside somewhere just so he didn't have to talk with the Reverend as he'd been told that sometimes he spoke with the children to find out how they were. A nice gesture but not one that Robbie wanted to partake in. This time though, there was no escape. And looking around, it didn't take more than a millisecond to realise any other children that were in the sleep hall had quickly scattered.

Here he came, led by Sister Meredith. Robbie would have probably welcomed Old man Joe to visit him rather than the Reverend. It's not that he seemed like a bad man, but it was the mundane agony of talking to him and answering his questions about this place. He knew from what some of the other children had told him that Reverend Holland was in charge of overseeing how Saint Vincent functioned and the funds. He was in a state of denial thinking it was a pleasant place to live and if anybody told him otherwise or questioned it, it was like an attack on his leadership.

There was no escape: no window to jump out of; no wardrobe to hide in or tree to climb and wait in until he had passed. Instead, he lay there like an unsheltered mouse with a buzzard hovering just overhead. He came straight over with Sister Meredith on his tail, so close she was almost stepping on his too-long tunic that must have been getting filthy from trailing on the dusty floor.

'And I see we have one boy enjoying the realms of the indoors this afternoon. A time to oneself - a time for solitude. And what's this?' He leant down to pick up Moby Dick. 'Ahh, a classic tale of adventure and revenge. I just love the end when the line gets tangled around the captain's neck as he gets dragged away by the whale.'

Right, that's it then, no need to read the damn book after all, Robbie thought.

'And how are you today, my boy?'

The question was said with a slight smile which on any other person would have looked welcoming, but on the Reverend, unfortunately it just looked disturbing.

'Actually,' Sister Meredith jumped in, looking down at Robbie with a slight smirk, 'Robinson here is grounded for deliberately wounding another boy in the town.'

'Oh, I see.' The smile faded. 'Well.....' he put a hand on Robbie's leg. 'That is not good, not good at all. So this is not a time of relaxation or study. Indeed, it is a time of reflection. You see my boy, one cannot just go around hurting other children. You don't want to give this place a bad name now, do you?'

Was he serious?

'Well, I'm sure you won't do it again.' He gave a quick squeeze before retracting his hand.

'Robinson is one of our newest residents. He joined us shortly before the end of the war as both his parents died.' Robbie thought he could hear a hint of pleasure in her voice as she spoke. Surely she couldn't be that evil, to take pleasure in him becoming orphaned?

The Reverend's smile attempted a temporary return. 'Is that right? Yes, many families were destroyed. Just be glad you had somewhere to come that keeps a roof over your head and you are looked after, hmm?'

He was serious.

The hand returned to Robbie's leg. 'You will be alright. I know that doesn't exactly sound like the most believable thing right now, but you will see. In time, you will learn to live without them. There is always someone more unfortunate than you. We just have to be thankful for what we have.'

'What do I have to be thankful for?' Robbie asked, somewhat agitated.

This question displeased the Reverend. He wasn't used to any child answering back in such a manner and without the customary "sir" to follow. Usually children would just nod along, sheep-like and accept what he was saying, no matter how much of it was nonsense.

'What do you have to be thankful for? Why, what a question. Any time you are alive, you are fortunate. Your life is anything you can make of it. Follow the word of God and the wisdom of your superiors and you will find divine peace, my son. Listen and learn is what I always say.' With that he pursed his lips and gave Robbie's leg one final squeeze and a slight slap as he looked up at Sister Meredith. He then stood up and, as if Robbie wasn't there anymore, said that they would need to get on. Robbie guessed the Reverend's job with him was done. All his problems suddenly worked out. *Thanks Rev*, he thought as he was glad to be watching the backs of the two of them walk away.

~

Over the next few days, his accomplice had stolen more food for him. To say she had come through was an understatement and after the third or fourth trip, Robbie had to admit he was feeling guilty for asking Mollie to keep bringing him food, even though she seemed okay with it. It was difficult to stop - the adrenaline rush was almost as tempting as the food.

One problem though, was that, because he was eating all this nice food that he knew was predominantly earmarked for the nuns and not the other children, the food he was being served was near impossible to stomach. There was no way he was filling himself up on nice bread and fruit and then eating the disgusting slop they expected him to live on. He had refused to eat on several occasions. This had prompted the nuns to think he was on some sort of hunger strike.

The sun shining through the window high above his bed was also torture. It was like a beacon summoning him to come outside and play, fading away with disappointment when he didn't obey.

He longed to be outdoors. That evil witch Sister Meredith was winning, despite his accomplishment of eating their food without them knowing. He was tall enough to peer over the window ledge if he stood on the back of his bed.

As he looked on, he could see out to the main street. The usual mundane things were going on. People were pottering about trying desperately to make ends meet for just one more day. The wheat cart that delivered the grain every day was parked outside the general store, the horse making dust clouds with its hooves as it waited patiently. All of a sudden, all these mundane things he was looking at didn't seem that mundane.

Perspective can be a funny thing.

'Robbie, be careful, you'll fall.'

The unexpected voice behind him was Sister Athena's and, ironically, it almost did make him fall. He turned and climbed carefully down.

'If you fall off there and somehow break your leg, you will be grounded for a lot longer than you are now.'

'Sorry, Sister. I was just trying to get a look outside.'

She looked almost pitifully at him. 'I hear you had a talk with Reverend Holland.'

A talk? More like listening to him waffle on about nonsense.

'Yeah, he came by. I couldn't leave. He talked. I listened. He left.'

'Don't be too bitter, Robbie. This won't last for much longer. Sister Meredith is getting tired of making sure there is always someone around to watch over you. She's ever so vexed at your defiance of her. And she wanted me to come and have a talk with you about you not eating much of your food. A few times now, you've not even touched it. Is it out of protest? You don't look pale or look like you've lost weight, which is good.'

Oh, great. Now he was going to have to lie to Sister Athena and he really hated that. She was always so kind to them and didn't deserve to have him lie to her, but in this instance he was going to have to push the truth just a little. Just a small white one.

'I'm not on any hunger strike or nothing, Sister. I guess it's maybe because I ain't using up no energy that I don't feel hungry. And I don't usually have much of an appetite when it's hot out.'

This appeared to make sense to Sister Athena. She nodded with acceptance or maybe she just wanted to believe there was no hunger strike going on. 'That's pretty much what I thought. Just don't be pulling any stunts in an attempt to disobey Sister Meredith again. I want to see you out of trouble and back doing what you like doing. You're a tough one to handle, Robinson Harvey, but we're getting there with you, aren't we?'

'It's this place Sister. How can you stand it?'

'This is where I do my work, that's all.'

'I'll make one promise to you, Sister. One day, somehow, I'll get out of this place, you'll see….. they'll all see.'

Chapter XVII

"Karma is a cruel mistress."
Kelley York

Punishment – it comes in all forms. From an early age we are taught to live by the rule of reward and consequence. This doesn't change throughout our lives. Even as an adult, one's actions should result in reward or consequence. We learn as we go along that this simple system does not always ring true. Sometimes, a wrongdoing can go unpunished and an act of kindness or achievement can be overlooked. How much of this we experience can define us later in life.

Sometimes, punishment comes from doing no wrong. For example, was it right that I was punished for losing both my parents? Or that Jack-Jack was born with a stutter?

Was it right for Sister Meredith to use her cane so avidly?

Was it right for me to be grounded for punching Richie, even though Richie had said those vile things?

There is no right or wrong answer. The only thing we can do is adapt our minds to accept the punishments handed out to us or not.

Arnie Took's punishment for almost striking Sister Athena with the spade had been a few days in the town jail while the potential assault and the theft from the store had been investigated. It had proved impossible to provide sufficient evidence of the theft and it was true that no assault had actually occurred, thanks to the intervention of Constable Pennileason. It was fair to say that the Constable was unhappy that charges could not be brought and he had consequently not been too urgent in concluding his investigations, thus providing a certain justice of his own by having Arnie spending at least a few days in jail.

Word got round that he was to be released later on that morning. Mollie and Jack-Jack came rushing in to tell Robbie the bad news. He was currently doing his best to make the indent on his bed a permanent feature with his ankles crossed, staring up at the ceiling.

'Robbie, Robbie, I just heard Arnie Took is going to be released from jail,' Mollie panted as she tried her best to steady her breathing.

Robbie sat up, startled but now alert. 'What do you mean? When?'

'Later today. I just got word from some of the ladies in town, you know, the gossipers.'

'Are they sure?'

'They say they heard it from the Constable himself. He wasn't able to be charged because he never actually hit Sister Athena.'

'But he was going to, hang it all. If Constable Pennileason hadn't come when he did, he would have done it for sure.'

'Don't matter though, does it? He's about to be released. They can't hold him any longer.'

A worried look came over Robbie's face. Arnie Took was not the kind of man to learn from his mistakes and consider the fact that his actions would have consequences. He doubted whether he thought of much at all.

'What about the theft? The money he stole? Surely, they can keep him locked up for that?'

'Nothing doing there either. Far as I heard, no-one could prove it was him even though he told the Constable that the money was his. There's just no evidence to say he stole it.'

'Well, he can't get me when I'm in here.'

'But you won't be in here forever.'

'Won't I? Sure feels like it.'

'Some time or another you'll be out there and so will he. I don't think he'll have learnt his lesson and he'll be after you. He's had a thing about you ever since he thought you killed his chicken.'

'I know, I know. I'll just have to watch my back is all. You'll have to try and find out as much as you can and report back to me.'

Mollie acknowledged this. She couldn't help but be worried about that man. It was clear he had no trouble in being physical towards anyone – children, women, even nuns.

Mollie and Jack-Jack left before Sister Beatrice – who was lurking ominously at the other end of the room - had had enough of them being in there with Robbie.

Robbie, on the other hand, went back to his crater on his hard, uncomfortable bed, ankles crossed, staring up at the ceiling. The exact same position he had been in before the disturbance. Only his thoughts had changed.

~

Arnie Took was released just in time for the annual Arm Wrestling Competition. Not much happened in Fellowood Marsh, but this was one thing that was never missed. It was a spectacle for some of the more meatier shaped men in town.

The competition divided the town. Some were enthusiastic and looked forward to it every year whereas others did not. They thought it was a barbaric event for the men just to show off their masculinity, usually fuelled by copious amounts of alcohol. For those in favour, exciting events were few and far between and what little entertainment was provided usually sparked up a great deal of interest.

The flyers had been up for weeks:

"Come test your feat of strength and wits at the annual Arm Wrestling Contest."

"First Prize – A whole leg of lamb, not to mention pride!"
"Second Prize – There is no second prize, only joint losers!"

"Enter if you're feeling brave."
"No women or children allowed in the audience."

And so, the day after Arnie's release, the competition was at hand. The men cheered, swigged beer and patted each other on the back. It was in full flow. There hadn't been this much joviality in Fellowood Marsh since last year's event and they were lapping it up.

Arnie had already beaten two men by the time he sat down opposite a burly looking man called Frederick Willingham.

Frederick Willingham - or Butch as some knew him as – was the town blacksmith, with arms the size of tree trunks. The two men stared and snarled into each other's eyes. Sweat poured down both of their brows and drool leaked out through their gritted, yellow teeth. There was more than a leg of lamb provided generously by the local butcher at stake. The winner of the competition would be revered the whole year round until he could defend his crown.

A clammy paw from each contestant clasped together and with a countdown from the referee, it was time to wrestle. The bout started very evenly but after a few grunts and groans by both men and drops of sweat and saliva splashing down on the rickety table, Butch seemed to have the upper hand. The roars grew and the bodies leaned further forward as most of the men could see the arms were tilting in Butch's favour. Arnie could also see he was in trouble. He did not want to lose. He couldn't lose. The desire for asserting himself in the town following his release was too great. Of course, being arrested for almost battering a nun with a spade and potentially stealing from the town's general store hadn't done his reputation any good and he knew what the town thought of him.

Their veins pulsated and the table shook under the pressure. Arnie's groans got louder and with victory in sight, Butch's eyes widened. He was almost there. Surely there was no coming back from this.

Arnie's eyes also widened but not for the same reason. His strength gave way in an instant as Butch slammed his arm down hard on the table just as Arnie took one last groan and slumped on the table before falling off his chair in a heap on the ground.

It was an unusual way to lose the contest. No-one ever fell off their chair just by surrendering to the power of the other man, but sure enough, Arnie lay face down, not moving. The cheers faded and Butch rose to look over the table at his defeated opponent. One man went over to check on Arnie as the crowd looked on, now quiet.

After a few moments: 'Why, this man's dead.'

A hushed gasp swept through the men before some chitter-chatter began. Arnie had pushed himself too far, not wanting to succumb to his opponent. The other men didn't know what to do. A few started gathering around closer as if this would help Arnie come back to life. But he didn't.

'Go and get the Constable someone,' a voice said. And off one man went, slipping in the mud as though he was using his legs for the very first time. Some of the other men decided to pick Arnie's body up, which was no mean feat. He wasn't the smallest of men and he was now just a dead weight.

They moved him into a house close to where the arm wrestling was taking place and soon enough the Constable arrived, shortly followed by the doctor.

Word quickly spread as always. Within moments, some of the men had dispersed like mice that have just had their shelter disturbed and gone to tell their loved ones and their friends. The whole town knew about Arnie's death in a matter of minutes, including Robbie.

'He was like a statue or an ugly-looking doll apparently, one of the men said. He had his eyes open but not really looking at anything. He said he could tell he was gone even before the doctor got to him.'

Mollie and Jack-Jack had been towards the upper end of town when the commotion had erupted. It was clear something major had happened and it didn't take long to get wind of what it was. They had raced back and Mollie had given her account to Robbie who was as shocked as anyone, but relieved more than most.

Nothing seemed to happen in the aftermath. The only thing Robbie knew was he was still locked up. It had been just over a week now and it was clear that Sister Meredith had meant what she said. But she was getting annoyed at having him around and having to keep an eye on him. It was more of a burden than she cared for and, reluctantly, she gave in.

This meant freedom. He had never felt so free. He had taken freedom for granted but no more; how good the outdoors smelled; how green the trees looked. A week inside the orphanage had felt like a year in prison to him. But standing outside on the pale concrete steps of the orphanage, he felt a sense of indifference. He should have been feeling elated. His dealings with Arnie were now over. He was gone and would trouble him no more. So why wasn't he screaming for joy? The town's atmosphere was what was stopping him. There were fewer people around and those who were appeared very sombre. Did the town think more of Arnie than he had thought? Whatever the reason, he didn't like it.

He caught a glimpse of Virgil sweeping his front porch. He hadn't spoken to Virgil in a while. Now would be a good time to catch up on the latest gossip and find out anything he could about Arnie.

'Hello, Virgil,' he said as he approached the raised porch. One thing about Virgil: he always did his upmost to keep the outside of his property very tidy. Maybe this was because the inside was such a cluttered mess of all his carvings.

'Ah, Robbie, my lad. I hear you've been at the mercy of the Mother Superior over there.'

Robbie hated hearing her being addressed as that.

'Yes, that's right. But I'm free now. Feels like I've been in there for not a day less than forty years. The witch had me locked up for..... well, something.'

'For striking that Curruthers boy. I know.

'He deserved it, Virgil. Honest. He made fun of my parents.'

'That I don't doubt. But you have to rise above such things. Look at what happened. You're the one who paid the price.'

Virgil had a wise way about him and Robbie had to admit, he was right.

'Virgil, what happened to Arnie Took?'

'Well, collapsed didn't he? Right over there during that arm wrestling contest.'

'What did they do with him?'

'Took him away but I don't know where. They'll quickly be organising his funeral I shouldn't wonder. My guess is not many will be turning up to it though. Not a liked man round here. Everybody scared of him so they were.'

A sense of relief went through Robbie.

Virgil continued after a moment's thought, 'He wasn't a nice fellow. He bullied his way around this place for many years. I should think a fair many people are glad he's dead. Not that anyone should be glad of anyone's passing, mind you.'

'So if no-one liked him, how come the whole town is so..... subdued?'

Virgil looked around as if every tree and shrub had a set of ears. 'You know what people are like around here, Robbie. I don't need to tell you. They're troubled souls. Many fear he might come back and haunt those whom he don't like. Just like Old man Joe.'

'But why would they think that? Old man Joe was cursed by that witch. Arnie just fell down dead. That ain't the same.'

'That may be so, my boy. But the mind can betray even the most sensible of folk. And these people around here aren't sensible folk. They are sheep. I've seen them throughout the years. They'll listen to word-of-mouth and believe what their neighbour believes.'

'So you don't believe it, all that business with Old man Joe?'

He shot Robbie a look and stopped the broom that had continued for the duration of their conversation.

'That reminds me. Come and sit down by me. Word has gone round that you intend to go looking for that glass eye of his.'

Richie. That blabbermouth.

'I never said that. If you heard that from that no-good Richie Curruthers then he's telling lies.'

'That also may be so, but I've heard it from *you* in the past at times too. Ever since you learnt about that tale you've been interested in that glass eye. It's been like a pirates' treasure to you. But I have reservations, I have to be honest.'

'What do you mean?' Robbie said, looking up at Virgil.

'Robbie..... I've seen a lot of things in my time. Some things I wish I hadn't. And I'm not saying I know everything there is to know about this world. There are some things I don't pretend to know about. But there are things out there that frighten even the likes of me. Unexplained – it's a word for a reason. In the past there have been things happen that no-one has been able to explain. All there has been is talk and belief. People seem to be pretty good at filling in the blanks all by themselves.

'The story of Old man Joe is not one I understand. What I do know is something isn't right there. I know I told you about the handyman, Billy, amongst others. You asked me about him going to look for the eye, but that was only presumption. There are many other possibilities. But yes, many believe he went looking for the eye and never came back. I know he was a simple man but he was an adult nonetheless and you are just a child still. I don't know what happened to the other men and that Billy fellow, but I do know they didn't return.'

Robbie thought on this for a second or two.

'What about the land in the woods?'

'What about it?'

'Well, I've been told Fellowood Marsh got its name for a reason. The land surrounding the town is marshland. Could it be that they got in to trouble somehow and never made it out? They might not have even found Old man Joe's cabin at all.'

'Like I said, I don't have all the answers. The only thing I know is that bad news surrounds that man and his glass eye and I don't want you out there trying to find it, regardless of if I've got the story straight or not. Hear me?'

Robbie gave a slight nod. Virgil made a lot of sense but, because of his adventurous nature, he still couldn't help but be intrigued.

~

Is it right to be glad when someone's dead? Who decides if this is a just emotion to have? The question was, was Robbie glad or just relieved? Arnie Took had shown himself to be an unpredictable, dangerous man. There was no denying it. Not that Robbie was buying into this religious thing but, if he had, Arnie's passing would surely have been the answer to prayer.

Names carved in stone.

What would be written underneath Arnie's name?

"Sorely missed?"

"In loving memory?"

Robbie knew what he would put if it was up to him: "Here lies Arnie Took. A vile beast of a man. No-one will miss him."

Much better. But Robbie wasn't in charge of what went on Arnie's tombstone. He didn't know who was, but he did know who would be etching the words into the stone.

The funeral wasn't going to be far away and Arnie's spot in the cemetery was beckoning. Drayton was hard at work when he went to see him, chiselling away behind the stone masons.

'Hi, Drayton.' He sat down on some of the piled-up stone. 'Arnie's, huh?'

'That's right. Father said I needed to get a move on with it. The funeral is going to be soon. They're not messing about for some reason.'

'So, what's going to be written on it?'

'Father told me just to put his name.'

'What, nothing else? Not even a date of birth?'

'No, nothing. No-one seems to know when he was born. There's nothing in the records. He had no next of kin either. So it was decided just to put his name and nothing else. Seems kinda cold.'

'Fitting, I'd say. A cold tombstone for a cold man. He was a bully and I'm glad he's dead.'

'Robbie, I'd be careful about saying things like that if I were you.'

'How come?'

'Just risky, is all. He's gone but maybe not really gone.'

'Nonsense.'

'Is it though? He might come back to haunt you like Old man Joe.'

'That's different. Old man Joe was cursed. And besides, it's all cobblers.'

'It ain't neither. All I know is I would be treading carefully about the things I were saying. You might think you know what's real and not real but strange things happen and I wouldn't be so sure taking that risk.'

The words resonated in Robbie's ears. Now that Arnie was gone, he couldn't deny he felt totally at peace. Sure enough, this was a strange place with strange goings on.

He watched until Drayton had finished the tombstone. It stood there almost intimidatingly so – staring him straight in the eyes.

"Here lies Arnold Took"

~

As Robbie walked to the waterhole, he couldn't shake what Virgil had told him. About Old man Joe. About that curse. He felt consumed by it all. Is this what had happened over time to the whole town? Was he feeling what they had felt all these years? He was being drawn in to the superstition more and more.

He needed to tell the other two about it. Sure, his friends were younger than him but they were all he had in this place; the only ones whom he could talk to and open up to without sounding like a crazy person.

They were waiting by the waterhole. Mollie lay on the grass making a rather impressive daisy chain as Jack-Jack swung three feet off the ground from a branch of a small tree. As Robbie approached, they could see he was in deep thought.

'What's the matter, Robbie?' Mollie inquired.

'I went to see Virgil. I wanted to know if he knew anything about what happened with Arnie.'

'Robbie, leave it. He's gone now. He can't do anything more to us.'

'No, I know that. I was just curious that's all. Death is a funny thing, don't you think?'

'I'm not sure I know what you're getting at.'

'Death – funny.'

'I guess. And you're referring to.....'

'No-one knows why those who went off looking for the glass eye never returned.'

'Knew it.'

'What I'm saying is there could be many explanations.'

'Other than what? That they found the cabin and somehow never made it out? We don't know anything for sure. And we don't even know how many went looking for it. It's all tales. Nothing but tales. The only one we've been told about was Billy and that was from Sister Athena. And even she doesn't know what happened. She only told us what the town thought about it all.'

'But don't you see? That's my whole point. Nobody knows for sure.'

'I..I..I think Old man J..J..Joe got him, Robbie,' Jack-Jack said after listening as he usually did.

'Don't be silly, Jack-Jack.'

'Let him speak, Robbie. He never says anything. He's got as much of a right to say what he thinks.'

Robbie looked sheepish as he let Jack-Jack continue.

'Place is c..c..cursed. Old man Joe is c..c..cursed. He gets anyone w..w..who tries to t..t..take his eye. That's why th..th..they don't come back.'

'Look, Robbie. I know what you're thinking but it ain't no good. You've only heard these tales for a short time. I heard 'em all my life, we both have.' Mollie nodded at Jack-Jack. 'Come on. Put it out of your mind. Let's head back before it gets too late. We don't want to get you into any more trouble than you've been in.'

Robbie didn't object. They wandered back through the thick trees with his mind still ticking over. Consumed..... that's what he was. Consumed.

The sun was starting to set on their return, creating a deep glow over the tops of the buildings and trees. The town almost looked at peace for once - a silhouette against a fiery backdrop. It was very quiet everywhere as they went inside. All the other children were entertaining themselves in the sleep hall but there were no nuns around keeping their beady eyes on them.

'This is strange,' Robbie whispered. 'Where are they all?'

Just then, amongst the quiet, they could hear muffled voices from down the corridor. It was the nuns, but they were too far away to hear properly. Robbie knew something was up and wanted to get a better position to earwig.

'Robbie, don't go. They'll catch you. Do you want to be grounded again?'

The voice of reason – so commonly ignored. 'It'll be fine, come on.'

Like sheep to the slaughter, the other two followed again. As they got closer, it was clear the nuns were having some sort of debate about something of some importance. A few of the voices were urgent but one was calm - that of Sister Meredith. They were congregated in the kitchen. The children hid behind a wall a good distance away, to escape if needed.

'It's treason, I tell you,' panicked one nun.

'Outright theft,' hissed another.

'Ladies, calm yourselves. I am aware of what has happened here. And believe you me, the culprit will be reprimanded and dealt with.' Sister Meredith was the mediator, but what were they talking about?

'It was one of those little rats and I don't mean the ones that scurry about on four legs with a long tail. Our precious food has been stolen. Nothing like this has ever happened before. What are we going to do?'

Mollie's skin suddenly went cold and prickly as she listened. The food, of course it was the food. She knew she had taken too much and been careless the more she had got away with it. She was no thief, that wasn't who she was. But under Robbie's influence and feeling the way she did about the orphanage, she had thrown caution to the wind, and now the wind had thrown it back.

'The question is, Sister, what do we do about it? There is no way of knowing who did this. No-one saw anything. We've only found out about it now because Cook alerted us to it.' Sister Klara, the mathematics teacher sounded apoplectic.

'They need to be punished,' Sister Beatrice announced to nods of agreement. And sure enough, the ideas came flooding out.

'Ordinarily, a thief would have their hands caned, front and back,' one said.

'Caning is too good for a food thief. I say we lock them up in the coal shed all day and all night. That should teach them.'

'The best way to teach someone who steals food is to deny them exactly what they stole. Starve the little traitor before they think they can do it again. We'll see how clever they are when they're begging for food instead of stealing it from under our noses.'

The children listened. Mollie's stomach was in knots and she felt at any moment she would heave her guts up and blow their cover. It almost seemed like the nuns enjoyed coming up with different ways to punish her. In fact, that's exactly what it seemed like. As usual, Sister Athena appeared not to have been invited to the party.

'Ladies, ladies.' Sister Meredith had to take some kind of control. 'Let me remind you that we still don't know who did this. I assure you I will be looking into this fully. You have my word. I will not allow a meagre child to steal from us. Food is short as it is, following the conclusion of the war. We cannot and will not let this happen. Now, please, back to your duties and no more on this for the time being.'

The meeting was over and before Sister Meredith could finish her sentence, the children were away up the corridor, Mollie's insides still doing cartwheels. Why did she listen to Robbie? Why?

My Regret

As you may have gathered by now, I am no saint. Far from it. In life, we make good decisions and we make bad decisions. It is no excuse, but if my parents hadn't been taken away from me at such an early age then maybe I would have made fewer bad decisions, but this remains conjecture.

When I reflect back on my time at Saint Vincent's, it is undeniable that my biggest regret is asking Mollie to steal that food for me. At the time it felt rebellious. On reflection, it feels selfish. The truth is I was selfish back then. I was swept up in my own tragic tale of woe and misery. This blinded me to the fact that at times I didn't think about the others around me whom I cared for dearly. Using Mollie to steal food from the kitchen was like using her as my very own pawn in a losing chess game; my very own plaything to puppet as I saw fit.

My voice of reason became my accomplice. It didn't seem that big of a deal but, then again, my underestimation of Sister Meredith and her troops also didn't seem like that big of a deal.

I was wrong.

Chapter XVIII

"Do I not destroy my enemies when I make them my friends?"
Abraham Lincoln

The conversation between the nuns had unnerved Robbie. Guilt plagued his insides. He didn't think they would have missed such a small amount of food but, then again, he had been locked up for longer than he anticipated and Mollie had been relentless in her thieving duties. He had meant to stop it but didn't. Just how much food had she smuggled and he consumed? It was a selfish act but nothing could change that now.

It was evident that Sister Athena wasn't at that meeting held so sinisterly in the kitchen. Listening to the nuns spout out punishments like they were enjoying it made him feel sick. He was getting a better idea of what Saint Vincent's really was the longer he stayed there.

He found Sister Athena doing some writing in her quarters. A quick knock on the door and an invitation to come in, soon found him sitting opposite her in an exceptionally old looking chair that looked as though it would struggle to hold his weight for more than a few seconds.

'What are you writing?'

'I write a little poetry every now and then. I find it soothes my tension.'

'You have tension?'

A rare smile. 'Contrary to what you may think, yes. This place can get to me at times too you know. But my tension usually stems from seeing you children unhappy. Beautiful words on paper counter this for some reason. Don't you ever find that reading something of beauty takes you away from everything and puts you in a place of tranquillity?'

'I ain't never really thought about it.' His badly spoken grammar sounded ridiculous following Sister Athena's elegantly spoken words.

'Well, maybe you should. It will be inside you. It's inside everyone. Maybe one day you'll write your own novel about your time here.'

'I wouldn't want to frighten anyone with that.'

Sister Athena chuckled with a hint of sorrow. She laid her pen down next to the small inkpot. 'So, what have you come to see me about? Not that it's not a pleasure to see you.'

'Am I interrupting though?'

'I'm always delighted to be interrupted if I'm needed.'

Robbie looked about as sheepish as he ever had and at first the words struggled to come out. 'I'm troubled. You see….. and I don't know quite how to say this, but when I was locked up, I got Mollie to steal the food from the kitchen for me. I didn't think at the time. I thought it was funny in a way, but I know it ain't now. I just….. I don't want her to get in to trouble or nothing.'

Her face dropped, not so much out of disappointment in Robbie – although he would have deserved it – but out of concern.

'I see. I had heard about the stolen food and it's got many of the ladies' backs up. In fact, I've not seen some of them so belligerent before. Food in these hard times means a great deal to them. I appreciate you coming to tell me about it but I'm not sure what can be done. I'm glad you have, as I've always told you to come to me with any problems and that honesty is always the best policy, but telling Sister Meredith what you have done is probably not the best thing to do right now.'

Robbie shook his head in disappointment at himself after hearing his confession out loud. 'I am sorry. It was stupid. Maybe you could have a word with her instead?' He knew it was a long shot.

'I'm afraid that wouldn't do much good either. She doesn't listen to me very often unless it's something she agrees with. I think the best thing to do for now would be to keep this under our hats. Does anyone else know?'

'Mollie of course and Jack-Jack but, to be honest, I'm not sure how much attention he has paid to it. He's been a little distant lately.'

'Yes, I've noticed that too. I'll keep an eye on him. But as for this, don't tell anyone else. The other nuns are perplexed and fractious about it now but it'll pass. There is still food. It'll be forgotten fairly shortly, I'm sure. But you've learnt a lesson here, I hope.'

'I have.'

'Was there anything else?'

Robbie thought a moment as he looked around her small enclosure. 'How can you stay here in such a depressing space?'

'Simple really, because I love you children and this is my purpose here. I do not need to be entertained every minute of the day and I'm certainly not like you – always looking for adventures in the outdoors.'

'But you've been here so long. You must know a lot about this place, huh?'

'It's safe to say I suppose I do, yes.'

Robbie considered telling her in that moment about the stash of toys they found under the floorboard in the attic but decided against it. He didn't want to impart that little secret right now, even if it was to Sister Athena - like a pirate's buried treasure.

Instead, he decided to be cryptic. 'Do you think the walls have secrets?'

'What a question. I suppose everyone and everything has secrets to tell, Robbie. The question is, do we want to hear them?'

Her answer was just as cryptic. He looked at her and could see the warmth in her eyes. He liked her, and he was glad she was here.

There was nothing more to say. The meeting had been short and to the point. A weight had been lifted from his shoulders but he still wasn't sure if it had been the best thing to do, even though he knew Sister Athena would keep it to herself. He left her to write her poetry. Beautiful words on paper.

~

It was typically raining. The sun wasn't prepared to shine down today. It was as though it knew what today was.

Today was Arnie Took's funeral. Gloom was the only ambience that suited. The procession was going to go through the town to the cemetery where he had a spot already dug out.

Processions in Fellowood Marsh were usually a fully embraced event. Everything closed and everyone would line the street as the cart got pulled along with the coffin in the back. A number of family members usually walking behind. You could argue that this was just another thing captured in the past that hadn't caught up with the times. The cart was pulled along by a solitary horse, with the cart itself looking about a hundred years old.

Today however, there were no family members. The horse looked like it should have been retired years ago as it struggled to pull the lonely cart through the sticky mud. The rain poured down but was easing off slightly. There were only a few people standing sheltered under the canopies of shops and businesses and these seemed to solely be there out of curiosity. Not the abundance of gatherers a procession would normally bring.

Arnie Took was obviously not well liked or respected in the town, that much was clear. As Robbie, Mollie and Jack-Jack stood watching the horse's hooves march slowly past, Robbie couldn't help but feel a tang of misery for him, regardless of everything.

The coffin looked sodden, the wood wet through, Arnie's still body probably soaked through inside. The horse looked dejected having to see its task through and the people didn't look sad – they looked wet and bored.

'Come on, let's go. I think we've seen enough,' Robbie stated. 'This is nothing but sad. He's gone. That's the end of it.'

They walked away behind the stores, feet traipsing along in the mud. They had no destination, nothing to do today. As they wandered around the back of the stores, they heard a few low, muffled voices. It wasn't the usual voices of people working or conducting some sort of business - these were children's voices obviously trying to keep quiet with a secretive undertone.

Cornering the end of the row of buildings they could see why. A small gathering of children was stood circling a small, wooden table with two sitting on chairs opposite each other – Richie being one of them. What they were doing became clear. They were having their own secret arm wrestling contest, clearly trying to stay out of sight and sound so as not to seem disrespectful during Arnie Took's funeral.

Richie was in the midst of defeating another boy, his hand hovering ominously just above the surface of the table, and with one last effort the back of his hand hit it with some force. He was defeated as whispered cheers went up with the victory. Now the contest was over, the attention was focused on the new onlookers.

'Hey, what are you doing here, creeping around?'

'We ain't creeping around. We heard voices,' Robbie replied. 'Bit disrespectful, ain't it? Today of all days.'

'What do you care? As I heard it, you and Mr Took over there weren't exactly best buddies.'

'That's not the point.'

'Hey, look. We have this contest every year just like they do. Only this year there happens to be a funeral. Why should we reschedule?'

Richie was still sporting a rather juicy black eye. Robbie really had clocked him good this time. Unfortunately, he was also sporting his usual bad taste. They were most probably just having their own contest as an act of rebellion. They probably didn't even have it every year. If they did, this was the first any of the three had heard of it before.

'So,' Richie continued, 'now that you're here, are you going to ante up? Feeling lucky?'

It was an inevitable challenge. Robbie was yet again faced with his arch enemy, his bully turned punch bag. The predicament was less than ideal – not long come out of being grounded for striking Richie and faced with the other boys staring at him now. Lessons hadn't been learned. He accepted and took his place on the sodden wooden chair opposite Richie. Even as he sat down, he knew this wasn't a good idea. But then again, he'd made such an endless list of bad ideas, why stop now?

This was just Richie's way of trying to make amends for himself in front of his crew. He put his winning elbow on the table and opened up his hand as he stared eagerly at Robbie with his one good eye. Robbie obliged and without speaking, both boys clasped hands together as the rain fell on their heads, locked in another battle.

Another boy, acting as referee, counted down, 3 – 2 – 1 go. And they were off. The two boys tugged and pushed with all their might. Robbie was surprised at how strong Richie actually was, but today was not a day to succumb.

He knew he was going to win before he even sat down and sure enough, he quickly got the better of his opponent. Richie quickly grasped that he was in immediate trouble and widened his eyes in desperation as his arm started to fall backwards. A few seconds later it hit the table with some velocity and the two boys released their grip. Richie was yet again defeated.

Robbie didn't gloat, he just celebrated by way of a coy smirk.

'That's not fair. I've already fought a bunch of other boys. I'm worn out. And you just sit down all fresh. Of course you were going to win!'

The excuse made things worse. It sounded pathetic and weak and Richie knew it. But before Robbie could get out a response, he was yanked out of his chair by the collar of his shirt.

'What the hell do you think you are doing?' The bellowing voice said, full of anger.

'Pa, it's okay. We were just.....' Richie was cut off by his father, still holding on to Robbie's shirt. It seemed he was quite adept at having his shirt grabbed by adult men.

'I don't want to hear it. Having an arm wrestling contest on today of all days. I bet this was your idea wasn't it, sonny?' he said, aiming his accusation at Robbie. Richie didn't correct him. 'You should be ashamed of yourself. You're the one who hit my boy, aren't you? I should have known. Boys like you have no respect, no morals. It's what I should expect from a boy with no parents. No-one to give guidance. You're just a bad influence on every other child in this town.' He released his grip on Robbie, not a moment too soon, as the collar was starting to dig into his skin.

Richie's father took Richie by the arm and led him away, muttering something under his breath that was too stifled to hear. The rest of the boys scattered and Robbie - next to a solemn Mollie and Jack-Jack - stood a little shaken, with the rain pouring down on his head – victorious but, yet again, in some way defeated.

~

The rest of the day was somewhat of a blur. How did this keep happening to him? At times it felt as though he was the one with the curse upon his head. The rain had eased off just in time – as if a dark cloud had been present for the sole purpose of making Arnie Took's funeral as miserable an occasion as it could – and parted now it was over. Job done.

So, with Mollie and Jack-Jack leaving Robbie to his thoughts, he found himself wandering through the town wondering what sort of trouble he was going to get into next. Why fight it? Instead, what happened next was unexpected; Richie of all people came around the corner - no father in tow.

'Oh, great. What now? Where's your father? Or is he the next one to come round the corner to finish what he started?'

'Easy, easy. I escaped out the house. I wanted to come and apologise for what my father said to you. It made me feel really bad when he said it – about you being an orphan and all. I now regret what I said to you at the Old Rectory.'

This surprised Robbie. 'Oh, that. Don't sweat it. I'm used to it.'

Richie held out his hand in a truce-like manner with a remorseful look on his face that seemed genuine.

'Still. I am sorry. He doesn't have much control over what he says. I never really looked at it from your point of view until he said that. It must be pretty tough being without your parents and having to live here.'

'Tough doesn't even begin to touch the sides.' Robbie took his offered hand and shook it. They both sat down on the wall. It was wet from the rain but neither boy seemed to care.

'I also didn't mean to rag you on about going to look for Old man Joe's cabin. That was just teasing in front of my friends.'

'That's okay. Everyone seems to know an awful lot about Old man Joe and his glass eye. I guess I'm just getting up to speed.'

'It's meant to be extremely valuable, you know.'

Robbie turned to look at him. 'Valuable?'

'Yeah, says my pa. Says it's enough to get any man out of this stinking town and live a life of luxury, whatever that means.'

'So, why doesn't he go and look for it?'

'Says it's a fool's errand. He says no man in his right mind would try such a thing after a few have tried and gone missing. And even if they did, they wouldn't be able to pick it up because it'd be hotter than hell. He says that, because Old man Joe sees into people's souls even after he's gone, the fire still burns inside the eye. It'd be like trying to carry a hot piece of coal and it would burn through any material you would carry it back in.'

'I've only heard about the one man. His name was Billy – he was the handyman at the orphanage years ago.'

'Yeah, I heard about him. Pa says he was a simple soul who didn't understand what going after the glass eye meant. But there were others before him. He was supposedly just the last to go after it, or so everyone thinks. Pa says it's not even guaranteed that it's still in the cabin.'

'How come?'

'Well, Old man Joe got banished from here and, so people say, went and spent the rest of his days deep in the forest in the cabin. But because everyone was afraid of him, no-one actually knows if he stayed there the rest of his life or not. It's all just rumour around here.'

'And what do you think?'

'I don't think much of it either way. I listen to what my pa says, but he's just like the rest of the town. Stuck in the past - afraid.'

'Do you think the legend is true? Do you think he visits folk when they're asleep?'

'I don't want to answer that. There are strange things that I don't know about and Old man Joe is one of them.'

The question had obviously unnerved Richie, and Robbie thought better than to push him on it. Richie's father had been around for a lot longer though and he had said the eye could be very valuable: *enough to get any man out of this stinking town and live a life of luxury.*

That was certainly worthy of some thought.

Chapter XIX

**"There are no foreign lands. It is
the traveller only who is foreign."**
Robert Louis Stevenson

He did indeed think. At times, there are only our thoughts to accompany us. They can be both a comfort and a burden. Robbie's right now felt more like a burden than anything. They certainly weren't giving him much comfort. He was fast becoming consumed and he needed to unload the burden. He would talk to Mollie tonight but would have to be quiet. He did not want any of the nuns or other children catching wind of what was on his mind.

Meanwhile, Jack-Jack had been moved into a room of his own on account of his nightmares returning. The orphanage was big and had many rooms from when it housed a lot more children. The rooms were small, however, and were a way down the corridor from the sleep hall. They were secluded and one would argue that putting Jack-Jack in a room all by himself would only manifest his nightmares. Still, that was the reality.

The lights were off and everyone was trying their best to get comfortable and settle down to another mediocre night's rest. Mollie lay in her bed just next to Robbie. She could tell something was on his mind; she always could. She was very instinctive that way.

'Will you shut your mind off please, Robbie? I can't sleep,' she whispered.

'If you know where the off switch is, please let me know.'

'Okay, okay. What's on your mind this time? Is it what happened with Richie's father?'

'No, in fact, I'm not thinking about that at all. Richie found me and apologised about that. I'm just thinking about what he told me.'

'Which is?'

'It's about Old man Joe's glass eye. He says it could be very valuable.'

'Robbie, not this again.'

'No, listen. I knew there was always a chance that it could be valuable, but think about it. He says that because of its curse and its legend, if anyone was to find it, it would be more valuable than ever. It's not just a glass eye, don't you see? That witch cursed it and sent him away. She cursed it so he could see into people's souls even after his death. It's not just a glass eye – it's a cursed glass eye. Who knows how much someone would pay for something like that, especially after it's well known that men have gone off looking for it and never returned. That would make it almost unattainable and even more valuable. It's one of a kind.'

'Robbie, listen to yourself. You're starting to sound like one of the town-folk. And where did you learn a word like "unattainable"? Nothing good can come from that eye, not even riches. It scares me and at the moment, you're scaring me. Please try to leave it alone.'

He just lay there, half listening to what Mollie had to say, half staring into the dark ceiling above him. In the dark, her voice took on the role of his voice of reason even more so, but again he wasn't taking much notice of it. All he knew was that eye may be his only way out of this place.

~

The room was strange and cold. He felt just as strange and even colder. There was one window too high up to see out of, with bars across it and grey curtains that were too thin to keep the ominous moonlight from half lighting up the room. It wasn't enough light, however. It left half the room in total darkness and created shadowed shapes in the other half. He cursed the unwanted moon as he lay in his creaky bed with the blanket pulled up just under his nose.

They had said the reason for him to move in to this tiny room by himself was because he was disturbing the other children during the night. His nightmares had come back and by all accounts were getting the better of him. But this room alone was a nightmare. It was empty save for a big cabinet in the corner that looked like it housed more bugs than clothes and, of course, his bed which was tucked in the corner under the window. It had to be dusted off from cobwebs when they first brought him in. In doing so, it was like the nuns were providing him with a brand-new bed which he should be grateful for.

Every time he moved, it creaked. They could be right, he might not have any more nightmares in here but that was only because he might not sleep ever again. In here, Old man Joe could visit him easily; much easier than if he were with the others in the sleep hall. And no-one would know. How long were they planning on keeping him in here?

A bird or an owl flew past his window outside. As it did, a shadow swooped across his room which made him jump. The bed creaked. His blanket raised up a few inches higher. His shivering was part due to being scared and part due to the cold. He was a way down the corridor too, far away from everyone else. In his head it seemed like he was in a totally different building. He couldn't hear any voices or sounds. Did that mean everyone, even the nuns, were asleep or did it mean he was too far away to hear anything?

He tried in vain to close his eyes. Maybe if he did, it would be better. He wouldn't be able to see the half moonlit room or his imagination. With his eyes closed, he could imagine he was somewhere else. But that did no good. He was old enough to know he wasn't somewhere else. He was here, in this room, alone with his nightmares. But he knew all too well that he might not be alone for long.

I see you.

~

The chalk scratched, the chairs grated and the dust kept getting up his nose, but the only thing on Robbie's mind was where he was going after class today. He had thought long and hard through the night until the weight of his eyelids had finally got the better of him.

The cart that went daily to and from Savannah's Bridge would be making its errand from the general store after lunch. If he was stealthy enough, he could climb aboard and ride it all the way there. There he would enquire as to any potential buyers of one rare, valuable glass eye. He sure wasn't going to find anybody in Fellowood Marsh, so he would have to venture further afield. He would have enough time to scout around before catching a ride back. He should be back at the orphanage in time for mealtime and, hopefully, no-one would miss him during the afternoon.

The only problem was that the storekeeper who sent the cart wasn't exactly what you would call punctual. Leaving wouldn't be too much of a problem; he knew it never left before the end of lunchtime, but the time coming back could be varied and he didn't want another run-in with Sister Meredith if she found out where he had been.

The trip was, in his mind, both adventurous and productive - the adventure part appealing to him more so. He hadn't been to Savannah's Bridge before. He had only heard of it from the occasional passer-by. Apparently, it was a rundown, dirty, hustle and bustle type of a place that was swarming with people in the centre with a wide river running through it.

Savannah's Bridge got its name in unfortunate circumstances: many years ago, the daughter of a rich merchant committed suicide by throwing herself off the bridge. Of course, her name was Savannah. She was sixteen. No-one truly knew the reason for the sudden act but, as it was broad daylight, many people saw – women, children, even some of the poor girl's family. The town was in mourning for a great many weeks before the council decided to honour her death by naming the town after her. In fact, this put the future of the town in darkness as it was a stark reminder of what had happened and prevented the town from moving on from the tragedy. Still, the name remained.

As lunch ended, he left with the others but, without word to anyone, he skulked off and away around the back of the buildings near to the general store. Sure enough, as if it knew he wanted to climb aboard, the cart stood with the horse patiently waiting for its orders to leave.

There were times when the cart would leave empty-handed, but this was not one of those times. Fortunately, there were some bags of something or another in the back. This was part of the plan, as Robbie wouldn't be able to sneak in to Savannah's Bridge without cover. Everything was falling in to place.

He climbed on the back with relative ease and took his spot between several woven bags.

Manure. Great. It was going to be a long, smelly ride.

~

Long and smelly it was, but Robbie was overwhelmed by the sense of adventure and rebellion. Here he was, taking a secret trip to the larger, neighbouring town and no-one knew about it. He felt free as a bird, albeit a free bird surrounded by bags of stinking manure. Still, it might help him blend in once he got there. If the smell clung to him, maybe people would take him for a poor beggar-boy and leave him alone.

Eventually the cart – driven by one of the storekeeper's less-than-intellectual sons – arrived at its destination. He couldn't help but have a feeling of trepidation now he was here. He was used to making bad decisions, but this could potentially be the most stupid of all. He was exposed and could be in a world of danger.

There was no turning back now. He jumped off the back of the cart and scurried away amongst the crowd of people. He needed to make sure he didn't get lost, however. He turned back to quickly make a mental note of where the cart was and hoped it would be here when he needed to return.

Savannah's Bridge was just like the picture in his mind created by the stories he'd heard. It *was* dirty and it *was* filled with people hustling away their frantic lives. Smoke rose up from the rooftops. People shouted bargains from the market stalls. Children ran in and out of people's legs chasing one another. It was a hive of activity and Robbie loved it.

The river that ran through the town was right next to the market place. It was bigger than he had imagined and looked cold with its brown water flowing steadily downstream. And there it was, the bridge that young Savannah had jumped off. It was higher than he had imagined and now he was looking at it, the stories became all too real. He imagined the sight of her falling to her death in front of all those people. The screams mixed with gasps of horror. He shuddered, but not because of the cold.

He turned. Enough of that. Now to business. But where to start? He admitted to himself that he might be in over his head, but if you were going to grow up, that would have to happen once in a while. Strangely, he didn't feel scared. He felt excited. The kind of excitement that makes you feel like you want to pee, even though you know you don't.

He decided to wander around for a bit but not stray too far from the cart or the market place. The contrast between here and Fellowood Marsh was vast. It was almost as though Fellowood Marsh didn't exist and yet it wasn't too far away.

The forgotten town.

Before long, he came across a shop that looked ever so intriguing. It was smaller than its competitors, squashed in, looking like it shouldn't fit. It had all sorts of trinkets in the window and cobwebs in all the corners. *Bits of Bob's* it was called, the writing above the shop in dire need of a touch-up. Still, this might be just the place that would be interested in such a thing as Old man Joe's eye.

Robbie pushed the door open to a pungent smell, but not quite as bad as the manure he had travelled so closely to. The inside looked more like a museum. Things hung from the ceiling. There was barely enough room to walk around. Currently he was the only one there. With all the junk cluttering up the pathway around the shop he almost didn't see the tiny man staring at him with his glasses perched on his nose and his few strands of hair combed to one side in a vain attempt to look like time hadn't been cruel.

'Can I help you?' The words came out high-pitched with a certain wobble.

'I'm just looking around,' he lied. 'You got some unusual stuff.'

'You can find almost anything you want in here. And anything you don't want. Got anything in mind?'

Robbie bolstered up what nerve he had in him. 'I bet you don't have one thing.'

'And what's that?'

He walked up to the counter – if you could call it that – the surface of which probably hadn't been seen in years. The man was so tiny they were pretty much eye to eye.

'There's one thing I don't see in here, mister. Something that would make this place stand out from all those other shops.'

'Which is?'

'Have you heard of tales of a cursed glass eye?'

'Have I? Boy, I've heard many a tale in my time but none as fraught with trouble as that. What business you got coming in telling me about that?'

Robbie was suddenly on the back foot. 'I was just wondering, if you had that glass eye in here, it would sell for buckets, wouldn't it?'

'I wouldn't have that thing anywhere near my shop. I've known people go out of their minds because of that thing.' His voice lowered now. 'And you, what do you know about it?'

'I err..... was just seeing if anybody would be interested in buying it, you know, if it were around.'

'Buying it? Great goose hunters. Why would anyone want to do something like that? Something of that peril should be left well alone. And you'd do yourself a good service not going around frightening folk over it too. Land you in hot water one day if you ask me.' The door opened behind Robbie as a customer came in. 'Now, I'll ask you politely to leave at once. Take that voodoo stuff elsewhere. It's not wanted here.' The wobble in the man's voice became a bit more distinct before he turned his attention to the man who had just walked in.

Robbie walked out dejected. That had not gone to plan. It seemed as though Fellowood Marsh was not the only place reeling from the tales. It had spread like ripples in a pond.

Maybe this shopkeeper was just more scared than most people were. After all, he'd only spoken to one person. He hadn't expected to be that nervous bringing up the subject. It felt like the words were taboo as they rolled off his tongue.

He walked up the street a bit further but there was nowhere else he saw that he thought might be interested in buying the eye. He didn't want to stray too far from the market place so he went up a small side street that was narrow and cobbled. It looked authentic. The kind you would read about in a classic novel.

A lady was throwing a bucket of water – or at least he hoped it was water – in the gutter and a few boys were sitting on the kerb playing with marbles. The further up the tiny street he went, the darker it seemed to get. Even if there were someone interested up here, it didn't seem like they would offer up any sort of substantial amount of money. This was quickly telling to be a waste of time.

After a bit more exploring after leaving the unusual street, Robbie eventually sat down on a barrel by the docks. Along the way he had found a comforting stick to scrape along the walls and bat at the floor with. But it had done no good. He had not managed to summon up the nerve to talk to anyone else about it and not seen anywhere that might be able to relieve him of his valuable treasure.

The hustle hadn't stopped. He was beginning to think that maybe it didn't stop, day or night. Just as he was starting to poke at the remainder of what looked like an ants nest under the barrel, a man set himself down on the barrel next to him, making him jump. This man looked worse for wear and smelled something awful. He wore ragged clothes and mud-coated boots. He sported an even more raggedy beard that was clearly a result of rough living rather than purpose grown and as he turned to look at Robbie, he could see his years of rough sleeping had not been kind.

His voice was gritty. 'Strange place for a young boy to be sat. Lost, are we?'

'Not exactly.'

'That's good. Not a good idea to be lost in a busy place such as this. So why if not lost are you sat on a barrel of Savannah's Bridge's finest, poking at ants with a stick?'

The man did appear to be amiable, albeit slightly odd looking, but Robbie didn't appreciate that smell he had brought with him. 'I'm sort of on an errand.'

'An errand, ey? Not a fool's one I hope.'

'I'm asking around for a friend about a bit of treasure he knows of. He sent me to try and find someone who might be interested in buying it. He's errm, not well, you see.'

'That so? Not much treasure comes through these parts. What sort of treasure are we talking?'

Robbie knew better than to just talk to a stranger on the docks but there were enough people around that he was confident nothing bad was going to happen. Besides, what did he have to lose?

'The treasure is a glass eye. One of some importance.'

The man eyeballed him for a few seconds. Robbie didn't like it. Then the man made a sort of grunting noise before rubbing his long, matted beard. 'Importance meaning?'

'I guess you could say it's famous but for reasons best left unsaid.'

'And your friend is wanting to sell this illustrious eye to someone, is he?'

Robbie nodded even though he wasn't sure what *illustrious* meant.

The man stared out into the water in front of them. 'I might know someone who would be interested in buying Old man Joe's eye from you.'

Robbie's attention was grabbed. The man knew whose eye he was talking about.

The man continued like an aged storyteller, 'That man has haunted people from both his infamous cabin and in death, just like she said he would. I lived in the town years ago. I came here when my father wanted to leave one day. I've never been back. That witch put a cloud over that town that will never clear.' He came out of his trance and looked at Robbie. 'And this friend of yours, he has this eye, does he?'

Robbie didn't know how deep to go into the lie. 'I'm not really supposed to say. He just wanted me to see if there was anyone around here that might want to buy it for a handsome sum. But walking around I got the feeling that wasn't possible.'

'It's possible. You go tell your friend that Fergus knows someone who would and yes, would pay handsome for it too.'

The man looked like the last person who would know of anybody who would pay a large sum of money for anything. But Robbie, filled with new enthusiasm, leaped off the barrel – he couldn't stand the smell anymore anyway – and started to head back to catch his ride back to Fellowood Marsh, hoping it hadn't left without him. But before he could leave, Fergus grabbed him by the arm and leaned in so close Robbie could smell his pungent breath.

'Remember what I said. Fergus knows someone that will pay for it. I'll be waiting here. Now, go get me that glass eye, boy. And don't let me down.'

The cart was still there and he knew it couldn't be long before it would depart back to town. He climbed aboard and took up his spot between what thankfully were no longer bags of manure but bags of wheat, as he had expected. Good, he couldn't be doing with the return journey between bags of manure again.

Before he left, Fergus had told him that he was always around this section of the docks and to tell his friend to come and find him with the so-called treasure and he would find *his* friend to do some sort of deal. It wasn't what Robbie had expected, but it was better than nothing. He couldn't wait to tell the others of his adventure. But first he had to sneak back without being noticed.

That wasn't going to be easy.

~

Having a stutter can be difficult to live with. Jack-Jack had never known where his had come from and throughout his short life it had held him back. He was usually quiet, but Sister Athena noticed he was more withdrawn than normal. Being moved into his own room, away from everybody, may have had something to do with it, but she wanted to check on him regardless. The walk down the narrow, dark corridor was longer than she realised. It really wasn't good to have a young child this isolated from everyone in such a big place as this, she thought. This really wasn't the answer to a child having nightmares, but as usual it wasn't her decision.

The door was slightly ajar. She knocked, then pushed on it gently and peered inside. Jack-Jack was laid on his side on his bed, facing away from the door. The emptiness of the room became apparent when she looked inside. It was no place for a boy of his age.

'Jack, can I come in?'

He turned to face her, still lying down with his hands tucked under his face. She went to sit on the side of the bed. It creaked.

'I wanted to check to see if you were alright in here on your own. Can I get you anything?'

As if not even hearing her question, Jack-Jack asked, 'W..w..what was the other b..b..boy like? You know, th..th..the one you told me a..a..about?'

She thought a moment. 'What was he like? Like I told you before, I can't remember him that well. I told you about him in the hope that it would help you. You could see that there have been other boys with the same issue you do and still be happy and confident. The only thing I can really remember was how he was always helping the handyman with his chores. We used to say: "a hard worker is a happy worker".'

'I d..d..don't seem anything l..l..like him.'

'Well, you have to remember that we no longer have a handyman. You can't help the handyman if there isn't one to help.' She gave him a smile. She didn't like seeing him like this and would say almost anything to help.

'I w..w..would help if we h..h..had one.'

'I know you would. I think you can do anything you put your mind to. You're a smart boy and I don't want you thinking anything different.'

'W..w..why was he here? Was he an o..o..orphan?'

'I can't recall that far back, Jack. I've seen so many children in my time, after a while it all becomes a blur.'

'I'm n..n..not even an orphan. My m..m..mother didn't even w..w..want me. Why? Why d..d..didn't she want me?'

The question threw Sister Athena a little. She hated seeing Jack like this. He was right. He wasn't an orphan. His mother's family had left him in their care, ironically due to their religious beliefs. It was a very difficult question to answer. As children grew up, they became more curious about where they had come from. It was a task that Sister Athena had always struggled with. There was no easy way to tell a child that their parents had to give them up, for any reason.

'I can't give you a reasonable answer that will make all the pieces of the puzzle fall into place, Jack. Sometimes people do things that seem like the best option at the time. Whatever happened, your mother did what she did out of love for you.'

Jack-Jack listened to what she was saying but it was hard to take in. All his life he had felt inferior to every other child he had come across. It did make him feel better, knowing he hadn't been the only one to live at Saint Vincent's who had struggled with a stutter, but from what Sister Athena had told him, the other boy had been a lot more confident and happier than him.

That's what made them different.

'So, can I get you anything?' she repeated.

'No th..th..thank you, S..S..Sister.'

He turned back around to face the wall.

Sister Athena stood up to leave, her heart troubled. She was no more content than when she came in, but it would have to do for now.

~

The cart pulled up behind the store. Robbie quietly disembarked - the storekeeper's absent-minded son none the wiser. He made it into the orphanage and quickly went for a wash, undetected. No-one had noticed and as far as he was aware, no-one had suspected he'd been gone. But to be sure, he had to see Mollie.

She was arranging some books on the bookshelf as instructed by one of the nuns.

'And where have you been? I didn't see where you went after lunch. It's not like you to disappear for so long.'

'Has anyone asked about me?' he said, avoiding the question.

'No.' She shook her head. 'Why, should they have?'

'Not exactly. Don't you want to know where I've been?'

'I just asked you where you've been.'

He got closer. There were no nuns nearby. 'I took a little trip.'

'A trip?' She had stopped putting the books up on the shelf. 'Where to?'

'I went into Savannah's Bridge. I took the horse and cart. Only way to travel.'

'You what? Robbie, what the hell are you thinking?'

'I wanted to do some research. See if anyone might be interested in buying Old man Joe's eye.'

He must have expected the look he was now getting. He had had many a disappointed look from Mollie but this one was different.

'You idiot. Do you know how much danger you put yourself in without anyone knowing where you were?'

'I was fine. It was exciting. And I found someone who would be interested in it.'

'You did? Who?'

'This bum who smelled like he just crawled through a pigsty told me he has a friend who is very wealthy.'

'Robbie, listen to what you've just said. A what, a homeless man told you this?'

'Well, yeah.' Now he said it in the open, he realised how it sounded. And his excitement halted. What had he been doing going to Savannah's Bridge to find someone who would buy the eye? Now he was back, the whole excursion seemed pointless and very dangerous. Regret seeped in. Mollie got back to her book-stacking.

Still, he believed what Richie had said about the eye being valuable. How could it not be? Even if he couldn't find anyone in Savannah's Bridge to buy it, there must be some other option.

Either way, he still had to have it.

Chapter XX

"No-one gets left behind, remember?"
Mitch Alborn

Sister Meredith had called one of her special meetings. These meetings usually meant that she had something on her mind – that she had already made up – and wanted confirmation from the other nuns. As usual, the outcast that was Sister Athena was not invited.

They all gathered around her table in the corner of her office, the coldest and darkest corner, and discussed what Sister Meredith had on her agenda: the children. As far as she was concerned, some of the children were getting out of hand. And by some, she meant Robbie.

The conversation quickly circled around to him. As she saw it, Robbie had been a fly in the ointment ever since arriving but lately he had become a menace. She didn't like menaces.

'He should be worked harder,' Sister Beatrice piped in.

'He needs to be taught a little respect,' another nun answered. 'That's the trouble with these children nowadays. They think they can go around having no respect for the Lord at all. It vexes me.'

'And I, Sister.' Sister Meredith had her proverbial stirring spoon handy. 'As you all know, Robinson Harvey has been somewhat troublesome as of late and quite frankly, I'm getting tired of it. Now, I had hoped that a little persuasion of mine would do the trick, but that boy is a law unto himself and I quite simply can't have it here at Saint

Vincent's. There is no room for it. Now, Sisters, I called you here today in the hope that you will back me on this. I want you to keep an eye on that one. I do not want him swaying the other children as is so easily done in these situations. The last thing we need is more Robinsons on our hands.'

'Can we not just get rid of him?' one of them said.

'He has been assigned to us in good standing. We are to be his protector. I would like to think we can do the Lord's work, but we may have to be a little more heavy-handed. As you can plainly see, what we are doing at the moment is not working.

'Now, he was grounded for assaulting another boy. I know, one of many issues we have had to endure from him. But I do think it made him think twice. I want to thank you all for your part in supervising him and I assure you, if I can keep from doing that again, I shall. I know it took its toll on some of you. After all, he is a child of God but like all God's children, at times they must be punished. We will be forgiven for laying the law down a little harsher if required.'

'We are not all here. Will you be having this conversation with Sister Athena?' Sister Beatrice asked.

'Sister Athena, unfortunately, has a tendency to be too lenient. She has been with us a great many years but she lacks the discipline needed to be a true nun, hence why she is not here at this moment in time. I shall deal with Sister Athena in my own way, but she is not fit to improve Robinson's troublesome ways. If anything, she enhances them.

'So, are we all clear? I need all your support on this.'

All nodded in agreement. Meeting adjourned. They all left, except for Sister Meredith who, without another word to the rest, sat with her hands clasped in front of her – deep in thought.

~

There are moments in life that are defining. There are decisions that are made that last the length of time. Fellowood Marsh had had its fair share of those. Another was to come its way that would send the town into utter turmoil.

It all started with a simple game of conkers. Robbie had been sitting on his usual wall with his usual stick when Richie – now somewhat of an ally – had approached him excitedly with two conkers on pieces of string.

'Look at these beauties. My pa made them for me with some of the conkers I collected. These two were the biggest. Here, you take this one.' He handed Robbie what looked to be the smaller of the two but, as there was nothing else to do, Robbie took it.

'Now, go on. I'll let you have first swing. But I must warn you, I'm a master at conkers.'

Challenge set. Robbie was not about to yield to such a boast. He took up his position and struck.

It was fair, but only fair. Richie was next and struck an equally fair blow.

After a few more, they got the attention of a few other boys, including Drayton and his younger brother Phillip, a short boy who was slightly younger than Jack-Jack.

The boys cheered as if their lives depended on it, but the two mighty conkers could not be defeated. One turn after another, with their tongues sticking out to the side for extra concentration, they swung true, connected, and had to relent as it was not enough. The tension was high for a meagre conker contest. Boys were shouting for one side then the next. Nobody cared who won but that wasn't the point. Just like the arm wrestling, this was competition and it filled them with such joy. All they wanted to see was the impending disintegration of one of the battling conkers.

Richie hit Robbie's with a venomous strike which cracked it but it did not break. It held firm onto the string. He was on the ropes but with the very next try, Richie's conker obliterated in to tiny shards on the ground and the rest of the boys erupted. The larger conker had been defeated in some style and the rest of the boys yelled with elation. The excited look on Richie's face evaporated. He had been beaten and in front of a crowd too. His claim of being a master was short-lived.

With the contest at an end and with no other conkers to continue, the excitement faded and the boys started to go on their way, all except Drayton and his brother. He wanted to stay and rub it in a little.

'What say you now, master of the conker?' Drayton teased.

'Alright alright, I knew I should have given Robbie the other one. I had a feeling about that one. It's always the smaller one that is better. Must be something to do with the size. It's got more surface to get hit, of course. I'll know next time, mind you.'

'So now what are we going to do?' Robbie asked, still beaming in victory.

'There ain't nothing to do round here,' Richie exclaimed. 'That's why I were so excited to get pa to fix them conkers. And you had to go and smash mine up. He won't do me anymore now, he's too busy.'

They all set off walking like it had been decided they would head off a certain way, kicking at the pebbles and dust. Robbie picked his stick back up and was proceeding to whack whatever wall or fence was in reach. A little down the way, they happened upon Fletcher's house. No-one had seen nor heard of Fletcher since he had been accused of stealing the money. Not that that was unusual. It was hard to say he'd gone into hiding over it as he always seemed to be in hiding. His house sat at the bottom of the street, almost as if someone had pushed it away from the rest of the town.

The four boys stood in the street looking over towards the house. Still, he was nowhere to be seen. It was a conspicuous place to be so they ran and hid on the edge of the woods at the back of the house. Then Richie caught a glimpse of something that returned his excitement.

'Check it out. There. You can just see the hatch to his cellar is open.'

'Where? I can't see nothing!' Drayton stated.

'Right there,' this time with a point. 'The hatch, it's open I tell you. I've heard things about his cellar. Things that's too awful for a young-un's ears to hear. Things that'll make your skin crawl.'

'No you ain't. What kind of things?' Drayton asked, unconvinced.

'I don't like to say. Not with little one here.'

'He ain't that little. He's old enough, he's just short is all. He's alright. What you heard?'

Robbie interjected, 'I don't think we should be telling stories. We know how they can get out of hand.'

'Yeah, but these are all true. He's a right weird one, that one. No-one's ever been inside his cellar. Keeps it locked and bolted with about ten different locks. It takes him about five minutes just to unlock them all.'

'So, what's down there? Spit it out.' Drayton said impatiently.

'My pa says he keeps stuffed animals down there. Like a museum. Not like teddy bears or anything. I mean, real animals. Animals of all kinds too. Creepy as hell, it is. He kills them sometimes just so he can stuff them and make them his own pets. Dead pets.'

'Your pa says? Oh, heck. That's just probably something he's made up to scare you.'

'Hey, my pa tells the truth about stuff. Besides you've seen Fletcher about town. He's creepy. Never says a thing to anyone and is always up to something. He's probably down there right now carving up one of them animals right now, getting ready to stuff it and make it lifelike. Probably sits down there with them and talks to them. Hang it all, they probably even talk back to him. That's probably why he never says anything. Only talks to dead animals.'

The story was starting to grip Drayton and even more so, Phillip, only in a more blood-curdling way.

They all stood, staring at the house, the hatch still open around the back and no sign of Fletcher anywhere. But Drayton, not wanting Richie to sound like the big know-it-all, thought he'd bring him down a peg or two. 'Dare you to go down there then. So you can prove your pa's stories.'

Richie was suddenly caught unawares. With the coin suddenly flipped, he didn't answer straight away. When he did, it didn't come out with as much conviction as he would have liked. 'Why would I want to do that? He might turn me into one of his animals. Probably put me between an unfortunate deer and rabbit or something that he killed on purpose.'

'You're scared is what I think. Scared as a damn rabbit.'

'No I ain't. I just don't think it's a good idea to go roaming around a cellar filled with dead animals.'

'Scared.'

'Alright. You asked for it. I'll do it. But only if you come too. Then I can show you them.'

'Okay then. We'll all go. But we all come back out together. No-one gets left behind.'

'Not me.' Robbie had been quietly watching the house, hoping they weren't being watched from inside. Fletcher had to be around somewhere as his hatch was open. He didn't like the prospect of going anywhere near his house.

'What do you mean? You gotta come. You're the grand conker champion. Can't back out now.' Richie's attempt to goad Robbie only had an adverse affect.

'You guys are on your own. I'm off. I want no part of it.' And with that, not wanting to be swayed even more, he turned and went back up the street, leaving the other three still facing Fletcher's house – none of them seemingly that bothered to go after him.

'Go on then,' Drayton said, as none of them had moved yet.

'Alright, watch me.'

'Hang on. If we somehow get separated, we all meet back there in the woods where no-one can see us. Got it?' Phillip saw him point to an area of the woods away from Fletcher's house.

'Yeah, yeah, whatever.'

Richie moved, set off around the edge of the trees surrounding Fletcher's house and crouched down behind an outhouse near the open hatch.

'I'm telling you. Dead animals. That what you want to see?'

'Well, as long as they're down there.'

Richie was going to have to bite the proverbial bullet. So, without another thought he jumped the low fence and sprinted to the hatch. He peered inside. There were some concrete steps leading down to the floor but he could see nothing else from this position. As there was no sign of Fletcher either, he turned and gestured to the other two to follow him. Seeing the coast was clear, they did.

With trembling knees, they went down slowly. Not one of them would admit to the others how anxious they felt, least of all Phillip who, being the youngest, was just along for the ride.

At the bottom of the stairs, the cellar was a large room that looked like it stretched the length of the house. It was cluttered with wooden crates, chests and tubs but nothing that would suggest anything to do with dead animals.

'So, where are all the stuffed animals, huh?' Drayton whispered.

'They got to be here. My pa wouldn't lie. Maybe they're in those crates and he just gets them out sometimes.'

'Forget it, Richie. You're pa's full of it. I'm out of here. Come on, Phillip.'

'Wait. Now that we're down here, don't you want to have a snoop around? We're making history here. No-one's ever been down here before. Who knows what we might find.'

He didn't wait for an answer. Richie walked forward and started looking inside some of the crates and fingering the shelves. After the previous silence, he seemed to be making an awful lot of noise.

'Richie, pack it in.' Drayton's whisper had an urgency about it now. 'Let's get out of here.'

'I'm frightened,' Phillip said as he clung on to Drayton's arm.

'One sec. I need to find something I can take back with me to show the others. Something that will prove I've been down here. You guys go on up. I'll see you up there.'

'No way. No-one gets left behind, remember?'

'You're such a stick-in-the-mud. Look, there's a door. I wonder what's behind it.'

There was one closed door that looked chipped and worn like it hadn't been opened for some time. Richie was pushing his luck and anytime that happens, the luck runs out. Before he could take another step towards the door, they heard what sounded like a key turning in the door at the top of the stairwell that led up to the house.

'Quick. Up the hatch. Sharp's the word.'

At Richie's panicked whisper they all darted back for the stairs leading up to the open hatch. Their footsteps were less quiet than when they went down but they didn't care. They made it out and began to run back, retracing their steps back to the fence and up the street. Drayton stumbled but carried on towards Marley's Store. Richie was hot on his heels without a trinket of memorabilia.

When you're spooked and running away from something, your body doesn't seem to function properly. You feel like you lose all control of your limbs. Your body doesn't feel your own. Drayton arrived at the back of the store in a cloud of dust, shortly followed by Richie who skidded to a halt. But in the cloud of dust, Drayton realised Phillip was no longer by his side, clinging on to his arm. In the mad panic they had fled, forgetting all about Phillip in the process.

He was younger and his legs weren't as long or near as fast. This had escaped Drayton as he was, ironically, making his own escape. Now the three boys were just two and a panic set in that neither of them had experienced before in their short lives.

'Where's Phillip? Richie, where's my brother!? Didn't you see him running with us?'

Richie tried to catch his breath but wasn't succeeding. He looked around as if by doing so would magically make Phillip appear. He shook his head. 'We just ran. That was the deal. If anything goes wrong, just run. That's what we did.'

'Oh my God, Phillip!'

'That weirdo has got him, I tell you. He's caught him. We have to go tell someone.'

'We need to go back. We need to see if he's there.'

'We can't go back. He'll get us too. We need to go tell someone what's happened.'

'I'm going back. I can't leave him!'

Drayton didn't wait for confirmation. He went back down the street. Richie reluctantly followed. His bravery had all but left by this time. They sneaked around so as not to be seen but by the time they arrived, there was no sign of Phillip or Fletcher and the hatch to the cellar was now shut. If it was possible, the panic increased inside Drayton.

His mind wasn't working right and he had no clue of what to do, except to go and tell his father. Tears streamed down his face now as they quickly went back up the street.

He arrived home in a frenzy and proceeded to tell his father that Fletcher had kidnapped Phillip. Richie stood idly by as Drayton lied to his father about how Fletcher had run after them as they were too close to his house and caught Phillip but they hadn't noticed. When they had turned around, he was gone, Fletcher having probably taken him into his house. He also refrained from disclosing the part about sneaking down into Fletcher's cellar.

Upon hearing the news, Cliff told Drayton, "*Stay there!*" and hurried straight to Fletcher's house, calling out to Constable Pennileason about what had happened as he raced by the police station. Drayton did as he was told and stayed behind. He had done enough – or hadn't as the case may be. He had left his little brother behind despite his own instruction to not leave anyone behind. The nauseous feeling creeping up inside him was now all too real. All he could do was sob. He put his head in his hands and sat down at the kitchen table as his father left.

Why did they have to go there? And why did they have to go down into that cellar. Fletcher Mane was a strange man and the worse thing they could have done was go sneaking around a strange man's cellar, all because boys will be boys and egg each other on to do stupid dares for a bit of fun.

But this was not fun. This was anything but fun. He had persuaded Richie to go down there, putting his own brother in danger by doing so. His brother meant the world to him. He was supposed to be the one protecting him and now he had been kidnapped by that man. He saw no good way out.

He felt sick and there was nothing that anyone could say that was going to make him feel okay about all this.

His brother had been kidnapped and it was all his fault.

Chapter XXI

"The gold you have to dig for is not the real gold."
Marty Rubin

Fletcher's door burst open with venom. Cliff stood at the doorway and stared at Fletcher who was in the kitchen, facing him. With a few short strides, Cliff was upon him, grabbing him by his shirt with both hands.

'Where's my boy? What have you done with him?' he yelled.

No words left Fletcher's mouth.

A moment later, Constable Pennileason entered through the open door. 'Cliff, wait.'

Cliff turned his head to look at the Constable and threw Fletcher in his direction. 'Here, you hold him. The freak's not answering.'

Fletcher landed in the grasp of the Constable as Cliff searched the house. He checked everywhere he could, including the cellar, but there was no sign of Phillip. In the meantime, the Constable detained Fletcher, saying nothing to one another.

The search was a clumsy and frantic one from a desperate father but revealed nothing. Out of breath and sweating, Cliff came once again in front of Fletcher to repeat his earlier question. 'What have you done with him, you filth? Tell me!'

'Cliff, this is doing us no good. I'm taking Fletcher to the jail and we can question him there. This is getting us nowhere.'

Constable Pennileason fumbled Fletcher Mane out of his own house and marched him to the jail under the now watchful eyes of many a spectator. Yet again Fletcher Mane was the accused, but the welfare of a young boy was far more important than some stolen money. He was imprisoned in the jail.

Constable Pennileason called for a guard to watch the jail so he could help search for Phillip. The guard was a man who was assigned the job when called upon, one of a number who had volunteered their services if ever there was a need. The need was rare except in times of crisis - and this was a crisis.

In the meantime, Cliff had followed and gone straight to gather a few men to inform them of Phillip's disappearance.

'Phillip is missing,' he informed them as soon as they had gathered around him after seeing the commotion. 'That piece of dirt in there (he motioned to the jail with his head) has done something with him but is refusing to say what and Pennileason has now locked him up. My guess is that he won't say anything so we have to search his place. I've already had a look myself but not enough of one. If he doesn't show up, we need to keep looking. The day is getting on so there's no time to waste.'

Just as Cliff was finishing his speech, Constable Pennileason joined the men. This sort of thing was a little out of his depth and he knew it. He had been a soldier in the war prior to being Constable of a lonely, forgotten town. This had enabled him to acquire such a position but he wasn't the strongest of characters and some of the men in town had always suspected his lack of leadership skills. They would be tested now.

As the day settled around them and the light began to give itself up, the men began their search. It was a sight to see. They were swarming Fletcher's house like bees searching for honey where there was none. The news hadn't fully made its rounds and so some of the other people in town had come out to see what was going on, most of them unaware until being told by someone in the know. The murmurs started, some of interest, some of panic. The gossipers amongst the women were in full flow.

Cliff had no reason to doubt Drayton. He was sure that Fletcher had taken Phillip and they would find him, but there was no sign of his boy in the house.

The search didn't confine itself to just the house. The garden was also searched but did not need much time spent on it as it was evident there were few places he could be. In sheer petulance, the garden was trashed at the hands of the ever-growing frustrated mob. The ground was dug up and the rose bushes and shrubbery were pulled out and discarded on the ground, leaving a wake of destruction.

The light was growing ever dimmer. The day was coming to an end and still there was no sign of Phillip. Cliff was in full panic mode and his band of men were not showing signs of resting. But it was getting harder. There was still a need to search the woods behind the house, but it was getting more and more difficult to see and the darkness was drawing in.

Drayton's head felt clammy in his hands. He had not left the table since his father had left. His thoughts plagued him.

How could he have been so neglectful?

Now he was in a dilemma. They were out searching whereas he'd been told to stay put. What troubled him was the lie he had told his father. The truth was, they had been running so fast away from Fletcher's house, that he didn't see Fletcher grab Phillip and take him into his house. He also didn't tell his father about their excursion into the cellar. He didn't lie to his father often for good reason and now he had probably told the biggest lie ever. It was eating him up inside and there was no way out of it. His only hope was that Phillip would be found safe and sound. After all, that was all that mattered.

~

Word had got back to the orphanage about what had happened. Upon leaving the other three boys behind, Robbie had gone back to the orphanage feeling rather inadequate. He rarely turned his back on a chance to be adventurous, but this was just one step too far. He had always disliked the assumption that Fletcher Mane was a bad man and resented the other children using him as a pawn for their cruel pranks. He hadn't liked the idea of going down Fletcher's cellar from the moment it had been mentioned. That was more trouble than he cared to participate in, and leaving the small group behind had felt both the right thing to do at the same time as being a betrayal of his childhood wiles.

On the way back, he had thought about what they were doing and if they had indeed gone down through the hatch. A few times he had almost gone back but decided against it. He regretted not trying to persuade them more not to go but instead had simply declined to follow and left. The burden would be all theirs and he could only hope they didn't get into trouble.

Only they did get into trouble. The three children were in the orphanage when the word made its way to them by way of one of the other children. One of the boys not much older than Jack-Jack came in hastily but also with a bit of stealth. For some reason, he didn't want to be seen. He wasn't paid attention by the nuns, but he was noticed almost immediately by the other children. He came up to where Robbie, Mollie and Jack-Jack were sitting to impart the information.

'A boy's gone missing!' he said, trying to keep his breathing under control.

'What do you mean, "a boy's gone missing"?' replied Robbie.

'I'm telling you, a boy in town has gone missing. That Fletcher man has taken him.'

Robbie's skin began to crawl. He felt cold hearing the words. He knew instantly what the boy was talking about. He waited for him to continue when no-one said anything. By this point, a few more children had gathered round.

'Phillip, his name is. He took him from the street. Some of the men are now out looking for him and Fletcher's been arrested.'

With that, the children tried to look out of the window, climbing on some of the bed frames. Sure enough, what they saw was some movement and fuss going on towards the bottom of the street. It was hard to make out.

'Why are they looking for him if they know Fletcher took him?' Robbie asked the messenger.

'When he got arrested, Phillip wasn't there.'

'And how do you know what's going on?'

'I heard it from one of the men in the street before they all went off in a panic.'

The others still watched from their windowsill, fascinated. All but Robbie who, without letting on, was worried now about what was unfolding down the street.

'What's going on here?' The unexpected voice made them all jump. It was Sister Meredith. They all turned, some of them climbing down, some of them frozen.

Robbie decided he would be the speaker, 'Sister, there's something going on down the street. A boy has gone missing. We were just trying to get a look.'

Ordinarily, this may have been cause for some form of discipline, but instead Sister Meredith, after having a glance through the window, seemed to be more interested in what Robbie was talking about.

'I need to go and find out what is happening. Nobody is to leave, do you hear? Everybody stays here until I can get more of a grasp of what is going on.'

With that, she turned and walked out. The group slunk down into a huddle, sitting on the beds. Whatever was happening out there was now becoming real as the minutes wore on and children being children, needed to make their own sense of it all.

'What do you think that Fletcher has done with him?' one boy said to the group.

'He's a scary man. I think he's got him hidden somewhere in his house that is difficult to find,' another slightly older boy said.

'Listen, he ain't guilty of anything yet. What do we know stuck in here? We can't just say Fletcher's got him hidden somewhere. They'll find him, you watch.' Robbie's interjection was another attempt at defending the lone man living at the bottom of the town. He had always believed Fletcher Mane to be an innocent man just getting on with his life, but at the same time, there were more and more circumstances that were pointing to his defending of him possibly being incorrect.

He wished he knew what had happened after leaving the other three behind. But now it was too late. Phillip was only young and he was missing.

'I think that man is evil,' one of the girl's piped in. 'I think he's kidnapped children before, in the past. Just no-one's ever known about it or caught him. I've heard a few people talk about him. He's strange.'

'What have people been saying?' The question came from the young messenger.

As if telling a campfire story, she continued, 'Some of the women in town talk about him a lot. They think he stays away from people because he's got too much to hide and he'll get found out. So he stays in his house and tends to his garden where no-one can see him. I think they're afraid of him but just leave him be.'

'What if he's done really horrible things to other children in the past?' another boy said. 'Children have gone missing before, haven't they? You know, in past years.' He kept his voice lower now, 'He might have taken them too.'

'And done what with them?'

'Kidnapped them and then killed them, maybe. Never to be found again.'

The children were beginning to make their own superstitions. A trait of the town rubbing off on them.

'But people would have found out.'

'Not if he hid the bodies somehow.'

'How?'

'Buried them in his back garden, that's how. Think about it, no-one can see his garden from the street. He could do it in the dark too. No-one would ever know.'

Robbie had listened long enough. 'Wait a minute. You're going too far. You can't say things like that,' he said lowering his voice as if the nuns might be listening. 'You're all getting carried away.'

'Robbie's right,' Mollie said after also listening to the children's minds and mouths running away with them. 'Listen to what you're saying.'

'But it's not just gossip,' the other girl said. 'Look at what's going on now. That Phillip boy is missing and apparently Fletcher took him and no-one can find him.'

Everyone fell quiet. It was true, they were letting themselves get carried away as children did, but Phillip was missing and, so far, no-one knew where he was.

Once the children had finished their meeting, Robbie, Mollie and Jack-Jack reverted back to their small group of just the three of them.

'What are you thinking, Robbie?' Mollie asked, seeing he was in deep thought.

'I'm thinking I need to know if Fletcher Mane is what everyone thinks he is.'

'What do you mean?'

'Do you think what the others were saying could be true? I've heard about children going missing and never turning up again from this town and even from this orphanage in the past. Mostly, it's been put down to all the dangerous places around here, but what if it's true?'

'What, that Fletcher Mane has actually kidnapped them all?'

'Yes, and buried them in his garden, like they said.'

Mollie didn't reply.

'I need to see for myself.'

'Robbie, stop it. Now, you're scaring me. I don't know what's going on, but Phillip's missing. I just hope they find him quickly.' She stood up and left. Where to? Robbie wasn't sure seeing as they weren't allowed to go anywhere. As for him, he sat alone now, staring out of the window, thinking.

~

Robbie was beginning to think that his sense for adventure was getting out of hand. Now that he had planted this latest seed, he knew without reservation that it was going to grow. After his chat with Mollie he had thought about his plan some more. The first thing was to get out of the orphanage. That meant he would need to get the keys to the large wooden main doors and there were only two of the nuns who had the main door keys: Sisters Meredith and Beatrice. He was not about to tackle Sister Meredith so he decided that if nothing had changed by night-time, then he would sneak into Sister Beatrice's chambers when she was asleep and take the keys.

He didn't know if Mollie had taken him seriously during their brief talk but he wasn't about to tell her he was following through with it. He plucked up the nerve and left his bed and the sleep hall. Fortunately, Sister Beatrice's chamber was relatively close to the main doors. He already knew some of the nuns were unusually relaxed about leaving their doors unlocked at night. He only hoped he was right.

Sure enough, her door was unlocked. He opened it with a minor creak and peered inside. She looked asleep and he could only pray she was. This was risky business, but it was too late to turn back now; the drive in him was just too strong.

The word was that she kept her keys on a hook at the bottom of her bed. It was dark, but sure enough he could see them glinting in the moonlight that shone lightly through the window. He cautiously took them and snuck back out of the room, closing the door behind him. It was the perfect stealth mission.

The main doors were surprisingly easy to unlock for such old doors and before he could sensibly talk himself out of this particular fool's errand, he was outside. It felt odd. He hadn't been outside at this time before. The moonlight shone down covered loosely by some delicate clouds and somewhere off to his right there was a distant owl making a call. It almost sounded like it was telling on him.

After his talk with Mollie, he had lain there figuring out the integral parts to his plan, one of which was where he was going to get a spade to dig with; he certainly wasn't about to use his hands. The only thing he could think was to take a midnight walk back to a place he never wanted to set foot in again - Arnie Took's farm.

His only hope was that someone hadn't cleared it out yet after the funeral.

Even though the search party had retreated for the day, it didn't mean the town slept. He could see lights in houses. The men were still awake and probably talking about Phillip. He would need to be extra careful not to be seen.

After a long, clumsy walk, he arrived at the farm. The place looked even more desolate than it had done the times he had been here in the daytime. He knew the tools were in the shed he had hidden behind before. There was a selection of spades hanging up on hooks alongside a plethora of other tools. Even though it was hard to see, he chose one that looked easy to carry and not too heavy.

Then he was away. He didn't really believe in ghosts even with all the talk of Old man Joe, but being here alone at night with a thirteen year old's imagination and his history with Arnie Took, he wasn't about to hang around to find out one way or another. He ran, tripping and stumbling in the dark, hairs standing on end and a cold shiver running down his spine.

Fletcher's house, thankfully, was lit up just enough with the moonlight to see where he was going. After having a good look to see he was in fact alone, he crept around the back, over the fence and into the garden. The hatch was closed and now he was here, his mind pictured the three of them escaping – well, two of them anyway. The cold shiver was back.

In the dark it was difficult to see exactly where he was stepping. He knew that Fletcher took great care of his garden, but it was clear to see it had been recently disturbed.

Now or never.

He picked a spot and stuck the spade in and began to dig. The soil was thankfully quite soft and easy to penetrate. One became two which soon became three and before he knew it he had dug a small hole.

If Fletcher had killed any children in the past (which deep down, he still refused to believe), then he wouldn't have thought he would spend a lot of time digging too deep. Even if he did it at night, he wouldn't have wanted to be caught. Even that thought gave Robbie chills – chills that he needed to push away. He wasn't scared. He couldn't be scared. He had decided to do this and he had to be brave.

He moved to another spot. The garden was bigger than he had pictured in his mind and the small spade was doing little to cover a good-sized area. It was also harder work than he anticipated and, feeling a little out of his depth, he stopped to stretch his back.

The owl was still in full voice as again and again the spade plunged into the soil and created a small dent in the vast garden. And with each one, another bead of sweat dripped down Robbie's face over his lips. It tasted salty. He could really be doing with a drink right now. The work was tiring and even though he was used to Work Detail, he was working himself harder than he had done since his arrival. This truly was the work of a handyman – and a handyman wouldn't be stupid enough to do this in the pitch dark either.

A while later and after many a sigh and a back stretch, Robbie stood in the middle of a number of shallow holes. Still nothing. So far, he had only concentrated on the main area of the garden. He went towards the back, away from the shrubbery and rose bushes that were scattered on the ground. He found an area that didn't look like it had been disturbed like the rest. He plunged the spade in and stood on it. It went in again quite easily.

He dug deeper here for some reason. He couldn't answer as to why. Inch by inch he lifted the soil out of the ground creating little craters and drop by drop the sweat poured off him, more so because he knew he was doing something indecently wrong.

Then, the spade hit something - something hard. It stopped him in his tracks. The spade rested on whatever it was he'd hit. He couldn't bring himself to move. He couldn't see anything. Whatever it was, was still covered in dirt under the tip of the spade.

Then the owl stopped.

He turned his head to where the owl had been making its incessant noise. In the distance - in the silence - he swore he could hear someone approaching: footsteps, crunching slowly on twigs and leaves. He couldn't be totally sure but, nevertheless, the sensation of needing to pee was back. He quickly ran out of the garden in the opposite direction to where he thought the footsteps were coming from, taking the spade with him. He was away, over the fence and into the trees.

He stayed there a while, the only sound his heart trying to jump out of his chest.

What was he doing here? Had he really gone this mad?

He had to get back to the orphanage. His midnight grave-digging was done.

~

The mind is a cruel thing to carry around with you wherever you go. You can't leave it behind because you don't feel like looking after it today. You can't tell it to behave and not play tricks on you. It does what it wants. The mind has a mind of its own.

He had not seen anyone or heard anything more of any footsteps after retreating into the trees. He had waited there a short while before making his way back up to the orphanage, disposing of the spade around the back (no-one would know or even speculate on where it had come from). Getting back inside was just as easy as it had been to leave, but once inside, he had suspected one of the nuns was up and about. He was pretty sure that this time it wasn't his mind playing cruel tricks and, not wanting to be caught, had quickly found his way to his bed as quietly as humanly possible and stashed Sister Beatrice's keys under his bed. He would just have to put them back later.

The entire process had felt like a dream. Now that he was back in bed, he wholeheartedly wished he hadn't set out in the first place. It had all happened so quickly and for many reasons it had been far too risky.

His heart still felt like it was going to protrude from his chest at any second and it was all he could do to control his breathing as he lay as still as possible, hoping no-one was awake and had seen him return.

Looking out of the window at the impending dawn, his mind whirled.

Questions circulated in his head: *Who did the footsteps belong to? Did they see him and recognise him? Would they find the holes he'd dug?*

And most importantly of all: *what did he hit?*

My Decision

To this day, I can't really tell you why I felt so compelled to go digging in Fletcher's back garden. The conclusion I had made up in my mind was very rash. There was no need to jump to such a morbid outcome after the discussion all the children had, but something was changing in me. I didn't dare admit it but I could feel it - something I couldn't explain; something outside of me.

The idea that this man Fletcher would do something like that was not what I would have normally thought of him, but you know how children are – they have wild imaginations that get carried away and I got carried away too. I was so adamant about what I was going to do that I snuck out in the middle of the night with a subconscious intent. My mind wasn't my own. It's hard to explain and I'm sure you're reading this with at least one of your eyebrows in a frowning position.

I had never thought of Fletcher Mane as a bad man. In fact, I was always the one who would stand up for him even though he wasn't there. He seemed to just be a quiet man who lived on his own at the bottom of town. What was wrong with that? Well, according to the people in the town, a lot was wrong with that. When you live somewhere for a long time you create a persona for yourself. Fletcher Mane had evidently done that. Maybe it was his intention, to keep people at a distance. If it was, it had certainly worked.

My midnight excursion frightened me more than I would dare to admit to anyone back then. As a thirteen year old boy who has a desire for adventure, it is not so easy to admit that you get frightened. You have to push it down, far away so no-one can touch it - so no-one can touch you. Just as my altercations with Arnie Took or my many with Sister Meredith, I couldn't show fear even though it was within me. But during that one night, there was no-one else with me to put on such a facade. I was alone. Or so I thought.

As I was digging, I didn't truly believe that there were bodies of children under there. How could there be? It was preposterous. Fellowood Marsh was many things but a town where someone murdered children and then buried them in his back garden was one thing it was not, at least not in my head. But when my spade made that dull thud, all my thoughts changed. I couldn't move. Not until the footsteps crunched in my direction.

It was a stupid thing to do but I was starting to become the master of stupid decisions.

It wouldn't be my last.

Chapter XXII

**"Life is rather like a tin of sardines –
we're all of us looking for the key."**
Alan Bennett

As soon as the morning broke through the darkness, the search was in full flow once again. Cliff had chosen to carry on through the night, desperately searching for Phillip on his own. Many of the men hadn't managed to sleep well during the night but were now back, eager to continue in the search. Cliff, having not slept, was now exhausted but he didn't care.

And so the search continued, which included Constable Pennileason. The morning, thankfully, was a good one – weather-wise. Some of the men split into small groups; this was not a collective decision, it just happened. One of these small groups was made up of three men, all of whom worked down the mines and arguably could be viewed as the outcasts of the miners. Their level of intelligence and demeanour set them aside from the other miners. They had been roped into this search but it was evident they weren't pleased about it.

'Why have *we* got to do this anyway? Have they not got enough men out here to find just one boy? It's that no-good constable if you ask me. Don't have a clue what he's doing.'

At this time, these three men were searching around the back of Fletcher's house just inside the wooded area.

'The quicker we can find him, the quicker it'll all be over and we can get back to normal. Couldn't get a wink last night with all that chatter and Cliff going on and on.'

'I always knew that Fletcher Mane was no good. Been saying it all along. Haven't I been saying it? If I was in charge of this thing, he'd have been hung up by his boots and beaten until he gave up what he done with him.'

'But, he don't talk.'

'I'd get him to talk. Tongue or no tongue. He'd tell me or he'd be turned the other way and hung up proper.'

The men continued to beat the overgrowth with their sticks, searching for the missing boy, but not with as much purpose as they should have.

~

The porridge had a bitter taste to it this morning; more than usual. Same colour though. The whole place had a bitter taste to it.

The night had been filled with a sort of thunderous silence. Not many of the children had slept, their thoughts working in overdrive, trying to make some sense of it all.

No-one was saying anything during breakfast. No-one had said anything all morning. The only sounds were the incessant clinking of metal utensils and the nuns' footsteps on a cold concrete floor.

Robbie played with his food, spooning the grey slop with his spoon and letting it fall down slowly. He wasn't hungry. Not one bit. Mollie sat opposite him. He knew she was eyeing him with suspicion. He still hadn't told anyone.

The large room seemed colder this morning and it wasn't from the gaps in the boards that were still covering some of the damaged windows from the storm. This was an atmosphere of coldness. None of the other children knew what to say or do and there was no comfort coming from the even colder nuns.

Robbie wasn't bothered about any of it. The only thing he could focus on was standing in that shallow hole as he plunged his spade down, hitting whatever it was he'd hit. The idea that he may have hit the skull of someone, possibly a child, sent a shiver through him he couldn't deny. It had been too dark to see anything at all and besides, the hard substance was still underneath the soil. The anonymous footsteps had disturbed him just at the wrong time. He didn't know if he would have been bold enough to examine what he had hit if he hadn't been disturbed and made a run for it. But now it was too late. The hole remained along with the others. And whatever it was under there also remained.

He tried to tell himself he was being silly. He was letting his mind run away with him again. It was under the soil, after all. It's quite conceivable that it was nothing but a rock - just a rock under the ground where you would usually find such things. Only, it hadn't felt like just a rock. It hit with more of a dull thud than a ting that would be expected when metal met rock. This was more like metal meeting bone.

Another quick shiver.

He looked up. Mollie was still looking at him. Neither of them had had a mouthful as of yet. The taste would excuse that. But she was focused on him, not the food. She wanted to ask him where he went last night but, as the room was quiet but for the shovelling of spoons into tiny mouths, she couldn't.

The silence was unexpectedly broken by a boy towards the other side of the table. 'Please Miss, will that Phillip boy be okay?'

It was directed towards Sister Klara who was standing guard against the wall with a non-expressive look on her face. She turned to where the question had come from and walked over.

'I beg your pardon?' as if acting like she hadn't plainly heard the question.

'The boy, will he be okay?' a little quieter a second time.

'That is none of our affair. It is in the hands of the authorities. You just get it out of your mind, do you hear me?'

'But I just wanted to ask if he would be okay.'

'And I told you not to concern yourself with it. That goes for the rest of you,' addressing the rest of the room. 'I will have no more talk of this. Is that understood?'

There was no group response other than heads looking down and spoons digging into bowls. Sister Klara turned back to the boy and looked down at him.

'Is that understood?'

'I just wanted to make sure. That he wasn't hurt or nothing.'

'Right, that's it.' She took him by the ear and stood him up. She led him away down the corridor. 'I warned you,' she chuntered as she left with him leaving the rest of the children still concentrating on their breakfast while trying to keep it down.

'I really hate this place,' Robbie whispered to himself as a gloop of porridge fell atop the mass still in his bowl.

~

Drayton stayed in the house as instructed, but was getting wind of the unease of the men conducting the search. He was in turmoil. He couldn't forgive himself for leaving Phillip behind like that and felt guilty as sin. He couldn't bring himself to eat or sleep.

Drayton's mother had died of tuberculosis when Phillip was just a baby. Ever since, it had just been the three of them. Drayton had begun to help his father in the stonemasons from a young age, taking precedence over schoolwork so as to keep the family trade running.

The three of them were very close and the prospect of something like this happening was unfathomable. He knew his father would be beside himself out there – frantically searching, hoping that at any minute he or someone would come across Phillip and the nightmare would be over. For Drayton, the nightmare was all too alive for him, alone in the house with nothing but his guilt to haunt him.

Cliff's stick battered the overgrowth harder than most. Drayton's perception of what his father was feeling was very accurate. He had unsuccessfully searched through Fletcher's house with an eerie feeling in the pit of his stomach.

The whole night had been agonising. It had been the longest night of his life. His two boys were all he had after his wife had died, leaving them to fend for themselves. The protective father inside him had felt like he had failed. Meanwhile, Fletcher Mane sat in the jail cell. He couldn't help but think he wasn't telling the truth about where Phillip was, but he could do nothing about that. He was out here and just had to find him, somewhere.

The dreaded feeling was, even if he did find him – would he find him alive?

~

Just as everyone was finishing breakfast and preparing to go and wash up ready for a day of isolation, Sister Beatrice came rushing up the corridor to the other nuns. They gathered around like flies. Something was up and all the children instantly noticed, including Robbie who still hadn't touched a morsel of his porridge.

After some chatter, Sister Meredith went back down the corridor and returned with haste. Some of the nuns went just as urgently into different rooms and again, returned with haste. It was like watching ants panic as their nest was being destroyed, trying desperately to preserve it. Then it all became clear once Sister Meredith stood in front of the watching children.

She clapped her hands together even though all attention was already on her.

'There seem to be some keys missing, children. Now, I need every one of you to go to the sleep hall and stand in front of your beds at once. No questions asked and no going to wash up. Quickly now.'

Everyone did as they were instructed. Within moments, all the children were lined up in military fashion in front of their unmade beds. The loss of keys to the nuns was a disaster. They were usually so pedantic and being seen to have lost keys was a catastrophic mistake, hence Sister Beatrice's concerned look.

Robbie stood next to his bed knowing full well the keys they were talking about were the ones currently hiding under his bed. He just hadn't been able to return them because of one of the nuns almost catching him sneaking back in. He had planned on trying to return them after breakfast but his mind had been elsewhere. He regretted that now.

Even though there were a few nuns loitering around as Sister Meredith sorted herself out, he tried pushing them a bit further under the bed without being too obvious but it didn't do any good.

Sister Meredith came down the makeshift aisle between the beds like a General ready to conduct his business. She was ready to conduct hers.

She sauntered down the aisle very slowly, meeting every child with her cold stare, putting icy fear in them as she always did.

'Sister Beatrice's keys appear to have gone missing and I have a sneaking suspicion that they may not be too far away,' she accused. 'In my experience, I have found that children seem to have a habit of taking things for no reason. I don't know why but it happens. I hope this is not the case here, but we cannot find the keys anywhere else. At least not anywhere Sister Beatrice has been since she realised she had lost them.' She got to the end of the aisle and turned around to walk back.

'So I am going to make an inspection of the hall. I don't want you to move, not even to go to the toilet. No-one here is young enough to be incapable of holding it, so don't even ask.'

She commenced with her search in total silence. Heartbeats pounded and palms became sweaty. One bed after another she searched high and low and one bed after another, she found nothing.

Even though she would not let on, it was clear she was becoming desperate. Even Sister Meredith couldn't deal with some keys going missing. There were just too many problems that came with it.

Robbie stood fast knowing she was getting nearer. He didn't have to wait long. He was next. She came and stood in front of him.

'Mr Harvey. Are you going to tell me that my prior searches have been futile? That I should have started here?'

He said nothing.

'Let's see, shall we?.'

She started going through his possessions, then his bed. It didn't take long. She stood back up with a jingling in her hand. The keys.

That was it. She had caught him red-handed. How could he have been so careless? So much for keeping your nose clean. Maybe that was just an impossibility.

'Oh, look. Look what I've found.' She turned. 'Sister Beatrice, your keys.'

Sister Beatrice came over all embarrassed and took the keys from her.

'Make sure they are all there,' she said as she handed them over. 'And Sister, be more careful.'

Sister Beatrice bowed her head and walked off. Sister Meredith turned back to Robbie.

'Another misdemeanour. And here I was thinking we were past all that. Now, you've resorted to stealing. And keys of all things. Will you not learn, boy?'

She took up her hand and slapped him across the back of the head. It was unexpected but Robbie just stood there. He would not react to her pettiness.

'You need a good lesson that you clearly did not get growing up. Thou shalt not steal. Ever heard of that one?' She slapped him again in the same place, only harder this time.

'Stop it!' The cry came without stutter from an unlikely source. It took Sister Meredith by surprise, as it did everyone else in the room.

Jack-Jack stood, red-faced, regret etched all over it as she stared at him. She walked over to him now as she clicked her fingers to one of the nuns standing by.

'I'm sorry? What was that? Did I hear a demand come out of your impertinent mouth?'

Jack-Jack couldn't say a word. He was riveted where he stood. The impulse was an unfortunate one. The other nun returned with Sister Meredith's cane; the clicking of the hands a clear message as to what she wanted.

'Put out your hand.'

He did.

Thwack.

Not once, not twice or three times - but four. The same hand. Jack-Jack winced and gritted his teeth. The other children could feel the sting as they stood, trying not to watch.

With her deed done, she addressed the rest of the children, 'Thou shalt not steal. And thou shalt not give me demands. Not in my own house. I want you all to take note. I will not be disrespected. Now, get on with your washing and your day.'

As she reached the doors, she turned to Robbie, 'Jack's red-hand is on your head.'

She left, leaving the hall in a foul atmosphere.

~

Sister Athena had been down in the kitchen during the impromptu inspection. She was not aware of anything to do with the keys. On her return, she sensed a morose atmosphere. Jack-Jack was lying on his bed. She approached him.

'Jack? Whatever's the matter?'

He turned. She saw the redness of his hand immediately.

'Oh my goodness, what happened here?'

Robbie came up behind her. 'She caned him, badly this time. In front of everyone.'

Sister Athena held his hand between her own without turning to look at Robbie. There was nothing that she could say. The whole situation was pretty dire. Robbie declined saying anything about her smacking him on the back of his head. Jack-Jack was more important and he wanted her to focus on him.

As she stayed to comfort him as much as she could, Mollie came up to them.

'Robbie, can we talk?'

Nothing good ever came from that sentence. They couldn't go outside so he followed her over to the bookcase. No-one else was in the close vicinity so she decided to confront him about where he had been during the night.

'The keys. I know you went out. Where did you go?' The question came out with a hint to it that she already knew the answer.

'I went to Fletcher's didn't I. Like I said I would.'

'You seem keen on taking too many risks,' she kept her voice low. 'Robbie, what is the matter with you? Do you know what would have happened to you if you had been caught? It wouldn't have just been the Sisters you would have been in trouble with, it would have been the Constable too.'

'But I didn't get caught, did I?'

'But you could have. That's the point. You got caught with the keys which led to Jack-Jack taking a hiding.' They both went quiet for a moment. 'And did you find anything?'

Robbie looked at a book he had picked up to make it look like they weren't talking. 'I'm not sure.'

'What do you mean, you're not sure?'

'I did it. I went to Arnie Took's farm and got a spade. Then I went to Fletcher's garden and started digging. I wasn't expecting to find anything and well, I didn't as such.

But I hit something that didn't feel like a stone or a rock or nothing.'

'Well, what did it feel like?'

'It's hard to say. It sort of felt like..... bone.'

'Bone? Stop it, Robbie. You're just letting your imagination run away with you. Either that or you seem intent on trying to scare me.'

'I ain't, I swear. I hit something, I tell you.'

'And that's it? You just left without finding out what it was?'

He debated whether to carry on. 'Something spooked me. Maybe I just spooked myself. I don't know. It was too dark anyway. I just ran and came back here. I know it wasn't a good idea.'

The voice of reason shot him a "told-you-so" kind of look with her arms folded. 'So, what now?'

'I don't know. I left. I wanted to stay but I ran back into the trees and then back here.'

'Well, you can't go back now. It's too risky.'

'I know, I know.'

'So, you think you hit a child's skull? Is that what you're telling me? After the others convinced you he killed and buried children in his garden?'

He looked at her without answering. He didn't think Fletcher had done such a thing, regardless of going there in the middle of the night to dig up his garden. Now, he wasn't quite sure.

The one thing he didn't know, was the bad news that awaited Fletcher.

Chapter XXIII

"The temper of the multitude is fickle."
Niccolo Machiavelli

As the day moved along, the plight became more urgent. There was still no sign of Phillip and the sun beating down made the search even more difficult.

In a small section of the woods, the three undesirable characters had searched the area with no success, all the while grumbling and moaning about having to be out there in the first place. Their topic of conversation had centred around what they wanted to do to Fletcher Mane – most of which was somewhat unpleasant.

The drag of searching the dense undergrowth had taken its final toll on them and, being separated from the rest of the men, they had decided on a break. This break involved being hidden, sitting against a large tree stump and drinking beer which had been fetched from one of their houses.

Adding alcohol to a situation like this was like adding fuel to a fire. Albeit, the cold beer had both quenched their thirst and cooled them down, but it had also heightened their annoyance at being out there on a hot day, looking for a child that, in their minds, they were not going to find.

'This is hopeless. We're not getting anywhere, are we? Let's face it.'

'I think the only way of getting to the bottom of this, is to get it out of him directly. The sooner he tells us what he's done with him, the sooner this can all be over.'

'I'm thinking we go over there and make him tell us.'
'But, there's a guard.'
'He won't stand in our way. We'll get it out of him.'
'So, what are we waiting for?'

The decision didn't need mulling over for long. In agreement, the three beer-drinkers marched out of the woods and up towards the jail. On their way, they passed Fletcher's house. The state of the garden looked different to when they were there the day before pulling up the rose bushes.

'Look, there. Seems as though there's something amiss,' one of them observed.

They went and had a quick look and came upon the various shallow holes that Robbie had dug in the night.

'What's this? Holes? Why would there be holes here?'

'It didn't look like this when we were here. Someone must have come back after us.'

'But why? What's the meaning of this?'

'I say we go and find out.'

The guard stood at the door to the jail and stood up as he saw the men approach.

'Gentlemen, what's going on here?' he said with not much conviction in his voice.

'We're here to speak to that no-good piece of dirt you've got hiding away in there.'

They stood intimidatingly in front of the guard. 'I'm afraid that's not possible. The Constable is with the search and no-one is to see or speak to the prisoner.'

'The Constable doesn't know what he's doing, and that man in there knows something and is refusing to speak.'

'I'm going to have to ask you gentlemen to leave. There is nothing I can do for you.'

'You can let us in so we can put an end to this.'

'I can't let you in. I don't have the keys. They are with the Constable.'

This put a dent in the men's plan. They hadn't considered the guard wouldn't even have the keys to the jail. Disappointed, and without being able to get inside, they had to resort to other tactics.

'This isn't over!' one shouted at the locked door. 'You hear me? This isn't over!'

One of the other men went to the side of the small jail wall, underneath a tiny barred window. 'Yeah, this isn't over! We know you can hear us in there. We'll get to you sooner or later. You just see if we don't! We know you've done something with that boy and we'll get to you if it's the last thing we do! We saw the holes in your garden! Whatever it is you're up to we'll get you for it!'

The guard had no answer. He was in no position to stop the men almost shouting the walls down. He stood by, letting them get their frustrations out before they left. Fletcher Mane however, remained silent inside his cell. For now, the small mob had left him alone, but not before spurting out their threats.

~

Meanwhile, with the men continuing their search, the women of the town were left to do what they did best – gossip. A gossiping tongue can be a mischievous tongue. Instead of saliva, fabrication drips from it. The women knew all too well how to do this.

Like wires connecting electricity to subsequent posts, the word spread from one house to another, inventing and construing along the way.

'I think it was that old fellow. He's taken him.'

This came from one of the more notorious gossips among the group.

'Hear yourself talk. What do you mean?' another of them said.

'He visits people and takes things, doesn't he? Well, who's to say he can't up and take a whole child?'

'You really think he could?'

'Who's to say he can't? He's not from this world, I tell you. If he wanted to, he could. Up and vanish just like that. I swear that's what's happened to that young boy.'

'Our men are out there. They'll find him, you just see if they don't. Nothing like that has happened to him.'

'I say it's happened before. Why, I know of at least several young children in my time who have gone missing. Not a hair of them turned up. It's him. He's been here amongst us all and taken them away.'

The unusual circumstances were starting to play havoc with the minds of the fickle. The women were terrible gossips at the best of times but, like the children, they were letting their minds run away with them. Once one rumour starts, it can snowball. There are always two paths for it to go down. The women were becoming scared of their own words and it was clear to see.

The folklore of Old man Joe was rooted deep within the residents of Fellowood Marsh. People were frightened, whether they would like to admit it or not. Up to now, the tales had been rife and many believed that any wrong-doing was down to Old man Joe. Now they had a dilemma on their hands – was it Fletcher, locked up in his cell, or Old man Joe who had done something with Phillip?

The answer was becoming more and more of an enigma.

~

The stick Cliff was holding flattened the tall grass that was lining the floor of the woods. With every swipe, he flattened more and more. The grass was so dense in the area just on the outskirts of town, that it meant taking far too much time. Cliff's arms were getting tired but he persisted.

Most of the small groups were searching in similar areas. They could be seen doing the same movements through the woods, inch by inch. Almost every man in town was out looking for his boy. However, it was painstaking as the woods circled the whole town. At the moment, their efforts were isolated to areas close to Fletcher's house.

Cliff's group was even smaller than most; his consisted of just himself and Constable Pennileason, both of whom were bent over, attacking the grass as they went with an air of desperation.

If Phillip was somewhere in the woods, it would be very easy to miss him due to the denseness. The search of

Fletcher's house and garden had been fruitless and no time had been taken to decide on moving to the outer-rim of the woods below the house. The sun was becoming hotter as the day wore on and energy and willing were waning fast.

'What if we don't find him?' Cliff said with a hint of desperation.

'We will, Cliff. Trust me. He's got to be around somewhere.'

'While that man sits in the jail saying nothing. Why doesn't he speak?'

'I don't know. I'm not even sure he can.'

'He'll speak when I get my hands on him. If we don't find Phillip soon, he'll have me to answer to. And by God, he'll answer.'

The Constable could see Cliff's anxiety and chose not to respond to the final statement. Cliff was closely becoming a man on the edge and the Constable's lack of experience was shining through. He only hoped that sooner or later they would happen upon Phillip and the whole ordeal would be over. They must keep looking. But he knew that eventually, Cliff would be wanting to take matters into his own hands. If that happened, he couldn't be sure of what might happen.

~

Robbie's thoughts were all over the place. The feeling inside the orphanage was not one of contentment. No-one was really talking or doing anything. Jack-Jack was around the back somewhere after getting the harsh punishment once again from Sister Meredith and Mollie was doing some washing of sorts.

He couldn't help thinking about Phillip and where he could be. He couldn't help thinking about Drayton and what he must be going through. The search outside was still in the full throe of the day and still to produce Phillip. But one thought on his mind aside from all this was Fletcher's garden. It was daytime and he couldn't help but think about what it was he hit under the ground. When it was dark, he had no chance of seeing before getting spooked. Now, temptation was urging him to go back and find out what it was.

He had to admit, the talk between the children had got him thinking. It was far-fetched that this man at the bottom of town would have buried children in his back garden and when he was digging, he didn't believe it. But the spade had made him think.

With everything going on, it was too risky to go back now. But he was doing nothing sat in here. He wanted to join in with the search but he knew that wouldn't do - children were not allowed and that was that. But he had to see Drayton. He wanted to see how he was doing.

Drayton would likely be in his house as his father was out looking for Phillip. Robbie snuck out undetected and went around the back of the stores and down to Drayton's house. He crouched down behind the wall and peeked inside. Drayton was sitting at the kitchen table. With a throw of a tiny stone to the window, he got his attention.

'Robbie, what's going on?' he said as he opened the window.

'I wanted to see how you were doing. Any news from your father?'

'No, nothing. He's not even been back. I keep wanting to go and find him but he told me to stay here. But I heard some men go up to the jail and start hounding Fletcher. They were yelling at him and saying they saw some holes in his garden. I don't know what that means. Why would there be holes there?'

So his digging *had* been noticed. Robbie's heart started to beat faster in his chest. He wondered if the men Drayton was referring to were who he had heard approaching during the night.

'Drayton, I dug those holes.' The words were out before he could stop them.

'You did? I don't understand. Why are you digging holes in Fletcher's garden?'

This was bad. How could he now explain what he was doing in the middle of the night, digging for possible buried children while Phillip was still missing? He wished he hadn't said anything, but it was too late.

'I don't want to upset you and it sounds so stupid now, but some of the children were talking and saying that Fletcher has probably buried children in the past in his garden.'

'So you went to dig them up?' Drayton looked physically upset and Robbie wanted desperately to make it all go away.

'I didn't believe it at first. I went there last night in the dark and just started digging. I wanted to prove them wrong. But then, when I was digging, I hit something strange with the spade. Just as I did, I heard someone coming through the trees and I ran away.'

Drayton looked at him oddly. 'What do you think it was that you hit?'

'I don't know, but it wasn't a rock. It didn't sound like a rock. Now it's light, I want to go back and see what it was.'

'Robbie, that's dangerous.'

'Don't you want to find out too?'

The truth was, Drayton did. He was upset that his little brother was still missing but what Robbie was saying sounded intriguing. 'Okay, but we can't be seen. We'll be in so much trouble.'

'We'll creep around the back. The search seems to have gone further into the woods now. No-one will see us.'

That was all the convincing Drayton needed. Even though by leaving the house, he would be disobeying his father, the temptation to see what Robbie was talking about was too great. They crept around the back of the houses and quickly ran across the street into the trees next to Fletcher's house. As Robbie had said, the search was further away now into the trees. It was surprisingly quiet – eerily quiet. They climbed the fence and yet again, Robbie found himself in Fletcher's back garden. But his excitement quickly faded into disappointment. Now he was here, it didn't look like he had imagined. The holes he had dug weren't in the places he had thought and it was just a big mess. The men who had come across it had also evidently walked around as their boot-prints were all over the place. Robbie simply couldn't remember where he had hit what he had hit. There was no way to tell.

Dejected, as they were about to leave, Robbie looked over and noticed that the hatch to Fletcher's cellar was closed, but something drew him to it. He went over and tried to lift one of the two doors. It came up. He dropped it, making a loud bang that startled Drayton.

'What are you doing?' he said quietly, as if his voice would all of a sudden get them caught.

'Drayton, the hatch. It wasn't locked.'

'So?'

'I know we're not supposed to be looking for Phillip, but imagine if he's down there and we find him.'

Drayton looked at it. 'Do you think he could be?'

'He's still missing, isn't he? He could be down there.'

'I don't know. I'm not sure about any of this, Robbie.'

'Come on. We can do this together. We have to do something. We can't just sit around while all the men look for him. He's your brother.'

The words resonated through Drayton. Phillip was his younger brother and he wanted nothing more than to find him. Robbie was right. If he was down there and they didn't go down, he would regret it for the rest of his life.

Both boys peered into the grim darkness. Drayton once again descended the concrete steps and before they knew it, they were at the bottom, staring into the open space underneath Fletcher's house. The relatively empty room was just as they had left it: crates turned over; shelves disturbed. The only difference was the chipped door that had been closed before, was now open.

They both steadily walked towards it with apprehension. Their footsteps on the cold solid concrete echoed around the hollow room. They could already see it was pitch black on the other side of the open door.

Standing at the entrance, both boys felt their hearts pumping and their hands shaking. They hadn't said anything to each other since setting foot on the cellar floor. Now they looked at each other, willing each other to go inside. It was hard to tell whether it was a room or just a cubbyhole. With no light, it was impossible to see what was inside. Was this where Phillip was? The door was closed when Drayton was last down here.

Robbie leant his head forward to peer inside to see if he could see anything. He put his hand out and immediately touched the wall. It was just a cubbyhole and with their eyes adjusting to the dark, they could both see there was nothing but a few tools inside haphazardly strewn about.

Just as they realised that there was nothing inside the door, the silence was harshly broken by the flapping of wings as a pigeon burst past them, out of the cubbyhole and out of the hatch. The boys almost jumped out of their skins. Robbie embarrassingly let out a scream that he thought was only fit to come out of a little girl's mouth and then they both had to compose themselves.

'That's it,' Drayton said finally. 'I'm done. I'm out of here. My ticker can't hack this. Phillip's not here, is he?' he said disappointingly.

'I guess not,' Robbie replied still out of breath from the scare.

With one captured pigeon released, they left, closing the hatch behind them.

Chapter XXIV

"Sometimes I arrive just when God's ready to have someone click the shutter."
Ansel Adams

'I never had a brother. I sometimes wish I had. I can't imagine what Drayton's going through. You should have seen his face when we realised that Phillip wasn't down the cellar. I'm not sure I believed it myself when I convinced him we should help in the search, even though we knew children weren't supposed to. I just wanted to help. I wanted Phillip to be found. I was thinking we would find him alive and then run back to town to scream the place down that we had found him and everyone would be happy. They would be happy with us.

'Drayton looked utterly soulless. Yeah, soulless – that's the best way I can describe it. I didn't do it out of selfishness, you understand? I really did want to help Drayton and his father. Most of all I wanted to help Phillip. But the biggest problem here is, no-one still knows where Phillip is. The men are over there right now, searching every inch they can, looking for him tirelessly. It's such a sad sight. I just don't know what to think. I do know one thing, I don't know what possessed me to go digging in his garden. I could have so easily been caught. Some of the men apparently found the holes I'd dug, according to Drayton. He was ever so upset until I told him it was me. I just had to. I couldn't let him think that those holes might have been dug for Phillip. I could have really messed things up.'

Mollie and Jack-Jack ambled along the path on the way to the waterhole listening intensely to Robbie spout out his thoughts as if they weren't there. He needed to vent. And they were letting him.

The path to the waterhole was in the opposite direction to the area the men were searching and, after leaving Drayton back at home, Robbie had gone to fetch the others. The decision to go to the waterhole had been primarily to get away from the ugly scene that was unfolding. They just needed some space.

~

The small group of three men had returned to the search after leaving the jail, getting nowhere with their quest. They had felt embarrassed about leaving without an answer. That didn't mean they didn't still want one.

The search was progressing slowly further into the woods. By now, some of the other men were starting to tire and lose hope that Phillip would be found as the woods were so dense. One could not help but think that he really could be anywhere.

Several other men had joined the three. They were tired, frustrated and angry. More beer had been fetched and once again they sat leant up against a tree, beer in hand, only this time in a slightly larger group.

'I still say that Fletcher has done something to that boy. We could search for two weeks and not find him in these woods. I'm sick and tired of that useless constable thinking he knows what he's doing. He hasn't got a clue.

Tell me, has he ever had to deal with anything like this before?' The question was directed at no-one in particular.

'He's out of his depth. Nothing will happen if this is all left to him. Someone else needs to take charge,' one of the other men said.

'I've never liked that Fletcher character. He's weird. I said so in the meeting a while back. He doesn't belong here. But no-one seems to do anything about it. I'll bet he did take that boy. I'd bet my life-savings on it. He's taken him and stashed him somewhere secret out of fear of getting caught. Minds like his don't think like ours. That's why we can't find him. Everyone out here looking in the woods won't do no good.'

A few of the other men chatted amongst themselves after this speech in their newly formed unofficial committee. It was clear to see there was no purpose to the meeting, but it was taking on a sinister intention. Like blood to wolves, the talk between the men was too compelling to ignore. They were filling each other's minds with negative thoughts, strengthening the way they thought about Fletcher.

'So what are we going to do about it? Continue to search when we all know it is pointless?'

'I think something needs to be done.'

'Like what?'

'We need to go back to the jail.'

'To make him talk?' asked one of the other men who hadn't spoken yet.

'He's had plenty of time to talk. He's way passed that now. He needs making an example of.'

'So we're all in agreement?'

The men nodded in the circle. More beer was drunk before they once again headed back up to the jail, only this time in stronger numbers.

By now, the Constable was back at his post to relieve the stand-in guard that, after his altercation with the three men, was glad of it. The guard had been dismissed but not before revealing his unsavoury encounter with the three men.

Cliff had joined a group of men in his search further into the woods, and Constable Pennileason had reluctantly left him to return to his post.

He was now sitting on a chair by the entrance to the jail when he looked up to see the mob of angry men walking up towards him.

'Gentlemen, what is the meaning of this?'

'Constable, we mean no disrespect by this, but that man needs making an example of. He has had chance to reveal what he has done with that boy and yet he remains silent.' The evident head of the men spoke in a firm tone.

The Constable was on edge faced with the mob, but he did his best to stem the anger he could see rising in them. 'Gentlemen, please. This is not the right way to go about this. I understand your frustrations but that is why everyone is out there searching for the missing boy. Believe me, no-one wants to find him more than I.'

'And yet he has still not been found.' The man took a step towards the Constable. The situation was taking an ugly turn. 'Give me the keys, Constable.'

The drink on the man's breath was unmistakable. 'I will not. Go back to your homes. You've been drinking. Please, let me handle this.'

'You've had your chance, Constable. And so has he.' The man charged at Constable Pennileason and grappled for the keys. It wasn't difficult. The angry man and his friends, fuelled with beer, were too much of a match for the Constable. In an instant, they had the keys from him and had stormed the jail, unlocking the door before a few of the men dragged a fragile Fletcher outside, locking the Constable inside in the process.

Fletcher had only been in the jail overnight but by the look of him, could have been in there over a month. He stood in front of the leader of the men, held by two other men on either side.

'So, filth, the Constable here seems content on keeping you locked away. We have other ideas. We know you did something with that boy. You don't belong here. You never did. Look at me when I'm talking to you.' He lifted Fletcher's face up by his chin. The other men behind him were obviously swept up in what was unfolding.

The man turned to the other men, 'The prisoner seems to still be refusing to reveal what he has done with the boy. Whatever shall we do with him?'

The roars rose up of "hang him"; "string him up"; "let him swing".

Mob mentality.

'To the tree,' the man announced.

~

Meanwhile, the three children continued their journey to the waterhole, unaware of what was happening back in town. They had decided to go to the waterhole to gather their thoughts. It was their favourite haunt. Everything seemed to make more sense there. It had a sort of mystery about it and besides, it was theirs.

They emerged through the thick shrubbery into the clearing. It was like opening a door to another world with the waterhole poised perfectly in the middle of the clearing.

As they came into view, they disturbed a deer that was peering into the waterhole, *probably trying to get low enough to get a drink of spring water*, Robbie thought. Not that it would; the water was too far down.

The deer was immediately spooked and with a quick look at the intruders, darted off with a bounce through the trees on the other side of the clearing. They walked towards the waterhole and, after several crunches through leaves and twigs, they heard a faint, low cry.

They stopped.

They looked at each other, knowing full well they had all heard the same thing. They all thought the same thing too. They rushed towards the edge of the waterhole and looked in.

It was Phillip. He was at the bottom of the waterhole, looking up at them with tears streaming down his face, holding his left leg that seemed to be contorted in a weird position.

'Phillip!' Robbie yelled louder than was necessary. 'My God, are you okay?'

Phillip's reply was feeble. His declaration that he was hurt came out like a wheeze more than anything. He said that his leg was hurt and he felt "poorly".

It wasn't too far to the bottom and they could see him quite clearly but it looked too treacherous to climb down to rescue him. Robbie had carefully climbed down the waterhole in the past but he couldn't climb back up with Phillip.

'Robbie, what are we going to do?' Mollie asked vehemently.

He hadn't taken his eyes off Phillip. Here he was, clear as day, down the waterhole of all places. And alive. Not hidden somewhere in Fletcher's house or in his cellar, but here, down the waterhole. And they were the only ones who were here with him. Phillip looked scared and weak. He must have been down there since the boys went to Fletcher's house, but he was alive. That was the most important thing.

'We have to get him out. I don't know how.'

'It's too dangerous. We can't get him out by ourselves.'

'And Fletcher!' It occurred to Robbie all of a sudden. 'He's in the jail at this very moment and Phillip is here. We have to go and tell someone!'

'You go back to town and get someone here to help get him out. Me and Jack-Jack will stay with Phillip.'

The voice of reason was right. There was no time to waste. Robbie was filled with a new sense of urgency. His initial feeling had been right. Fletcher hadn't done anything to Phillip. And he was the one who was going to tell them that they had got it wrong. He took off back through the thicket towards the town faster than he had done before.

But would he be too late?

~

The tree that the man had referred to was a large, sturdy tree that stood firm, just off the main street on a grassy knoll. If you were to look at it, you could swear it had been placed there for the sole purpose of conducting hangings.

The small mob pushed and shoved Fletcher away from the jail, towards the tree. He stumbled and tripped, at one point falling over only to be roughly hauled back to his feet without hardly missing a step.

Once on the grassy knoll, within an instant, a noose formed from a large rope which had been brought by one of the men, was put around his neck as two men held him. There was no escaping; he was too weak to even attempt it.

The pending hanging was now in full swing. The town was undoubtedly steeped in its own history – bogged down, unable to escape the quagmire that it was stuck in. But to carry out a hanging was barbaric even for Fellowood Marsh. However, that was exactly what was about to happen. Some of the men, swept up in the excitement, began spitting on Fletcher as he stood there at their mercy as a few others threw the rope over a considerably large branch that stuck out like a purposeful arm. A crate had been fetched and Fletcher bungled on top of it.

At that moment, Cliff appeared from the trees and quickly came up to the grassy knoll, just as the vigilantes were about to carry out their own form of justice.

'What are you doing?!' he shouted as he rushed up to where they were.

No-one replied. Instead, all the men just looked in his direction, as if he were ruining their fun on purpose.

'Phillip has not yet been found. You cannot do this! He needs to tell me where my boy is!' Cliff's desperation was clear to see as he saw what was about to unfold before him.

'But he won't, Cliff. He won't speak. He's had his chance. Now the town needs to be rid of him once and for all.'

Cliff tried to catch his breath after the shock of the sight in front of him had taken it away temporarily. As if convinced in an instant, with uncontrollable emotions running through him, he walked up to Fletcher and grabbed him by his dirt-stained shirt and pulled him to his face. 'Please! Tell me what you have done with my boy!'

Fletcher shook his head frantically like a frightened child as if he wanted to cooperate but couldn't. He was beyond scared. What was happening to him terrified him as he stood with the rope around his neck. He opened his mouth, but it just quivered in response to Cliff's angry demand.

Cliff saw this. 'What?!' he demanded harder. 'Speak! Tell me, damn you!'

'He won't, Cliff!' The leader of the mob was losing his patience and before Cliff could reply, he gave out the instruction, 'Pull the rope!'

But before the rope could be pulled, Robbie burst onto the scene, emerging from behind the group from the direction of the waterhole. He froze in his tracks, shocked by the horrific situation facing him. He had seen the small group of men and rushed over to them, not seeing Fletcher until now.

All the men focused their attention on the newest member of the mob as he tried to get his words out in the right order.

'Its..... its Phillip! We've found him! He's down the waterhole!' The words came out like a screech. He still looked at Fletcher, realising he had arrived in the nick of time.

'What are you talking about, boy?' one man said who was standing near the trunk of the tree. He was holding the rope. 'What waterhole? What are you talking about?'

Before Robbie could answer the man's questions, Cliff came over to him and grabbed him by his arms, pressing them firmly against his body.

'What do you mean, "you found him"? You found Phillip?!'

'Yes. He's fallen down the waterhole in the middle of the thicket.' He wanted to point in the general direction but couldn't raise his arm under Cliff's force.

'What waterhole? What are you talking about? Take me to him!' He then turned back to the mob. 'Take that thing off him, we might need it!'

Robbie, swept up in the urgency and realism of the panic couldn't take his eyes off Fletcher.

'What are you waiting for boy, move!'

He did as he was told and set off in the direction of the waterhole. Every other person in the mob followed, but not before taking the noose off from around Fletcher's neck, leaving him alone standing under the large branch on the knoll.

~

Mollie was doing her best to calm Phillip when the others arrived. The young boy was clearly distressed, but her calming manner and soothing voice appeared to be doing the trick. She heard the manic stampede through the trees and turned to see them flood through the thicket. Robbie was leading them and brought them to the edge of the waterhole. They all gathered round and peered in.

'Phillip!' Cliff screamed, louder than needed. 'Don't worry. We'll get you out of there. Hold on!'

He looked around to the mob member who was carrying the rope which had not long ago almost been Fletcher's undoing. 'Give me that.'

He took it and threaded it down the waterhole but Phillip was too weak to hold onto it to be hauled up.

All the men were too big to fit between the rocks to descend to get him, so Robbie, being a lot smaller, was nominated. Just like it had been around Fletcher's neck, the rope was tied around his waist.

'You pick him up steady-like when you get down there. Hold him tight and don't drop him. We'll pull you back up when you've got him.'

Cliff's instructions were clear and precise. Robbie was lowered as he palmed his way down the slick, wet rocks to Phillip. Once at the bottom, he could see Phillip's leg was in a bad way. He had been incredibly lucky to have fallen the way he had and land in such a spot. There was a small pool of crystal-clear water right next to him. If he had landed in it with his injured leg the way it was, he would have been in even bigger trouble.

There was very little room and as Robbie looked up towards the opening above them, a sense of claustrophobia swept over him. It looked further up from the bottom than it had from the top. The amount of times they had been to the waterhole and had been careful not to slip and fall down it and here he was, standing in a tiny space on a rock, looking up at the opening.

He picked Phillip up as best he could, trying not to aggravate his leg. It wasn't easy. Robbie wasn't that strong and the space didn't lend itself to much manoeuvring. Somehow, he picked him up and shouted up that they were ready. The ascent was a lot harder than he had assumed and a couple of times, he almost let go of Phillip. His waist was killing him. The rope dug into his flesh and burned, but he wasn't about to complain about such a thing. And he wasn't about to drop his precious cargo.

Thankfully, they made it to the top and were roughly pulled up and out onto the ledge of the waterhole. Cliff scooped Phillip into his arms, being far less delicate with his leg than he should have been. Robbie loosened the rope which was near to slicing him in half before Mollie and Jack-Jack found him in the crowd to see if he was okay.

The rescue complete, the mob-turned-rescue party headed back to town so Cliff could tend to his son.

No-one thanked Robbie for a job well done.

~

Phillip had been found. Once in his bed, the doctor had been called right away to check on his leg. He had broken his ankle as well as having some bad bruising and cuts-and-scrapes. The doctor bandaged him up and told Cliff that he would visit Phillip later. Unfortunately, it was going to take some time for Phillip to fully recover.

The story went that Phillip had stumbled and fallen and when Fletcher had tried to help him up, Phillip had panicked and tried to run off. He hadn't seen which way Drayton and Richie had gone and so, remembering what his big brother had said when they were on the edge of the woods, had gone into the woods to try and look for them. He hadn't found them and just kept on walking. Before long he had got lost and became frightened. He had come into the clearing and simply hadn't been paying attention to the waterhole.

Upon hearing Phillip's story, Fletcher had been officially redeemed. But the damage had already been done. He had almost been falsely hanged. How could anybody remedy that?

When the rescue party had returned to town, everyone was caught up in getting Phillip home. No-one had seen Fletcher upon their return. He was no longer standing under the branch of the tree. Had he simply gone back home to his simple life and his destroyed garden?

Fletcher had been innocent and they had taken the law wrongly into their own hands with almost catastrophic consequences. There was nothing great enough that anyone could say to apologise for such a misunderstanding.

And besides, how would you apologise to someone who couldn't speak anyway?

Chapter XXV

**"You can't plough a field simply by
turning it over in your mind."**
Gordon B. Hinckley

The whole dynamic of the town had changed. What was once a sleepy town containing sleepy people, was now living within its own self-destruction. The people in it were anything but sleepy. So many things had happened in such a short space of time that it was too much for them to comprehend.

A man had nearly been killed by their own doing, and wrongly so. They had been so quick to come to carry out their own form of justice, that they had almost committed murder. Now, everyone was confined in their own metaphorical shell, unable to face the reality of their actions.

Every aspect of Fletcher Mane's existence had been invaded: his house; his garden; his cellar; his dignity. The only assumption was that he had silently retreated back to his house once the rope had been taken off, into his own shell that had protected him for so many years.

The people of Fellowood Marsh had watched him from afar throughout these years, judging him and moulding his personality through their own contorted ideas. No-one had ever had the chance or created the chance to get to know him and as soon as something terrible had fallen upon the town, awaking it from its slumber, they had condemned him at the drop of a hat. Guilt covered the town like a plague, weighing down on troubled hearts.

Order had also broken down. Constable Pennileason had had his authority exposed in the worse way. He had been walked over, dismissed like a child to a school bully by the fickle army. How would he redeem himself after showing his weakness at such a crucial point?

And so, the town took the shape of a ghost town once again. When anyone passed each other in the street or conducted their business, it was done with minimal interaction.

Life in the orphanage also made a half-hearted attempt to carry on as normal. As Robbie sat gazing out of the window at the world he was trying so hard to become part of, the scratching of chalk on slate brought him out of his trance. Sister something-or-another was doing her best to teach them all something really boring. There was just no way he was going to be able to concentrate. The outside was filled with adventure and mystery. He had seen it now. Experienced it. His thoughts kept jumping from one thing to another, rolling them over in his mind.

He had always longed for adventure. The setting of Fellowood Marsh should be the last place to find such things. Now he was back in a stuffy old classroom listening to the ramblings of a nun who was making a poor effort to enrich children's minds with her monotone voice.

As he listened to the screeching of the chalk and the even more tiresome screeching of her voice, only one thing was plaguing Robbie's mind: Old man Joe's glass eye. He just had to have it and he knew it was waiting for him out there, somewhere. He had listened to the tales about the other men who went off to find it, all supposedly in vain. He was starting to wonder if these tales were just a ruse to discourage him from going to look for it himself. They knew his lust for adventure. He hadn't tried to hide it. If the stories fraught with danger were an attempt to warn him off, they were having the opposite effect.

~

The little black bodies scuttled around in all directions, bumping into one another. Some carried bits of leaves and sticks. Some carried the dead – sacrificed soldiers for the good of the colony. *It was all part and parcel of being an ant*, Jack-Jack thought. He watched them ever so intensely, darting back and forth as if every one of them had just been told their life was about to end.

He was lying on the grass just around the back corner of the orphanage not far from where Robbie sometimes chopped up wood. He'd always had an interest in watching the behaviour of small insects. He liked how they acted in their tiny world, not seeming to know of the giant boy lurking above them.

It was interesting to Jack-Jack that he could destroy their world if he wanted to; the world that they had obviously spent so much hard work to construct. But he wouldn't. He loved observing them going frantically in and out of the dusty mound and he would never ruin what they had created. He respected them too much.

He wasn't sure where the fascination came from. Maybe it was because they were so small in such a big world - the way *he* felt sometimes. That must be the connection.

It was the day after the big misunderstanding about Fletcher Mane and it was a beautiful one. It was as if the sun was caressing the earth with its rays, trying to smooth it over, to portray that everything was okay. But Jack-Jack felt far from okay. No-one had really paid him much attention during the whole upsetting event. He had just gone along with it as he always did. He was good at that. That way, he could go unnoticed. He liked being unnoticed. Sometimes he wished he were as small as an ant.

The sun was scorching the soil that formed the entrance to the nest. He wondered if he could do anything about it. He didn't want them to be too hot as they tirelessly worked to build what he hoped was a magnificent world right underneath where he was lying. Maybe a few twigs and a large leaf from the big tree he was under might act as a good shelter.

It did. He picked a large, bright green one and propped it up with two twigs that he poked through at each end. It created just enough shade to cover the whole of the mound. But he knew how the sun worked. It would move. He would have to come and move the shelter as the sun moved. On a day like today it would be out until really late.

A smile etched its way onto his face as he thought he could tell the ants had a bit more energy from this newfound shade. He had helped. That was a good thing. He started to wonder whether anyone would help him. He was struggling with everything that had passed. The sight of seeing Phillip down the waterhole frightened him. Robbie had always been so strict about being careful around the edge of it. The risk of slipping or tripping and falling in was just too great. Phillip had not been so careful.

The nightmares hadn't left him completely either. The only reason he had been moved back into the sleep hall was because of what was going on in town, otherwise he would still be there, face to face with the shadows that were quickly becoming part of his subconscious. He didn't like the shadows. They moved. They talked. Even though he knew that wasn't possible, in a mind so young as his it was all too real.

He wished right then that he were an ant. He would work really hard at being an ant. Then he could carry sticks, leaves or even the dead deep into the world beneath him.

That world must surely be better than this one.

~

The talk in town was that Fletcher had retreated back to his house and no-one had seen him since his vindication. The finding of Phillip at the bottom of the waterhole should have been enough to clear Fletcher's name but when a name has been tarnished with such a thick coat, it can be hard to wash off.

Fellowood Marsh was a town built on gossip. It was a town fuelled by gossip. And it was a town desecrated by gossip. The town-folk simply couldn't resist. It was built into their blood ever since the witch had cursed Old man Joe. From then on, reality took on a different dimension.

Two men, both in their forties – one early, one late – stood in the queue in the general store waiting patiently for the keeper to ring the goods through of the other customers in front of them.

These two men knew each other very well and hadn't had chance to talk of the recent events as of yet. Now was as good a time as any.

'Even though that Fletcher Mane character was cleared of that boy's disappearance, I still think he's no good.' The man behind whispered in his friend's ear. He was slightly overweight with a stooped posture from working down the mines for so many years. His friend was also a miner but had a sturdier build.

'They should have continued with the hanging regardless,' sturdy man replied.

'Better for everyone if he wasn't around, I say. Him being in that old rundown house of his, alone at the bottom of the town there is like a rat at the bottom of the cupboard. The quicker he's taken care of, the less chance he'll have to spread his disease.'

Sturdy man gave a little chuckle at the comparison. 'Someone will take care of him sooner or later. That Constable hasn't got a clue how to deal with scum like that. He's never fit in around here. It's a shame we don't have a witch here right now who could put a curse on him and then maybe he'd go away and live somewhere deep in the woods where no-one would ever see him again.'

'I'd like to know why he don't speak. Did he lose his tongue? I was there in the crowd when they were going to string him up. He didn't say nothing even then. I know if it were me I'd be saying something.'

'I was there too. I was left holding the rope when Cliff told me to take it off him. I was ready, I tell you. Ready to kick that crate from under him.'

'I think you two should find something more profitable to discuss when in public.'

Sturdy and Stoopy both flinched with surprise at the deep voice behind them. They were next in line but hadn't noticed Councillor Grayson joining the queue behind them. He had been hanging on every word. They both cowered like two bullies being caught in the playground by the headmaster.

'We were just talking, Councillor, nothing more,' Stoopy said in a muted response.

'You know as well as I do that talk like that can do damage. Enough damage has been done here recently and we don't need the likes of you two making things any worse. I'd advise you pay for your goods and go back home, keeping whatever sordid thoughts you have behind your tongues. Do I make myself clear?'

They nodded, reluctantly. The sturdier one of the two didn't like being told off by a man of similar age but the rank of Councillor as against miner suggested that this conversation was better closed off and so they silently paid for their goods and left the store. The feelings expressed by the men probably echoed those of many in the town. Fletcher Mane had been spared and supposedly vindicated but that meant little in a town such as this.

Mud sticks. And Fellowood Marsh was covered in mud.

~

Robbie and Mollie hadn't spoken since the rescue. With normal life resuming, that also meant Work Detail. He caught her when she got back from the kitchen. Jack-Jack was somewhere outside and hopefully wouldn't be back anytime soon on such a lovely day.

'Why aren't you of all people outside on such a day like this?' said Mollie as she took off her greasy apron.

Robbie was lying on his bed but sat up when she arrived. 'I'm concerned about Jack-Jack.'

'What's to be concerned about?'

'This place, that's what. Just look at where we live, Mollie.'

'Not this again.'

'Yes, this again. Can't you see? This whole town is going crazy bit by bit. It's making me crazy and I know it's affecting Jack-Jack now more than ever.'

'He's been here a lot longer than you, Robbie. But I do sort of know what you mean. I hate that he had to stay in that room all by himself. He must have been so frightened.'

'That's what I'm talking about. How can you grow up in this place of all places? It's evil, I'm telling you. And the nuns are evil with it.'

'Robbie, you're being very intense. What are you trying to say?'

'Look at what's happened recently. From that damned chicken of Arnie Took's to Fletcher Mane almost getting hanged because of some stupid misunderstanding. And what's been done about it? Nothing, that's what. No-one takes responsibility for anything around here. I didn't care much for it at first but after being here for a while and especially recently, I can see it for what it is. I was hanging around the store today when I heard two men talking. They were still talking bad about Fletcher. Nothing will ever change these people's minds. We have to get out of here, Mol.'

'Get out of here? How?'

'I need Old man Joe's eye,' he whispered.

'Robbie, you're taking this too far.'

'It's out there somewhere, Mol. It's waiting for me.'

'Just like it waited for everyone else?'

'We don't know that.'

'We know no-one has come back with it though, don't we?'

He paused. Mollie usually won their debates. But this was more than a debate to him. This was bigger than a debate, bigger than him, bigger than anything. His need for the eye had manifested itself into an obsession, he knew that now. 'Listen, I know what I'm saying sounds crazy. But I've figured it out. It can be our passage away from here – you, me and Jack-Jack. I'll go and find it and come back for you. Then we can leave and take it to Savannah's Bridge. I'll find someone there who will buy it off us so we can go somewhere far away from here. I don't know where but we'll find somewhere and start a new life, just the three of us.'

'Okay, I've listened. Now you listen to me. You sound like some madman on a wild goose chase. A dangerous one. And what about Jack-Jack? He's too young and fragile for anything like that.'

'I can't just stay here, Mol. Not like this, even if it isn't forever. I'll die here.'

Their conversation had fizzled out with no agreement. The way Robbie had talked to her had troubled her. She had never seen him with such intent in his eyes. The way he talked about the glass eye. She needed to talk to someone about him, to share her concerns. There was no-one other than Sister Athena whom she trusted. Tomorrow - she would talk to her tomorrow.

Meanwhile, as the day was drawing to a close, Jack-Jack had come inside and was playing on the bed with some pebbles he had brought in. Robbie was still engrossed in his thoughts and hadn't received the confirmation he was looking for from Mollie. He leaned over to Jack-Jack's bed.

'Jack-Jack. I need to talk to you about something. It's something of mighty importance and I need you to listen to me.'

Jack-Jack turned to him but didn't say anything.

'You don't like it here, do you?' He didn't wait for an answer. 'I have a plan. I'm thinking of going to find Old man Joe's glass eye which is very valuable and then we can sell it and leave this place.'

The look on Jack-Jack's face changed. 'Th..th..the eye, Robbie? B..b..but it's cursed!' he said in as low a whisper as he could contain.

'Don't worry about that. It's just an eye that is very famous. People will pay handsomely for it.'

'No, no. I d..d..don't want you to.'

'Jack-Jack, calm down. What's the matter?'

'It's him. H..h..he's been visiting me. With h..h..his one eye!'

He looked positively terrified and Robbie was taken aback slightly by his sincerity.

'Jack-Jack, those are just dreams. It's all superstition and in your mind. Old man Joe hasn't been visiting you. It was only because you were in that room all by yourself. Don't you see? Your mind played tricks on you. They're just nightmares.'

'It w..w..was him. It was h..h..him, Robbie!'

Jack-Jack was getting louder and the other children were starting to look their way. The whisper had turned into a panicked cry almost and alerted the attention of the nuns. Robbie quickly jumped on his bed next to him and hugged him in the hopes he would calm down.

Sister Beatrice arrived next to the bed with her hands on her hips. 'What's going on here? That boy is causing a disturbance.'

'It's alright. He's just scared over something. It ain't nothing,' Robbie pleaded so she would go away.

'It's O..O..Old man Joe! He's here. All the t..t..time, he's here!' Jack-Jack was becoming hysterical and Robbie could feel him tense up in his arms.

'Right, that's it. You come with me. You cannot be acting this way in here.' Sister Beatrice took Jack-Jack by his arm and ripped him away from Robbie.

'Hey! What are you doing? Get off him!' he shouted.

A few other nuns came over to deal with Robbie. It was no use. Sister Beatrice took Jack-Jack back down the corridor to the other room. 'You need to calm yourself down. While you're in this state, you can't be sleeping in here with all the other children and disrupting them.'

An angry Robbie could do nothing but stand there as Jack-Jack sobbed, being pulled along on his way once again back to the secluded room.

The other children looked on.

My Connection

There is nothing in words that you can read that could make you understand the pull that Old man Joe's eye had on me at that moment in time. The best I can do is try to explain it but that still won't do it justice.

I wanted that eye more than anything. It was as if having it in my possession would somehow complete me, give me back what I had lost. I didn't even know what that meant. My subconscious knew but I did not and we didn't speak that much. We live through our subconscious; it dictates our thoughts and feelings to us and yet we do not question nor reason with it. We simply just allow it to rule over us like a higher power that we can't see. I'm sure if my subconscious was writing this down as I am now, it would surely be able to explain why I wanted the eye better than I can.

I could see that Mollie was concerned about me. It did not escape me. She was always concerned about me but this was different. I knew she could see that for some reason or another, the eye had a hold on me. I'm sure she couldn't explain it either. Maybe in life there are some things we can't explain and I've since learnt that some are better left unexplained.

Looking back on one's childhood can be a troublesome errand indeed. I did things as a boy that I am far from proud of. Growing up, they call it. Well, I'm not too sure about that. Can every wrong you do in your early years be put down to "growing up"? Can every mistake? Can every error of judgement?

I was selfish back then. The trauma of losing my parents so young may have had something to do with it but I was not qualified to decide one way or the other. Needing the eye made me even more selfish. It kept me awake at night, staring at the darkness above me, my eyelids hardly moving.

I had heard the numerous tales about Old man Joe; tales that sounded like they would belong more suitably in a somewhat dark children's book rather than reality. But they were real enough. They were real to the people of that town. They told them with such vigour.

If Old man Joe had been run out of town and went to live in a cabin deep in the woods, legend suggested that he never left there. If he never left there, then he would have died there. If he had died there, then his body would still be there. And if his body was still there, then his eye would still be there.

I wanted to be the one to find the eye. Nobody had ever found it – or so they say. The idea was to find it and sell it somehow so I could get enough money to get us out of there. My only problem was, if I did get my hands on it, would I ever be able to let it go?

Chapter XXVI

"The confessions of your mouth are the measure of your faith."
Sebastien Richard

When does a boy become a man? Is it when the digits reach a numerical milestone? Is it what he goes through in pre-adulthood? Nothing is written in stone.

Throughout life there are various Rites of Passage; some are planned, some are not; some are good, some are not. They come along at all ages and they shape us as a person.

What Phillip went through would shape him as he grew. Equally, what Jack-Jack had gone through would also shape him, but in what mould was undetermined. The fallout from Phillip's disappearance was starting to subside. In truth, nothing was really happening. Talk of Fletcher had started to die down; or rather been swept under the metaphorical carpet.

Robbie found Drayton down by the stream, rod in hand. Fishing was something Robbie had enjoyed doing since arriving in Fellowood Marsh. It gave him an escape – an escape into nature. He had never been much into fishing mainly because there hadn't been a decent place to do it. But here was different. The stream and surrounding area offered an ambience much to a fisherman's dream. With all that had been going on, fishing had taken a leave of absence. Seeing Drayton stood on the bank now with his line dipped in the edge of the stream, he realised how much he had missed it.

There was no "have you caught anything yet?" or "hey, what's for dinner today then?" Instead, Robbie just casually walked up next to Drayton as he fished and said nothing. He wasn't sure how Drayton was feeling after everything with Phillip, but he sure wanted to find out. Awkward situations were not his strong point.

'The fish are quiet today,' Drayton said at last.

'No bites, huh?'

'Not one. I'm not really bothered. I just needed to get out for a bit. Dad's looking after Phillip and there wasn't much else going on.'

'I wanted to ask you how he was doing.'

A tense silence spread itself between the two boys. 'Thank you for finding him.'

Robbie wasn't expecting an offering of gratitude. They didn't do that kind of thing as two best friends. Anything like that was considered "sissy stuff" but maybe on this occasion, Drayton didn't care about unwritten adolescent politics, maybe he was just grateful that he had his brother back.

'How is he doing?' Robbie said eventually.

'Not bad. He's just got to rest and dad's worried about his leg getting infected, but the doctor says it'll be okay. Don't think dad trusts what he says though. What are you doing here, anyway?'

'I needed to get out too. I couldn't stay in that place for much longer.' A frown formed on Robbie's brow. 'They took Jack-Jack off to a secluded room again. He didn't do nothing neither. He got a bit worked up over some nightmares he's been having and they dragged him off. I couldn't do anything about it. I hate them, Drayton. I really do.'

Robbie had gone off this morning without telling anyone where he was going. He seemed to be doing that a lot lately. Ordinarily, it was always the three of them going everywhere together. Recently, it seemed like their relationship was being tested. He hadn't seen Jack-Jack since being taken off to the other room and Mollie had gone to breakfast before he had woken up. He wasn't interested in breakfast so had snuck out before anyone could see him.

'Just nightmares? That's it?'

'Well, he says they're not nightmares. They're real to him but they're just bad dreams. He's young and I can't blame him, living in that place all his life. I'd have nightmares too at that age. But he don't deserve to be hauled off to a room all by himself just for that. He deserves better than that place and I'm going to give it to him, somehow.'

'No-one's ever thought much of that place according to dad. He says it's a place of evil when it should be a place for good. I don't know much about it.'

'All I know is there's got to be something better out there, for everyone. Too many children have come and gone in that place for too many years.'

Drayton's line dipped down sharply under the surface of the water. All of a sudden a new urgency entrapped both boys.

'You got a bite! Haul him in!'

'I'm trying, I'm trying!'

'Here, give me it. You're not doing it right.'

'I'm doing just fine. Leave off, leave off!'

Robbie's hands wrapped around Drayton's as he tried to take over the battle between man and fish. Drayton resisted his attempt by trying to prise it away from his friend. The two boys grappled at the rod before they both fell and let go. They landed on the muddy bank and watched as the rod got dragged into the murky shallows of the bank and disappeared under the surface of the water.

'Great! Look what you did,' Drayton said annoyed as he stood up and wiped his hands on his trouser leg. 'Now what am I going to do? That's my only rod!'

Robbie embarrassingly stood up slowly, hands just as muddy with a sheepish look on his face. 'I'm sorry. I don't know what came over me. I just had to have it. I don't even know why. What's wrong with me?'

Drayton looked over at his friend, still annoyed but seeing a disconcerted look on Robbie's face. 'I don't think any of us know what's wrong with us at the moment. Don't worry too much about it. I'll just tell my dad that I caught a real big one and I couldn't hold it and that it almost dragged me into the water unless I let go. At least then he might be slightly impressed that it was a huge fish that I almost caught before losing my rod.'

'You can tell him the truth, you know.'

'No, I'd rather him think that I almost caught a big fish. He's always teasing me that I don't catch anything of any size and that I'll never be as good a fisherman as him. Maybe this way he'll get me another rod. Then maybe one day I *can* be as good as him.'

Both boys stood gazing out into the water with the sun glistening off it in tiny ripples, the rod lost to its depths. Robbie felt bad. He had only come to find Drayton to see how Phillip was doing and now his actions had lost his friend his beloved fishing rod. When would he grow up and learn? Hopefully soon, and fast.

~

As Robbie was making a usual nuisance of himself, Mollie was struggling with a problem of her own. Her concern was the change that she was seeing in Robbie. Up to now, even with the trauma he had gone through when they first met, he had always been a level-headed character. Even the unkindly ways of the nuns hadn't penetrated his icy exterior. But ever since his obsession with Old man Joe's glass eye had begun, he had become more and more unlike his old self. Maybe this was the hold the glass eye had on people.

Yesterday, she had told herself she would speak with the ever-reliable Sister Athena. She hadn't talked to Sister Athena for a while. With everything going on, the only kind nun in the establishment had been a little reclusive of late. Now would be as good a time as any.

It was the middle of the day. Nothing much was happening and, for once, Robbie wasn't with her. She didn't know where he was and, therefore, didn't know when he would be back.

Sister Athena wandered down the corridor connected to the sleep hall when Mollie spotted her. She beckoned her over.

'Mollie? Is everything alright?'

'I'm not sure. I mean, it is, but I just wanted to talk to you about something.'

'Well, what is it?'

'It's concerning Robbie.'

Sister Athena could see he wasn't around. 'What about Robbie?'

'It's about this glass eye. It's hard to explain, but it's really got underneath his skin. There's something about it - something wrong.'

'There are many things wrong with that glass eye. That's what I've been trying to tell you children all along.'

'So you have. And we listen, we really do. Even Robbie listens, sometimes too intently. He's becoming a bit obsessed with it and I fear that with everything that's been going on that he will go off in search of it.'

'Whatever gives you that impression? Has he said so?'

'In a manner of speaking. But it's more than just wanting to go off on some sort of adventure. It's like it has a hold on him or something. Like some sort of wicked spell.'

Sister Athena took a moment to think. She could see the distress on Mollie's face. 'Do you want me to have a talk with him? Are you worried that he will go off one day in search of it?'

'I'm not really sure what I'm worried about. That's the strange thing. With the disappearance of the Phillip boy and all that, we've not really talked much about it. But he's changed and I'm sure it's to do with that.'

'Robbie has always been into his adventures. This could just be another one of his schemes to keep us on our toes. He's a bright boy but also in need of some guidance. What he went through before coming here was awful and another example of the atrocities of war.'

'He has been through a lot and Sister Meredith hasn't helped matters with him. She doesn't know how to handle him, which is why they clash so often. Like when he wasn't allowed to leave the orphanage after striking Richie. She locked him up without even getting to know the whole truth of what happened. I was there. I saw how Richie was with him, what he said. He was lucky Robbie only hit him the once. It just wasn't fair. I hated seeing him punished for something that he didn't start. That's why I.....' She broke off from what she was saying, having realised her tongue was running away with her.

'Why you what, dear?'

Mollie was unsure whether to carry on but she knew anything she told Sister Athena would stay confidential. The burden of stealing the food for Robbie had weighed heavily on her and now might be the time to unburden herself. 'That's why I did what I did for him. I mean it wasn't my idea or anything but I couldn't help seeing him like he was. I felt sorry for him so I stole the food from the kitchen for him. It was me.'

Timing is everything in life. Sometimes things just happen at the wrong time and there's nothing you can do about it. What's worse is you can't reverse it.

The timing of Mollie's confession was about as bad timing as it could possibly have been. How she hoped her confession had been in a little booth instead of sitting on her bed in the middle of a large sleep hall with concrete walls that carried sound.

At that very moment, Sister Meredith happened to be walking past the beds towards the other side of the room.

Mollie, caught up in what she was saying, simply hadn't noticed her.

'What did I just hear you say, girl?'

The menacing voice startled both Mollie and Sister Athena alike. Before they knew it, she was upon them, looming over Mollie like a sinister shadow; the black tunic a stark advocate.

Mollie couldn't say a thing. Her confidential confession had gone completely wrong.

'So it was you.' Sister Meredith hadn't needed an answer to her question. 'Of all the sneaky little rats in this place, I never would have thought it would have been you. They say you have to watch out for the quiet ones.'

'Please, Mother Superior, I was just talking to Mollie here about.....'

'Silence!' Her voice reverberated around the room as she cut Sister Athena off mid-sentence. 'I do not need an explanation or an excuse from the likes of you. You're the reason this sort of defiance happens around here. You forget your place, Sister.'

Humbled, Sister Athena withdrew. Right now, Sister Meredith had the floor.

'So you feel as though it is your given right to steal precious food from our kitchen. You feel as though the rules of society and our Lord do not apply to you. You feel as though you are above everyone else here, is that so?'

Mollie could not and did not answer. Her joints were frozen, her throat tight. Soon the other children gathered after being alerted by the raised voice and palpable tension. Jack-Jack, who had come in from outside was standing by the entrance. All eyes were centred on the unusual victim of Sister Meredith's tirade.

'These are pressing times. We cannot afford to be careless with what is valuable. Losing something is one thing, having it stolen is quite another. In my experience, the punishment for stealing something of value is to have something of value taken from your person. Our food is valuable to us. And I know your hair is valuable to you.'

Sister Meredith gestured to one of the other nuns with her hands. As if by telepathy, she was brought over a large pair of scissors. Mollie's eyes widened with the realisation of what was about to happen.

Her hair was what set her aside from everyone else. She had been gifted with the most exquisite, jet-black flowing head of hair that all the other girls were envious of. It would glisten in the sunshine, absorbed by its beauty. Robbie had always compared it to a shimmering waterfall of darkness.

Sister Meredith, now with the scissors, put a hand on Mollie's shoulder and moved her so she was facing away from her. Mollie was now terrified as the other children in the hall looked on.

'Mother Superior, you absolutely cannot do this!' Sister Athena shouted mercifully.

'Sister! I have already told you. I will not tell you again. Do not test me. "Superior" is correct. I am in charge here, not you.'

'But this is wrong. This is not the way to go about things. This is just a young girl.'

'A young girl? A young thief more like it. If one is old enough to commit a crime, then one is old enough to receive the punishment. Now, let me do my duty or I promise you will regret it.'

As she turned back towards Mollie, Sister Athena stepped forward and took hold of Sister Meredith's arm. Stunned by her behaviour, Sister Meredith gave her a seething look as if she wanted to strike out. But instead she did something that she knew would hurt Sister Athena much worse. Sister Athena had always been the square peg in Sister Meredith's round hole of an organisation. But no more.

'Sister Athena. You forget your place as you have so regularly. I suggest to you that your place is no longer here. You are hereby banished from this establishment. Do not return. I do not want to see you here, again. Leave now!'

Sister Athena stared at her in bewilderment, moisture forming in the corners of her eyes. Regardless, she would not give her the satisfaction by allowing a tear to fall. With not a single other word, she let go of her arm and left the sleep hall. She had been the only shining light in this dark place and now that light had been cruelly extinguished.

After she had left, no other words were spoken. The only sound in the hall was the sound of metal blades scraping together as Mollie's beautiful hair fell bit by bit to the ground. Her head jolted to and fro as she winced at the rough hands of Sister Meredith. No-one said anything. Hands were clasped over the mouths of a few of the other children. Within minutes, the deed was done. The waterfall was no more. It lay in tatters on the cold floor, no longer attached. Locks of dark hair covered the bed.

Sister Meredith walked away and down the corridor prompting, the other nuns to do the same. Slowly the other children dispersed not knowing what to do or where to take themselves. The only one who went over to Mollie was Jack-Jack, unable more than ever to find words to leave his mouth. He sat on the bed next to Mollie as she put her head in her hands and began to weep, her head now feeling substantially lighter than it was before.

~

The place had a strange feel to it. Robbie walked up the large concrete steps with an uneasy feeling in his stomach. It's odd how you can feel the aura of somewhere as if something bad has happened. This was how it felt to Robbie. He walked into the sleep hall and over to his bed where Jack-Jack sat distressed.

'Jack-Jack, what on earth is wrong?'

He turned to Robbie but was struggling to control his breathing. He was visually upset and shook every time he breathed in. He opened his mouth to try and tell Robbie what unfortunate event he had missed out on but the words just didn't want to come out. His stutter didn't allow him.

'It's okay. Calm down.' He put his arm around Jack-Jack and could feel him shaking. As he looked around, there was no-one else at all in the hall – no children or nuns. Something was very wrong. 'Take a deep breath. Steady now. Where's Mollie?'

As if waiting for her cue, Mollie walked in from the wash area, revealing her new haircut. Robbie was aghast. The girl walking towards him looked broken. The sublime waterfall that he admired so much had been replaced by a knotty, ragged mess.

'Mollie! What the.....?' He leapt up and went to meet her as she burst into more tears against his shoulder. 'Tell me. What the hell has happened here?' Again he looked around as if expecting the next surprise to walk in.

'Sister Meredith – she overheard me confessing to Sister Athena that it was me that stole the food from the kitchen. She cut off my hair. It hurt, Robbie. It really hurt.'

'She did this to you? And no-one stopped her?'

'Well.....'

'Well, what?'

'Sister Athena tried. But to no avail. Sister Meredith banished her. She was told to leave and not come back. I don't know where she's gone. But she's gone, Robbie. Oh, it's awful.' She continued to weep.

'Banished? For good? That's it. Do you see, now? We have to leave.' He grabbed Mollie by her head and looked into her watery eyes with urgency in the hope that now she would see sense. 'Do you understand, Mol? We cannot stay here. You must see that. Wherever we go, it won't be here.'

Mollie nodded.

'Come and sit down and listen to me.'

All three sat down on the bed that was still feathered with Mollie's hair. Robbie spoke quietly.

'We leave together – not just me. We will be okay. It can't be worse than here. This entire place has gone crazy as I knew it would. Now, Sister Athena said that Old man Joe's cabin was to the east.'

'But we don't know where, Robbie. No-one does.'

'That may be so, but I have the compass my father gave me. We got to try something. I ain't staying here no longer and I ain't leaving you behind. That cabin is somewhere in those woods. And Old man Joe's body is in that cabin. If he died there like so many people say, then his glass eye will still be with him. We can get it and sell it to make enough money to leave this place for good.'

'Do you know what you're saying sounds crazy?'

'Yes. Yes I do, Mol.'

He held her tightly and ran his fingers through her tattered hair.

Sister Meredith.

Before leaving, there was one other thing he must do.

Chapter XXVII

"Where two or three are gathered, a seemingly difficult task gets done."
Utibe Samuel Mbom

This was rock bottom. No more excuses.

As far as Robbie was concerned, the whole orphanage could go to hell (if in fact they weren't already there). The only decent part of the whole place had been banished. What was to happen to Sister Athena? He had no way of knowing. Sister Meredith had apparently told her not to be seen again and by all accounts, she was sticking to that order. He had not even seen her go and his heart ached for her predicament. He was very fond of her. She had always been the protective mask in the face of adversity. She had always been the only one who had any compassion or humanity about her. She had been here for so long he always wondered how she could stand it. She was unique and a beautiful person inside. Now, Sister Meredith had sent the only good thing in Saint Vincent's away, not caring a jot about where she would go or what would become of her.

And for what, because she didn't yield to Sister Meredith's way of doing things? The proverbial black sheep in her flock of miscreants. Sister Athena had seemingly simply disagreed with Sister Meredith's methods and tried to step in for the right thing and been punished for it. There seemed to be no end to Sister Meredith's harsh punishments. It was as if she thrived on it, which Robbie strongly suspected she did.

If it was possible, the orphanage now radiated an even darker feel about it. Nobody was talking. Mollie was trying her best to adorn her new hair style while Jack-Jack remained enclosed within himself. As for Robbie, he was doing nothing else but think - so hard his head hurt. He needed a plan of action and an accomplice. That accomplice would be Drayton. He knew Drayton would agree to it, if he worded it right.

He had his word around the back of Drayton's house but far enough away to not be overheard by suspecting eavesdroppers.

'We're leaving,' he said while making circles in the dirt with yet another stick.

'What do you mean, you're leaving? Leaving to where?'

'At this moment, I don't know. Anywhere but here. But I need to do something first. And I need you to help me.'

Drayton didn't say anything.

Robbie continued, 'I need to get rid of that place so it doesn't continue doing what it's doing. I'm thinking we could get some dynamite from down the mines and set it alight, just enough to blow a big enough hole in it so it's ruined.'

'And then what?'

'Then we're going. But I'll figure that part out later. Will you help me?'

'Those damn nuns didn't seem to show concern for Phillip when he was lost or worse, so I have no allegiance towards them. But what about the other children?'

'That's where I need your help. I was thinking you could come rushing up during a break in the school day and say that there's a deer stuck in the mud or something in the woods. Anything so all the children will go off to see. Then once they see there is no deer you can just act like it got free. If I do it right, the dynamite should have gone off by then.'

'What about the nuns, if they don't go or some are inside?'

'Hopefully they won't be, but if they are, I'm not really thinking about them.'

Drayton could see the determination in Robbie's face and hear it in his voice. He liked the idea of being party to something which sounded so exciting and out of the ordinary but he also knew that if anything was to go wrong, there would be huge consequences. 'I'm in.'

As if Robbie knew Drayton would concur, he continued, 'I need to sort out a few things but I'm thinking we sneak down the mines tomorrow after everyone has finished work and stash the dynamite behind the orphanage where the chopped wood is. Then I need to get some provisions for us and hide them somewhere. But once the dynamite is put in place, we'll need to do it the next day before someone finds it.'

'I might be able to get you some food and stuff but you're going to need to be able to carry it.'

'We'll be fine. This just needs to work and I need to tell Mollie the plan so that she can look after Jack-Jack. She'll probably try to talk me out of it, but she's ready to leave after what's happened. Jack-Jack's too young to understand and I can't risk him blurting something out. Thing I need most from you is to not say anything to anyone.'

'Promise, I won't.' Drayton made a cross sign over his heart before Robbie stood up.

'I'll meet you here, tomorrow, once everyone's finished work and it's safe to sneak down.'

Drayton nodded in acceptance.

Robbie left.

~

It was so easy in his mind: he would stash some provisions at the waterhole beforehand, then he would get some dynamite and fuse from the mines and hide it behind the orphanage, get Drayton to create a distraction, then get Mollie and Jack-Jack to meet him at the waterhole, before blowing what he assumed would be a sizeable hole in the rundown hell hole he called a home.

It all sounded so easy; he knew the undertaking may not be so. He didn't care about being caught anymore. What was the worst that could happen?

After leaving Drayton with his strict instructions, he went back to find a still-deflated Mollie and quietly told her his plan, but not to say anything to Jack-Jack about it.

'Robbie, that's all so risky and dangerous. You don't know the first thing about lighting dynamite. And if you do get caught, it's more than just a cane to the hands. What if something goes wrong? What if someone's still in the building?'

'It won't. It'll all be fine. We have to get out of here and I'm not going and leaving this place to carry on its evil deeds. It's all planned out in my head. It'll work, I'm telling you.'

'Is this just about revenge, Robbie or something else?'

'It's way past revenge.' The look on Robbie's face was unmistakable. Mollie agreed that they would leave and after hearing of his plan for Drayton to cause a distraction, would go to the waterhole with Jack-Jack and wait for him there.

~

They hid behind some rocks as they watched the miners climbing up the embankment on their way out of the mines. Obtaining some provisions from the kitchen had been surprisingly easy and Robbie understood why Mollie hadn't been caught.

This was the reason for his wanting to seek revenge on Sister Meredith. It wasn't just the fact that he felt anger towards her but also the guilt he felt about Mollie.

The stolen provisions had been scrupulously stashed at the waterhole amongst some large stones to keep them hidden from wildlife or any passers-by. He had managed to acquire some bags from the kitchen to carry the food in and some blankets from the store in case they got cold. He would also have his compass, which would now prove its usefulness in helping them find their way through the woods. In truth, he didn't know what to prepare for and he didn't like to admit it to himself, but he was feeling slightly out of his depth.

This next task was not going to be easy.

'How long do we wait before we go down there? What if someone's staying behind for some reason?'

'They don't as far as I know,' replied Drayton. 'Dad says they all come out together. It's not like an office where someone finishes up some paperwork or something. But I think we should give it a little while just to be sure.'

"Give it a little while" was what they did and then, when it looked like the coast was clear, ventured once again into the deep dark hole of the mines. Just like last time, Drayton lit a match and there was just enough light to see. Miners weren't the tidiest of people; the saying "leave a place in the state you found it" obviously didn't mean anything to them.

They quickly found the alcove. This time the door was only half open but it was enough for them to squeeze through without disturbing it. The crate of dynamite and the fuses were still there.

'How much are you going to take?'

'I have no idea now I'm here. I don't even know how to set it off. Do you stick the fuse wire in the end and light it?' Robbie was beginning to realise that things might not be as simple as he thought.

'My dad told me once that it's someone's job to look after the dynamite and he connects the fuse wire somehow. It has to be long enough that he can get away safely before it explodes.' Drayton winced as the match burnt to the end. He lit another one.

Drayton pointed. 'Hey, there's a stick with a fuse wire attached already. It must be ready for tomorrow. That's got to be dangerous, leaving it like that.'

Robbie picked it up carefully, wondering how long it would take for the fuse wire to burn.

'Look, Robbie, now we're here do you really think this is a good idea?'

'I don't know. But I don't feel like it's a bad idea,' he said without taking his eyes off the loot. He took the fused stick of dynamite and wrapped it up in a small blanket he had brought down with him. Then the two boys headed back out of the mines. Robbie couldn't help but think how surprisingly easy it was for anyone to go down the mines when no-one else was there. Maybe after this, security would tighten up.

It felt like every set of eyes in town were on them as they walked through the street with the blanket under-arm. Robbie was used to the idea that he was suspected for anything and everything. A young boy was guilty until proven innocent. At least that's the way it seemed with him. The walk was nerve-racking but eventually they made it up to the orphanage. The coast appeared clear but Robbie didn't want to risk any needless suspicion so he told Drayton to hang behind and he would stash the dynamite alone.

He knelt down and took one more look around before unwrapping the blanket and taking out the stick of dynamite. He placed it carefully between the pieces of wood that he himself had chopped up.

Job done.

It would be a miracle if someone saw it or stumbled across it by accident. He'd borrowed the matches from

Drayton and taken them with him, tucked down his trousers.

As he watched Drayton leave, he was conflicted with what he was doing. He had taken some risks in the past and he had enjoyed the thrill. He thrived on it. Maybe this was why he went digging in the dead of the night. Yes, he wanted to help matters and solve the conundrum of what had happened but in his heart it was the ecstasy of being part of something like that.

But this - this felt different. This was dangerous. Did he really have the courage and the fortitude to light the stick and have it blow up? He would only know when the time came.

And that wasn't going to be far away.

~

'We have to go tomorrow.'

'Tomorrow? But Robbie, that's too soon. I'm not ready. Jack-Jack.....'

'It has to be tomorrow. There is too much risk otherwise.'

It was dark and quiet. The two were talking - well, whispering in bed that night. Jack-Jack on the other hand was fast asleep. He had been placed back in the sleep hall, having only spent one night in the secluded room. It had become too much of a burden for the nuns to keep watch on one child in a separate room.

'At break time tomorrow, I want you to take Jack-Jack to the waterhole and wait for me there. I will come and find you and then we'll leave. I've placed some provisions by the waterhole. It should be enough for us to carry and be okay until we find the cabin.'

'But Robbie, what if we don't find it? What if it's not even there by now?'

'I don't know. We'll just have to come to that but hopefully we won't have to. We'll continue on to Savannah's Bridge and find somewhere to stay, somehow. I was planning on going there after we find the eye anyway to sell it to someone.'

'But Savannah's Bridge is miles away. What about Jack-Jack?'

'We'll just have to do the best we can. There's nothing for it. We can't stay here. We're on our own, Mol.'

They went quiet after that, bedding down but knowing that the probability of either of them getting to sleep was slim to none. Robbie entwined his fingers together and rested them on his stomach as he stared up at the ceiling into the darkness.

Nothing but darkness – that's all this place was anyway.

~

Fortunately, it was sunny. If it hadn't been, most of the other children would have likely been indoors. As it happened, everyone tried to be outside as much as possible. It beat being inside the orphanage with a limited amount of things to do and was far less depressing.

The time for Mollie and Jack-Jack to leave was now. The waterhole was in the opposite direction to where they were hiding behind the orphanage but they could make a big loop round once covered by the trees.

'Remember, wait for me there. I won't be too far behind you.'

Mollie wasn't going to argue anymore. She took Jack-Jack by the hand and fled into the trees behind them.

They were gone. Robbie turned back to the children. Some were playing, some were sitting in groups, but thankfully all outside. The real reason he was so desperate to get rid of Mollie and Jack-Jack was Drayton. Where was he? He had given him strict instructions to divert the children away from the orphanage soon after break had started. But as of yet, he was nowhere to be seen.

If break time finished and they all went back into class, his plan would be foiled. But just then, Drayton did appear from the trees on the opposite side to where Robbie was. It was just like he had pictured it in his mind. Drayton came running up shouting to everyone that there was a deer stuck in the mud and needed help. His acting was very convincing because sure enough, all the children immediately stopped what they were doing and, without caring about getting into trouble, followed Drayton back into the woods, closely followed by the nuns as they shouted after them.

This was it. Robbie pushed the stick of dynamite as far as he could into a hole in the mortar of the wall. He waited for a few seconds before taking the box of matches out of his pocket and striking one. It lit instantaneously. He lowered it to the fused stick of dynamite. The match fizzled out. He quickly tried again. Suddenly, the fuse spluttered into life and Robbie got up and ran as fast as he could into the trees. As he ran, he hoped he wouldn't slip. He hoped the fuse wouldn't be faulty. He hoped he hadn't underestimated the scale of power of the dynamite. He hoped.....

The explosion was immense behind him. So much so that he went deaf for a few moments after. It sent him crashing to the floor and he boxed his ears tightly with the sting of it. Even though he had made it quite far into the woods before the actual explosion, the force of it was greater than he had predicted in his mind. All of a sudden, he felt a surge of regret at what he had done. This was real. What if someone had been hurt or worse? Up to now, it had just been a plan. The shock and reality of it was too much. He laid there on the ground and looked through the trees. There was certainly a fireball of some kind but from here he couldn't tell just how big. The only thing he could wish for was that no-one did get hurt. This had been for everyone's good. Surely, it had to be.

No more *porridge walls*.

He got up unsteadily. His balance was all off but he had to get moving. Mollie and Jack-Jack would have heard the blast. He only hoped they would be there, waiting. He knew they would be but there was a niggling doubt rising up inside him. He staggered through the dense woodland and headed for the waterhole.

They were there. But they were panicked. As he emerged, they rushed over to him and checked if he was okay. Mollie was desperate to know what had happened but the ringing in his ears was still hurting.

They gathered up the provisions that, thankfully, were still there. Robbie quickly checked his compass and they headed off east, supposedly in the direction of Old man Joe's cabin. Every part of the plan had gone smoothly (if you can call it that), but it had taken more out of Robbie than he first thought. A plan in one's mind is somewhat different to the undertaking. What was worse, he had no way of knowing what the extent of the damage had been.

Would he ever know?

Chapter XXVIII

"Children see magic because they look for it."
Christopher Moore

The first initial steps had been taken in silence, each of them buried in their own thoughts.

Robbie's were of the destruction he had just left behind. Was *his* worse than the destruction the nuns had imparted on the countless children who had passed through their doors? He also couldn't shake the unknowing of whether the other children had escaped being part of his act. Drayton had done his part well, but there was still no telling if anyone had been hurt or worse. The magnitude of what he had done was weighing him down, making his feet drag with every step of their journey.

Mollie's thoughts were more of concern for their future. This was against everything she believed in and it was as if she was walking not to freedom, but against the grain. She was usually the voice of reason and she now had doubts as to what reason even was.

Sister Meredith's haircut had affected her deeply and with it she had become a different person. Reasoning seemed to be a thing of the past. It was too late to go back on anything now. The thing she couldn't fathom was just how much danger they were in. The picture? Three children all alone wandering through woods which to them were nothing more than a stranger welcoming them deeper inside. Everyone had been warned off going deep into the woods, so why were they here?

And Jack-Jack. Well, his were thoughts of many things, most of which would not be shared with the other members of the group. Jack-Jack had become much more reclusive of late, something which had not gone unnoticed by his two companions. They knew it, they just didn't know what to do about it. Right now, he would simply do as he always did and go along with whatever happened, but what was that massive explosion about and why were they running away?

And so, with the bags slung over their shoulders and their feet carefully searching for the correct path, they trundled on together. As they walked, Mollie told Jack-Jack what had happened. He listened quietly, soaking it all in.

That was Jack-Jack's way.

The weather was kind and forgiving. A good while after the explosion and the remnants left behind, the birds were out chirping their happy call and the leaves blew with a gentle wave that fanned their journey. It was like they were the only ones in the world at that moment. Regardless of everything, all three of them couldn't deny that this was the most free they had felt in a very long time.

The woods surrounding Fellowood Marsh were dense and unspoilt – a place of fairy tales that looked like no-one in the history of the earth had ever dared set foot. There were no pathways, no sign of human life. At this rate, if the woods didn't at least open up somewhat, they would surely pass right by Old man Joe's cabin. The chance meeting as it was, was thin at best. The information from Sister Athena that it was to the east was vague, but that was all they had to go on. Robbie was outwardly confident, but inwardly suspected that they might not come across it at all. The consequence of this possibility had not yet been formed in his plan. He hoped it wouldn't have to be.

They had not walked that far, but it felt as though they were the only ones in this new, surreal world. Everything had changed so fast. The walk was a time to reflect. Robbie's thoughts shifted from Fletcher Mane to Sister Athena.

Poor Sister Athena. He wondered where she was. She was better than that place and, in his eyes, had wasted most of her life being there when she could have been of much more use elsewhere. He knew she would have argued that opinion. She loved what she did and had loved being at Saint Vincent's all those years. And now she was gone. He just hoped wherever she was, she was okay.

Jack-Jack's legs were shorter than the other two. He was short even for his age. This was a hindrance during a trek through the woods. It was harder for him to step over fallen branches and foliage. If it were not for his unfortunate speech impediment the complaining would have surely already begun.

The first person to break the silence was Robbie and he broke it by asking Mollie the strangest of questions: 'Do you think the power of the glass eye transfers to whoever has it in their grasp?' He asked the question quietly so as not to disturb the sleeping nature around them.

Mollie hadn't quite taken in the question. 'The power?' was her only response.

'Yes, the power. To see.'

'Robbie, I'm not sure I know what you're getting at.'

'The witch cursed Old man Joe and his glass eye, didn't she? She told him he would forever see into people's souls even after he was gone. Well, he possesses the eye. If someone else took it, would they have the same power?'

The fact that Robbie was even asking her this question unsettled her. 'I think you're expecting far too much if you believe a piece of glass has magical powers. Is this why you've been so weird lately? Do you want that power?'

'I've not been weird.'

'You've not been yourself. There's been something wrong, strange, almost unworldly about you and I've been a bit worried.'

'Well, there's no need to worry anymore. I'll take care of everything. You'll see. Everything will be alright.'

Even as he spoke, the words seemed to get lost somehow, captured by the trees. It was a strange question to ask. The whole time, he had just been looking down as they walked. It was almost as if he was trying to convince himself that they would be alright. After all, he had brought them along on this escapade with no certainty of knowing what they would find or if everything *would* in fact be alright.

~

Time passed and still they walked, compass in hand. But they would have to stop. Enough distance had been covered for Jack-Jack to start complaining that he was tired. A while back, the thick woods had transformed. Now it was much more open and easier to walk, allowing them to go a bit faster. But even Robbie had to admit he was in need of sitting down for a bit. They chose a spot just underneath a large tree not unlike The General. With their backs to the huge trunk, they relaxed their legs.

'How far do you think we've come so far?'

'Feels like miles,' Mollie said in response to Robbie's question.

'What do you think is happening back there?' He never referred to it as home but it had been the only home he had known for the past year.

'I don't know.'

'Do you think anyone would know it was me?' Not that he cared, not really.

'There's no telling. I still can't believe what happened. It's almost like it's not real. What if someone got hurt?'

Robbie didn't assure her that he didn't think anyone would have been. Instead he asked Mollie his next strange question: 'What has it been like growing up there? You and Jack-Jack aren't even orphans. Were you okay staying at an orphanage all that time?'

Being out in the wilderness was making them behave differently. It was making them talk differently. Suddenly there was more of a maturity about their speech.

'I don't know if I am or not. I was found. I don't know if I'm an orphan or not. I don't even know if I had another name or what it was. The orphanage saved me and it was home. I didn't know anything else. I knew it wasn't a nice place but I didn't feel like I belonged anywhere else.'

Robbie could sense the hurt in her voice and once again was sorry for having asked the question.

'As for Jack-Jack here, he's always just gone with the flow. The only thing he got told was that he had to be given up because of religious reasons.' She leaned over and gave him a hug so as not to seem like she was talking about him as if he wasn't there. The three of them were close, but Mollie and Jack-Jack had always been like brother and sister. They had only ever had each other.

'One day, we'll find a good home to live in. I don't know where, but it'll be different from anything you've known, you'll see.'

Robbie's promise had a coating of doubt. He couldn't be sure of that in their future, but he wanted so much for the two of them to know what it was like to have a loving home. He had lost his; an atrocity of war. What was war but to build empires, all the while destroying homes and lives?

Once on the move again, it was clear just how unpopulated this area was. They hadn't come across anyone or anything that resembled life. Green trees were all that lay ahead. They could have even passed the cabin and not known it. Robbie tried to stay optimistic, at least in his own head.

The terrain had changed. Under foot had become softer and unsteady. Fellowood Marsh got its name for good reason. They had been told of the marshes in the surrounding area; wet and uneven. It had slowed them down considerably. There was no path and up to now, Robbie had been concentrating on making sure the needle of the compass always pointed due east.

Even though they were heading in a straight line, their trek was about to take a turn for the worse. Robbie, who was leading the other two, took a large step over a big rock straight into a muddy bog and his leg sank quickly up to his thigh. He fell off balance, his other leg following the fate of the first and he sank even deeper. The mud ate him up and before he knew what was happening, he was waist deep and could feel himself still sinking. The other two were not far behind but it had happened so fast, neither could do anything to stop it. As the mud sucked down his lower body, he tried grappling at the ground to pull himself free, but it was no use. Mollie, who was following behind, realised and looked up. She saw Robbie sinking fast into the earth and rushed over.

'Robbie!' she shrieked.

He was facing away from her, but managed to shout out a belated cry for help. He knew he was in trouble. The marsh was devouring him like it had just been given its first meal in a long time and wasn't going to let it go to waste. The bag he was wearing didn't help as it was weighing him down. Mollie rushed around the side of him and could see he was in a panic. The attempt at freeing himself had been utterly in vain.

Mollie looked around quickly for a strong looking branch. She could see one that should do the trick over on the ground. She rushed over to fetch it. Meanwhile, Jack-Jack was in tears standing at the side of the camouflaged bog. He didn't know what to do as the mud was now up to Robbie's chest.

Mollie lay down at the edge of the bog and held out the branch. She wasn't sure if it was long enough but, fortunately, it reached him. As long as it didn't break.

'Jack-Jack! Come here. Hold this with me. Quick!'

Still crying, he did as he was told. He lay down next to her and held the branch as Robbie tried desperately to claw his arms out of the sticky mud. He reached out and grabbed the end of the branch and the two of them hauled with all their might to pull him free.

It was gripping him like tar. They heaved and they tugged. At first, it didn't seem like he was going to budge but, eventually, the tug of war between children and earth started to go in their favour. He pulled himself up one hand over the other. The mud was down to his waist again but the wet marsh didn't want to give up. It grabbed his legs, trying to swallow him up as he clambered out to the side of the bog where the other two were. Finally, looking half human - half swamp monster, he was free and resting on the side, no longer being devoured.

It had only taken a matter of moments. He stayed there, all three of them breathing heavily. Jack-Jack clung to Robbie. Robbie put his muddy arm around him and hugged him back. I think now he realised just how close he had come to being eaten up by the marsh. Every footstep now would need to be more carefully trodden.

~

'I'm going back.'

'Back to what? We can't. Don't you see we can't? We have to keep going. That eye is out there somewhere. I..... *we* have to find it.'

After gathering themselves from the side of the bog, and with the mud clinging to Robbie's clothes quickly hardening, the three explorers were now sitting on some large rocks, much like the ones at the waterhole. But this was very different from sitting at the waterhole telling fairy-tale stories; this was no fairy tale. Mollie's statement came from the realisation that they had put themselves in a life-threatening situation. Robbie had survived the bog, but it had been too close a call and there was no telling what other dangerous terrain lay ahead of them. They were not equipped for an expedition like this and if they weren't careful they were going to run out of food stuck out in the middle of nowhere. In Mollie's mind, the need to escape the orphanage had been desperate, but now she was scared.

'Robbie, there's no way of knowing where the cabin is. Head east, that's all we know. That's all we've done. And we don't even know how true that is. It might not even be there and if it is, we can't be certain we can sell the eye to anyone anyway. This is stuff of myths and legends. What are we doing here?' The final words were spoken as her head dropped.

Without responding, all Robbie did was put his arm around her. After a while, despite Mollie's concerns, they decided they had to keep on walking.

The sun beat down hard on them from above, firing streaks of light through the gaps in the trees - a flourishing desert. This sun did nothing to temper the now ongoing complaints coming sporadically from Jack-Jack's mouth. He had not been involved in any discussions about the past nor about any decisions going forward. When he did use his voice it wasn't beneficial. He was young, tired, scared, hungry and confused. He was weighing them down more than the bags each one of them carried.

The dried-up mud on Robbie's clothes was heavy, although, with the sun drying it, fortunately he had managed to peel and scrape some of it off.

In an attempt to divert the talk away from Jack-Jack's protests, Mollie asked Robbie a very personal question, a question that she may never have asked were it not for their predicament: 'Do you miss your parents?'

Robbie didn't look shocked or surprised at this. It was a relevant question for a friend of his who hadn't brought up the subject in all the time that she had known him.

'Yes, I do,' was his immediate answer. 'More than I can probably tell you, Mol. You might see a brave face more often than not but it's pretty painful underneath. They were taken. They didn't leave. They weren't lost. They were simply taken away from me. I didn't have a say in the matter. All I've heard for the past year is God this and God that. Well, He's the one that took them away, so screw Him.'

'Is that why you've been so rebellious since arriving?'

'Maybe. I was never like this when I was at home when everything made sense. I'm not even sure when the last time anything did make sense. It certainly wasn't since the war started.'

'The war was hard on us too at the start. Everything changed. It wasn't too bad before that. You only got to see it at the back end of the war. The whole town didn't know how to deal with the impact it had.'

The two friends talked adult-like for a while on the subject; a chance to clear their minds of what had been plaguing them for so long. Out here in the open, in the wilderness it seemed to get swallowed up by the trees. Relief exonerated.

A few more obstacles had stood in their way during the afternoon. First there was the grass snake that Jack-Jack stood on which frightened him half to death - fortunately, it slithered its thin green body off into the undergrowth before any of them really knew what had happened.

Next there was the stream that was just a little too wide and deep to walk across. The inventive minds of exploring children used a large log to get across it which in the grand scheme of things was actually quite fun.

Then they came across a cave. Of course, Jack-Jack was none too thrilled about this find, having got lost in the last one he was in. There was no time for exploring this one. They simply shouted into it, which threw their own voices back at them. Robbie was at least hoping to disturb some bats but, to his disappointment, the cave looked empty.

The day passed and before long the sun began to set. They had walked and walked but they hadn't gone as far as their young minds had led them to believe. The walking was slow and laborious. It hadn't been easy.

'We are going to have to stop and set up camp,' Robbie said, as he looked up to the trees.

'We don't have anything to set up camp with. I didn't know we were going to be sleeping out here.' Mollie had overlooked the possibility of not finding the cabin and making it to Savannah's Bridge all in one day. Now, looking back, she could see that was an oversight on her part. Would it have changed things back when they were in town? She doubted it, but now it was too late. The day had run out and they would have to sleep out here in the woods.

They laid out the blankets which Robbie had stolen and huddled together, covering themselves with what was left. There was no way of knowing exactly what time it was. The sun had set behind them. It left a glowing sheet of thick orange that dimmed until darkness consumed it. Once it was dark it not only looked dark but it felt dark. It closed in all around them as if the trees were trying to huddle up to them to keep them warm. Fortunately, it was still the back end of summer so the temperature was still relatively warm. There was no wind either so the trees stood very still, as if trying not to disturb them.

Jack-Jack lay close up to Mollie. 'W..w..will there be any c..c..creatures at night?'

He was evidently frightened. The darkness was one thing in a big sleep hall or in a secluded room, but out here it was altogether more scary.

'They won't bother us,' was Mollie's answer. But she didn't sound convincing, even to herself.

'We'll be fine. Just stay close to each other and shut your eyes. We'll keep each other warm and fall asleep pretty soon 'cause we're so tired from walking.' Robbie had heard of the need to huddle up tight so as to share body warmth and it was working. He wasn't cold but the reality of being out here in the dead of night was making him feel vulnerable.

A child's mind is a fickle thing. It is a plaything for the subconscious. It has the ability to tease and mock for its own amusement. As the calls of numerous owls and the scuttling creatures in the undergrowth became louder, it didn't take long for phantom thoughts to creep in. Shadows became alive and rustling leaves echoed with merciless amplification. The woods were a vision of beauty during the day but became unforgiving at night.

~

As exhaustion enveloped them, each one gave way to the phenomenon of hallucination:

Robbie, in his half-awake, half-asleep state, saw his parents walking towards him through the trees, assuring him they were okay and everything was alright - to be strong for his young companions.

Mollie saw visions of Sister Meredith wielding the pair of scissors that now looked bigger than they did when they were ravishing her cascading, jet-black hair and sending it floating to the floor, never to be attached to her again.

And Jack-Jack saw *him*. Once again, a silhouette in an already darkened wood with his back to him. He was standing alone, barefoot in the soil and leaves, this time with no sticky door to be pushed open. Old man Joe was out here in the open. They had found him. But he wasn't dead.

Jack-Jack waited for the inevitable turning of the head, waiting to be stared at by the bright burning eye. But it didn't happen. He didn't turn his head. Instead, he walked off into the dense black trees as they opened up before closing in like a curtain. Then he was gone, leaving Jack-Jack standing alone in the woods; no silhouette, no Robbie, no Mollie. Nothing.

His feet burned with the coldness of the earthy floor. Then he fell to the ground in a cloud of ash, burned from the inside out.

That's when he jolted awake, making the other two jump. It was still dark, but Old man Joe was nowhere to be seen. The curtain of trees had taken him away, at least for now.

As they all tried to get back to some form of sleep, Robbie looked out once again to the dead of the night with only the abundance of glistening stars to watch over them. He had only one thought left before sleep reluctantly took him: *had they indeed gone too far and missed the cabin?*

My Responsibility

Is looking back the same as hindsight? It is quite clearly not, but sometimes it feels that way. In hindsight, my decision to take Mollie and Jack-Jack along on this excursion was a selfish act on my part. Looking back, of course I wish I hadn't. If it had not been for Sister Meredith's despicable and callous act, I may have gone by myself and come back later for them. But like I have mentioned before, I don't have any reservations about how I may come across to you during this story, the telling of which is not intended to put me in a good light.

Many times in my life I have been focused on the wrong thing. At this particular point, of course, it was the glass eye. I was captivated by the stories, the tales and the men who had supposedly gone in search of a prize, a treasure, dare I say a relic?

I had listened to Sister Athena and Virgil tell of Billy the handyman and how he had been good to the boy with the stutter, whom many later saw as his sidekick. I had listened to how many thought he had gone in search of Old man Joe's glass eye and never returned. He had been a simple soul however, which I took to meaning that anything could have happened to him. Most blamed the curse of the eye, but at the time I didn't buy into it.

I had listened to the countless warnings of Sister Athena, telling me time and time again to forget about it and how it was nothing but pure evil and to stay away. Of course, she was talking from a particular bias. Whatever her bias, I never wanted to go against her or disobey her in any way. Deep down she was a friend, a confidante. But this was different. This wasn't about being disrespectful or about friendship.

My only concern was getting my hands on that unattainable treasure, and on more than one occasion, reality would slap me in the face of the danger I had put not only myself in, but Mollie and Jack-Jack too. I cared for them like siblings. And like siblings, sometimes you don't always do what's best for them. Sometimes siblings follow the oldest and learn from his bad examples. Mollie was much too switched on for that, well, most of the time anyway. As for Jack-Jack, he was more like a lost sheep trying to find his way in the field. It was quite easy to pity him, which I always tried not to do. He didn't deserve that. Not from me or anyone else. He was much stronger than most people gave him credit for. I could see that in him, I just needed him to see it too.

I'm not going to lie and say I was confident or comfortable with our predicament at that particular time. I'd much rather say I was apprehensive. But the truth is I was scared out of my wits. I didn't have any clue what was going to happen to us. Leaving town didn't seem like that big of a deal, which I know must sound strange after the explosion I had caused. But because we were still there it felt like we were safe. I suppose it's similar to leaving the shore on a small boat, venturing into the big wide ocean, paddling frantically with the oars, trying to break the crest of the waves as they do their best to push you back to shore – the water's way of telling you to go back, it's not safe out here. But we broke the waves easily and found ourselves out in the big wide ocean.

An ocean of trees.

How I longed for a couple of paddles.

Chapter XXIX

"Show me your hidden skeletons and I will show you closets hidden by my monsters."
Efrat Cybulkiewicz

The morning sun did its best to rouse up the young explorers. They were sleep deprived and disorientated. They hadn't managed to get any real sleep, only the inevitable slumber that exhaustion had thrust upon them. It had been colder than they had anticipated. The three of them had huddled up as close as they could and joined in a game of synchronised shivering. Now it was time to try and get up and continue on with their journey.

The strangest of things happened between Robbie and Mollie. The tide had turned overnight in the realm of opinion. Before eventually falling asleep, Robbie had stared up at the stars watching them shine and twinkle above him, peeking at them through the trees. His mind had turned over and over and betrayed him. He had thought about all the superstition they had left behind. What if it was all nothing but people gone mad making something out of nothing? What if Old man Joe never even lived in a cabin? What if it wasn't there at all and they were hunting around in this wilderness for nothing? The word "nothing" bothered him. It was a word that had painted itself on his mind and now it was safe to say he was having doubts.

Mollie on the other hand went the other way. She had managed to sleep enough to have a dream or two, albeit short ones. Her dreams had filled her with hope of someday living in a big open house and to be cared for. She had dreamed it so vividly it was almost as real as the cold, damp ground she was waking up on.

Reality.

The birds were shouting at them to get started. It was alright for them, they were used to this and had feathers to keep them warm. There was no way they were going to let the children sleep in.

They all stirred at the same time, an unspoken acknowledgment that they needed to stand up and brush themselves down. Eventually they were ready to set off.

Robbie looked at his dirty clothes. 'This damn mud is incredibly uncomfortable. Look at it. It looks like I've slept in a pigsty all night.'

'It's almost all off now,' said Mollie.

'But it's still made my clothes all hard and feels strange.'

'Well, that's what happens when you sink into a bog.' It sounded like she was trying to be funny but he knew she didn't mean to be.

'Oh, what are we doing out here, Mol?'

'What do you mean?'

'This. This whole thing. What happened back in town. Where we are now. What if it's all for nothing?' There was that word again.

'But this was your plan. This was.....'

'I know it was,' he cut her off. 'I had it all figured out: the explosion, finding the eye, selling it. I have to admit I don't know what happens after that, but I just figured we would be okay and find somewhere to go, to live. Anywhere.'

'Well, maybe we will.'

'But I've brought you out here on this mission and we don't know anything about Old man Joe really, do we? Old tales from crazy people, that's all it is. The story could be true….. but the curse? I'm thinking maybe we should go back after all.'

'Regardless of what is real or not, we are going to find what we're looking for and get far away from here. You'll see, everything will be fine. We have to keep going. We've come too far. You said it yourself.'

Mollie was right. The voice of reason had struck again. Robbie just needed a vote of confidence. He knew in his heart that he wanted to carry on. And he knew that they would. They had to stick together and be strong for one another.

~

Just like the day before, they packed up their bags and set off walking. How strange that no-one knew they were here. Alone in a sea of green.

They were just starting to lose hope when it happened.

It was during a steady climb up an incline. The woods seemed to get denser for a moment, but there didn't seem to be a way around the mound. It inclined like a wave in the sea of green. Climbing up was not easy. It was slippery underfoot and they were carrying a bag each. With the help of some protruding branches and small trees to act as leverage, they eventually made it to the top where a surreal sight awaited them.

Almost at the same time, all three of them straightened their backs at the top of the mound and stared straight ahead at what looked like a mirage. But they couldn't all be seeing it at the same time. On the contrary, this was about as real as it got.

If it wasn't for it standing directly in front of them, they could have been forgiven for not seeing it at all. It looked like it had been purposely hidden, camouflaged in the thicket, decisively positioned amongst the trees.

The cabin.

Moss and ivy stretched itself around it like a parcel ready for shipping. Tree branches bound it together and sheltered it from above. Decay swamped it. Time had not been a friend to the elusive cabin but here it was; not a myth, not a legend anymore – but real. To Robbie, it was the most beautiful thing he had ever seen. It was vindication and validation all rolled into one. He had led them to it. They hadn't missed it or gone past it.

'Robbie,' Mollie let out the faintest of whispers.

'I know.' That was it. That was all he could muster. His mouth wasn't working but his heart was. In fact, it was working harder than it ever had. Thumping in his chest, he took a step towards it, then another. He wanted to touch it to make sure it was real.

It was real enough. Mollie and Jack-Jack followed his steps. They walked up to the cabin. It was a picture of beautiful decadence.

At first, there was no way of telling where the entrance was as the immense amount of foliage was so thick and overgrown. Robbie dug his hands in and pulled it apart. It was tough but he managed to reveal the wood hiding beneath. It was dark and looked like it was built to last. Mollie did the same, trying to pull apart some of the twigs and branches while Jack-Jack just stood and watched. This did not feel like it was his job to do.

They circled the cabin, stepping over yet more branches before meeting up around the other side. That's where they found the door. It was covered and impossible to open. Some gardening would need to be done.

They set to it. Bare hands ripped and tugged at whatever they could get their hands on. Eventually there was enough of the door to see and get through.

Robbie tried the big black latch that was the handle but it was no good. It didn't open.

'God knows when this thing was last opened. It's jammed all right. We need to clear more of this stuff,' which was exactly what they did.

With a few more handfuls, they made a clearing at the bottom of the door where some of the wood had been eaten away and damaged. There was just enough room to get a few sets of young hands around. Both of them pulled and pulled. It gave way and opened just wide enough to get a child's body through.

Robbie looked at the prised opening. 'Who's going in first then?'

Mollie looked at him. 'Well, I'm not. It looks dark in there.'

'Of course it's dark in there,' he said as he crouched down and slid his body through the gap.

Then he was gone.

Mollie was next, followed by Jack-Jack.

They were confronted by the second surreal sight.

~

It smelled of damp. It smelled of death.

It was completely silent, even the birds seem to have left this place for dead.

The cobweb-laden cabin looked like something out of a derelict museum. The sun shone through the many gaps in the broken roof, streaking the inside. Ivy had penetrated the walls and had climbed up to the ceiling to spread itself out. A fireplace stood to their right with a half-used bucket of coal and an axe that lay on the hearth. Next to that was a small table with two chairs that stood under a small, dirty window. The table still had cups and plates on top of it which were covered in dust and cobwebs. Next to that, along the right wall was a chest of drawers with a fishing rod propped up against it. To their left was a small cot bed and another against the far wall.

Only one of the beds was empty.

It was the bed against the far wall that all six eyes were focused on. Nothing else in the room mattered. The unmistakable shape of a body looked to be lying on its back, covered by a dirty old grey-coloured sheet or blanket.

Mollie and Jack-Jack both gripped Robbie's arms.

'That must be him. That's Old man Joe. We've found him.' The words didn't exactly come out right, he was so nervous.

The other two didn't say anything. They just kept their eyes pinned on the motionless shape, not more than a few feet away from them.

Mollie and Jack-Jack released their grip on Robbie and stayed where they were as he walked towards the bed. He stood over the body and reached one trembling hand out to the edge of the blanket. He held it and peeled it back. From head to toe, the shape turned into a skeleton as the blanket was pulled away.

It lay there, head tilted back with its jaw open, teeth on show. It was clutching a large red book across its chest. A rusted gold medallion was held by one of the skeleton's hands which rested on the book.

It was an overwhelming sight to behold for such young eyes, each of them knowing they weren't quite taking it all in. Robbie was, however, focused on one thing. He looked at the eye sockets of the skeleton, but there was no glass eye, not even a dusty one. Then his mind told him, if Old man Joe's body had decayed around the glass eye, there would be nothing to hold it in place. Of course, it would have dropped into his skull. He leaned cautiously forward and peered into the dark cavities but saw nothing. Disappointment embraced him.

'It's not here,' he announced to the others. 'Nothing, no glass eye.'

'What about what he's holding? The book.' The most she could manage was a whisper, as if anything louder would awaken the sleeping bones.

Robbie's disappointed eyes shifted to the dusty red book, held tightly by the arms of bones. He took hold of one of them and carefully, picked it up with his fingers and slid the book out. To say how long it had most probably been there, it came out surprisingly easily. He held it in his hands and looked at it. It was old and frail. The once white pages looked yellow from the outside and age had made the corners a mouldy black. He ran his hand over the front cover to expel the dust. A light cloud formed around him before attempting to settle by his feet.

There was a string hanging out of the bottom between some of the pages.

He opened it.

The bookmarked string had clearly signified the last entry to what looked like some sort of diary. Robbie read aloud from the beginning of the entry:

I hesitate to write this but I feel as though I must.

This final excerpt in my diary should be viewed as the confession I have held within me for far too long. The rest of the diary will describe what I am ashamed to know and even more ashamed to have done nothing about. I have left it here to reveal the truth that has plagued my heart with a bitter taste; the written words that I was unable to speak.

If someone is reading this, you have found my son, Billy.
When I was banished from the nearby town of Fellowood Marsh because of a curse that was put upon me, I came here, to this cabin. I was forced out of town but not before taking the one thing left dear to me – my son. He was just a young boy at the time. His mother had died a year before and I was all he had. I took him with me.

I brought him here to this - the only place I knew of that would most likely be vacant. And it was.

We lived here together, but not well. I couldn't go back and I knew word would have spread about me. I wasn't welcome anywhere. So we tried to live off the land which was difficult and, as Billy grew, he became – different. I am to blame for that. He lived out here with no-one, with nothing. It became apparent to me that Billy didn't act right, or think right.

The biggest mistake I could have made was persuading him to go and find a job in town. However, if he was to do so, I made it clear to him that he was never to mention anything about me or where we were. I wasn't sure he understood and had to convince myself that this was a good idea for him. I thought it might give him some normality and some purpose.

The only thing he managed to get was to be some sort of handyman at the orphanage. At first I was overjoyed, but it was short-lived. He turned bad and, once it started, there was nothing I could do to stop it.

I saw it.

I may only have one good eye but I saw what he was doing, in a manner of speaking.

He was abusing some of the boys, one in particular. He would come home sometimes with their toys that he had stolen. He told me about places in the orphanage where he stored some of them instead of bringing them home. He would tell me many other things, most of which I will not write here. These I will take to my grave with me.

He seemed to enjoy it, and he seemed to enjoy telling me about it, in his manner of broken words. He didn't realise how much I detested hearing about it and how much I had grown to detest him.

I could and should have done something, but I didn't. This is why this is more than a diary. It is a revelation of my cowardice. I created all this from the start. None of it would have happened if it wasn't for me bringing him here to grow up in total seclusion, without any human contact. I should have found some other way, but I didn't.

The last straw was when he came home with the pendant. I have left it here along with my diary.

He stole it from the boy who, in his words, "followed him around". In my words, he made him his slave. I would hear how he would treat this boy and pick on him because he was the weakest. I believe he had a speech impediment, a stutter or something. Billy would sometimes mimic him, which would make me sick to my stomach.

When he came home with the pendant, he told how he had been looking for it for so long. He knew it was the pendant the boy's mother had left with him when she abandoned him at the orphanage as a baby. It was very dear to him and that made Billy want it all the more.

I was scared of Billy, that I admit, but my cowardice would come to an end tonight.

I picked up the axe and drove it into the back of Billy's skull when he had his back to me. He didn't die instantly. He tried saying something to me but I couldn't make out what it was. I think I'm better off not knowing.

I dragged him with all my might onto the bed and covered him over before leaving him with my diary and the pendant. How long he will stay here, I do not know.

It does not exonerate me for what I did and what Billy became, but it stopped the abuse of those poor boys. I am too ashamed and have to leave.

Where I will go, I'm not quite sure.

I have nothing else to write.

Robbie closed the book.

He set it down on the bed behind him before going to the head of the occupied bed. He slid his hand carefully under the skull and leant over to take a look. Sure enough there it was: a perfectly penetrated slit right down the middle. He just had to be sure.

Robbie then took the pendant off what he now knew to be Billy's fingers.

It was gold and aged. He opened it and read out loud the inscription inside:

"To my Fletcher. As long as you keep this, I will be with you. Your loving mother."

Chapter XXX

**"What is lost is returned to me,
what is far away is near me today."**
Patrizia Cavalli

The haunting atmosphere encircled the room, pinching their cheeks as it floated by. The sun was beaming through the broken planks of wood but it felt colder than when they first entered. Jack-Jack sheltered next to Mollie, clinging on to her as he had done while Robbie read from the diary. The mould-eaten confession lay on the empty bed, having thoroughly done its job. Robbie stood gripping the pendant, the chain dangling from his hand. And Billy..... Billy lay still in front of all three of them, his fleshless bones sleeping peacefully after his identity had been revealed.

Fletcher.

Robbie couldn't quite believe it. As he'd read out the inscription, the words had come out in a kind of wobble. So the boy with the stutter who helped Billy around the orphanage all those years ago was Fletcher. And he wasn't helping him, he was being abused by him. Fletcher had lived in the orphanage as well. His mother had evidently left him there with the pendant as a trinket to remember her by. When everyone thought Billy had gone looking for the glass eye and not returned, it wasn't true. He hadn't gone looking for it at all. This was where he had lived with Old man Joe all that time, working at the orphanage.

And Old man Joe had killed him.

'Robbie, what do we do?' Mollie said finally.

Instead of answering her, Robbie took the edges of the blanket and covered Billy back over. He grabbed the diary and, still holding the pendant, went back outside through the small gap. The other two followed him. All three sat on the ground next to their bags.

'We have to go back. We have to give the pendant back to Fletcher,' Robbie said.

'Go back? We can't. Not after.....'

'We have to. The glass eye isn't here anyway. It was Billy all along, not Old man Joe. Don't you see? Now that we know the truth of what has happened, we have to return this to Fletcher. Billy stole it from him when he was a child. His mother left it with him when she left him at the orphanage.' He was looking down at it, examining it with his fingers. The diary set down next to them. Disappointment turned into purpose.

'Will we make it back today? What's it going to be like when we get there?'

'I don't know. It's only been a day. Everything will still be in uproar, I guess. But I don't care. We have to get this back to him.'

Mollie looked at Robbie. He had a saddened look on his face now. She wasn't sure if it was the grim reality that they had recently learned or that the glass eye wasn't here after all. The pendant's return seemed to have replaced the importance of Old man Joe's eye.

'We'd better go then before we lose any more time.'

She was right. They didn't want to spend another night in the woods. Robbie packed the diary into his now almost empty bag. Food and drink were very low and he knew it. He had not managed to scavenge as much as was needed from the kitchen. It would have to suffice the journey back.

They set off, leaving the cabin with Billy inside, minus one diary and one pendant that he had been holding on to all these years.

As it was, the journey back was arduous but faster than anticipated. By the time they reached town they were very tired, very hungry and very thirsty, but their determination had carried them over every step of the way back.

Upon their return around dusk that very same day, their bodies felt beaten and their joints were aching. Their faces were dirty, as were their clothes - Robbie's in particular from the bog incident.

Finding their way back to town should have been easier, retracing their steps, but there were no steps to retrace. However, they had the compass to rely on which proved invaluable.

They came to the edge of the trees, almost exactly where they had fled after the explosion, which was pretty much the first thing they saw. As it turned out, the dynamite had not done as much damage as Robbie had anticipated: the whole corner of the orphanage was destroyed, but the rest looked to be intact. The town looked lively but for what reason they didn't know. More people than usual appeared to be gathered in the middle of the street and a fair amount of commotion was occurring.

Exhausted, Mollie said, 'Well, here we are.' She was inwardly more relieved than she let on.

'Come on, let's go. It'll be fine,' Robbie tried to assure her, unconvincingly.

They walked towards the crowd, bags on shoulders, looking like drifters who had had a bad time of it. As they approached, one person, then the next, turned to look at them. In a few seconds the entire group of people had stopped what they were doing and were staring at them.

Town-folk.

~

Numerous sets of eyes stared them down but were they concerned eyes or suspicious eyes? No-one had known at the time that Robbie had been the one to cause the explosion and no-one knew where they had been. They were about to get quizzed and Councillor Grayson would be the quizmaster.

'Children,' he said as he pushed through the crowd. 'What is the meaning of this? Look at the frightful state of you. Were you part of the orphanage?'

The fact that he didn't know showed how little he paid attention to the town's underprivileged residents. Robbie nodded.

'Goodness me. Well, where have you been?'

'We ran after the explosion. Into the woods. We ran and ran and didn't look back. Before we knew it we were lost. We've only just found our way back.' Robbie had to think quickly. The lie came out like water from a tap. It didn't seem plausible that they would be lost all day and night but the Councillor appeared to accept it.

'Heavens. All the other children have left for another orphanage and I'm afraid there is no more room. It's all happened so fast. I was sure we had accounted for everyone. If you ran in such a hurry, why do you have these bags with you? What are you up to?'

The bags. Of course.

Councillor Grayson took the one off Robbie's shoulder and rifled through it as Robbie told another lie: 'We found them in the woods by an abandoned campfire. They had a bit of food in them..... and a diary.'

He said this as the Councillor took the diary out of the bag and opened it. He didn't hold it open long enough to read anything from it and with his interest flagging, put it back.

'Yes well, I don't know anything about all that. But I don't know what we're going to do with you. There is just nowhere else to put three more children.'

'I'll take them!'

The deep voice came from somewhere in the middle of the crowd. It was a familiar voice to the three of them, a friendly one. It was Virgil. He pushed his way to the front of the wall of people.

'You, Virgil? Will take these three unfortunate orphans into your home?'

'I have that big old house all to myself. It's empty and could do with a bit of youth to bring it back to life.'

This was an easy escape for the Councillor and without even conferring with the children, granted Virgil's wish. Not that it mattered. All of them would have accepted had they been asked.

'Then it's settled. I can't for the life of me think why Virgil, but you have your wish. The children can stay with you and we can get back to sorting out this mess. What made that explosion is beyond me. I always said that orphanage was too old. There must have been a leak in the pipes or something. We'll never know. Come along then. Virgil, take these children to your place and have them cleaned up. They're your responsibility now and I won't have them walking around my town looking like that.'

They went with Virgil to his workshop of a house, Robbie clutching onto his bag containing Old man Joe's diary and Fletcher's pendant.

Fletcher had not been part of the so-called welcoming committee.

Usually they would sit on Virgil's porch with him and Robbie would bat stones around with one of his sticks as they talked about goings-on in the town, but now they were to live here. Mollie recalled a conversation they had earlier on in the summer about them wanting to live in a big house like this one day. She even picked out her room. Now this was to be their house.

'What happened to the nuns, Virgil?' Robbie asked as they walked up the porch steps.

'I saw them get shipped off in a wagon. Odd sight it was. I heard something about them going and being housed at various establishments away somewhere. Truth of the matter is, I don't rightly know but I think they'll be split up and put where they're needed.'

Robbie was glad to hear they would be split up. Maybe that way their evil gang wouldn't be so strong. Take away the queen bee and the rest will die.

However, there was one exception. Mollie was the first to raise the question. 'Virgil, do you know what happened to Sister Athena? She was always very kind to all of us.'

'That's true, Virgil,' Robbie chimed in. 'She's the one who deserves something better than being shipped off with the rest of them.'

'I don't rightly know,' replied Virgil. 'We will have to ask around tomorrow.' And with that, the three of them followed Virgil into their new home.

The house had four rooms upstairs, most of which were cluttered. There was a bed in all but one. Some work would be needed in order to get the place into a decent enough state to occupy three new, young guests but they didn't mind. The prospect of it seemed quite exciting.

Mollie went into the room she had picked from outside and looked out of the window. This particular room had the mark of a feminine touch. It was dusty and felt like it hadn't been lived in for many years. She sat on the bed - it was twice the size of the one she had in the orphanage.

'This was my parents' room, back in the day,' Virgil said as he stood in the doorframe. 'I decided not to put anything in here or change it too much. Sorry it's not the cleanest it's ever been, I wasn't expecting to invite three children to live with me today.'

'It's lovely, Virgil, really.'

'I'd like you to have it. It's not been lived in for so long. I think you could make it very homely in here.'

Mollie looked around her – her own room.

After Robbie and Jack-Jack had cleaned themselves up a bit and decided on sharing a room until they could get something better sorted out, Robbie saw Drayton out of his window walking past the front porch. He quickly went downstairs.

'Drayton.'

'Somebody said you were back, I didn't know where though.'

'We're going to live here.'

'And you're okay with that? I thought you wanted to get out of this place.'

'I wanted to get out of *that* place,' he nodded in the direction of the wounded orphanage. 'Fellowood Marsh isn't the most ideal town but Virgil's a good guy and we didn't have anything else. Can you keep a secret?'

'I haven't told anyone about the dynamite,' as if proving his worth. 'It's been kinda nice having a secret that no-one else knows.'

'The real reason we left was to go and look for Old man Joe's cabin and find his eye.'

'You did what?'

'But he wasn't there. We found the skeleton of Billy who used to be the handyman at the orphanage. Turns out he was Old man Joe's son.'

Drayton took it in. 'So, where's Old man Joe?'

'Don't know. Looks like he killed Billy and then left.'

'Wow, this place just keeps getting weirder. Regardless, I'm glad you're back.'

'I am too. Relieved anyway. I'm not sure I know what I was thinking going out there. I put the other two in danger.'

'Don't worry about it. Hey, once you're settled in, we'll go do a bit of fishing.'

Fishing sounded pretty good right now but it would have to wait.

~

The next errand was one for all three of them to carry out.

Fletcher's house looked as solemn as ever. He was in the garden tending to his beloved roses – trying to recover what he could – when the children walked around the side of the house.

He was surprised to see them. He stood up. What impact had almost being hanged had on him?

Both sides were apprehensive. Standing there, suddenly, Robbie felt inadequate. He didn't know what to say, but he knew he had to say something.

'Fletcher. We have something for you.'

To his surprise, Fletcher walked towards them, taking off his gloves. Robbie held out his hand and produced the rusted gold pendant. Fletcher looked at it. He stared at it as his past stared back at him. He dropped to his knees, took it from Robbie's hand and opened it. For the second time, Robbie saw the inscription. Then he saw the look on Fletcher's face. It was a look of contentment.

'Th.....thank.....you.'

This was the first time they had heard him speak. His voice was coarse and his stutter evident.

Robbie smiled. 'You're welcome.'

Inside, Fletcher's house was not at all what they had imagined. It was clean, tidy, some would say immaculate. Not a thing was out of place. It looked as though he never lived in there. Maybe there was some truth in that. He loved his garden too much.

Fletcher still held on to the open pendant he hadn't seen since Billy stole it from him when he was just a child, hidden under the bed with his blanket. He asked where they had found it. Robbie proceeded to tell him the entire tale of their short journey to the cabin, sleeping under the stars, almost drowning in the marsh and eventually finding his tormentor's bones holding onto his mother's gift.

He listened like a little child being told a fairy tale. It was obvious he was having a hard time comprehending everything Robbie was saying, but he continued to tell him about Old man Joe and the diary; how it revealed everything about Billy and what Old man Joe "saw" Billy do over the years, admitting that he hadn't read anything apart from the final entry.

'What should we do? Do we tell someone about the cabin? About Billy and Old man Joe?'

Fletcher thought for a moment. 'N.....no.' His stutter was stronger than Jack-Jack's. This was the first time Jack-Jack had heard anybody other than him speak with one. Here was the grown form of the boy that Sister Athena had told him about.

'If.....anyone.....w.....wants to f.....find him, they'll h.....have to f.....find him themselves.'

Robbie thought hard about whether to tell Fletcher about the hidden treasure they had found in the orphanage attic. Maybe some things were better left buried with their memories.

He placed the diary on the side next to Fletcher. 'This should stay here with you, even if you don't ever open it.'

Fletcher looked at it and thanked Robbie with his eyes before Robbie ushered the other two to the door. It was time to leave. No more words needed to be exchanged. The pendant had been returned to its rightful owner.

They would see him around, hopefully more often, and maybe even have a chat every now and then. For now, they parted ways.

~

As he had promised, Virgil asked a number of towns-people if they had seen or heard what had happened to Sister Athena. Some speculated that she had been sent away to another orphanage with the other nuns, but Robbie didn't think so. Others suggested that she had travelled to Savannah's Bridge, but the truth was, nobody knew.

Life carried on with relative normality in Fellowood Marsh after that.

The three children settled in with Virgil with surprising ease.

The whole town had a new feel to it. It was as though the dark cloud had disappeared now that the orphanage wasn't in operation – like it had had a sinister hold on the whole town the entire time. The ruin still stood at the head of the street – the porridge walls now providing a hollow emptiness.

Over a short period of time, Virgil and Jack-Jack became really close. Virgil was becoming the father figure that Jack-Jack had never had. He taught him to whittle; something Jack-Jack was becoming really good at and, in turn, Virgil willingly took fishing lessons.

On a crisp morning one weekend, as Robbie was sitting out on the porch, Virgil came out to sit with him.

'Bright morning this morning.'

'Going to be a nice day, I reckon.'

'Good for tree climbing or going on adventures?'

'I think I'll lay off the adventures for a while.'

'And the tree climbing?'

'Oh no, tree climbing will still get done.' He smiled as the sun shone down on the white planks of the porch. Just then, he pictured himself being as high as he'd ever gone up The General. That might be something that would be challenged later on in the day.

A few silent moments passed before Virgil opened his mouth again.

'Since you got here, Robbie, there's something I've been meaning to ask you.' Robbie looked up. 'What do you think it was that you hit when you dug into Fletcher's back garden?'

Robbie was stunned. How did he.....?

'I was the one who spooked you that night. I could hear something going on when everyone was supposed to be indoors. I thought I'd check it out. I saw you digging and was going to come over to you but you heard me and ran off into the trees. I couldn't call out to you in case I alerted someone.'

Robbie felt pretty stupid. He hadn't known who it had been but had been sure he'd got away without anyone knowing it was him. But Virgil had known all this time.

'I'm sorry, Virgil. I just wanted to help.'

'That's okay, my boy. I'm not here to scold.'

Robbie was glad to hear it but still felt embarrassed.

'So, you didn't answer my question. I heard and saw you hit something in the ground there at the back edge of Fletcher's garden. What do you think it was?'

'I don't know. I guess I'll never know. Maybe it wasn't anything at all, just a big rock or something.'

'Didn't sound like a rock.'

They both sat there a good while before either of them moved or said another word. It was true, maybe Robbie would never know what it was - if it was anything at all - still buried over there at the back of Fletcher's garden.

Fletcher - at least he had his pendant back. He was glad of that much. The whole experience had taught him one valuable lesson: never judge a book by its cover for the cover will almost certainly prove you wrong.

It had been a strange experience. It had been a strange year; the year that a storm revealed a hidden treasure, the year of the boy and the body.

My Gift

I did not know I had the capability to blow anything up with dynamite, let alone attempt the destruction of an entire building. As it happened, I did not succeed. The building was only partially damaged but it was enough to never be used again. It stood as a ruin for many years, decaying from the inside out. I watched from down the street as I grew up; a painful reminder of my short time there.

As I suspected I would, I thought about Sister Meredith and her bandits of intolerable cruelty on many an occasion. I wondered where she had ended up and if she ever got the comeuppance she so rightly deserved. This is one loose end I cannot tie for you. As for the superhero to her villainy, I thought about Sister Athena too. Wherever she was and whatever she was doing, I knew that she would be okay because she was strong enough.

I also did not know I had it in me to go on a hunting adventure in search of a superstition. My mind got so fixated after everything that had happened that year, it just seemed to manifest at every opportunity. Unveiling a skeleton was not something that was on my list to do before I reached adulthood.

I am not with you for very much longer and I want to thank you for lending me your time. Before I leave you, I want to take you some years down the line.

We had a very decent upbringing from the moment we resided with Virgil and also had to attend the schoolhouse. Now that we were not tainted with being from the orphanage, we were accepted and fitted in surprisingly well. However, we were in separate classes and, at Virgil's, we had our own rooms, so inevitably, we were not as close as before.

Mollie and I eventually grew up. We both moved far away and I don't see her very often.

Jack-Jack, on the other hand, became Virgil's right-hand man. He stayed with him as Virgil got older and looked after him. He had found a purpose in life and did a good job. He continued to carry on Virgil's craft and became quite the whittler; adding to the already extensive museum that I got so accustomed to living amongst.

After leaving the town, the three of us sort of drifted apart and got on with our own lives. Yes, we were like family when we were children. We were there for each other during a torrid time but, like a lot of families, eventually you part ways and grow apart. That's exactly what happened to us.

Virgil died on a cold, autumn Thursday morning.

Although I had stayed in touch with Virgil and Jack-Jack, writing to them occasionally, it would be my first time returning to Fellowood Marsh for Virgil's funeral.

The day of the funeral was a far from pleasant one and not just in mood but in climate too. The clouds were plentiful and they were angry – waiting to unleash their misery upon the congregation when the timing was right. It's funny how the darkness of bad weather seems to seek out the darkness of a funeral - as if it thinks if it rains it will somehow mask the tears of the mourners.

Virgil was to be buried in the cemetery of the local church, adding to the names carved in stone that Mollie and I had so flippantly darted around after we created our game of seek out the oldest date we could find; Virgil's would become the newest, at least for a while. In truth, there wasn't much room for many more neighbours.

I had decided not to attend the whole service. I had waited outside until the procession made its way to the cemetery. I stood a good distance away. I don't know why. Maybe it was my way of keeping the sorrow at a good arm's length. Maybe I was a coward and couldn't face saying goodbye. Maybe I didn't fancy being the proverbial shoulder for Mollie's tears to run down; I had seen her but only briefly and hadn't gone to say hello. I'm not even sure if she knew I was there.

We all have our own way of coping in these situations.

The rain wasn't heavy. It pattered down gently on the black coats, hats and umbrellas, making them glisten. I didn't bring an umbrella and I certainly wasn't interested in sharing. The rain could fall all it liked on my face but it wasn't to mask any tears - they would fall from the inside.

I watched the proceedings. I watched him be lowered into earth's final mouth. I watched Jack-Jack stand on the edge of the hole and thought at any moment he would cast himself in there too. He looked sad and I felt bad for him. He had grown into a very handsome, robust man. He stood alone as I did. But I would not be alone for long.

As I watched with only the sound of rain for accompaniment, a figure joined me. He appeared out of nowhere and stood next to me as we then both watched.

'Hello again.....R.....Robbie.'

Fletcher.

I didn't even need to turn, the stutter was so distinctive. But I did have a slight glance towards him in a faint way of acknowledging his greeting. He looked a lot older - not that everyone doesn't when stood at a funeral in the pouring rain. The new lines on his face drew a picture of so many words.

'Hello, Fletcher. It's been a long time. What are you doing here?'

'I w.....wouldn't miss it for the.....world.'

It wasn't going to be a long conversation. We spoke relatively quietly, for what reason I'm not sure because we were far enough away that no-one would hear anyway.

Fletcher continued the somewhat muted dialogue, 'He was.....a good m.....man.'

'He was. Thank you.'

'I was.....hoping to see you.....h.....here.'

This time, I did look at him.

'You d.....didn't find the glass eye. D.....did you?'

Fletcher's words froze my already cold heart. I didn't need to reply. The question was said rhetorically. I could tell he already knew my answer. I didn't know what to make of the strange statement. How had he known? And what was he saying that for? Had he just come back to mock me?

There was no need to wait for an answer that wasn't coming. Like memorising a well-rehearsed play, he continued, 'You.....r.....returned something v.....very dear to me. I.....wanted to r.....repay the gesture.'

He took out a small wooden box from his coat pocket. Surprisingly, it wasn't dry. He handed it to me from the side without turning.

I took it and looked down, examining the tiny box. There was nothing to it – just an old, wet box.

When I looked back up, Fletcher was already walking away from me and away from the funeral. No stuttered goodbye, no nothing. Just a small gift I now held in my hands.

I watched him leave.

I recalled a rhyme that I remembered Virgil saying to us when we saw Fletcher walking past the house. In a bereft voice, I said it to myself:

'There he goes - the rogue that bears the name..... Fletcher Mane.'

A man pitied by some, feared by others, misunderstood by most.

Once of out sight, my attention returned to the box.
I opened it.
Inside sat a small glass eye looking straight up at me – boring into my soul.

1901

(Eighteen years prior to Robbie's dig)

I know who the man is sitting in front of me, slumped over my table with his hands reaching out in search of one last strand of help.

I think he's dead.

Actually, I know he's dead. When someone dies right in front of you, you just know; no need to check for signs of extinguished life.

It's quite late. He had stumbled through my back door and given me the shock of my life. I had helped him into the chair he sits in now. He was very confused; kept chuntering on about how he saw it all. He said that even though he only had one good eye, he saw it all and how he was sorry. I didn't know what he was talking about.

The man looks very old and frail. I don't know where he's been at this hour or what he was doing wandering around in his condition, but it's obviously finished him off. I offered him a glass of water but he declined. He did most of the talking, I just listened. I prefer it that way anyway due to my infernal stutter. Funny how I don't stutter in my thoughts. It's only when my thoughts turn to words.

He had collapsed, arms spread out in front of him. It was a bit horrible to watch. Now, I'm just looking at him. I think I'm waiting for him to wake up so he can leave me alone, but I know he won't.

When he was talking, he said he had come back because of unfinished business. I think he was about to tell me what that was before he collapsed on the table. I also think he knew he was dying. I haven't got there yet so I don't know what that feels like. The only thing he did say was that he didn't want anybody in town to know he was back.

That's why I know who he is.

But now what do I do with him? There's a part of me that wants to go and get somebody, but then, what will they think? People around here already think I'm strange. What will they think if they find a dead body in my house with no witnesses other than me?

The old man didn't want anybody knowing he was here.

I decide to bury him in my garden. No-one ever comes into my garden. He'll be safe here.

I choose a patch at the back of my garden away from my rose bushes. I don't want his corpse tainting the roots and ruining them.

It takes me ages to dig the hole but I think it's deep enough. After I drag him from the chair in the kitchen to the waiting orifice, I look down at his lifeless body in the ground and stare into his absent face.

He won't miss it.

I am unaware of how to conduct a proper burial. I take a solitary rose from one of my bushes and drop it into the hole.

An ample trade for the glass eye I have just taken.

Printed in Great Britain
by Amazon